INTO THE
WIDENING
WORLD

OTHER PERSEA ANTHOLOGIES

AMERICA STREET
A MULTICULTURAL ANTHOLOGY OF STORIES
Edited by Anne Mazer

GOING WHERE I'M COMING FROM
MEMOIRS OF AMERICAN YOUTH
Edited by Anne Mazer

FIRST SIGHTINGS
CONTEMPORARY STORIES OF AMERICAN YOUTH
Edited by John Loughery

IMAGINING AMERICA
STORIES FROM THE PROMISED LAND
Edited by Wesley Brown and Amy Ling

VISIONS OF AMERICA
PERSONAL NARRATIVES FROM THE PROMISED LAND
Edited by Wesley Brown and Amy Ling

PAPER DANCE
55 LATINO POETS
Edited by Victor Hernández Cruz, Leroy Quintana, and Virgil Suarez

POETS FOR LIFE
SEVENTY-SIX POETS RESPOND TO AIDS
Edited by Michael Klein

IN THE COMPANY OF MY SOLITUDE
AMERICAN WRITING FROM THE AIDS PANDEMIC
Edited by Marie Howe and Michael Klein

INTO THE
WIDENING
WORLD

EDITED BY
John
Loughery

INTERNATIONAL
COMING-OF-AGE
STORIES

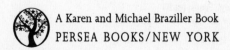
A Karen and Michael Braziller Book
PERSEA BOOKS/NEW YORK

PERSEA BOOKS, INC.
171 Madison Avenue
New York, New York 10016

Library of Congress Cataloging-in-Publication Data

Into the widening world : international coming-of-age stories /
edited by John Loughery.
p. cm.
Summary: A collection of twenty-six short stories about young
people, from twenty-two different countries.
ISBN 0-89255-204-2 (pbk.) : $11.95
1. Adolescence—Fiction. 2. Youth—Fiction. 3. Short stories.
[1. Short stories.] I. Loughery, John.
PN6120.95.A3I58 1994
808.83'108352055—dc20
94-13805
CIP
AC

Designed by REM Studio, Inc.
Printed on acid-free, recycled paper and bound by The Haddon Craftsmen,
Bloomsburg, Pennsylvania
Cover printed by Lynn Art, New York, New York

01 02 03 04 05 RRD 10 9 8 7 6 5 4

For
Patricia Loughery Timm
and Christopher and Melissa Timm

CONTENTS

CONTENTS

INTRODUCTION

When I was in high school in the early 1970s, we read Shakespeare and Shaw, Hardy and the Brontës, Steinbeck, Thomas Wolfe, J. D. Salinger, and Richard Wright—worthy writers all, and still part of the lives of most literate students, I hope. It was a satisfying line-up, but it had one drawback: the idea that novels, stories, and plays of equivalent power and importance had been written in Brazil or China or India would never have occurred to us. Even in college, the central place of the American and British tradition in world literature was in a way affirmed by the rarity, the *strangeness*, of the occasional elective in Japanese Novels or Modern African Fiction.

Of course, there are good reasons why most of us knew *David Copperfield* better than any coming-of-age story set in Asia or Latin America or why, in college, "Egypt" always meant Lawrence Durrell rather than Naguib Mahfouz. Writers in one's own language know the common codes, the ways of perceiving reality and sifting experience that we are apt to need if the literature is going to mean much to us at first reading. Those writers tend to be easier to talk about and easier to teach. An even more significant fact, perhaps, is that translations from other languages into English vary widely. A flawless knowledge of grammar and vocabulary is never enough. All too often, well-meaning translators lose the flavor (if not some of the meaning) of the original prose or verse, making flat what should be unpredictable and dynamic. Like the sensation of looking at a painting behind glass in a museum, a bad translation keeps us at an uncomfortable distance from the texture, the feel, of the thing. Read enough works in translation and you begin to feel that a first-rate translator is as uncommon as a first-rate novelist. Good writers who want international audiences have to wait for good translators.

Still, the obstacles of translation notwithstanding, the newfound interest in this country in the cultures of the wider world was a long time in coming and can only be seen as a positive development. It implies a useful rethinking—at the end of what has been called the American Century—of the world, our place in the world, and the nature of literature. This anthology, then, aims to be part of that process. The twenty-six stories collected here, from twenty-two countries, make no pretense to "representing" the seven continents. Rather, they might serve as a very general introduction to the riches of a literature that includes, but is not exclusively defined by, American and British storytellers; that encompasses a variety of styles and voices; that suggests ways in which certain situations and emotions might be common to all societies, yet how different other countries and people really are or might be—or how different their writers' concerns might be.

The last point is the tricky one. The tendency to assume that we should be able to "relate" immediately to all experience foreign to our lives is as debatable as the assumption that Americans and Europeans have nothing in common with other cultures. The ever-shifting gap between the universal and the strange, the known and the exotic, provides us with a healthy tension we're well advised to live with. The awakening to adult entanglements faced by Alice Munro's teenage Canadian narrator in "The Turkey Season" could just as easily be taking place in Vermont or California, but the world of the Australian Aboriginals in B. Wongar's "*Babaru*, the Family" or the nature of the Parsi community in Rohinton Mistry's Bombay story "One Sunday" requires a greater imaginative leap. The Japanese writer Yukio Mishima makes unusual demands on all his readers, and the issue at the heart of Peter Carey's "American Dreams" can be understood only by someone who can imagine what it would be like to live in a country of troubled origins and an unsettled identity. The more we are willing to attempt those precarious leaps, the greater the body of literature that will be available to us and the more we are apt to learn about the world.

Like its companion volume, *First Sightings: Contemporary Stories of American Youth*, this collection of stories has a specific focus: childhood and adolescence, a time of life that might have been neglected in the past but that has inspired some of the best contemporary short fiction. The protagonists of the stories range in age from infancy to the nervous verge of adulthood. The child in Margareta Ekström's "The Nothingness Forest" is just old enough to walk and has a vocabulary of only a few words when she innocently wanders off and encounters for the first time what lies beyond the borders of home, family, and her identity there. In Ben Okri's "In the Shadow of War," little Omovo has his own initiation in the forest—the fact of adult cruelty and unspeakable violence—while the narrator of *"Babaru*, the Family," a child in the Australian outback, struggles to make sense of her mother's disappearance, racial distinctions, illness, and the idea of a confusing universe beyond her village, a heartless world of white men, technology, and anger. If these children have one attribute in common, it is curiosity: life invites exploration, wandering. The narrator of Naguib Mahfouz's "The Conjurer Made Off with the Dish" sets out on a errand for his mother but ends by engaging in a wider, more mysterious search, not unlike the boy in Nissim Aloni's "Turkish Soldier from Edirne," whose preoccupation with the stories of a wounded Turk lead him farther and farther from the known and the secure. "I am in foreign territory, I said to myself, going after him," the narrator reflects at one point. But dangerous or just confusing, that territory has to be traversed, examined, understood.

Sometimes experience is not even sought, but presents itself unbidden. Petya in Tatyana Tolstaya's "Date with a Bird" vaguely comprehends that his grandfather is dying and that he likes the neighborhood eccentric Tamila ("she was an enchanted beauty with a magical name") more than his cynical, conventional Uncle Borya. Tamila suggests a mysterious world of dragons, secrets, and wild flight, while Borya is dull and smug. That the two personae might overlap would not occur to Petya until circumstances arrange otherwise. The main character of Ha Jin's story "In Broad Daylight" witnesses with some terror adult reactions to sexual transgressions in a context that also involves the frightening politics of his society: a hoard of indignant villagers want the adulterous Mu Ying to suffer, but the Chinese Red Guard play their part in the proceedings as well. In a more humorous or offbeat vein, V. S. Naipaul re-creates the haplessness of schooldays in the Caribbean ("They don't pay primary schoolteachers a lot in Trinidad, but they allow them to beat their pupils as much as they want . . . Mr. Hinds, my teacher, was a big beater") as a favored pupil and an unwanted goat cross paths. "Columba" by Michelle Cliff tells a lyrical story set in Jamaica of an imperious aunt, a twelve-year-old girl from America, and the native boy she unexpectedly befriends in a culture rife with taboos and class distinctions.

Once a certain age has been reached, the challenges and the problems change; young people "know" the world to one degree or another and now struggle to find their place in it. The protagonist of Charles Mungoshi's "Who Will

Stop the Dark?" is torn between his mother's wish to see him spend his days in school becoming an educated African man and his own desire to be in the forest with his grandfather, a loving relic of another age and another way of seeing the world. The teenage boys in "On Sunday" by Mario Vargas Llosa confront the limits of *machismo* in their pack, just as Kersi Boyce, cricket-player and rat-killer in Rohinton Mistry's "One Sunday," faces the unnerving truth of what it will mean to be a man in a world that defines manhood in terms of decisiveness and "heroic" aggression. The young man in John McGahern's "Christmas" has less to lose; he has been sent from the Home, farmed out to a rural Irish family, and the knowledge of adult folly is almost liberating. The stories by Mercè Rodoreda, Gabriel García Márquez, and Shirley Geok-lin Lim all deal with young women reacting to or contemplating their first relationships with the opposite sex, and in the case of Lim's dramatic "Mr. Tang's Girls," this takes place in the context of a polygamous society and a tradition in Malaysia of arranged marriages for teenage girls. On the other hand, Alice Munro's narrator in "The Turkey Season" is only fourteen and not yet ready for her own relationships, but she observes a great deal about the sexually intricate ways of the world while gutting Christmas turkeys at the Turkey Barn. In contrast, Nadine Gordimer's protagonist in "Some Are Born to Sweet Delight" is only too ready to link her life with a man she doesn't really know and to trade the identity of "daughter" for that of "wife."

The question of identity forms something of an undercurrent in this book. In "Borders" by Thomas King, we read from a thirteen-year-old's point of view about an Indian family from Canada undertaking a journey to the United States only to be caught between both sides when the mother refuses to declare herself either Canadian or American. "Blackfoot," she describes herself, in what soon becomes a media cause. The townspeople, and especially the central character, in Peter Carey's "American Dreams" have to wonder just what it means to be Australian in a world where American culture and American values (and American money) so often call the shots. Shawn Patel of Poughkeepsie, New York, is the son of an Indian father and an American mother and, like his Vietnamese-American buddy Tran, is a product of innumerable cultural threads. In Bharati Mukherjee's "Saints," Shawn labors to find and maintain that emergent *self* under the combined pressure of raging hormones, out-of-control parents, and life in the suburbs. Even the identity that comes from education can present its own problems. The highly intelligent young women in Margaret Drabble's "The Gifts of War" and Zoe Wicomb's "When the Train Comes" find that their schooling might have simply substituted one barrier or role for another.

For that matter, this theme of indeterminant identity extends even to some of the writers themselves. Thomas King, who is part-Cherokee, has lived for a time in the United States and currently resides in Canada. He is generally discussed as a Canadian author but might, like his narrator's mother in "Borders," question the accuracy of the designation "Canadian" in a world that is moving beyond borders, that rightly wants to honor tribes and regions, or internationalism itself, more than "nations." Likewise, Bharati Mukherjee would certainly seem to most people to be the name of an Indian writer, and indeed Mukherjee was born in India. Yet, a United States citizen now, she is as American as Bernard Malamud or Alice Walker. The late Mercè Rodoreda was Catalan, proudly so, but since the time of Franco, Catalonia has had to struggle to maintain its separate culture. B. Wongar is the pseudonym of a man born in Eastern Europe who traveled to Australia, married an Aboriginal woman, and who has since devoted himself to Aboriginal causes. But the issue remains: in Australia, or America, what is an "authentic" citizen in a land of constant immigration and emigration? The old demarcations look increasingly ambiguous or irrelevant.

Finally, a word about style. Not all the authors in this collection write in the realist tradition that has been brought to near-perfection by writers like Alice Munro, Nadine Gordimer, and John McGahern. In Jorge Edwards's "Weight-Reducing Diet," we have a touch of the Magic Realism that Latin American novelists have cultivated in the last few decades as an overweight young girl realizes her wish that the more she eats, the lighter she will become—to the point of floating above her house. "Exchange Value" by Charles Johnson has the quality of a nightmare or a fable as an eighteen-year-old young man of the black ghetto dishonestly comes by a large sum of money. The stories by Tatyana Tolstaya and Peter Carey also involve some wonderfully fantastic, "anti-realistic" elements. And as we enter the dormitory of Yukio Mishima's "Martyrdom," we are entering a vivid realm of boyish competition and affection, spectacle and sadism.

As one of the greatest storytellers of the century, Vladimir Nabokov, once observed, fiction must make its primary appeal to the imagination—not to political conscience or sociological curiosity or even the heartstrings—and surely he was right. These stories matter, in the long run, because they transport us by means of remarkable language to the fairy-tale maze of the sun-baked alleys of Cairo, to a hidden grove in Jamaica where doves are killed and innocence is thwarted, or to a country house in Russia where a bird of death waits on a dying grandfather and a little boy learns about life, sex, and deception. What we will remember and carry with us, if the story is good, is not so much an idea or a theme as the flavor of a distinctive personality or setting, a haunting climax or an unexpected mood, the force of new images brought to life by an original writer—images culled not only from our own backyard now but from the many yards that span the globe.

•   •   •

My thanks to those people who suggested stories or authors for this book or helped in other ways: Karen Braziller, Ty Florie, Virginia Loughery, Thomas Orefice, and Lillian Zietz.

JOHN LOUGHERY
New York, 1994

SOUTH AMERICA
AND
THE CARIBBEAN

COLUMBA

Michelle Cliff

Jamaica

When I was twelve my parents left me in the hands of a hypochondriacal aunt and her Cuban lover, a ham radio operator. Her lover, that is, until she claimed their bed as her own. She was properly a family friend, who met my grandmother when they danced the Black Bottom at the Glass Bucket. Jamaica in the twenties was wild.

This woman, whose name was Charlotte, was large and pink and given to wearing pink satin nighties—flimsy relics, pale from age. Almost all was pink in that room, so it seemed; so it seems now, at this distance. The lace trim around the necks of the nighties was not pink; it was yellowed and frazzled, practically absent. Thin wisps of thread which had once formed flowers, birds, a spider's web. Years of washing in hard water with brown soap had made the nighties loose, droop, so that Charlotte's huge breasts slid outside, suddenly, sideways, pink falling on pink like ladylike camouflage, but for her livid nipples. No one could love those breasts, I think.

Her hair stuck flat against her head, bobbed and straightened, girlish bangs as if painted on her forehead. Once she had resembled Louise Brooks. No longer. New moons arced each black eye.

Charlotte was also given to drinking vast amounts of water from the crystal carafes standing on her low bedside table, next to her *Information Please Almanac*—she had a fetish for detail but no taste for reading—linen hankies scented with bay rum, and a bowl of soursweet tamarind balls. As she drank, so did she piss, ringing changes on the walls of chamber pots lined under the bed, all through the day and night. Her room, her pink expanse, smelled of urine and bay rum and the wet sugar which bound the tamarind balls. Ancestral scents.

I was to call her Aunt Charlotte and to mind her, for she was officially *in loco parentis.*

The Cuban, Juan Antonio Corona y Mestee, slept on a safari cot next to his ham radio, rum bottle, stacks of *Punch, Country Life,* and something called *Gent.* His room was a screened-in porch at the side of the verandah. Sitting there with him in the evening, listening to the calls of the radio, I could almost imagine myself away from that place, in the bush awaiting capture, or rescue, until the sharp PING! of Charlotte's water cut across even my imaginings and the scratch of faraway voices.

One night a young man vaulted the rail of a cruise ship off Tobago and we picked up the distress call. A sustained SPLASH! followed Charlotte's PING! and the young man slipped under the waves.

I have never been able to forget him, and capture him in a snap of that room, as though he floated through it, me. I wonder still, why that particular instant? That warm evening, the Southern Cross in clear view? The choice of a sea-change?

His mother told the captain they had been playing bridge with another couple when her son excused himself. We heard all this on the radio, as the captain reported in full. Henry Fonda sprang to my movie-saturated mind, in *The Lady Eve,* with Barbara Stanwyck. But that was blackjack, not bridge, and a screwball comedy besides.

Perhaps the young man had tired of the coupling. Perhaps he needed a secret sharer.

The Cuban was a tall handsome man with blue-black hair and a costume of unvarying khaki. He seemed content to stay with Charlotte, use the whores in Raetown from time to time, listen to his radio, sip his rum, leaf through his magazines. Sitting on the side of the safari cot in his khaki, engaged in his pastimes, he seemed like a displaced white hunter (except he wasn't white, a fact no amount of relaxers or wide-brimmed hats could mask) or a mercenary recuperating from battle fatigue, awaiting further orders.

Perhaps he did not stir for practical reasons. This was 1960; he could not return to Cuba in all his hyphenated splendor, and had no marketable skills for the British Crown Colony in which he found himself. I got along with him, knowing we were both there on sufferance, unrelated dependants. Me, because Charlotte owed my grandmother something, he, for whatever reason he or she might have.

One of Juan Antonio's duties was to drop me at school. Each morning he pressed a half-crown into my hand, always telling me to treat my friends. I appreciated his largesse, knowing the money came from his allowance. It was a generous act and he asked no repayment but one small thing: I was to tell anyone who asked that he was my father. As I remember, no one ever did. Later, he suggested that I say 'Goodbye, Papá'—with the accent on the last syllable—when I left the car each morning. I hesitated, curious. He said, 'Never mind,' and the subject was not brought up again.

I broke the chain of generosity and kept his money for myself, not willing to share it with girls who took every chance to ridicule my American accent and call me 'salt'.

I used the money to escape them, escape school. Sitting in the movies, watching them over and over until it was time to catch the bus back.

Charlotte was a woman of property. Her small house was a cliché of colonialism, graced with calendars advertising the coronation of ER II, the marriage of Princess Margaret Rose, the visit of Alice, Princess Royal. Bamboo and wicker furniture was sparsely scattered across dark mahogany floors—settee there, end table here— giving the place the air of a hotel lobby, the sort of hotel carved from the shell of a great house, before Hilton and Sheraton made landfall. Tortoise-shell lamp- shades. Ashtrays made from coconut husks. Starched linen runners sporting the embroideries of craftswomen.

The house sat on top of a hill in Kingston, surrounded by an unkempt estate—so unkempt as to be arrogant, for this was the wealthiest part of the city, and the largest single tract of land. So large that a dead quiet enveloped the place in the evening, and we were cut off, sound and light absorbed by the space and the dark and the trees, abandoned and wild, entangled by vines and choked by underbrush, escaped, each reaching to survive.

At the foot of the hill was a cement gully which bordered the property—an empty moat but for the detritus of trespassers. Stray dogs roamed amid Red Stripe beer bottles, crushed cigarette packets, bully-beef tins.

Trespassers, real and imagined, were Charlotte's passion. In the evening, after dinner, bed-jacket draped across her shoulders against the soft trade winds, which she said were laden with typhoid, she roused herself to the verandah and took aim. She fired and fired and fired. Then she excused herself. 'That will hold them for another night.' She was at once terrified of invasion and confident she could stay it. Her gunplay was ritual against it.

There was, of course, someone responsible for cleaning the house, feeding the animals, filling the carafes and emptying the chamber pots, cooking the meals and doing the laundry. These tasks fell to Columba, a fourteen-year-old from St Ann, where Charlotte had bartered him from his mother; a case of condensed milk, two dozen tins of sardines, five pounds of flour, several bottles of cooking oil, permission to squat on Charlotte's cane-piece—fair exchange. His mother set up house-keeping with his brothers and sisters, and Columba was transported in the back of Charlotte's black Austin to Kingston. A more magnanimous, at least practical, landowner would have had a staff of two, even three, but Charlotte swore against being taken advantage of, as she termed it, so all was done by Columba, learning to expand his skills under her teaching, instructions shouted from the bed.

He had been named not for our discoverer, but for the saint buried on Iona, discoverer of the monster in the loch. A Father Pierre, come to St Ann from French Guiana, had taught Columba's mother, Winsome, to write her name, read a ballot, and know God. He said he had been assistant to the confessor on Devil's Island, and when the place was finally shut down in 1951 he was cast adrift, floating around the islands seeking a berth.

His word was good enough for the people gathered in his seaside chapel of open sides and thatched roof, used during the week to shelter a woman smashing limestone for the road, sorting trilobite from rock. On Sunday morning people sang, faces misted by spray, air heavy with the scent of sea grapes, the fat purple bunches bowing, swinging, brushing the glass sand, bruised. Bruises releasing more scent, entering the throats of a congregation fighting the smash of the sea. On Sunday morning Father Pierre talked to them of God, dredging his memory for every tale he had been told.

This was good enough for these people. They probably couldn't tell a confessor from a convict—which is what Father Pierre was—working off his crime against nature by boiling the life out of yam and taro and salted beef for the wardens, his keepers.

Even after the *Gleaner* had broadcast the real story, the congregation stood fast: he was white; he knew God—they reasoned. Poor devils.

Father Pierre held Columba's hand at the boy's baptism. He was ten years old then and had been called 'Junior' all his life. Why honor an un-named sire? Father Pierre spoke to Winsome. 'Children,' the priest intoned, 'the children become their names.' He spoke in an English as broken as hers.

What Father Pierre failed to reckon with was the unfamiliar nature of the boy's new name; Columba was 'Collie' to some, 'Like one damn dawg,' his mother said. 'Chuh, man. Hignorant smaddy cyaan accept not'ing new.' Collie soon turned Lassie and he was shamed.

To Charlotte he became 'Colin', because she insisted on Anglicization. It was for his own good, she added for emphasis, and so he would recognize her kindness. His name-as-is was foolish and feminine and had been given him by a *pedophile*, for heaven's sake.

Charlotte's shouts reached Columba in the kitchen. He was attempting to put together a gooseberry fool for the mistress's elevenses. The word *pedophile* smacked the stucco of the corridor between them, each syllable distinct, perversion bouncing furiously off the walls. I had heard—who hadn't?—but the word was beyond me. I was taking Latin, not Greek.

I softly asked Juan Antonio and he, in equally hushed tones, said, 'Mariposa . . . butterfly.'

Charlotte wasn't through. 'Fancy naming a boy after a bird. A black boy after a white bird. And still people attend that man . . . Well, they will get what they deserve,' she promised. 'You are lucky I saved you from that.' She spoke with such conviction.

I was forbidden to speak with Columba except on matters of household business, encouraged by Charlotte to complain when the pleat of my school tunic was not sharp enough. I felt only awkward that a boy two years older than myself was responsible for my laundry, for feeding me, for making my bed. I was, after all, an American now, only here temporarily. I did not keep the commandment.

I sought him out in secret. When Juan Antonio went downtown and while Charlotte dozed, the coast was clear. We sat behind the house under an ancient guava, concealed by a screen of bougainvillea. There we talked. Compared lives. Exchanged histories. We kept each other company, and our need for company made our conversations almost natural. The alternative was a dreadful loneliness; silence, but for the noises of the two adults. Strangers.

His questions about America were endless. What was New York like? Had I been to Hollywood? He wanted to know every detail about Duke Ellington, Marilyn Monroe, Stagger Lee, Jackie Wilson, Ava Gardner, Billy the Kid, Dinah Washington, Tony Curtis, Spartacus, John Wayne. Everyone, every name he knew from the cinema, where he slipped on his evening off; every voice, ballad, beat, he heard over Rediffusion, tuned low in the kitchen.

Did I know any of these people? Could you see them on the street? Then, startling me: what was life like for a black man in America? An ordinary black man, not a star?

I had no idea—not really. I had been raised in a community in New Jersey until this interruption, surrounded by people who had made their own world and 'did not business' with that sort of thing. Bourgeois separatists. I told Columba I did not know and we went back to the stars and legends.

A Tuesday during rainy season: Charlotte, swathed in a plaid lap-robe lifted from the *Queen Mary*, is being driven by Juan Antonio to an ice factory she owns in Old Harbour. There is a problem with the overseer; Charlotte is summoned. You would think she was being transported a thousand miles up the Amazon into headhunter territory, so elaborate are the preparations.

She and Juan Antonio drop me at school. There is no half-crown this morning. I get sixpence and wave them off. I wait for the Austin to turn the corner at St Cecilia's Way, then I cut to Lady Musgrave Road to catch the bus back.

When I return, I change and meet Columba out back. He has promised to show me something. The rain drips from the deep green of the escaped bush which surrounds us. We set out on a path invisible but to him, our bare feet sliding on slick fallen leaves. A stand of mahoe is in front of us. We pass through the trees and come into a clearing.

In the clearing is a surprise: a wreck of a car, thirties Rover. Gut-sprung, tired and forlorn, it slumps in the high grass. Lizards scramble through the vines which wrap around rusted chrome and across black hood and boot. We walk closer. I look into the wreck.

The leather seats are split and a white fluff erupts here and there. A blue gyroscope set into the dash slowly rotates. A pennant of the Kingston Yacht Club dangles miserably from the rearview.

This is not all. The car is alive. Throughout, roaming the seats, perched on the running board, spackling the crystal face of the clock, are doves. White. Speckled. Rock. Mourning. Wreck turned dovecote is filled with their sweet coos.

'Where did you find them?'

Columba is pleased, proud too, I think. 'Nuh find dem nestin' all over de place? I mek dem a home, give dem name. Dat one dere nuh Stagger Lee?' He points to a mottled pigeon hanging from a visor. 'Him is rascal fe true.'

Ava Gardner's feet click across the roof where Spartacus is hot in her pursuit.

Columba and I sit among the birds for hours.

I thank him for showing them to me, promising on my honor not to tell.

That evening I am seated across from Charlotte and next to Juan Antonio in the dining room. The ceiling fan stirs the air, which is heavy with the day's moisture.

Columba has prepared terrapin and is serving us one by one. His head is bowed so our eyes cannot meet, as they never do in such domestic moments.

We—he and I—split our lives in this house as best we can. No one watching this scene would imagine our meeting that afternoon, the wild birds, talk of flight.

The turtle is sweet. A turtling man traded it for ice that morning in Old Harbour. The curved shell sits on a counter in the kitchen. Golden. Delicate. Representing our island. Representing the world.

I did not tell them about the doves.

They found out easily, stupidly.

Charlotte's car had developed a knock in the engine. She noticed it on the journey to the ice factory, and questioned me about it each evening after that. Had I heard it on the way to school that morning? How could she visit her other properties without proper transport? Something must be done.

Juan Antonio suggested he take the Austin to the Texaco station at Matilda's Corner. Charlotte would have none of it. She asked little from Juan Antonio, the least he could do was maintain her automobile. What did she suggest? he asked. How could he get parts to repair the Austin; should he fashion them from bamboo?

She announced her solution: Juan Antonio was to take a machete and chop his way through to the Rover. The car had served her well, she said, surely it could be of use now. He resisted, reminding her that the Rover was thirty years old, probably rusted beyond recognition, and not of any conceivable use. It did not matter.

The next morning Juan Antonio set off to chop his way through the bush, dripping along the path, monkey wrench in his left hand, machete in his right. Columba was in the kitchen, head down, wrapped in the heat of burning coals as he fired irons to draw across khaki and satin.

The car, of course, was useless as a donor, but Juan Antonio's mission was not a total loss. He was relieved to tell Charlotte about the doves. Why, there must be a hundred. All kinds.

Charlotte was beside herself. Her property was the soul of bounty. Her trees bore heavily. Her chickens laid through hurricanes. Edible creatures abounded!

Neither recognized that these birds were not for killing. They did not recognize the pennant of the Kingston Yacht Club as the colors of this precious colony within a colony.

Columba was given his orders. Wring the necks of the birds. Pluck them and dress them and wrap them tightly for freezing. Leave out three for that evening's supper.

He did as he was told.

Recklessly I walked into the bush. No notice was taken.

I found him sitting in the front seat of the dovecote. A wooden box was beside him, half-filled with dead birds. The live ones did not scatter, did not flee. They sat and paced and cooed, as Columba performed his dreadful task.

'Sorry, man, you hear?' he said softly as he wrung the neck of the next one. He was weeping heavily. Heaving his shoulders with the effort of execution and grief.

I sat beside him in silence, my arm around his waist. This was not done.

WEIGHT-REDUCING DIET

Jorge Edwards

Chile

A meteor crossed the night and someone said three wishes could be made.

"What are your wishes, Chubby?"

The fat girl considered. "First," she said, "to fly."

"To fly?"

"Yes," said the girl. "I would like to be able to fly."

"But that's impossible."

"I know," said the girl, "but I would like to. Don't I have the right to ask for anything?"

"All right," they told her. "This means you lose your first wish. What's the second one?"

"The second?" The girl laughed. "I would like to own a pastry shop," she said, "so I could eat pastry all the time . . . with no one bothering me . . ."

The smell of the pastry shop made her mouth water.

"And the third one?"

The girl thought again with her finger on her lips and seemed about to say something, but held it back. She pressed her lips and closed her eyes tightly to drive off the wish—an insane, murderous wish. She thought she had a black soul, a monstrous soul. Later, she recalled that virtue does not lie in lacking evil desires. The devil is continuously active, blowing in our ears the fetid breath of his insinuations. The devil's daring led him to approach Jesus himself. And with the most dangerous and treacherous of temptations, that of power, as the parish priest—who also seemed to feel power's allure—had said, hissing with anger. Virtue, then—and the tone of his voice had, since the conclusion was so logical, descended along a curve of fatigue—consists in rejecting temptation with an iron will, digging your nails into the palms of your hands until they hurt and stamping your foot on a rock.

"What's wrong?"

"Let's go," she said, ill-humored.

When they reached the path, Sebastián hugged her from behind.

"Meanie!" he said.

"Let me go!" she screamed in fury, jabbing his stomach with her elbow.

"Bitch!" howled Sebastián, doubled over.

The light in her mother's room was on. "Tough luck!" thought the girl. She climbed up to her bedroom on the tips of her toes, and the first thing she did was to lift the pillow. All the lumps of sugar had disappeared. "The bedroom is out," she thought.

"Maria Eugenia!" her mother called.

Her pale face glistened with cold cream, and it seemed she had drunk little that night, and was in a bad mood.

"Who gave you permission to go out after dinner?"

The girl lowered her eyes. "They came and picked me up," she said.

"Furthermore," said her mother, "I found the lumps of sugar. If you weigh one gram more than last week your father will punish you. I'm warning you. So don't complain later."

"Let's see . . ." said her father.

"Last week I weighed myself without shoes," protested the girl.

"Well, then, take your shoes off."

She had examined the scale beforehand from all sides, searching for a little screw. Now she stepped barefoot on the scaffold's rubber platform, holding her breath. With her mind she tried to levitate. But the executioner wore his thickest pair of glasses and the inexorable machine showed an overweight of about three hundred grams.

"What's happening is that I'm growing," said the girl. "How could I not increase a little as well?"

"Yes, of course. And what about the lumps of sugar Mommy found under the pillow?"

The girl bit her lower lip. "She turned me in," she said to herself. She put her feet into her shoes without bending. She turned completely red before the cold, sparkling glasses.

"Tomorrow you can't go out at all. Not until you understand!"

"It's not my fault!" cried the girl, biting her lower lip in an effort to stop her tears.

"Not your fault! You spend the whole day eating. Ruminating like a cow!"

The girl burst into tears and ran toward her room hiccupping, sodden, her head lowered. She flung herself on the bed and sobbed for a long time with her face crushed against the bedspread. She would have liked to destroy the flashing glasses, to pierce them with a stiletto so that the eyes would spill like the white of an egg; to suffocate the sharp voice whose inexorable precision drove her up the wall. "One peach only," said that voice. "Stop playing with those crumbs," it said. "Bread is strictly forbidden." And she had an urge to do away with all the bread on the table; to lick the crumbs up on all fours; to empty the platter of peaches and devour five plates of bean soup, deep plates filled to the brim, with fat sausages floating in the center. She imagined that her parents took off and left the pantry open. She settled on the floor among pots of marmalade, jars of peaches in syrup and bricks of quince paste in varied and fascinating shapes. It was a enchanted forest. The ecstasy made her float in the rarefied, sweetish air. . . . She stabbed the stiletto in and the glasses broke in thousands of pieces. The voice dried out. From pantries of fragrant wood fell torrents of sugar.

But the voice, after the departure to Santiago on Sunday afternoons, left a scientific list of instructions, weaving a metallic net for the rest of the week. No escape was possible. And the girl felt suddenly the desire to throw herself off the highest rock. Anguish left her breathless. To live this way, oppressed by an absurd fatality! Why not the other? But the question remained unanswered. Meanwhile, with its thread of saliva sustained by the gelid glow of the glasses, the voice strung its net of orders, arguments, contradictions, categorical assertions and interdictions. Nothing could stop its hellish fever. No human power.

"It's a real disease," said Perico. "A vice."

"She'll become thin later," said Uncle Gonzalo in a conciliatory attempt. "She has many years ahead of her."

"This little girl," said Perico, "suffers from a respiratory deficiency. And the problem is that the fat oppresses her diaphragm."

"But how can you prevent her from eating sugar!" exclaimed Alicia with a biting edge in her voice.

Uncle Gonzalo stared at her and arched his brows. How can you prevent her! And what does it matter! The diaphragm is one of those typical medical pedantries. Doctors enslaved him for years, until he stopped listening to them. We've got to die of something, haven't we? Those pedants, who believe themselves to be spokesmen for the truth, are the ones who poison the world. And, apropos of nothing, he turned the conversation to the European places he had visited between the two wars. He remembered them, elaborating unfavorable comparisons to the present moment, during his afternoon walk. Uncle Gonzalo spoke for a long time about Budapest, its beautiful women and magnificent restaurants.

"This was sometime in the Twenties, when the Chilean peso still was worth something."

He joined the fleshy tips of his fingers, and his sky-blue, watery eyes submerged in the evocation. The memories had left a painful scar, a scar whose edges opened from time to time like thirsty lips. He kept a few faded pictures with dedications inscribed on them in oblique lines; some wrinkled and yellowed post cards. Pictures and cards which now served to convince him that he hadn't dreamed it all. The process of doubt and verification set into motion the lips of the scar covered with brine and tortured by an insatiable thirst. Lowering his head, Uncle Gonzalo tried to console himself with a sip of his drink.

"It's like the man," he said, "who returns from the future with a flower, after having flown in the time machine. That flower is the irrefutable proof. Do you remember?"

Perico raised his eyes. To save himself further explanation he said yes. "Each day more tiresome and senile," he thought. He was going to tell Alicia to keep him within bounds. But what is gained by saying anything to Alicia! She is completely impervious to reason, to common sense. She nods with her head, very much in agreement, and in a second forgets the whole thing.

"How's that?" asked the girl from her observation post by the swinging door.

"Oh! So you were there!" exclaimed Uncle Gonzalo. "And did not come to greet me!"

The girl approached him and kissed a dry cheek which had a peculiar odor, something between camphor, tobacco, cologne and other undefined substances.

"What's that about the man who flew?" asked the girl.

"He did not fly in space," said Uncle Gonzalo, pleased at being asked, "but rather in time. He'd go in a machine beyond the year two thousand and then he'd return."

Perplexed, the girl stared at him while her father half concealed an interminable yawn. Uncle Gonzalo said that now communism had put an end to all that. That world was gone. Irremediably. And everywhere, due to the insidious influence of communism, which uses thousands of subterfuges, the good things, the real pleasures of the spirit, were beginning to be erased from the map.

"Communism, taxes, the socializing measures, the masses, like locusts, invading and destroying even the remotest corners, the last vestiges of beauty, flattered by unscrupulous demagogues, softened by television, living in a regime of robots, a whole nation brought up with the mentality of a shopkeeper. . . . The only things they have not succeeded in spoiling are the sea and the mountain range, not for lack of wanting to, but insofar as the work of man is concerned. . . . Observe the marvels of modern Santiago! Now it's impossible to go anywhere without being forced to rub against the rabble. One should emigrate, but where to? With the progress in communication, the world, instead of enlarging, has become frightfully reduced. If you travel to the remotest hamlet in the Orient you'll find the same Coca-Cola advertisements, the same trash, while the Communists, like ants, ambushed or in broad daylight, gnaw away at the institutions . . ."

The girl was stunned. Uncle Gonzalo crossed his bloodless hands, covered with stains the color of tobacco, and stared over his shoulder with shining eyes as if hostile hordes stood there, on the other side of the door, gathering in the shadows, ready to break into the room and provoke the final unraveling. Noticing that his only remaining listener was the girl, he put an arm around her waist. His right hand delved with difficulty in his trouser pocket and, trembling, he handed her a large bill. The girl made some slight resistance.

"Take it!" ordered Uncle Gonzalo. "Don't be a fool." And he added with a devilish glitter in his eyes: "So you can eat pastry until you burst!"

The eyes of the girl sparkled and remained absorbed, staring into the night. Her uncle stood up, pained. His lungs worked like a worn-out, leaky bellows.

"Your uncle is getting unbearably boring," said Perico.

"Poor old man!" exclaimed Alicia.

The girl felt the bill next to her belly button, pressed by her clothes. The hostile forces truly dominated the universe and the blockage became narrower every day. But she was not as pessimistic as Uncle Gonzalo. She had to defend herself with cunning, silently, without giving one single millimeter of ground, utilizing all the resources allowed by ineffective vigilance overly imbued with its false control and made lax by complacency.

Chewing on an enormous peach, Perico declared that Uncle Gonzalo was becoming completely mushy, totally gaga. The pair of guests, out of consideration for Alicia, smiled kindly.

"And do you know the true story of the pictures?"

"What story?"

Alicia, motioning toward the girl, gestured to Perico to be quiet.

"He used to have strange habits concerning photography. He was a fanatic photographer, fond of taking rather muddy scenes. Do you understand?"

"Perico!" begged Alicia.

"Later I'll explain," said Perico after spitting out the peach pit and wiping his lips with a napkin.

The girl thought of asking permission to eat another peach, but the confusing revelations of her father distracted her.

"Chubby," said her mother, "say good night and go to sleep."

At the first opportunity she would ask Uncle Gonzalo. The art of photography must hide an infallible weapon for dismembering the enemy, for relegating him to the outer shadows. One could make use of the secret, a darkroom protected from intruders and free from the laws that rule time and space. In that darkroom Uncle Gonzalo would bring to light from out of those shadowy depths weird characters: sinister dwarfs, youths with bluish thighs, a being with an enormous belly and the head of a bird, a nun who stuck her tongue out and who would suddenly raise up her skirt and show her behind. . . . "Who can say?" the girl told herself, surprised at her own wit. She and Uncle Gonzalo were accomplices. They were alone, surrounded by a multitude equipped with glasses, lancets, hair, a thick soft tongue which dripped saliva, red knobby noses. The secret darkrooms could be extended over the whole world, under the very noses of the others, but choosing the right ones presented delicate problems: they should be protected by natural or architectural elements, be outside the common haunts of the knobby-nosed men, and offer facilities for hiding and hoarding, for observing without being observed. . . . The girl thought the attic fulfilled these conditions. As soon as she entered it, she breathed differently. Her oppression evaporated as if by magic. The crossbeams, the sack of cement, the armchair with a broken leg, the old magazines, all received her with delight. The air crossed the small balcony, and became lost, humming joyfully amidst the beams. In the street, men seemed small and harmless, insects to be pitied. She was the queen of this high land. When she sat in her ancient throne, the spring emitted a triumphant chord. The treasure lay under a loose plank. Now the chests would open to receive with solemnity, in the midst of cheers and the roll of drums, a huge gift, a large bill, which now occupied the place of honor surrounded by the white guard of lumps of sugar under whose command there was a candy cane dressed as a marquis, with tassels, hangings and glittering inlay.

The silence in the rest of the house allowed her to hear better the frantic clamor of the multitude. The fat girl advanced down the center acknowledging the cheers with a slight bow and an aristocratic smile. She was dying of hunger, but would have to await the end of the ceremony before eating the lumps. At the end of her journey she saw from the little window the woman who sold pastry.

"Hey!" she yelled.

The vendor stopped and looked up.

"Do you still have any pastry?"

The vendor searched among the second-floor windows.

"Over here." The girl stuck out a hand.

"I have a few left," the woman said.

The girl rose high and showed her head.

"Could you go over to the back street?"

Confused, the vendor hesitated.

"To the street at the back," the girl insisted.

In the kitchen everything was in order, shining and empty. Celestina surely snored. Olga had left. And besides, Olga was not dangerous. And the siesta habit would keep Celestina for many hours out of commission, open-mouthed and covered with sweat. The girl ran noiselessly toward the wooden fence. She became restless seeing that the street was deserted, but soon the vendor tiredly climbed the slope.

The bill was enough to buy twenty pastries. After counting them all, only one remained inside the basket.

"Can't you throw it in?" asked the girl.

"All right," said the woman with a gesture of resignation.

"That's it," said the girl, staring behind her, suddenly assaulted by the fear that Celestina with a perfidious smile would be spying on her. "Don't tell anyone that you sold me these pastries, okay?"

Glum, the vendor shrugged her shoulders. "I don't have to go around telling things," she said. "Who would I tell it to?"

"My Uncle Gonzalo," said the girl, "gave me the money to buy the pastries, but . . ."

Expressionless, the vendor watched her attentively. She waited for a second, and since the girl did not complete the sentence, she took her leave. The servants' quarters were plunged in a quiet, sticky drowsiness, gently underlined by the hum of insects around the gladiolas at the edge of the yard. There, in the open, repressing a howl of Apache vengeance, the girl gave an enormous bite into the cake and then brandished it above her head. She was answered by the roar of a bloodthirsty mob. Singing hymns of war, the girl climbed up to the dark interior of her armored fortress, her nest of eagles.

Between the trees, the sea dazzled, tranquil as a cup of milk. The distant cries of swimmers became confused with the murmur of the waves. Her burden lightened, the vendor soon reached the road's curve and disappeared. The street was again deserted, heated by rays which made the light vibrate and gave to the sounds a spongy, sweet consistency. She licked her lips and decided to eat another one. They were extremely light; they melted in her mouth. She ate another, and the white crumbs, dissolving on her tongue, gave her a sense of ecstasy—something airy, angelic: pure delight. The wishes made on the falling star, to which she had candidly confessed, provoking the mockery of her obtuse, ignorant companions, had come true with added interest. For example, her granaries had become crammed with magical goods, among whose virtues was that of providing weight-lessness. The woman who had brought them to her advanced to the end of the street without touching the ground; as soon as she went around the bend of the road, she became smoke. She was, doubtless, a messenger from the secret alcoves of Uncle Gonzalo. Once there again, she would loosen her braids and emit siren-like cries, swinging her hips. During her mission she had faked a sullen, suspicious attitude while fulfilling the instructions which had been given to her. That way she could circulate fearlessly, protected by the hidden powers controlled by her masters. If Uncle Gonzalo, who had planned it all to the smallest detail, gave the girl a bill, it was so that the transaction would have all the appearance of normality. But the bill did not exist; it became smoke together with the vendor at the curve of the road. No one else saw the vendor. And the cakes needed only to enter into the cavity of her mouth to become foam, breeze, and the body that swallowed them was transformed into a balloon lighter than air: the breeze itself could lift it away.

At that moment there was a fanfare and the floodgates of the attic opened. All at once, light, and a mischievous, whimsical breeze entered, bringing the distant shouts of bathers and the quacks of a flock of wild ducks flying in a straight line. The clear, immense sky appeared. The girl barely had time to fish out two cakes for her journey; the breeze allowed for no delay or objection. The beating of her panic-stricken heart only quieted once she found herself above the hills, far from the danger of being torn apart by branches or the sharp edges of crags. Floating slowly, she thought that from his darkroom her Uncle Gonzalo controlled the operation and rubbed his hands with an ironic smile of satisfaction. She discovered that by blowing upward she descended, and that it was enough to move her hands as if they were wings to gain altitude. It was beautiful to contemplate the sinuous white line of the breakers which separated the coast line's reef from the peaceful, open blue. From time to time, over one or another elevation, a quiet jet of water sprang. It sprang and fell slowly and then broke out again at a more distant spot, while the successive ridges of the sea swelled till they reached the interior of the bay. When she observed them again, the flock of ducks appeared farther down, flying about halfway between herself and the water.

Blowing strongly, she neared the beach and watched the bathers at a closer distance. They, unaware of the unusual presence, continued their innocent games. The girl got bored with watching these fooleries and continued her flight toward the south. It was better to contemplate the seaweed covering the rocks by the shore; caressed and swept by the surge, they remained always in place, turgid, slippery, undulating and firm. She could imagine the suction of the foamy ebb, and the restless bubbling of the crabs, baffled in their holes by the sudden violence of the tide. They clasped the wall insanely with their tense musculature and, in the depths, the sea urchins mobilized their antennae and continuously devoured and digested, transforming all kinds of living organisms into elemental clay and yellow tongues.

She made out Perico and Alicia on a nearby beach and maintained a prudent distance. But a rare and lucid faculty allowed her to capture their conversation even to its slightest subtleties. Perico spoke of certain possible applications of science in the year two thousand. His glasses sent out sparks. Alicia, lying on her back, with her face protected by a hat, was thinking that cellulitis had definitely installed itself in her muscles; that her will could no longer combat it. She had already eliminated sugar, bread, cookies and cakes, but twilight would come and she could not resist the temptation of cocktails. At dusk, things were seen in a different light. What did cellulitis matter! Life was short and abstinence excessively sad. Afterward, nothing happened. Three or four times, totally drunk, she had climbed to a secondfloor bedroom with the husband of a friend or a passing bachelor. Perico, who boasted of his tolerance, who sustained modern, scientific ideas about these subjects, hit her one time with his thick open hand with all his strength. It's one thing to act with freedom; it's another to behave like a goddam whore! He pulled her out of the bedroom by one arm, not even alluding to the presence of the other fellow, who had spent better moments in his life. Without caring about appearances, he pushed her downstairs with a determination she had never imagined him capable of, and, in the garden, with one blow, he threw her to the ground, where, as she fell, she crushed one of the new, thorny bushes. "Shut up!" he ordered and pointed at the girl's window. But the girl, with no need for hysterical crying, had understood everything. She slept lightly. She knew by heart that voice, a little vulgar, lascivious, which two or three times in the last year had gone up the stairs followed by other steps, in search of the rear bedroom. The indistinct filthy murmur frightened her. She hid her head under the sheet, while her heart throbbed as if it were about to jump out of her mouth, and the idea that the door might suddenly open, that it might open and that the voice might enter and inundate the dark room filled her with terror. The night of the fight, she thought panic would no longer let go of her. She was covered with cold sweat. But the sobs which slowly tapered off in the garden, the gentleness of this crying, let her sink into a heavy sleep, bathing all her muscles in tranquilizing honey, and placed oil on her lips.

This happened two or three times to Alicia, but usually nothing came of it. Anyway, this was the same as nothing. Except for the dryness in her mouth, the undefined uneasiness, a pain which she could not locate with precision, the signs of hangover, and next morning cellulitis, which had made frightening progress. She ordered Celestina to prepare a bit of fish and a little lettuce for lunch, and there was to be no sugar on the breakfast table. Useless precautions, because as soon as darkness descended on the sea, after nine in the evening, things took on a different look. What did cellulitis matter!

Perico was saying that in the year two thousand an amputated arm or leg could be made to grow again under specific treatments. There would be ways of changing the human body in order to adapt it to new conditions of life, to supersonic speed, to regular trips to the moon and to explorations of other planets. A friend watched him, awed, thinking that doctors are fascinating, that she had been a fool to marry a poor bureaucrat, and Alicia, on the other hand, had gotten into bad shape; her legs were full of little lumps, really ugly, her only advantage being that she was such a shameless bitch—which is, one must admit, in current times an enormous advantage. Alicia had always been that way, even in school; she would introduce a friend to her, in all naïveté, and the following week he'd be taken. Afterward they would pass her by scarcely bothering to greet her. Over here a girl's got to be really alert! If you just look away for one second . . . Perico, swollen with satisfaction, continued his dissertation, sprinkling it with incomprehensible, fascinating words . . .

The girl, losing altitude, saw men whose veined eyes shone in the night like fireflies of incandescent blue. They possessed pointed ears; vibrating, transparent wings; legs like toothpicks, covered with long hair; and broad gristly feet. All of a sudden there was no one on the shore. Breathing was very hard. The sky took on an ashen, gloomy aspect, announcing cataclysms and afflictions. She noticed that the sea was boiling and that from the lower slopes of the hills came forth a great cloud of dust, as if the earth were quaking. On the beach and over the rocks there were fat fishes, with great perpendicular fins and light gray bellies turned upward. The difficulty in breathing became more desperate by the minute.

"How did you behave?" asked her father. "Did you eat anything between meals?"

"Nothing," said the girl. She stretched her arms, thrusting out her breasts, which were beginning to show, and then scratched her back. Slyly, she passed her tongue over her lips.

The cook had appeared on the living room's threshold. "Tell me, Celestina, did the girl eat anything between meals?"

"Nothing, it seems," said Celestina and shrugged her shoulders.

Her father joined his hands and, with a sigh, let himself fall into an armchair. Alicia told Celestina to bring ice, lemon and sugar. Uncle Gonzalo rubbed his eyes and signed in turn, in a prolonged and deep manner. At that moment, his facial tics were more rapid, more agitated than usual. They were accentuated by the nervous drumming of his fingers and the rocking of his right foot, which was crossed over the left.

"The afternoon was quite pleasant," said Uncle Gonzalo, who seemed to be thinking of something else.

"Pleasant," said Perico, covering a yawn.

"Shall I make drinks for everyone?" asked Alicia, cocktail shaker in hand.

"Yes," said Perico. "Why not? There's never enough for you . . ."

"I'm thinking of inaugurating a system of only one single cocktail an afternoon," said Alicia.

"Hum!"

Perico, with a mocking air, made himself comfortable.

The eyes of Uncle Gonzalo, lost beyond the windows leading to the garden, in the cluster of dark bushes, met the eyes of the girl and gave her a fast wink. The girl answered with a smile of complicity. With a shaking hand, Uncle Gonzalo grasped his cocktail glass. He drank the first sip with a grimace of distaste.

"Very pleasant!" he said before the grimace had disappeared completely. "A marvelous afternoon!" And the girl knew he was saying it to divert the attention of the others. She understood that he was thinking of something totally different. His fatigue filled with dissatisfaction, the rocking leg, the eyes wandering toward the bushes in the shade, everything was part of a subtle feint. Her uncle was an eminent artist of deceit. The girl realized it now perfectly. Light had come into her spirit—an overwhelming evidence. Just the merest wink and the circle of conclusions she had drawn that afternoon in the intimacy of her refuge closed itself. Uncle Gonzalo looked at her again and that gesture was the final confirmation, the missing detail for the day to attain its roundest culmination. The girl felt her own clairvoyance and observed the others, those who did not share the secret, with an attitude that had passed disdain and reached a compassionate, even friendly sympathy.

Translated by Susana Hertelendy
and Lita Paniagua

ON SUNDAY

Mario Vargas Llosa

Argentina

He held his breath for an instant, dug his fingernails into the palms of his hands and said very quickly: "I'm in love with you." He saw her blush suddenly, as if someone had slapped her cheeks, which were radiantly pale and very smooth. Terrified, he felt his confusion rising in him, petrifying his tongue. He wanted to run away, to put an end to it: in the gloomy winter morning there rose up from deep inside him the weakness that always discouraged him at decisive moments. A few minutes before, in the midst of the lively, smiling crowd strolling in Miraflores' Central Park, Miguel was still repeating to himself: "Right now. When we get to Pardo Avenue. I'll get up the nerve. Oh, Rubén, if you knew how much I hate you!" And still earlier at church, seeking out Flora, he had glimpsed her at the base of a column and, opening a path with his elbows without begging pardon of the women he was pushing aside, succeeding in getting close to her. Saying hello in a low voice, he repeated to himself, stubbornly, as he had that dawn lying in his bed, watching day break: "There's no other way. I've got to do it today. In the morning. You'll pay for this yet, Rubén." And the night before, he had cried for the first time in many years when he realized how that dirty trick was being planned. People were staying in the park and Pardo Avenue was deserted. They walked down the tree-lined promenade under the tall, densely crowned rubber trees. I've got to get a move on, Miguel thought, if I'm not going to foul myself up. Out of the corner of his eye he looked around him: there was no one about; he could try. Slowly, he stretched out his left hand until it touched hers; the contact made him aware that he was sweating. He begged for some miracle to happen, for that humiliation to be over. What do I say to her now? he thought. What do I say to her now? She had pulled back her hand and he was feeling forsaken and silly. All his brilliant lines, feverishly rehearsed the night before, had dissolved like soap bubbles.

"Flora," he stammered, "I've waited a long time for this moment. Ever since I met you, you're all I think about. I'm in love for the first time, believe me. I've never known a girl like you."

Once again a compacted white space in his brain—a void. The pressure could not get any higher: his skin gave way like rubber and his fingernails struck bone. Still, he went on talking with difficulty, pausing, overcoming his embarrassed stammer, trying to describe an impulsive, consuming passion until he found with relief that they had reached the first circle on Pardo Avenue, and then he fell silent. Flora lived between the second and third trees past the oval. They stopped and looked at each other: Flora was still red, and being flustered had filled her eyes with a moist brightness. Despairing, Miguel told himself that she had never looked more beautiful: a blue ribbon held her hair back and he could see the start of her neck as well as her ears, two tiny, perfect question marks.

"Look, Miguel," Flora said; her voice was gentle, full of music, steady. "I can't answer you right now. But my mother doesn't want me to go with boys till I finish school."

"Flora, all mothers say the same thing," Miguel insisted. "How's she going to find out? We'll see each other whenever you say, even if it's only on Sundays."

"I'll give you an answer but first I've got to think it over," Flora said, lowering her eyes. And after several seconds she added: "Excuse me, but I have to go now; it's getting late."

Miguel felt a deep weariness, a feeling that spread throughout his entire body and relaxed him.

"You're not mad at me, Flora?" he asked humbly.

"Don't be silly," she replied animatedly. "I'm not mad."

"I'll wait as long as you want," Miguel said. "But we'll keep on seeing each other, won't we? We'll go to the movies this afternoon, okay?"

"I can't this afternoon," she said softly. "Martha's asked me over to her house."

A hot, violent flush ran through him and he felt wounded, stunned at this answer, which he had been expecting and which now seemed cruel to him. What

Melanés had insidiously whispered into his ear Saturday afternoon was right. Martha would leave them alone; it was the usual trick. Later Rubén would tell the gang how he and his sister had planned the situation, the place and the time. As payment for her services, Martha would have demanded the right to spy from behind the curtain. Anger suddenly drenched his hands.

"Don't be like that, Flora. Let's go to the matinee like we said. I won't talk to you about this. I promise."

"I can't, really," Flora said. "I've got to go to Martha's. She stopped by my house to ask me yesterday. But later I'll go to Salazar Park with her."

He did not see any hope even in those last words. A little later he was gazing at the spot where the frail, angelic figure had disappeared under the majestic arch of the rubber trees along the avenue. It was possible to compete with a mere adversary, not with Rubén. He recalled the names of girls invited by Martha, other Sunday afternoons. Now he was unable to do anything; he was defeated. Then, once more, there came to mind that image which saved him every time he experienced frustration: out of a distant background of clouds puffed up with black smoke, at the head of a company of cadets from the naval academy, he approached a reviewing stand set up in the park; illustrious men in formal attire with top hats in hand, and ladies with glittering jewels were applauding him. A crowd, in which the faces of his friends and enemies stood out, packed the sidewalks and watched him in wonder, whispering his name. Dressed in blue, a full cape flowing from his shoulders, Miguel led the march, looking toward the horizon. His sword was raised, his head described a half circle in the air; there at the center of the reviewing stand was Flora, smiling. He saw Rubén off in one corner, in tatters and ashamed, and confined himself to a brief, disdainful glance as he marched on, disappearing amid hurrahs.

Like steam wiped off a mirror, the image vanished. He was at the door of his house; he hated everyone, he hated himself. He entered and went straight up to his room, throwing himself face down on the bed. In the cool darkness, the girl's face appeared between his eyes and their lids—"I love you, Flora," he said out loud—and then Rubén with his insolent jaw and hostile smile: the faces were alongside each other; they came closer. Rubén's eyes twisted in order to look at him mockingly while his mouth approached Flora.

He jumped up from the bed. The closet mirror showed him an ashen face with dark circles under the eyes. "He won't see her," he decided. "He won't do this to me; I won't let him play that dirty trick on me."

Pardo Avenue was still deserted. Stepping up his pace without pausing, he walked to the intersection at Grau Avenue. He hesitated there. He felt cold: he had left his jacket in his room and just his shirt was not enough to protect him from the wind blowing off the sea and tangling itself with a soft murmuring in the dense branches of the rubber trees. The dreaded image of Flora and Rubén together gave him courage and he continued walking. From the doorway of the bar next to the Montecarlo movie house, he saw them at their usual table, lords of the corner formed by the rear and left-hand walls. Francisco, Melanés, Tobias, the Brain— they all noticed him and after a moment's surprise turned toward Rubén, their faces wicked and excited. He recovered his poise immediately: in front of men he certainly did know how to behave.

"Hello!" he said to them, drawing near. "What's new?"

"Sit down," said the Brain, pushing a chair toward him. "What miracle's brought you here?"

"You haven't been around here for ages," Francisco said.

"I felt like seeing you," Miguel answered pleasantly. "I knew you'd be here. What's so surprising? Or aren't I one of the Hawks anymore?"

He took a seat between Melanés and Tobias. Rubén was across from him.

"Cuncho!" shouted the Brain. "Bring another glass. One that's not too greasy."

Cuncho brought the glass and the Brain filled it with beer. Miguel said, "To the Hawks," and drank.

"You might as well drink the glass while you're at it," Francisco said. "You sure are thirsty!"

"I bet you went to one o'clock mass," said Melanés, winking in satisfaction as he always did when he was starting some mischief. "Right?"

"I did," Miguel said, unruffled. "But just to see a chick, nothing else."

He looked at Rubén with defiant eyes but Rubén did not let on; he was drumming his fingers on the table and whistling very softly, with the point of his tongue between his teeth, Pérez Prado's "The Popoff Girl."

"Great!" applauded Melanés. "Okay, Don Juan. Tell us, which chick?"

"That's a secret."

"There are no secrets between Hawks," Tobias reminded him. "You forget already? C'mon, who was it?"

"What's it to you?" Miguel asked.

"A lot," Tobias said. "Got to know who you're going around with to know who you are."

"You lost that round," Melanés said to Miguel. "One to nothing."

"I'll bet I can guess who it is," Francisco said. "You guys don't know?"

"I do already," Tobias said.

"Me too," said Melanés. He turned to Rubén with very innocent eyes and voice. "And you, brother, can you guess who it is?"

"No," said Rubén coldly. "And I don't care."

"My stomach's on fire," said the Brain. "Nobody's going to get a beer?"

Melanés drew a pathetic finger across his throat. "I have not money, darling," he said in English.

"I'll buy a bottle," announced Tobias with a solemn gesture. "Let's see who follows my example. We've got to put out the fire in this booby."

"Cuncho, bring half a dozen bottles of Cristal," said Miguel.

There were shouts of joy, exclamations.

"You're a real Hawk," Francisco declared.

"A friendly son of a bitch," added Melanés. "Yeah, a real super Hawk."

Cuncho brought the beers. They drank. They listened to Melanés telling dirty, crude, wild, hot stories and Tobias and Francisco started up a heavy discussion about soccer. The Brain told an anecdote. He was on his way from Lima to Miraflores by bus. The other passengers got off at Arequipa Avenue. At the top of Javier Prado, Tomasso, the White Whale, got on—that albino who's six feet four and still in grammar school, lives in Quebrada, you with me? Pretending to be really interested in the bus, he started asking the driver questions, leaning over the seat in front of him while he was slowly slitting the upholstery on the back of the seat with his knife.

"He was doing it because I was there," asserted the Brain. "He wanted to show off."

"He's a mental retard," said Francisco. "You do things like that when you're ten. They're not funny at his age."

"What happened afterwards is funny." The Brain laughed. " 'Listen, driver, can't you see that whale's destroying your bus?' "

"What?" yelled the driver, screeching to a stop. His ears burning, his eyes popping out, Tomasso the White Whale was forcing the door open.

"With his knife," the Brain said. "Look how he's left the seat."

At last the White Whale managed to get out. He started running down Arequipa Avenue. The driver ran after him, shouting, "Catch that bastard!"

"Did he catch him?" Melanés asked.

"Don't know. I beat it. And I stole the ignition key as a souvenir. Here it is."

He took a small, silver-plated key out of his pocket and tossed it onto the table. The bottles were empty. Rubén looked at his watch and stood up.

"I'm going," he said. "See you later."

"Don't go," said Miguel. "I'm rich today. I'll buy us all lunch."

A flurry of slaps landed on his back; the Hawks thanked him loudly, they sang his praises.

"I can't," Rubén said. "I've got things to do."

"Go on, get going, boy," Tobias said. "And give Martha my regards."

"We'll be thinking of you all the time, brother," Melanés said.

"No," Miguel yelled out. "I'm inviting everybody or nobody. If Rubén goes, that's it."

"Now you've heard it, Hawk Rubén," Francisco said. "You've got to stay."

"You've got to stay," Melanés said. "No two ways about it."

"I'm going," Rubén said.

"Trouble is, you're drunk," said Miguel. "You're going because you're scared of looking silly in front of us, that's the trouble."

"How many times have I carried you home dead drunk?" asked Rubén. "How many times have I helped you up the railing so your father wouldn't catch you? I can hold ten times as much as you."

"You used to," Miguel said. "Now it's rough. Want to see?"

"With pleasure," Rubén answered. "We'll meet tonight, right here?"

"No, right now." Miguel turned toward the others, spreading his arms wide. "Hawks, I'm making a challenge."

Delighted, he proved that the old formula still had the same force as before. In the midst of the happy commotion he had stirred up, he saw Rubén sit down, pale.

"Cuncho!" Tobias shouted. "The menu. And two swimming pools of beer. A Hawk has just made a challenge."

They ordered steak with spiced onions and a dozen beers. Tobias lined up three bottles for each of the competitors and the rest for the others. They ate, scarcely speaking. Miguel took a drink after each mouthful and tried to look lively, but his fear of not being able to hold enough beer mounted in proportion to the sour taste at the back of his throat. They finished off the six bottles long after Cuncho had removed the plates.

"You order," Miguel said to Rubén.

"Three more each."

After the first glass of the new round, Miguel heard a buzzing in his ears; his head was a slow-spinning roulette wheel and everything was whirling.

"I've got to take a piss," he said. "I'm going to the bathroom."

The Hawks laughed.

"Give up?" Rubén asked.

"I'm going to take a piss," Miguel shouted. "If you want to, order more."

In the bathroom he vomited. Then he washed his face over and over, trying to erase all the telltale signs. His watch said four-thirty. Despite his heavy sickness, he felt happy. Now Rubén was powerless. He went back to their table.

"Cheers," Rubén said, raising his glass.

He's furious, Miguel thought. But I've fixed him now.

"Smells like a dead body," Melanés said. "Somebody's dying on us around here."

"I'm fresh as a daisy," Miguel asserted, trying to hold back his dizziness and nausea.

"Cheers," Rubén repeated.

When they had finished the last beer, his stomach felt like lead; the voices of the others reached his ears as a confused mixture of sounds. A hand suddenly appeared under his eyes; it was white with long fingers; it caught him by the chin; it forced him to raise his head; Rubén's face had gotten larger. He was funny-looking, so rumpled and mad.

"Give up, snot-nose?"

Miguel stood up suddenly and shoved Rubén, but before the show could go on, the Brain stepped in.

"Hawks never fight," he said, forcing them to sit down. "You two are drunk. It's over. Let's vote."

Against their will, Melanés, Francisco and Tobias agreed to a tie.

"I'd won already," Rubén said. "This one can't even talk. Look at him."

As a matter of fact, Miguel's eyes were glassy, his mouth hung open and a thread of saliva dribbled off his tongue.

"Shut up," said the Brain. "We wouldn't call you any champion at beer drinking."

"You're no beer-drinking champion," Melanés emphasized. "You're just a champion at swimming, the wizard of the pools."

"You better shut up," Rubén said. "Can't you see your envy's eating you alive?"

"Long live the Esther Williams of Miraflores!" shouted Melanés.

"An old codger like you and you don't even know how to swim," said Rubén. "You want me to give you some lessons?"

"We know already, champ," the Brain said. "You won a swimming championship. And all the chicks are dying over you. You're a regular little champion."

"He's no champion of anything," Miguel said with difficulty. "He's just a phony."

"You're keeling over," Rubén answered. "Want me to take you home, girlie?"

"I'm not drunk," Miguel protested. "And you're just a phony."

"You're pissed because I'm going to go steady with Flora," Rubén said. "You're dying of jealousy. Think I don't understand things?"

"Just a phony," Miguel said. "You won because your father's union president; everybody knows he pulled a fast one, and you only won on account of that."

"At least I swim better than you," Rubén said. "You don't even know how to surf."

"You don't swim better than anybody," Miguel said. "Any girl can leave you behind."

"Any girl," said Melanés. "Even Miguel, who's a mother."

"Pardon me while I laugh," Rubén said.

"You're pardoned, your Highness," Tobias said.

"You're getting at me because it's winter," Rubén said. "If it wasn't, I'd challenge you all to go to the beach to see who's so cocksure in the water."

"You won the championship on account of your father," Miguel said. "You're just a phony. When you want to swim with me, just let me know—don't be so timid. At the beach, at Terraces, wherever you want."

"At the beach," Rubén said. "Right now."

"You're just a phony," Miguel said.

Rubén's face suddenly lit up and in addition to being spiteful, his eyes became arrogant again.

"I'll bet you on who's in the water first," he said.

"Just a phony," said Miguel.

"If you win," Rubén said, "I promise you I'll lay off Flora. And if I win, you can go peddle your wares someplace else."

"Who do you think you are?" Miguel stammered. "Asshole, just who do you think you are?"

"Listen, Hawks," Rubén said, spreading his arms, "I'm making a challenge."

"Miguel's in no shape now," the Brain said. "Why don't you two flip a coin for Flora?"

"And why're you butting in?" Miguel said. "I accept. Let's go to the beach."

"You're both crazy," Francisco said. "I'm not going down to the beach in this cold. Make another bet."

"He's accepted," Rubén said. "Let's go."

"When a Hawk challenges somebody, we all bite our tongues," Melanés said. "Let's go to the beach. And if they don't have the guts to go into the water, we throw them in."

"Those two are smashed," insisted the Brain. "The challenge doesn't hold."

"Shut up, Brain," Miguel roared. "I'm a big boy now. I don't need you to take care of me."

"Okay," said the Brain, shrugging his shoulders. "Screw you, then."

They left. Outside, a quiet gray atmosphere was waiting for them. Miguel breathed in deeply; he felt better. Francisco, Melanés and Rubén walked in front; behind them, Miguel and the Brain. There were pedestrians on Grau Avenue, mostly maids on their day off in gaudy dresses. Ashen men with thick, lanky hair preyed around them and looked them over greedily. The women laughed, showing their gold teeth. The Hawks did not pay any attention to them. They walked on with long strides as the excitement mounted in them.

"Better now?" asked the Brain.

"Yeah," answered Miguel. "The air's done me good."

They turned the corner at Pardo Avenue. They marched in a line, spread out like a squadron under the rubber trees of the promenade, over the flagstones heaved up at intervals by the enormous roots that sometimes pushed through the surface like grappling hooks. Going down the crosstown street, they passed two girls. Rubén bowed ceremoniously.

"Hi, Rubén," they sang in duet.

Tobias imitated them in falsetto: "Hi, Rubén, you prince."

The crosstown street ends at a forking brook: on one side winds the embankment, paved and shiny; on the other a slope that goes around the hill and reaches the sea. It is known as the "bathhouse path"; its pavement is worn smooth and shiny from automobile tires and the feet of swimmers from many, many summers.

"Let's warm up, champs," Melanés shouted, breaking into a spring. The others followed his example.

They ran against the wind and light fog rising off the beach, caught up in an exciting whirlwind: through their ears, mouths and noses the air penetrated to their lungs and a sensation of relief and well-being spread through their bodies as the drop became steeper, and at one point their feet no longer obeyed anything but a mysterious force coming from the depths of the earth. Their arms like propellers, a salty taste on their tongues, the Hawks descended the slope at a full run until they reached the circular platform suspended over the bathhouse. Some fifty yards offshore, the sea vanished in a thick cloud that seemed about to charge the cliffs, those high, dark breakwaters jutting up around the entire bay.

"Let's go back," said Francisco. "I'm cold."

At the edge of the platform is a railing, stained in places by moss. An opening marks the top of the nearly vertical stairway leading down to the beach. From up there the Hawks looked down on a short ribbon of open water at their feet and the strange, bubbling surface where the fog was blending with the foam off the waves.

"I'll go back if this guy gives up," Rubén said.

"Who's talking about giving up?" responded Miguel. "Who the hell do you think you are?"

Rubén went down the stairway three steps at a time, unbuttoning his shirt as he descended.

"Rubén!" shouted the Brain. "Are you nuts? Come back!"

But Miguel and the others were also going down and the Brain followed them.

From the balcony of the long, wide building that nestles against the hill and houses the dressing rooms, down to the curving edge of the sea, there is a slope of gray stone where people sun themselves during the summer. From morning to dusk the small beach boils with excitement. Now the water covered the slope and there were no brightly colored umbrellas or lithe girls with tanned bodies, no reverberating, melodramatic screams from children and women when a wave succeeded in splashing them before it retreated, dragging murmuring stones and round pebbles. Not even a strip of beach could be seen, since the tide came in as far as the space bounded by the dark columns holding the building up in the air. Where the undertow began, the wooden steps and cement supports, decorated by stalactites and algae, were barely visible.

"You can't see the surf," said Rubén. "How're we going to do this?"

They were in the left-hand gallery, in the women's section; their faces were serious.

"Wait till tomorrow," the Brain said. "By noon it'll be clear. Then we'll be able to check on you."

"Since we're here, let's do it now," Melanés said. "They can check on themselves."

"Okay with me," Rubén said. "And you?"

"Me too," Miguel said.

When they had stripped, Tobias joked about the blue veins scaling Miguel's smooth stomach. They went down. Licked incessantly by the water for months on end, the wooden steps were smooth and slippery. Holding on to the iron railing so as not to fall, Miguel felt a shivering mount from the soles of his feet up to his brain. He thought that in one way the fog and the cold favored him: winning now did not depend on skill so much as on endurance, and Rubén's skin was purplish too, puckered in millions of tiny goose bumps. One step below, Rubén's athletic body bent over: tense, he was waiting for the ebb of the undertow and the arrival of the next wave, which came in noiselessly, airily, casting a spray of foamy droplets before it. When the crest of the wave was six feet from the step, Rubén plunged in: with his arms out like spears and his hair on end from the momentum of his leap, his body cut straight through the air and he fell without bending, without lowering his head or tucking his legs in; he bounced in the foam, scarcely went under, and immediately taking advantage of the tide, he glided out into the water, his arms surfacing and sinking in the midst of a frantic bubbling and his feet tracing a precise, rapid wake. Miguel in turn climbed down one more step and waited for the next wave. He knew that the water was shallow there and that he should hurl himself like a plank, hard and rigid, without moving a muscle, or he would crash into the rocks. He closed his eyes and jumped and he did not hit bottom, but his body was whipped from forehead to knees and he felt a fierce stinging as he swam with all his might in order to restore to his limbs the warmth that the water had suddenly snatched from them. He was in that strange section of the sea near the shore at Miraflores where the undertow and the waves meet and there are whirlpools and crosscurrents, and the summer months were so far in the past that Miguel had forgotten how to clear it without stress. He did not recall that you had to relax your body and yield, allowing yourself to be carried along submissively in the drift, to stroke only when you rose on a wave and were at the crest in that smooth water flowing with the foam and floating on top of the currents. He did not recall that it is better to endure patiently and with some cunning that first contact with the exasperating sea along the shore that tugs at your limbs and hurls streams of water in your mouth and eyes, better to offer no resistance, to be a cork, to take in air only when a wave approaches, to go under—scarcely if they broke far out and without force or to the very bottom if the crest was nearby—to grab hold of some rock and, always on the alert, to wait out the deafening thunder of its passing, to push off in a single movement and to continue advancing, furtively, by hand strokes, until finding a new obstacle, and then going limp, not fighting the whirlpools, to swirl deliberately in the sluggish eddy and to escape suddenly, at the right moment, with a single stroke. Then a calm surface unexpectedly appears, disturbed only by harmless ripples; the water is clear, smooth, and in some spots the murky underwater rocks are visible.

After crossing the rough water, Miguel paused, exhausted, and took in air. He saw Rubén not far off, looking at him. His hair fell over his forehead in bangs; his teeth were clenched.

"Do we go on?"

"We go on."

After a few minutes of swimming, Miguel felt the cold, which had momentarily disappeared, invade him again, and he speeded up his kicking because it was in his legs, above all in his calves, that the water affected him most, numbing them first and hardening them later. He swam with his face in the water and every time his right arm came out, he turned his head to exhale the breath he had held in and to take in another supply, with which he scarcely submerged his forehead and chin once again so as not to slow his own motion and, on the contrary, to slice the water like a prow and to make his sliding through it easier. With each stroke, out of one eye he could see Rubén, swimming smoothly on the surface, effortlessly, kicking up no foam now, with the grace and ease of a gliding seagull. Miguel tried to forget Rubén and the sea and the surf (which must still be far out, since the water was clear, calm and crossed only by newly formed waves). He wanted to remember only Flora's face, the down on her arms which on sunny days glimmered like a little forest of golden threads, but he could not prevent the girl's image from being replaced by another—misty, usurping, deafening—which fell over Flora and concealed her: the image of a mountain of furious water, not exactly the surf (which he had reached once, two summers ago, and whose waves were violent with green and murky foam because at that spot, more or less, the rocks came to an end, giving rise to the mud that the waves churned to the surface and mixed with nests of algae and jellyfish, staining the sea) but rather a real ocean tormented by internal cataclysms whipping up monstrous waves that could have encompassed an entire ship and capsized it with surprising quickness, hurling into the air passengers, launches, masts, sails, buoys, sailors, portholes and flags.

He stopped swimming, his body sinking until it was vertical; he lifted his head and saw Rubén moving off. He thought of calling to him on any pretext, of saying to him, for example, "Why don't we rest for a minute?" but he did not do it. All the cold in his body seemed concentrated in his calves; he could feel his stiffened muscles, his taut skin, his accelerated heart. He moved his feet feverishly. He was at the center of a circle of dark water, walled in by the fog. He tried to catch sight of the beach or the shadow of the cliffs when the mist let up, but that vague gauze which dissolved as he cut through was not transparent. He saw only a small, greenish-black patch and a cover of clouds level with the water. Then he felt afraid. He was suddenly struck by the memory of the beer he had drunk and thought: I guess that's weakened me. In an instant it seemed as if his legs and arms had disappeared. He decided to turn back, but after a few strokes in the direction of the beach, he made an about-face and swam as gently as he could. "I won't reach the shore alone," he said to himself. "It's better to be close to Rubén; if I wear out, I'll tell him he beat me but let's go back." Now he was swimming wildly, his head up, swallowing water, flailing the sea with stiff arms, his gaze fixed on the imperturbable form ahead of him.

The movement and effort brought his legs back to life; his body regained some of its heat, the distance separating him from Ruben had decreased and that made him feel calmer. He overtook him a little later; he stretched out an arm and grabbed one of his feet. Rubén stopped instantly. His eyes were bright red and his mouth was open.

"I think we've gotten turned around," Miguel said. "Seems to me we're swimming parallel to the beach."

His teeth were chattering but his voice was steady. Rubén looked all around. Miguel watched him, tense.

"You can't see the beach anymore," Rubén said.

"You couldn't for some time," Miguel said. "There's a lot of fog."

"We're not turned around," Rubén said. "Look. Now you can see the surf."

As a matter of fact, some small waves were approaching them, with a fringe of foam that dissolved and suddenly re-formed. They looked at each other in silence.

"We're already out near the surf, then," Miguel said finally.

"Yeah. We swam fast."

"I've never seen so much fog."

"You very tired?" Rubén asked.

"Me? You crazy? Let's get going."

He immediately regretted saying that, but it was already too late. Rubén had said, "Okay, let's get going."

He succeeded in counting up to twenty strokes before telling himself he could not go on: he was hardly advancing; his right leg was half paralyzed by the cold, his arms felt clumsy and heavy. Panting, he yelled, "Rubén!" Rubén kept on swimming. "Rubén, Rubén!" He turned toward the beach and started to swim, to splash about, really, in desperation; and suddenly he was begging God to save him: he would be good in the future, he would obey his parents, he would not miss Sunday mass, and then he recalled having confessed to the Hawks that he only went to church "to see a chick" and he was sure as a knife stab that God was going to punish him by drowning him in those troubled waters he lashed so frantically, waters beneath which an atrocious death awaited him, and afterwards, perhaps, hell. Then, like an echo, there sprang to his mind a certain old saying sometimes uttered by Father Alberto in religion class, something about divine mercy knowing no bounds, and while he was flailing the sea with his arms—his legs hung like dead weights—with his lips moving, he begged God to be good to him, he was so young, and he swore he would go to the seminary if he was saved, but a second later, scared, he corrected himself, and promised that instead of becoming a priest he would make sacrifices and other things, he would give alms, and at that point he realized how hesitating and bargaining at such a critical moment could be fatal and then he heard Rubén's maddened shouts, very nearby, and he turned his head and saw him, about ten yards away, his face half sunk in the water, waving an arm, pleading: "Miguel, brother, come over here, I'm drowning, don't go away!"

He remained motionless, puzzled, and suddenly it was as though Rubén's desperation banished his own; he felt himself recovering his courage, felt the stiffness in his legs lessening.

"I've got a stomach cramp," Rubén shrieked. "I can't go any farther, Miguel. Save me, for God's sake. Don't leave me, brother."

He floated toward Rubén and was on the point of swimming up to him when he recalled that drowning people always manage to grab hold of their rescuers like pincers and take them down; and he swam off, but the cries terrified him and he sensed that if Rubén drowned, he would not be able to reach the beach either, and he turned back. Two yards from Rubén, who was quite white and shriveled, sinking and surfacing, he shouted: "Don't move, Rubén. I'm going to pull you but don't try to grab me; if you grab me we'll sink, Rubén. You're going to stay still, brother. I'm going to pull you by the head; don't touch me." He kept at a safe distance and stretched out a hand until he reached Rubén's hair. He began to swim with his free arm, trying with all his strength to assist with his legs. The movement was slow, very laborious. It sapped all his power and he was hardly aware of Rubén, complaining monotonously, suddenly letting out terrible screams—"I'm going to die, Miguel, save me"—or retching in spasms. He was exhausted when he stopped. With one hand he held Rubén up, with the other he traced circles on the surface. He breathed deeply through his mouth. Rubén's face was contracted in pain, his lips folded back in a strange grimace.

"Brother," murmured Miguel, "we've only got a little way to go. Try. Rubén, answer me. Yell. Don't stay like that."

He slapped him hard and Rubén opened his eyes; he moved his head weakly.

"Yell, brother," Miguel repeated. "Try to stretch. I'm going to rub your stomach. We've only got a little way to go; don't give up."

His hand searched under the water, found a hard knot that began at Rubén's navel and took up a large part of his belly. He went over it many times, first slowly, then hard, and Rubén shouted, "I don't want to die, Miguel, save me!"

He started swimming again, dragging Rubén by the chin this time. Whenever a wave overtook them, Rubén choked; Miguel yelled at him to spit. And he kept on swimming, without stopping for a moment, closing his eyes at times, excited because a kind of confidence had sprung up in his heart, a warm, proud, stimulating feeling that protected him against the cold and the fatigue. A rock grazed one of his legs and he screamed and hurried on. A moment later he was able to stand up and pass his arms around Rubén. Holding him pressed up against himself, feeling his head leaning on one of his shoulders, he rested for a long while. Then he helped Rubén to stretch out on his back and, supporting him with his forearm, forced him to stretch his knees; he massaged his stomach until the knot began to loosen. Rubén was not shouting anymore; he was doing everything to stretch out completely and was rubbing himself with both his hands.

"Are you better?"

"Yeah, brother, I'm okay now. Let's get out."

An inexpressible joy filled them as they made their way over rocks, heads bent against the undertow, not feeling the sea urchins. Soon they saw the sharp edges of the cliffs, the bathhouse, and finally, close to shore, the Hawks standing on the women's balcony, looking for them.

"Hey!" Rubén said.

"Yeah?"

"Don't say anything to them. Please don't tell them I called out. We've always been very close friends, Miguel. Don't do that to me."

"You really think I'm that kind of louse?" Miguel said. "Don't worry, I won't say anything."

They climbed out, shivering. They sat down on the steps in the midst of an uproar from the Hawks.

"We were about to send our sympathy to your families," Tobias said.

"You've been in for more than an hour," the Brain said. "C'mon, how did it turn out?"

Speaking calmly while he dried his body with his undershirt, Rubén explained: "Nothing to tell. We went out to the surf and came back. That's how we Hawks are. Miguel beat me. Just barely, by a hand. Of course, if it'd been in a swimming pool, he'd have made a fool of himself."

Slaps of congratulation rained down on Miguel, who had dressed without drying off.

"You're getting to be a man," Melanés told him.

Miguel did not answer. Smiling, he thought how that same night he would go to Salazar Park. All Miraflores would soon know, thanks to Melanés, that he had won the heroic contest and Flora would be waiting for him with glowing eyes. A golden future was opening before him.

Translated by Gregory Kolovakas
and Ronald Christ

ARTIFICIAL ROSES

Gabriel García Márquez

Colombia

Feeling her way in the gloom of dawn, Mina put on the sleeveless dress which the night before she had hung next to the bed, and rummaged in the trunk for the detachable sleeves. Then she looked for them on the nails on the walls, and behind the doors, trying not to make noise so as not to wake her blind grandmother, who was sleeping in the same room. But when she got used to the darkness, she noticed that the grandmother had got up, and she went into the kitchen to ask her for the sleeves.

"They're in the bathroom," the blind woman said. "I washed them yesterday afternoon."

There they were, hanging from a wire with two wooden clothespins. They were still wet. Mina went back into the kitchen and stretched the sleeves out on the stones of the fireplace. In front of her, the blind woman was stirring the coffee, her dead pupils fixed on the stone border of the veranda, where there was a row of flowerpots with medicinal herbs.

"Don't take my things again," said Mina. "These days, you can't count on the sun."

The blind woman moved her face toward the voice.

"I had forgotten that it was the first Friday," she said.

After testing with a deep breath to see if the coffee was ready, she took the pot off the fire.

"Put a piece of paper underneath, because these stones are dirty," she said.

Mina ran her index finger along the fireplace stones. They were dirty, but with a crust of hardened soot which would not dirty the sleeves if they were not rubbed against the stones.

"If they get dirty you're responsible," she said.

The blind woman had poured herself a cup of coffee. "You're angry," she said, pulling a chair toward the veranda. "It's a sacrilege to take Communion when one is angry." She sat down to drink her coffee in front of the roses in the patio. When the third call for Mass rang, Mina took the sleeves off the fireplace and they were still wet. But she put them on. Father Angel would not give her Communion with a bare-shouldered dress on. She didn't wash her face. She took off the traces of rouge with a towel, picked up the prayer book and shawl in her room, and went into the street. A quarter of an hour later she was back.

"You'll get there after the reading of the gospel," the blind woman said, seated opposite the roses in the patio.

Mina went directly to the toilet. "I can't go to Mass," she said. "The sleeves are wet, and my whole dress is wrinkled." She felt a knowing look follow her.

"First Friday and you're not going to Mass," exclaimed the blind woman.

Back from the toilet, Mina poured herself a cup of coffee and sat down against the whitewashed doorway, next to the blind woman. But she couldn't drink the coffee.

"You're to blame," she murmured, with a dull rancor, feeling that she was drowning in tears.

"You're crying," the blind woman exclaimed.

She put the watering can next to the pots of oregano and went out into the patio, repeating, "You're crying." Mina put her cup on the ground before sitting up.

"I'm crying from anger," she said. And added, as she passed next to her grandmother, "You must go to confession because you made me miss the first-Friday Communion."

The blind woman remained motionless, waiting for Mina to close the bedroom door. Then she walked to the end of the veranda. She bent over haltingly until she found the untouched cup in one piece on the ground. While she poured the coffee into the earthen pot, she went on:

"God knows I have a clear conscience."

Mina's mother came out of the bedroom.

"Who are you talking to?" she asked.

"To no one," said the blind woman. "I've told you already that I'm going crazy."

Ensconced in her room, Mina unbuttoned her bodice and took out three little keys which she carried on a safety pin. With one of the keys she opened the lower drawer of the armoire and took out a miniature wooden trunk. She opened it with another key. Inside there was a packet of letters written on colored paper, held together by a rubber band. She hid them in her bodice, put the little trunk in its place, and locked the drawer. Then she went to the toilet and threw the letters in.

"I thought you were at church," her mother said when Mina came into the kitchen.

"She couldn't go," the blind woman interrupted. "I forgot that it was first Friday, and I washed the sleeves yesterday afternoon."

"They're still wet," murmured Mina.

"I've had to work hard these days," the blind woman said.

"I have to deliver a hundred and fifty dozen roses for Easter," Mina said.

The sun warmed up early. Before seven Mina set up her artificial-rose shop in the living room: a basket full of petals and wires, a box of crêpe paper, two pairs of scissors, a spool of thread, and a pot of glue. A moment later Trinidad arrived, with a pasteboard box under her arm, and asked her why she hadn't gone to Mass.

"I didn't have any sleeves," said Mina.

"Anyone could have lent some to you," said Trinidad.

She pulled over a chair and sat down next to the basket of petals.

"I was too late," Mina said.

She finished a rose. Then she pulled the basket closer to shirr the petals with the scissors. Trinidad put the pasteboard box on the floor and joined in the work.

Mina looked at the box.

"Did you buy shoes?" she asked.

"They're dead mice," said Trinidad.

Since Trinidad was an expert at shirring petals, Mina spent her time making stems of wire wound with green paper. They worked silently without noticing the sun advance in the living room, which was decorated with idyllic prints and family photographs. When she finished the stems, Mina turned toward Trinidad with a face that seemed to end in something immaterial. Trinidad shirred with admirable neatness, hardly moving the petal tip between her fingers, her legs close together. Mina observed her masculine shoes. Trinidad avoided the look without raising her head, barely drawing her feet backward, and stopped working.

"What's the matter?" she said.

Mina leaned toward her.

"He went away," she said.

Trinidad dropped the scissors in her lap.

"No."

"He went away," Mina repeated.

Trinidad looked at her without blinking. A vertical wrinkle divided her knit brows.

"And now?" she asked.

Mina replied in a steady voice.

"Now nothing."

Trinidad said goodbye before ten.

Freed from the weight of her intimacy, Mina stopped her a moment to throw the dead mice into the toilet. The blind woman was pruning the rosebush.

"I'll bet you don't know what I have in this box," Mina said to her as she passed.

She shook the mice.

The blind woman began to pay attention. "Shake it again," she said. Mina repeated the movement, but the blind woman could not identify the objects after listening for a third time with her index finger pressed against the lobe of her ear.

"They are the mice which were caught in the church traps last night," said Mina.

When she came back, she passed next to the blind woman without speaking. But the blind woman followed her. When she got to the living room, Mina was alone next to the closed window, finishing the artificial roses.

"Mina," said the blind woman. "If you want to be happy, don't confess with strangers."

Mina looked at her without speaking. The blind woman sat down in the chair in front of her and tried to help with the work. But Mina stopped her.

"You're nervous," said the blind woman.

"Why didn't you go to Mass?" asked the blind woman.

"You know better than anyone."

"If it had been because of the sleeves, you wouldn't have bothered to leave the house," said the blind woman. "Someone was waiting for you on the way who caused you some disappointment."

Mina passed her hands before her grandmother's eyes, as if cleaning an invisible pane of glass.

"You're a witch," she said.

"You went to the toilet twice this morning," the blind woman said. "You never go more than once."

Mina kept making roses.

"Would you dare show me what you are hiding in the drawer of the armoire?" the blind woman asked.

Unhurriedly, Mina stuck the rose in the window frame, took the three little keys out of her bodice, and put them in the blind woman's hand. She herself closed her fingers.

"Go see with your own eyes," she said.

The blind woman examined the little keys with her fingertips.

"My eyes cannot see down the toilet."

Mina raised her head and then felt a different sensation: she felt that the blind woman knew that she was looking at her.

"Throw yourself down the toilet if what I do is so interesting to you," she said.

The blind woman ignored the interruption.

"You always stay up writing in bed until early morning," she said.

"You yourself turn out the light," Mina said.

"And immediately you turn on the flashlight," the blind woman said. "I can tell that you're writing by your breathing."

Mina made an effort to stay calm. "Fine," she said without raising her head. "And supposing that's the way it is. What's so special about it?"

"Nothing," replied the blind woman. "Only that it made you miss first-Friday Communion."

With both hands Mina picked up the spool of thread, the scissors, and a fistful of unfinished stems and roses. She put it all in the basket and faced the blind woman. "Would you like me to tell you what I went to do in the toilet, then?" she asked. They both were in suspense until Mina replied to her own question:

"I went to take a shit."

The blind woman threw the three little keys into the basket. "It would be a good excuse," she murmured, going into the kitchen. "You would have convinced me if it weren't the first time in your life I've ever heard you swear." Mina's mother was coming along the corridor in the opposite direction, her arms full of bouquets of thorned flowers.

"What's going on?" she asked.

"I'm crazy," said the blind woman. "But apparently you haven't thought of sending me to the madhouse so long as I don't start throwing stones."

Translated by Gregory Rabassa
and S. J. Bernstein

THE RAFFLE

V. S. Naipaul

Trinidad

They don't pay primary schoolteachers a lot in Trinidad, but they allow them to beat their pupils as much as they want.

Mr Hinds, my teacher, was a big beater. On the shelf below *The Last of England* he kept four or five tamarind rods. They are good for beating. They are limber, they sting and they last. There was a tamarind tree in the schoolyard. In his locker Mr Hinds also kept a leather strap soaking in the bucket of water every class had in case of fire.

It wouldn't have been so bad if Mr Hinds hadn't been so young and athletic. At the one school sports I went to, I saw him slip off his shining shoes, roll up his trousers neatly to mid-shin and win the Teachers' Hundred Yards, a cigarette between his lips, his tie flapping smartly over his shoulder. It was a wine-coloured tie: Mr Hinds was careful about his dress. That was something else that somehow added to the terror. He wore a brown suit, a cream shirt and the wine-coloured tie.

It was also rumoured that he drank heavily at weekends.

But Mr Hinds had a weak spot. He was poor. We knew he gave those 'private lessons' because he needed the extra money. He gave us private lessons in the ten-minute morning recess. Every boy paid fifty cents for that. If a boy didn't pay, he was kept in all the same and flogged until he paid.

We also knew that Mr Hinds had an allotment in Morvant where he kept some poultry and a few animals.

The other boys sympathized with us—needlessly. Mr Hinds beat us, but I believe we were all a little proud of him.

I say he beat us, but I don't really mean that. For some reason which I could never understand then and can't now, Mr Hinds never beat me. He never made me clean the blackboard. He never made me shine his shoes with the duster. He even called me by my first name, Vidiadhar.

This didn't do me any good with the other boys. At cricket I wasn't allowed to bowl or keep wicket and I always went in at number eleven. My consolation was that I was spending only two terms at the school before going on to Queen's Royal College. I didn't want to go to QRC so much as I wanted to get away from Endeavour (that was the name of the school). Mr Hinds's favour made me feel insecure.

At private lessons one morning Mr Hinds announced that he was going to raffle a goat—a shilling a chance.

He spoke with a straight face and nobody laughed. He made me write out the names of all the boys in the class on two foolscap sheets. Boys who wanted to risk a shilling had to put a tick after their names. Before private lessons ended there was a tick after every name.

I became very unpopular. Some boys didn't believe there was a goat. They all said that if there was a goat, they knew who was going to get it. I hoped they were right. I had long wanted an animal of my own, and the idea of getting milk from my own goat attracted me. I had heard that Mannie Ramjohn, Trinidad's champion miler, trained on goat's milk and nuts.

Next morning I wrote out the names of the boys on slips of paper. Mr Hinds borrowed my cap, put the slips in, took one out, said, 'Vidiadhar, is your goat,' and immediately threw all the slips into the wastepaper basket.

At lunch I told my mother, 'I win a goat today.'

'What sort of goat?'

'I don't know. I ain't see it.'

She laughed. She didn't believe in the goat, either. But when she finished laughing she said: 'It would be nice, though.'

I was getting not to believe in the goat, too. I was afraid to ask Mr Hinds, but a day or two later he said, 'Vidiadhar, you coming or you ain't coming to get your goat?'

He lived in a tumbledown wooden house in Woodbrook and when I got there I saw him in khaki shorts, vest and blue canvas shoes. He was cleaning his bicycle with a yellow flannel. I was overwhelmed. I had never associated him with such dress and such a menial labour. But his manner was more ironic and dismissing than in the classroom.

He led me to the back of the yard. There *was* a goat. A white one with big horns, tied to a plum tree. The ground around the tree was filthy. The goat looked sullen and sleepy-eyed, as if a little stunned by the smell it had made. Mr Hinds invited me to stroke the goat. I stroked it. He closed his eyes and went on chewing. When I stopped stroking him, he opened his eyes.

Every afternoon at about five an old man drove a donkey-cart through Miguel Street where we lived. The cart was piled with fresh grass tied into neat little bundles, so neat you felt grass wasn't a thing that grew but was made in a factory somewhere. That donkey-cart became important to my mother and me. We were buying five, sometimes six bundles a day, and every bundle cost six cents. The goat didn't change. He still looked sullen and bored. From time to time Mr. Hinds asked me with a smile how the goat was getting on, and I said it was getting on fine. But when I asked my mother when we were going to get milk from the goat she told me to stop aggravating her. Then one day she put up a sign:

RAM FOR SERVICE
Apply Within For Terms

and got very angry when I asked her to explain it.

The sign made no difference. We bought the neat bundles of grass, the goat ate, and I saw no milk.

And when I got home one lunch-time I saw no goat.

'Somebody borrow it,' my mother said. She looked happy.

'When it coming back?'

She shrugged her shoulders.

It came back that afternoon. When I turned the corner into Miguel Street I saw it on the pavement outside our house. A man I didn't know was holding it by a rope and making a big row, gesticulating like anything with his free hand. I knew that sort of man. He wasn't going to let hold of the rope until he had said his piece. A lot of people were looking on through curtains.

'But why all-you want to rob poor people so?' he said, shouting. He turned to his audience behind the curtains. 'Look, all-you, just look at this goat!'

The goat, limitlessly impassive, chewed slowly, its eyes half-closed.

'But how all you people so advantageous? My brother stupid and he ain't know this goat but I know this goat. Everybody in Trinidad who know about goat know this goat, from Icacos to Mayaro to Toco to Chaguaramas,' he said, naming the four corners of Trinidad. 'Is the most uselessest goat in the whole world. And you charge my brother for this goat? Look, you better give me back my brother money, you hear.'

My mother looked hurt and upset. She went inside and came out with some dollar notes. The man took them and handed over the goat.

That evening my mother said, 'Go and tell your Mr Hinds that I don't want this goat here.'

Mr Hinds didn't look surprised. 'Don't want it, eh?' He thought, and passed a well-trimmed thumb-nail over his moustache. 'Look, tell you. Going to buy him back. Five dollars.'

I said, 'He eat more than that in grass alone.'

That didn't surprise him either. 'Say six, then.'

I sold. That, I thought, was the end of that.

One Monday afternoon about a month before the end of my last term I announced to my mother, 'That goat raffling again.'

She became alarmed.

At tea on Friday I said casually, 'I win the goat.'

She was expecting it. Before the sun set a man had brought the goat away from Mr Hinds, given my mother some money and taken the goat away.

I hoped Mr Hinds would never ask about the goat. He did, though. Not the next week, but the week after that, just before school broke up.

I didn't know what to say.

But a boy called Knolly, a fast bowler and a favourite victim of Mr Hinds, answered for me. 'What goat?' he whispered loudly. 'That goat kill and eat long time.'

Mr Hinds was suddenly furious. 'Is true, Vidiadhar?'

I didn't nod or say anything. The bell rang and saved me.

At lunch I told my mother, 'I don't want to go back to that school.'

She said, 'You must be brave.'

I didn't like the argument, but went.

We had Geography the first period.

'Naipaul,' Mr Hinds said right away, forgetting my first name, 'define a peninsula.'

'Peninsula,' I said, 'a piece of land entirely surrounded by water.'

'Good. Come up here.' He went to the locker and took out the soaked leather strap. Then he fell on me. 'You sell my goat?' Cut. 'You kill my goat?' Cut. 'How you so damn ungrateful?' Cut, cut, cut. 'Is the last time you win anything I raffle.'

It was the last day I went to that school.

NORTH AMERICA

EXCHANGE VALUE

Charles Johnson

United States

Me and my brother, Loftis, came in by the old lady's window. There was some kinda boobytrap—boxes of broken glass—that shoulda warned us Miss Bailey wasn't the easy mark we made her to be. She been living alone for twenty years in 4–B down the hall from Loftis and me, long before our folks died—a hincty, halfbald West Indian woman with a craglike face, who kept her door barricaded, shutters closed, and wore the same sorry-looking outfit—black wingtip shoes, cropfingered gloves in winter, and a man's floppy hat—like maybe she dressed half-asleep or in a dark attic. Loftis, he figured Miss Bailey had some grandtheft dough stashed inside, jim, or leastways a shoebox full of money, 'cause she never spent a nickel on herself, not even for food, and only left her place at night.

Anyway, we figured Miss Bailey was gone. Her mailbox be full, and Pookie White, who run the Thirty-ninth Street Creole restaurant, he say she ain't dropped by in days to collect the handouts he give her so she can get by. So here's me and Loftis, tipping around Miss Bailey's blackdark kitchen. The floor be littered with fruitrinds, roaches, old food furred with blue mold. Her dirty dishes be stacked in a sink feathered with cracks, and it looks like the old lady been living, lately, on Ritz crackers and Department of Agriculture (Welfare Office) peanut butter. Her toilet be stopped up, too, and, on the bathroom floor, there's five Maxwell House coffee cans full of shit. Me, I was closing her bathroom door when I whiffed this evil smell so bad, so thick, I could hardly breathe, and what air I breathed was stifling, like solid fluid in my throatpipes, like broth or soup. "Cooter," Loftis whisper, low, across the room, "you smell that?" He went right on sniffing it, like people do for some reason when something be smelling stanky, then took out his headrag and held it over his mouth. "Smells like something crawled up in here and died!" Then, head low, he slipped his long self into the living room. Me, I stayed by the window, gulping for air, and do you know why?

You oughta know, up front, that I ain't too good at this gangster stuff, and I had a real bad feeling about Miss Bailey from the get-go. Mama used to say it was Loftis, not me, who'd go places—I see her standing at the sideboard by the sink now, big as a Frigidaire, white flour to her elbows, a washtowel over her shoulder, while we ate a breakfast of cornbread and syrup. Loftis, he graduated fifth at DuSable High School, had two gigs and, like Papa, he be always wanting the things white people had out in Hyde Park, where Mama did daywork some-times. Loftis, he be the kind of brother who buys *Esquire*, sews Hart, Schaffner & Marx labels in Robert Hall suits, talks properlike, packs his hair with Murray's; and he took classes in politics and stuff at the Black People's Topographical Library in the late 1960s. At thirty, he make his bed military-style, reads *Black Scholar* on the bus he takes to the plant, and, come hell or high water, plans to make a Big Score. Loftis, he say I'm 'bout as useful on a hustle—or when it comes to getting ahead—as a headcold, and he says he has to count my legs sometimes to make sure I ain't a mule, seeing how, for all my eighteen years, I can't keep no job and sorta stay close to home, watching TV, or reading *World's Finest* comic books, or maybe just laying dead, listening to music, imagining I see faces or foreign places in water stains on the wallpaper, 'cause some days, when I remember Papa, then Mama, killing theyselves for chump change—a pitiful li'l bowl of porridge—I get to thinking that even if I ain't had all I wanted, maybe I've had, you know, all I'm ever gonna get.

"Cooter," Loftis say from the living room. "You best get in here quick."

Loftis, he'd switched on Miss Bailey's bright, overhead living room lights, so for a second I couldn't see and started coughing—the smell be so powerful it hit my nostrils like coke—and when my eyes cleared, shapes come forward in the light, and I thought for an instant like I'd slipped in space. I seen why Loftis called me, and went back two steps. See, 4–B's so small if you ring Miss Bailey's doorbell, the toilet'd flush. But her living room, webbed in dust, be filled to the max with dollars of all denominations, stacks of stock in General Motors, Gulf Oil, and 3M Company in old White Owl cigar boxes, battered purses, or bound in pink rubber bands. It be like the kind of cubbyhole kids play in, but filled with . . . *things:*

everything, like a world inside the world, you take it from me, so like picturebook scenes of plentifulness you could seal yourself off in here and settle forever. Loftis and me both drew breath suddenly. There be unopened cases of Jack Daniel's, three safes cemented to the floor, hundreds of matchbooks, unworn clothes, a fuel-burning stove, dozens of wedding rings, rubbish, World War II magazines, a carton of a hundred canned sardines, mink stoles, old rags, a birdcage, a bucket of silver dollars, thousands of books, paintings, quarters in tobacco cans, two pianos, glass jars of pennies, a set of bagpipes, an almost complete Model A Ford dappled with rust, and, I swear, three sections of a dead tree.

"Damn!" My head be light; I sat on an upended peach crate and picked up a bottle of Jack Daniel's.

"Don't you touch *anything!*" Loftis, he panting a little; he slap both hands on a table. "Not until we inventory this stuff."

"Inventory? Aw, Lord, Loftis," I say, "something ain't *right* about this stash. There could be a curse on it. . . ."

"Boy, sometime you act weak-minded."

"For real, Loftis, I got a feeling. . . ."

Loftis, he shucked off his shoes, and sat down heavily on the lumpy arm of a stuffed chair. "Don't say *anything.*" He chewed his knuckles, and for the first time Loftis looked like he didn't know his next move. "Let me think, okay?" He squeezed his nose in a way he has when thinking hard, sighed, then stood up and say, "There's something you better see in that bedroom yonder. Cover up your mouth."

"Loftis, I ain't going in there."

He look at me right funny then. "She's a miser, that's all. She saves things."

"But a tree?" I say. "Loftis, a *tree* ain't normal!"

"Cooter, I ain't gonna tell you twice."

Like always, I followed Loftis, who swung his flashlight from the plant—he a night watchman—into Miss Bailey's bedroom, but me, I'm thinking how trippy this thing is getting, remembering how, last year, when I had a paper route, the old lady, with her queer, crablike walk, pulled my coat for some change in the hallway, and when I give her a handful of dimes, she say, like one of them spooks on old-time radio, "Thank you, Co-o-oter," then gulped the coins down like aspirin, no lie, and scurried off like a hunchback. Me, I wanted no parts of this squirrely old broad, but Loftis, he holding my wrist now, beaming his light onto a low bed. The room had a funny, museumlike smell. Real sour. It was full of dirty laundry. And I be sure the old lady's stuff had a terrible string attached when Loftis, looking away, lifted her bedsheets and a knot of black flies rose. I stepped back and held my breath. Miss Bailey be in her long-sleeved flannel nightgown, bloated, like she'd been blown up by a bicycle pump, her old face caved in with rot, flyblown, her fingers big and colored like spoiled bananas. Her wristwatch be ticking softly beside a half-eaten hamburger. Above the bed, her wall had roaches squashed in little swirls of bloodstain. Maggots clustered in her eyes, her ears, and one fist-sized rat hissed inside her flesh. My eyes snapped shut. My knees failed; then I did a Hollywood faint. When I surfaced, Loftis, he be sitting beside me in the living room, where he'd drug me, reading a wrinkled, yellow article from the *Chicago Daily Defender.*

"Listen to this," Loftis say. " 'Elnora Bailey, forty-five, a Negro housemaid in the Highland Park home of Henry Conners, is the beneficiary of her employer's will. An old American family, the Conners arrived in this country on the *Providence* shortly after the voyage of the *Mayflower.* The family flourished in the early days of the 1900s. . . .' " He went on, getting breath: " 'A distinguished and wealthy industrialist, without heirs or a wife, Conners willed his entire estate to Miss Bailey of 3347 North Clark Street for her twenty years of service to his family. . . .' " Loftis, he give that Geoffrey Holder laugh of his, low and deep; then it eased up his throat until it hit a high note and tipped his head back onto his shoulders. "Cooter, that was before we was born! Miss Bailey kept this in the Bible next to her bed."

Standing, I braced myself with one hand against the wall. "She didn't earn it?"

"Naw." Loftis, he folded the paper—"Not one penny"—and stuffed it in his shirt pocket. His jaw looked tight as a horseshoe. "Way *I* see it," he say, "this was her one shot in a lifetime to be rich, but being country, she had backward ways and blew it." Rubbing his hands, he stood up to survey the living room. "Somebody's gonna find Miss Bailey soon, but if we stay on the case—Cooter, don't square up on me now—we can tote everything to our place before daybreak. Best we start with the big stuff."

"But why didn't she *use* it, huh? Tell me that?"

Loftis, he don't pay me no mind. When he gets an idea in his head, you can't dig it out with a chisel. How long it took me and Loftis to inventory, then haul Miss Bailey's queer old stuff to our crib, I can't say, but that cranky old ninnyhammer's hoard come to $879,543 in cash money, thirty-two bank books (some deposits be only $5), and me, I wasn't sure I was dreaming or what, but I suddenly flashed on this feeling, once we left her flat, that all the fears Loftis and me had about the future be gone, 'cause Miss Bailey's property was the past—the power of that fellah Henry Conners trapped like a bottle spirit—which we could live off, so it was the future, too, pure potential: can *do.* Loftis got to talking on about how that piano we pushed home be equal to a thousand bills, jim, which equals, say, a bad TEAC A–3340 tape deck, or a down payment on a deuce-and-a-quarter. Its value be (Loftis say) that of a universal standard of measure, relational, unreal as number, so that tape deck could turn, magically, into two gold lamé suits, a trip to Tijuana, or twenty-five blow jobs from a ho—we had $879,543 worth of wishes, if you can deal with that. Be like Miss Bailey's stuff is raw energy, and Loftis and me, like wizards, could transform her stuff into anything else at will. All we had to do, it seemed to me, was decide exactly what to exchange it for.

While Loftis studied this over (he looked funny, like a potato trying to say something, after the inventory, and sat, real quiet, in the kitchen), I filled my pockets with fifties, grabbed me a cab downtown to grease, yum, at one of them high-hat restaurants in the Loop. . . . But then I thought better of it, you know, like I'd be out of place—just another jig putting on airs—and scarfed instead at a ribjoint till both my eyes bubbled. This fat lady making fishburgers in the back favored an old hardleg baby-sitter I once had, a Mrs. Paine who made me eat ocher, and I wanted so bad to say, "Loftis and me Got Ovuh," but I couldn't put that in the wind, could I, so I hatted up. Then I copped a boss silk necktie, cashmere socks, and a whistle-slick maxi leather jacket on State Street, took cabs *every*where, but when I got home that evening, a funny, Pandora-like feeling hit me. I took off the jacket, boxed it—it looked trifling in the hallway's weak light—and, tired, turned my key in the door. I couldn't get in. Loftis, he'd changed the lock and, when he finally let me in, looking vaguer, crabby, like something out of the Book of Revelations, I seen this elaborate, booby-trapped tunnel of cardboard and razor blades behind him, with a two-foot space just big enough for him or me to crawl through. That wasn't all. Two bags of trash from the furnace room downstairs be sitting inside the door. Loftis, he give my leather jacket this evil look, hauled me inside, and hit me upside my head.

"How much this thing set us back?"

"Two fifty." My jaws got tight; I toss him my receipt. "You want me to take it back? Maybe I can get something else. . . ."

Loftis, he say, not to me, but to the receipt, "Remember the time Mama give me that ring we had in the family for fifty years? And I took it to Merchandise Mart and sold it for a few pieces of candy?" He hitched his chair forward and sat with his elbows on his knees. "That's what you did, Cooter. You crawled into a Clark bar." He commence to rip up my receipt, then picked up his flashlight and keys. "As soon as you buy something you *lose* the power to buy something." He button up his coat with holes in the elbows, showing his blue shirt, then turned 'round at the tunnel to say, "Don't touch Miss Bailey's money, or drink her splo, or do *any*thing until I get back."

"Where you going?"

"To work. It's Wednesday, ain't it?"

"You going to work?"

"Yeah."

"You got to go *really?* Loftis," I say, "what you brang them bags of trash in here for?"

"It ain't trash!" He cut his eyes at me. "There's good clothes in there. Mr. Peterson tossed them out, he don't care, but I saw some use in them, that's all."

"Loftis . . ."

"Yeah?"

"What we gonna do with all this money?"

Loftis pressed his fingers to his eyelids, and for a second he looked caged, or like somebody'd kicked him in his stomach. Then he cut me some slack: "Let me think on it tonight—it don't pay to rush—then we can TCB, okay?"

Five hours after Loftis leave for work, that old blister Mr. Peterson, our landlord, he come collecting rent, find Mrs. Bailey's body in apartment 4–B, and phoned the fire department. Me, I be folding my new jacket in tissue paper to keep it fresh, adding the box to Miss Bailey's unsunned treasures when two paramedics squeezed her on a long stretcher through a crowd in the hallway. See, I had to pin her from the stairhead, looking down one last time at this dizzy old lady, and I seen something in her face, like maybe she'd been poor as Job's turkey for thirty years, suffering that special Negro fear of using up what little we get in this life—Loftis, he call that entropy—believing in her belly, and for all her faith, jim, that there just ain't no more coming tomorrow from grace, or the Lord, or from her own labor, like she can't kill nothing, and won't nothing die . . . so when Conners will her his wealth, it put her through changes, she be spellbound, possessed by the promise of life, panicky about depletion, and locked now in the past 'cause *every* purchase, you know, has to be a poor buy: a loss of life. Me, I wasn't worried none. Loftis, he got a brain trained by years of talking trash with people in Frog Hudson's barbershop on Thirty-fifth Street. By morning, I knew, he'd have some kinda wheeze worked out.

But Loftis, he don't come home. Me, I got kinda worried. I listen to the hi-fi all day Thursday, only pawing outside to peep down the stairs, like that'd make Loftis come sooner. So Thursday go by; and come Friday the head's out of kilter—first there's an ogrelike belch from the toilet bowl, then water bursts from the bathroom into the kitchen—and me, I can't call the super (How do I explain the tunnel?), so I gave up and quit bailing. But on Saturday, I could smell greens cooking next door. Twice I almost opened Miss Bailey's sardines, even though starving be less an evil than eating up our stash, but I waited till it was dark and, with my stomach talking to me, stepped outside to Pookie White's, lay a hard-luck story on him, and Pookie, he give me some jambalaya and gumbo. Back home in the living room, finger-feeding myself, barricaded in by all that hope-made material, the Kid felt like a king in his counting room, and I copped some Zs in an armchair till I heard the door move on its hinges, then bumping in the tunnel, and a heavy-footed walk thumped into the bedroom.

"Loftis?" I rubbed my eyes. "You back?" It be Sunday morning. Six-thirty sharp. Darkness dissolved slowly into the strangeness of twilight, with the rays of sunlight surging at exactly the same angle they fall each evening, as if the hour be an island, a moment outside time. Me, I'm afraid Loftis gonna fuss 'bout my not straightening up, letting things go. I went into the bathroom, poured water in the one-spigot washstand—brown rust come bursting out in flakes—and rinsed my face. "Loftis, you supposed to be home four days ago. Hey," I say, toweling my face, "you okay?" How come he don't answer me? Wiping my hands on the seat on my trousers, I tipped into Loftis's room. He sleeping with his mouth open. His legs be drawn up, both fists clenched between his knees. He'd kicked his blanket on the floor. In his sleep, Loftis laughed, or moaned, it be hard to tell. His eyelids, not quite shut, show slits of white. I decided to wait till Loftis wake up for his decision, but turning, I seen his watch, keys, and what looked in the first stain of sunlight to be a carefully wrapped piece of newspaper on his nightstand. The sunlight swelled to a bright shimmer, focusing the bedroom slowly like solution do a photographic image in the developer. And then something so freakish went down I ain't sure it took place. Fumble-fingered, I unfolded the paper, and inside be a blemished penny. It be like suddenly somebody slapped my head from behind. Taped on the penny be a slip of paper, and on the paper be the note "Found while walking down Devon Avenue." I hear Loftis mumble like he trapped in a nightmare. "Hold tight," I whisper. "It's all right." Me, I wanted to tell Loftis how Miss Bailey looked four days ago, that maybe it didn't have to be like that for us—did it?—because we could change. Couldn't we? Me, I pull his packed sheets over him, wrap up the penny, and, when I locate Miss Bailey's glass jar in the living room, put it away carefully, for now, with the rest of our things.

BORDERS

Thomas King

Canada

When I was twelve, maybe thirteen, my mother announced that we were going to go to Salt Lake City to visit my sister who had left the reserve, moved across the line, and found a job. Laetitia had not left home with my mother's blessing, but over time my mother had come to be proud of the fact that Laetitia had done all of this on her own.

"She did real good," my mother would say.

Then there were the fine points to Laetitia's going. She had not, as my mother liked to tell Mrs. Manyfingers, gone floating after some man like a balloon on a string. She hadn't snuck out of the house, either, and gone to Vancouver or Edmonton or Toronto to chase rainbows down alleys. And she hadn't been pregnant.

"She did real good."

I was seven or eight when Laetitia left home. She was seventeen. Our father was from Rocky Boy on the American side.

"Dad's American," Laetitia told my mother, "so I can go and come as I please."

"Send us a postcard."

Laetitia packed her things, and we headed for the border. Just outside of Milk River, Laetitia told us to watch for the water tower.

"Over the next rise. It's the first thing you see."

"We got a water tower on the reserve," my mother said. "There's a big one in Lethbridge, too."

"You'll be able to see the tops of the flagpoles, too. That's where the border is."

When we got to Coutts, my mother stopped at the convenience store and bought her and Laetitia a cup of coffee. I got an Orange Crush.

"This is real lousy coffee."

"You're just angry because I want to see the world."

"It's the water. From here on down, they got lousy water."

"I can catch the bus from Sweetgrass. You don't have to lift a finger."

"You're going to have to buy your water in bottles if you want good coffee."

There was an old wooden building about a block away, with a tall sign in the yard that said "Museum." Most of the roof had been blown away. Mom told me to go and see when the place was open. There were boards over the windows and doors. You could tell that the place was closed, and I told Mom so, but she said to go and check anyway. Mom and Laetitia stayed by the car. Neither one of them moved. I sat down on the steps of the museum and watched them, and I don't know that they ever said anything to each other. Finally, Laetitia got her bag out of the trunk and gave Mom a hug.

I wandered back to the car. The wind had come up, and it blew Laetitia's hair across her face. Mom reached out and pulled the strands out of Laetitia's eyes, and Laetitia let her.

"You can still see the mountain from here," my mother told Laetitia in Blackfoot.

"Lots of mountains in Salt Lake," Laetitia told her in English.

"The place is closed," I said. "Just like I told you."

Laetitia tucked her hair into her jacket and dragged her bag down the road to the brick building with the American flag flapping on a pole. When she got to where the guards were waiting, she turned, put the bag down, and waved to us. We waved back. Then my mother turned the car around, and we came home.

We got postcards from Laetitia regular, and, if she wasn't spreading jelly on the truth, she was happy. She found a good job and rented an apartment with a pool.

"And she can't even swim," my mother told Mrs. Manyfingers.

Most of the postcards said we should come down and see the city, but whenever I mentioned this, my mother would stiffen up.

So I was surprised when she bought two new tires for the car and put on her blue dress with the green and yellow flowers. I had to dress up, too, for my mother did not want us crossing the border looking like Americans. We made sandwiches and put them in a big box with pop and potato chips and some apples and bananas and a big jar of water.

"But we can stop at one of those restaurants, too, right?"

"We maybe should take some blankets in case you get sleepy."

"But we can stop at one of those restaurants, too, right?"

The border was actually two towns, though neither one was big enough to amount to anything. Coutts was on the Canadian side and consisted of the convenience store and gas station, the museum that was closed and boarded up, and a motel. Sweetgrass was on the American side, but all you could see was an overpass that arched across the highway and disappeared into the prairies. Just hearing the names of these towns, you would expect that Sweetgrass, which is a nice name and sounds like it is related to other places such as Medicine Hat and Moose Jaw and Kicking Horse Pass, would be on the Canadian side, and that Coutts, which sounds abrupt and rude, would be on the American side. But this was not the case.

Between the two borders was a duty-free shop where you could buy cigarettes and liquor and flags. Stuff like that.

We left the reserve in the morning and drove until we got to Coutts.

"Last time we stopped here," my mother said, "you had an Orange Crush. You remember that?"

"Sure," I said. "That was when Laetitia took off."

"You want another Orange Crush?"

"That means we're not going to stop at a restaurant, right?"

My mother got a coffee at the convenience store, and we stood around and watched the prairies move in the sunlight. Then we climbed back in the car. My mother straightened the dress across her thighs, leaned against the wheel, and drove all the way to the border in first gear, slowly, as if she were trying to see through a bad storm or riding high on black ice.

The border guard was an old guy. As he walked to the car, he swayed from side to side, his feet set wide apart, the holster on his hip pitching up and down. He leaned into the window, looked into the back seat, and looked at my mother and me.

"Morning, ma'am."

"Good morning."

"Where you heading?"

"Salt Lake City."

"Purpose of your visit?"

"Visit my daughter."

"Citizenship?"

"Blackfoot," my mother told him.

"Ma'am?"

"Blackfoot," my mother repeated.

"Canadian?"

"Blackfoot."

It would have been easier if my mother had just said "Canadian" and been done with it, but I could see she wasn't going to do that. The guard wasn't angry or anything. He smiled and looked towards the building. Then he turned back and nodded.

"Morning, ma'am."

"Good morning."

"Any firearms or tobacco?"

"No."

"Citizenship?"

"Blackfoot."

He told us to sit in the car and wait, and we did. In about five minutes, another guard came out with the first man. They were talking as they came, both men swaying back and forth like two cowboys headed for a bar or a gunfight.

"Morning, ma'am."

"Good morning."

"Cecil tells me you and the boy are Blackfoot."

"That's right."

"Now, I know that we got Blackfeet on the American side and the Canadians got Blackfeet on their side. Just so we can keep our records straight, what side do you come from?"

I knew exactly what my mother was going to say, and I could have told them if they had asked me.

"Canadian side or American side?" asked the guard.

"Blackfoot side," she said.

It didn't take them long to lose their sense of humor, I can tell you that. The one guard stopped smiling altogether and told us to park our car at the side of the building and come in.

We sat on a wood bench for about an hour before anyone came over to talk to us. This time it was a woman. She had a gun, too.

"Hi," she said. "I'm Inspector Pratt. I understand there is a little misunderstanding."

"I'm going to visit my daughter in Salt Lake City," my mother told her. "We don't have any guns or beer."

"It's a legal technicality, that's all."

"My daughter's Blackfoot, too."

The woman opened a briefcase and took out a couple of forms and began to write on one of them. "Everyone who crosses our border has to declare their citizenship. Even Americans. It helps us keep track of the visitors we get from the various countries."

She went on like that for maybe fifteen minutes, and a lot of the stuff she told us was interesting.

"I can understand how you feel about having to tell us your citizenship, and here's what I'll do. You tell me, and I won't put it down on the form. No-one will know but you and me."

Her gun was silver. There were several chips in the wood handle and the name "Stella" was scratched into the metal butt.

We were in the border office for about four hours, and we talked to almost everyone there. One of the men bought me a Coke. My mother brought a couple of sandwiches in from the car. I offered part of mine to Stella, but she said she wasn't hungry.

I told Stella that we were Blackfoot and Canadian, but she said that that didn't count because I was a minor. In the end, she told us that if my mother didn't declare her citizenship, we would have to go back to where we came from. My mother stood up and thanked Stella for her time. Then we got back in the car and drove to the Canadian border, which was only about a hundred yards away.

I was disappointed. I hadn't seen Laetitia for a long time, and I had never been to Salt Lake City. When she was still at home, Laetitia would go on and on about Salt Lake City. She had never been there, but her boyfriend Lester Tallbull had spent a year in Salt Lake at a technical school.

"It's a great place," Lester would say. "Nothing but blondes in the whole state."

Whenever he said that, Laetitia would slug him on his shoulder hard enough to make him flinch. He had some brochures on Salt Lake and some maps, and every so often the two of them would spread them out on the table.

"That's the temple. It's right downtown. You got to have a pass to get in."

"Charlotte says anyone can go in and look around."

"When was Charlotte in Salt Lake? Just when the hell was Charlotte in Salt Lake?"

"Last year."

"This is Liberty Park. It's got a zoo. There's good skiing in the mountains."

"Got all the skiing we can use," my mother would say. "People come from all over the world to ski at Banff. Cardston's got a temple, if you like those kinds of things."

"Oh, this one is real big," Lester would say. "They got armed guards and everything."

"Not what Charlotte says."

"What does she know?"

Lester and Laetitia broke up, but I guess the idea of Salt Lake stuck in her mind.

The Canadian border guard was a young woman, and she seemed happy to see us. "Hi," she said. "You folks sure have a great day for a trip. Where are you coming from?"

"Standoff."

"Is that in Montana?"

"No."

"Where are you going?"

"Standoff."

The woman's name was Carol and I don't guess she was any older than Laetitia. "Wow, you both Canadians?"

"Blackfoot."

"Really? I have a friend I went to school with who is Blackfoot. Do you know Mike Harley?"

"No."

"He went to school in Lethbridge, but he's really from Browning."

It was a nice conversation and there were no cars behind us, so there was no rush.

"You're not bringing any liquor back, are you?"

"No."

"Any cigarettes or plants or stuff like that?"

"No."

"Citizenship?"

"Blackfoot."

"I know," said the woman, "and I'd be proud of being Blackfoot if I were Blackfoot. But you have to be American or Canadian."

When Laetitia and Lester broke up, Lester took his brochures and maps with him, so Laetitia wrote to someone in Salt Lake City, and, about a month later, she got a big envelope of stuff. We sat at the table and opened up all the brochures, and Laetitia read each one out loud.

"Salt Lake City is the gateway to some of the world's most magnificent skiing.

"Salt Lake City is the home of one of the newest professional basketball franchises, the Utah Jazz.

"The Great Salt Lake is one of the natural wonders of the world."

It was kind of exciting seeing all those color brochures on the table and listening to Laetitia read all about how Salt Lake City was one of the best places in the entire world.

"That Salt Lake City place sounds too good to be true," my mother told her.

"It has everything."

"We got everything right here."

"It's boring here."

"People in Salt Lake City are probably sending away for brochures of Calgary and Lethbridge and Pincher Creek right now."

In the end, my mother would say that maybe Laetitia should go to Salt Lake City, and Laetitia would say that maybe she would.

We parked the car to the side of the building and Carol led us into a small room on the second floor. I found a comfortable spot on the couch and flipped through some back issues of *Saturday Night* and *Alberta Report.*

When I woke up, my mother was just coming out of another office. She didn't say a word to me. I followed her down the stairs and out to the car. I thought we were going home, but she turned the car around and drove back towards the American border, which made me think we were going to visit Laetitia in Salt Lake City after all. Instead she pulled into the parking lot of the duty-free store and stopped.

"We going to see Laetitia?"

"No."

"We going home?"

Pride is a good thing to have, you know. Laetitia had a lot of pride, and so did my mother. I figured that someday, I'd have it, too.

"So where are we going?"

Most of that day, we wandered around the duty-free store, which wasn't very large. The manager had a name tag with a tiny American flag on one side and a tiny Canadian flag on the other. His name was Mel. Towards evening, he began suggesting that we should be on our way. I told him we had nowhere to go, that neither the Americans nor the Canadians would let us in. He laughed at that and told us that we should buy something or leave.

The car was not very comfortable, but we did have all that food and it was April, so even if it did snow as it sometimes does on the prairies, we wouldn't freeze. The next morning my mother drove to the American border.

It was a different guard this time, but the questions were the same. We didn't spend as much time in the office as we had the day before. By noon, we were back at the Canadian border. By two we were back in the duty-free shop parking lot.

The second night in the car was not as much fun as the first, but my mother seemed in good spirits, and, all in all, it was as much an adventure as an inconvenience. There wasn't much food left and that was a problem, but we had lots of water as there was a faucet at the side of the duty-free shop.

One Sunday, Laetitia and I were watching television. Mom was over at Mrs. Manyfingers's. Right in the middle of the program, Laetitia turned off the set and said she was going to Salt Lake City, that life around here was too boring. I had wanted to see the rest of the program and really didn't care if Laetitia went to Salt Lake City or not. When Mom got home, I told her what Laetitia had said.

What surprised me was how angry Laetitia got when she found out that I had told Mom.

"You got a big mouth."

"That's what you said."

"What I said is none of your business."

"I didn't say anything."

"Well, I'm going for sure, now."

That weekend, Laetitia packed her bags, and we drove her to the border.

Mel turned out to be friendly. When he closed up for the night and found us still parked in the lot, he came over and asked us if our car was broken down or something. My mother thanked him for his concern and told him that we were fine, that things would get straightened out in the morning.

"You're kidding," said Mel. "You'd think they could handle the simple things."

"We got some apples and a banana," I said, "but we're all out of ham sandwiches."

"You know, you read about these things, but you just don't believe it. You just don't believe it."

"Hamburgers would be even better because they got more stuff for energy."

My mother slept in the back seat. I slept in the front because I was smaller and could lie under the steering wheel. Late that night, I heard my mother open the car door. I found her sitting on her blanket leaning against the bumper of the car.

"You see all those stars," she said. "When I was a little girl, my grandmother used to take me and my sisters out on the prairies and tell us stories about all the stars."

"Do you think Mel is going to bring us any hamburgers?"

"Every one of those stars has a story. You see that bunch of stars over there that look like a fish?"

"He didn't say no."

"Coyote went fishing, one day. That's how it all started." We sat out under the stars that night, and my mother told me all sorts of stories. She was serious about it, too. She'd tell them slow, repeating parts as she went, as if she expected me to remember each one.

Early the next morning, the television vans began to arrive, and guys in suits and women in dresses came trotting over to us, dragging microphones and cameras and lights behind them. One of the vans had a table set up with orange juice and sandwiches and fruit. It was for the crew, but when I told them we hadn't eaten for a while, a really skinny blonde woman told us we could eat as much as we wanted.

They mostly talked to my mother. Every so often one of the reporters would come over and ask me questions about how it felt to be an Indian without a country. I told them we had a nice house on the reserve and that my cousins had a couple of horses we rode when we went fishing. Some of the television people went over to the American border, and then they went to the Canadian border.

Around noon, a good-looking guy in a dark blue suit and an orange tie with little ducks on it drove up in a fancy car. He talked to my mother for a while, and, after they were done talking, my mother called me over, and we got into our car. Just as my mother started the engine, Mel came over and gave us a bag of peanut brittle and told us that justice was a damn hard thing to get, but that we shouldn't give up.

I would have preferred lemon drops, but it was nice of Mel anyway.

"Where are we going now?"

"Going to visit Laetitia."

The guard who came out to our car was all smiles. The television lights were so bright they hurt my eyes, and, if you tried to look through the windshield in certain directions, you couldn't see a thing.

"Morning, ma'am."

"Good morning."

"Where you heading?"

"Salt Lake City."

"Purpose of your visit?"

"Visit my daughter."

"Any tobacco, liquor, or firearms?"

"Don't smoke."

"Any plants or fruit?"

"Not any more."

"Citizenship?"

"Blackfoot."

The guard rocked back on his heels and jammed his thumbs into his gun belt. "Thank you," he said, his fingers patting the butt of the revolver. "Have a pleasant trip."

My mother rolled the car forward, and the television people had to scramble out of the way. They ran alongside the car as we pulled away from the border, and, when they couldn't run any farther, they stood in the middle of the highway and waved and waved and waved.

We got to Salt Lake City the next day. Laetitia was happy to see us, and, that first night, she took us out to a restaurant that made really good soups. The list of pies took up a whole page. I had cherry. Mom had chocolate. Laetitia said that she saw us on television the night before and, during the meal, she had us tell her the story over and over again.

Laetitia took us everywhere. We went to a fancy ski resort. We went to the temple. We got to go shopping in a couple of large malls, but they weren't as large as the one in Edmonton, and Mom said so.

After a week or so, I got bored and wasn't at all sad when my mother said we should be heading back home. Laetitia wanted us to stay longer, but Mom said no, that she had things to do back home and that, next time, Laetitia should come up and visit. Laetitia said she was thinking about moving back, and Mom told her to do as she pleased, and Laetitia said that she would.

On the way home, we stopped at the duty-free shop, and my mother gave Mel a green hat that said "Salt Lake" across the front. Mel was a funny guy. He took the hat and blew his nose and told my mother that she was an inspiration to us all. He gave us some more peanut brittle and came out into the parking lot and waved at us all the way to the Canadian border.

It was almost evening when we left Coutts. I watched the border through the rear window until all you could see were the tops of the flagpoles and the blue water tower, and then they rolled over a hill and disappeared.

SAINTS

Bharati Mukherjee

United States

"And one more thing," Mom says. "Your father can't take you this August."

I can tell from the way she fusses with the placemats that she is interested in my reaction. The placemats are made of pinkish linen and I can see a couple of ironing marks, like shiny little arches. Wayne is coming for dinner. Wayne Latta is her new friend. It's the first time she's having him over with others, but that's not why she's nervous.

"That's okay," I tell her. "Tran and I have plans for the summer."

Mom rolls up the spray-starched napkins and knots them until they look like nesting birds on each dinner plate. "It isn't that he's really busy," she says. She gives me one of her I-know-you're-hurting, son, looks. "I don't see why he can't take you. He says he has a conference to go to in Hong Kong at the end of July, so he might as well do China in August."

"It's okay. Really," I say. It's true, I am okay. At fifteen I'm too old to be a pawn between them, and too young to get caught in problems of my own. I'm in a state of grace. I want to get to my room in this state of grace before it disintegrates, and start a new game of "Geopolitique 1990" on the Apple II–Plus Dad gave me last Christmas.

"Can you get the flower holders, Shawn?" Mom asks.

I take a wide, flat cardboard box out of the buffet.

She lifts eight tiny glass holders out of the box, and lines them up in the center of the table. She hasn't used them since things started going bad between Dad and her. When things blew up, they sold the big house in New Jersey and Mom and I moved to this college town in upstate New York. Mom works in the Admissions Office. Wayne calls it a college for rich bitches who were too dumb to get into Bennington or Barnard.

"Get me a pitcher of water and the flowers," Mom says.

In a dented aluminum pot in the kitchen sink, eight yellow rosebuds are soaking up water. Granules of sugar are whitish and still sludgy in the bottom of the pot. Mom's a believer; she's read somewhere that sugar in lukewarm water keeps cut flowers fresh. I move the pot to one side and fill a quart-sized measuring cup with lukewarm water. I know her routines.

It's going to be an anxious evening for Mom. She's set out extra goblets for spritzers on a tray lined with paper towels. Index cards typed up with recipes for dips and sauces are stacked on the windowsill. She shouldn't do sauces, nothing that requires last-minute frying and stirring. She's the flustery type, and she's only setting herself up for failure.

"What happened to the water, Shawn?"

It's a Pizza Hut night for me, definitely. I know what she's going through with Wayne. He's not at all like Dad, the good Dr. Manny Patel, who soothes crazies at Creedmore all day. Nights he's a playboy and slum landlord, Mom says.

Mom says, "Your father will call you tomorrow, he said. He wants to talk to you himself. He wants to know what you want this Christmas."

This is only the first Thursday in November. Dad's planning ahead is a joke with us. Foresight is what got him out of Delhi to New York. "Could I have become a psychiatrist and a near-millionaire if I hadn't planned well ahead?" Dad used to tell Mom in the medium-bad days.

Mom thinks making a million is a vicious, selfish aim. But Dad's really very generous. He sends money to relatives and to Indian orphanages. He's generous but practical. He says he doesn't want to send me stuff—cashmere sweaters and Ultrasuede jackets, the stuff he likes—that'll end up in basement cedar closets.

"I'll be late tomorrow," I remind Mom. "Fridays I have my chess club."

Actually, Tran and I and a bunch of other guys from the chess club play four afternoons a week. Thursdays we don't play because Tran has Debate Workshop.

"You know what I want, Mom. You can tell him."

I ask for computer games, video cassettes, nothing major. So twice a year

Dad sends big checks. Dad's real generous with me. It makes him feel the big benefactor, Mom says, whenever a check comes in the mail. But that's only because things went really bad two years ago. They sent me away to boarding school, but they still couldn't work things out between them.

At five, Wayne comes into our driveway in his blue Toyota pickup. The wheels squeal and rock in the deep, snowy ruts. Wayne has a cord of firewood in the back of the truck. Mom paid him for the firewood yesterday and for the time he put in picking up the cord from some French guy in Ballston Spa. Wayne's a writer; meantime he works as a janitor in the college. A "mopologist" is what he calls himself. It's so corny, but every time Wayne uses that word, Mom gives him a tinkly, supportive laugh. Janitors are more caring than shrinks, the laugh seems to say.

We hear Wayne on the back porch, cursing as he drops an armload of logs. For all his muscles, he's a clumsy man. But then Mom could never have gotten Dad to carry the logs himself. Dad would have had them delivered or done without them.

Mom takes five-dollar bills out of the buffet drawer and counts out thirty dollars. "For the wine, would you give it to him? I couldn't do a production all by myself on a weeknight."

"Why do a production at all?"

She stiffens. "I'm not ashamed of Wayne," she says. "Wayne is who he is."

Wayne finally comes into the dining room. I slip him the money; it's more than he expected. "I got some beer too, Mila." Mom's name is Camille but he calls her Mila. That's a hard thing to get used to. He drops my rucksack on the floor, turns the chair around and straddles it. There are five other chairs around the table and two folding chairs brought up from the basement for tonight. Under Wayne's muscular thighs, the dining room chair looks rickety, absurdly elegant. Red long-johns show through the knee rips of his blue jeans. He keeps his red knit cap on. But he's not as tough as he looks. He keeps the cap on because he's sensitive about his bald, baby-pink head.

"Hey, Shawn," he says to me. "Still baking the competition?"

It's Wayne's usual joke about my playing competitive chess. Our school team has T-shirts that we paid for by working the concession stands on basketball nights last winter. Tran plays varsity first board, I play third. Now we need chess cheerleaders, Wayne kids me. *"Hey, hey, push that pawn! Dee-fense, dee-fense, King's Indian dee-fense!"* Wayne isn't a bad sort, not for around here. Last year we went for trout out on the Battenkill. The day with Wayne wasn't bad, given our complicated situation. I went back to the creek with Tran a week later, but it was different. Tran's idea of fishing is throwing a net across the river, tossing in a stick of dynamite, then pulling it up.

"You'll like Milos and Verna," Mom tells Wayne. "They're both painters in the Art Department. From Yugoslavia, but I think they're hoping to stay in the States."

From the soft, nervous look she's giving Wayne, I know it isn't the Yugoslavs she's thinking of right at the moment. Wayne grabs her throat in his thick hairy hands. She lifts her face. Then she glances at me in a quick guilty way as if she's already given away too much.

I know about feelings. I've got a secret life, too.

"D'you have enough for a pizza?" Mom asks me. She's moved away from Wayne.

Yeah, I have enough.

From the Pizza Hut, Tran and I go back to Tran's place. Tran's sixteen and he owns a noisy used Plymouth. It's two-tone, white and aquamarine. I like the colors. Tran's a genuine boatperson. When he was younger, the English teacher made him tell the class about having to hide from pirates and having to chew on raw fish just to stay alive. Women on his boat hid any valuable stuff they had in their vaginas. "That's enough, Tran, thank you," the teacher said. Now he never mentions his cruise to America.

We skid to a stop inside the Indian Lookout Point Trailer Park where he lives with his mother in a flash of aqua. The lights are on in Tran's mobile home. Tran's mother's muddy Chevy and his stepfather's Dodge Ram are angle-parked. Tran's real father got left behind in Saigon.

"I don't know," Tran says. He doesn't cut the engine. We sit in the warm, dark car. "Maybe we ought to go on to your place. He never gets home this early."

It's minus ten outside, maybe worse with the wind-chill factor. I open the car door softly. The carlight on Tran's face makes his face look ochre-dingy, mottled with pimples.

"Mom's entertaining tonight," I warn him. The snow is slippery cold under my Adidas. I pick my way through icy patches to the trailer, and look in a little front window.

Tran's mom is at the kitchen sink, washing a glass. She's still wearing her wool coat and plaid scarf. Her face has an odd puffy quiver. There are no signs of physical violence, but someone's sure been hurt. Tran's stepfather (he didn't, and can't, adopt Tran until some agency can locate Tran's real father, and get his consent) is sitting hunched forward in a rocker, and drinking Miller Lite.

Like Tran, I've learned to discount homey scenes.

"That's okay," Tran says. He's calling out from the car. His sad face is in the opened window. "Your place is bigger."

It makes sense, but I can't move away from his little window.

"I can show you a move that'll bake Sato," he says. "I mean really bake his ass."

We both hate Sato but Sato isn't smart enough to wince under our hate or even smart enough to know when his ass has really been baked.

"Okay." There's that new killer chess move, and a new Peter Gabriel for us to listen to. Tran's chess rating is just under 1900. Farelli's is higher, but Farelli is more than arrogant. He's so arrogant he dropped off the team. He goes down to Manhattan instead and hustles games in Times Square or in the chess clubs. Tran's a little guilty about playing first board; he knows he owes it to Farelli's vanity. The difference between Farelli and Tran is about the same as between Tran and me. Farelli wants to charge the club four-fifty an hour for tutoring. He's the only real American in the club. The rest of us have names like Sato, Chin, Duoc, Cho and Prasad. My name's Patel, Shawn Patel. Mom took back her maiden name, Belliveau, when we moved out of Upper Montclair. We're supposed to be out of Dad's reach here, except for checks.

A week after Mom's dinner party, Tran and I are coming out of an arcade on Upper Broadway Street when we see Wayne walking our way. Upper Broadway's short and squat. The storefronts have shallow doorways you can't hide in. Wayne is with the Yugoslav woman, the painter who doesn't intend to go back to her country. They aren't holding hands or anything, they aren't even touching shoulders, but I can tell they want to do things. The Yugoslav has both her hands in the pockets of her duffle coat. A toggle at her throat is missing and the loop has nothing to weigh it down. The Yugoslav has red cheeks. With her red cheeks, her button nose and her long, loose hair, she looks very young. Maybe it's a trick of afternoon light or of European make-up, but she looks too young to be a friend of Mom's.

Wayne wants to hug her. I can tell from the way he arches his upper body inside his coat. He wants to sneak his hand into her pocket, pull out her fist, swing hands on Upper Broadway and be stared at by everyone.

I pull Tran back inside the arcade.

"I got to get to Houston," Tran says. We're playing "Joust," his favorite game, but his slight body is twisted in misery.

"It'll work out," I tell him. Wanting to go to Houston has to do with his mother and stepfather. Things always go bad between parents. "You can't leave in the middle of the semester. It doesn't make sense."

"What does?"

Tran has an older brother in Houston, in engineering school. Tran thinks his mother will come up with the bus fare south. She works at Grand Union, and weekends she waitresses. "My luck's got to change," he says.

Luck has nothing to do with anything, I want to say. You're out of the clutch of pirates now. No safe hiding places.

Wayne and his painter make us spend too many tokens on this Joust machine.

Mom's in the eating nook of the kitchen, reading a book on English gardens when I come in the back door. She's wearing a long skirt made of quilted fabric and a matching jacket. The quilting makes her look fat, and ridiculous.

She catches my grin. "It's warm, don't knock it," she says of her skirt. These upstate houses are drafty. Then she pulls her feet up under her and wriggles her raised knees gracelessly under the long skirt. "And I love the color on me."

I bleed. Mom should have had a daughter. Two women could have con-soled each other. I can only think of Wayne, how even now he's slipping the loops over Serbian toggles. It's a complicated feeling. I bleed because I'm disloyal.

"Your father's sent a present by UPS," she says. She doesn't look up from the illustration of a formal garden of a lord. A garden with a stiff, bristly hedged maze to excite desire and contain it. "I put the package on your desk upstairs. It looks like a book."

She means to say, Dad's presents are always impersonal.

Actually it's two books that Dad has sent me this time. The thick, heavy one is an art book, reproductions of Moghul paintings that Dad loves. Even India was once an empire-building nation. The other is a thin book with bad binding put out by a religious printing house in Madras. The little book is about a Hindu saint who had visions. Dad has sent me a book about visions.

May this book bring you as much happiness as it did me when I was your age, Dad's inscription reads. Then a p.s. *The saint died of throat cancer and was briefly treated by your great-uncle, the cancer specialist in Calcutta.*

Forty pages into the book, the saint describes a vision. "I see the Divine Mother in all things." He sees Her in ants, dogs, flowers, the latrine bowls in the temple. He keeps falling into trances as he goes for walks or as he says his prayers. In this perfect state, sometimes the saint kicks his disciples. He eats garbage thrown out by temple cooks for cows and pariah dogs.

"Did I kick you?" the saint asks when he comes out of his trance. "Kick, kick," beg the disciples as they push each other to get near enough for a saintly touch.

My father, healer of derangements, slum landlord with income properties on two continents, believer of visions, pleasure-taker where none seems present, is a mystery.

Downstairs Mom is dialing Wayne's number. In the whir of the telephone dial, I read the new rhythms of her agony. Wayne will not answer his phone tonight. Wayne is in bed with his naked Yugoslav.

It's my turn to call. I slip my bony finger into the dial's fingerholes. "Want to ball?" I whisper into the mouthpiece. My throat is raspy from the fullness of desire.

"What?" It's a girlish voice at the other end. "What did you say?"

The girl giggles. "You dumb pervert." She leaves it to me to hang up first.

The next night, a Friday night, Tran and I come down from my room to get Mountain Dew out of the fridge. Mom and Wayne are making out in the kitchen. He has her jammed up against the eating nook's wall. There are Indian paintings on that wall. She kept the paintings and gave Dad the statues and framed batiks. Wayne holds Mom's head against dusty glass, behind which an emperor in Moghul battledress is leading his army out of the capital. Wayne's got his knee high up Mom's quilted skirt. The knee presses in, hard. I see love's monstrous force bloat her face. Wayne has her head in his grasp. Her orange hair tufts out between his knuckles, and its orange mist covers the bygone emperor and his soldiers.

Tran's used to living in small, usurped spaces. He drops a shy, civil little cough, and right away Wayne lets go of Mom's hair. But his knee is still raised, still pressing into her skirt.

"Get outta here, guys," he says. He looks pleased, he sounds good-natured. "You got better things to do. Go push your pawns."

"Tell her about the painter," I say. My voice is even, not emotional.

"What're you talking about? What's the matter with you?"

Tran says, "Let's get the soda, Shawn." He picks up the six-pack and two glasses and pushes me toward the stairwell.

Upstairs, Tran and I take turns dialling the town's other insomniacs. "Do you have soft breasts?" I ask. I really want to know. "Yes," one of them confesses. "Very soft and very white and I'm so lonely tonight. Do you want to touch?"

Tran reads aloud an episode from the life of the Hindu saint. Reaching the state of perfection while strolling along the Ganges one day, the saint fell and broke his arm. The saint had been thinking of his love for the young boy followers who lived in the temple. He had been thinking of his love for them—love as for a sweetheart, he says—when he slipped into a trance and stumbled. Love and pain: in the saint's mind there is no separation.

Tran makes the last of our calls for the night. "You bitch," he says as he shakes his thin body in a parody of undulation. To me he says, "Mother won't come through with the bus fare to Houston."

Tonight Tran wants to sleep over in my room. Tomorrow we'll find a way to raise the bus fare.

I want to tell him things, to console him. Bad luck and good luck even out over a lifetime. Cancer can ravage an ecstatic saint. Things pass. I don't remember Dad in any intimate way except that he embarrassed me when he came to pick me up from my old boarding school. The overstated black Mercedes, the hugging and kissing in such a foreign way.

A little before midnight, Tran's moan startles me awake. He must be dreaming of fathers, pirates, saints and Houston. For me the worst isn't dreams. It's having to get out of the house at night and walk around. At midnight I float like a ghost through other people's gardens. I peer into other boys' bedrooms, I become somebody else's son.

Tonight I'm more restless than other nights. I look for an Indian name in the phone book. The directory in our upstate town is thin; it caves against my eager arms. The first name I spot is Batliwalla. Meaning perhaps bottle-walla, a dealer in bottles in the ancestral long-ago. Batliwalla, Jamshed S., M.D.

I dress in the dark for a night of cold roaming. It'll be a night of walking in a state of perfect grace. For disguise, I choose Mom's red cloth coat from the hall cupboard and her large red wool beret into which she has stuck a pheasant feather. She keeps five more feathers, like a bouquet, in a candy jar. The feathers are from Wayne the hunter. Wayne's promised to put a pheasant on our table for Thanksgiving dinner. I can taste its hard, stringy birdflesh and pellets of buckshot.

Like the Hindu saint, I walk my world in boots and a trance. But in this upstate town the only body of water is an icy creek, not the Ganges.

The Batliwallas have no curtains on their back windows. I look into a back bedroom that glows from a bedside lamp. A kid in pajamas is sitting up in bed, a book in his hands. He's a little kid, a junior high kid, or maybe a studious dwarf. The dwarfkid rocks back and forth under his bedclothes. He seems to be learning something, maybe a poem, by heart. He's the conqueror of alien syllables. His fleshy, brown lips purse and pout ferociously. His tiny head in its helmet of glossy black hair bumps, bumps, bumps the bed's white vinyl headboard. The dwarfkid's eyes are screwed tightly shut, and his long eyelashes look like tiny troughs for ghosts to drink out of. Wanting good grades, the dwarfkid studies into the night. He rocks, he shouts, he bumps his head. I can't hear the words, but I want to reach out to a fellow saint.

When I get home, the back porch is dark but the kitchen light is on. I sit on the stack of firewood and look in. I'm not cold, or sleepy. Wayne and Mom are fighting in the kitchen, literally slugging each other. I had Wayne figured wrong.

He isn't the sly operator after all. He's opened up my Mom's upper lip. It's blood Mom is washing off.

"Get out," Mom screams at him. This time I can make out all the words. I feel like a god, overseeing lives.

The faucet is running as it had done the day there were yellow rosebuds in a kitchen pot. Steam from the hot, running water frizzes Mom's hair. She looks old. "Get out of my house."

"I'm getting out." Wayne says. But he doesn't leave. First he lights a cigarette, something Mom doesn't permit. Then he flops down on one of the two kitchen stools, props his workboots on the other and starts to adjust the laces. "I wouldn't stay if you begged me."

"Get out, out!" Mom's still screaming as I turn my house key in the lock. She might as well know it all. "Do me a favor, get out. Lace your goddamn boots in your goddamn truck. Please get out."

I move through the bright kitchen into the dark dining room, and wait for the lovers to finish.

In a while Wayne leaves. He doesn't slam the door. He doesn't toss the key on the floor. The pickup's low beams dance on frozen bushes.

"My god, Shawn!" Mom has switched on a wall light in the dining room. She's staring at me, she's really looking at me. Finally. "My god, what have you done to your face, poor baby."

Her fingers scrape at the muck on my face, the cheek-blush, lipstick, eyeshadow. Her bruised mouth is on my hair. I can feel her warm, wet sobs, but I don't hurt. I am in a trance in the middle of a November night. I can't hurt for me, for Dad, I can't hurt for anyone in the world. I feel so strong, so much a potentate in battledress.

How wondrous to be a visionary. If I were to touch someone now, I'd be touching god.

THE TURKEY SEASON

Alice
Munro

Canada

When I was fourteen I got a job at the Turkey Barn for the Christmas season. I was still too young to get a job working in a store or as a part-time waitress; I was also too nervous.

I was a turkey gutter. The other people who worked at the Turkey Barn were Lily and Marjorie and Gladys, who were also gutters; Irene and Henry, who were pluckers; Herb Abbott, the foreman, who superintended the whole operation and filled in wherever he was needed. Morgan Elliott was the owner and boss. He and his son, Morgy, did the killing.

Morgy I knew from school. I thought him stupid and despicable and was uneasy about having to consider him in a new and possibly superior guise, as the boss's son. But his father treated him so roughly, yelling and swearing at him, that he seemed no more than the lowest of the workers. The other person related to the boss was Gladys. She was his sister, and in her case there did seem to be some privilege of position. She worked slowly and went home if she was not feeling well, and was not friendly to Lily and Marjorie, although she was, a little, to me. She had come back to live with Morgan and his family after working for many years in Toronto, in a bank. This was not the sort of job she was used to. Lily and

Marjorie, talking about her when she wasn't there, said she had had a nervous breakdown. They said Morgan made her work in the Turkey Barn to pay for her keep. They also said, with no worry about the contradiction, that she had taken the job because she was after a man, and that the man was Herb Abbott.

All I could see when I closed my eyes, the first few nights after working there, was turkeys. I saw them hanging upside down, plucked and stiffened, pale and cold, with the heads and necks limp, the eyes and nostrils clotted with dark blood; the remaining bits of feathers—those dark and bloody, too—seemed to form a crown. I saw them not with aversion but with a sense of endless work to be done.

Herb Abbott showed me what to do. You put the turkey down on the table and cut its head off with a cleaver. Then you took the loose skin around the neck and stripped it back to reveal the crop, nestled in the cleft between the gullet and the windpipe.

"Feel the gravel," said Herb encouragingly. He made me close my fingers around the crop. Then he showed me how to work my hand down behind it to cut it out, and the gullet and windpipe as well. He used shears to cut the vertebrae.

"Scrunch, scrunch," he said soothingly. "Now, put your hand in."

I did. It was deathly cold in there, in the turkey's dark insides.

"Watch out for bone splinters."

Working cautiously in the dark, I had to pull the connecting tissues loose.

"Ups-a-daisy." Herb turned the bird over and flexed each leg. "Knees up, Mother Brown. Now." He took a heavy knife and placed it directly on the knee knuckle joints and cut off the shank.

"Have a look at the worms."

Pearly-white strings, pulled out of the shank, were creeping about on their own.

"That's just the tendons shrinking. Now comes the nice part!"

He slit the bird at its bottom end, letting out a rotten smell.

"Are you educated?"

I did not know what to say.

"What's that smell?"

"Hydrogen sulfide."

"Educated," said Herb, sighing. "All right. Work your fingers around and get the guts loose. Easy. Easy. Keep your fingers together. Keep the palm inwards. Feel the ribs with the back of your hand. Feel the guts fit into your palm. Feel that? Keep going. Break the strings—as many as you can. Keep going. Feel a hard lump? That's the gizzard. Feel a soft lump? That's the heart. O.K.? O.K. Get your fingers around the gizzard. Easy. Start pulling this way. That's right. That's right. Start to pull her out."

It was not easy at all. I wasn't even sure what I had was the gizzard. My hand was full of cold pulp.

"Pull," he said, and I brought out a glistening, liverish mass.

"Got it. There's the lights. You know what they are? Lungs. There's the heart. There's the gizzard. There's the gall. Now, you don't ever want to break that gall inside or it will taste the entire turkey." Tactfully, he scraped out what I had missed, including the testicles, which were like a pair of white grapes.

"Nice pair of earrings," Herb said.

Herb Abbott was a tall, firm, plump man. His hair was dark and thin, combined straight back from a widow's peak, and his eyes seemed to be slightly slanted, so that he looked like a pale Chinese or like pictures of the Devil, except that he was smooth-faced and benign. Whatever he did around the Turkey Barn— gutting, as he was now, or loading the truck, or hanging the carcasses—was done with efficient, economical movements, quickly and buoyantly. "Notice about Herb—he always walks like he had a boat moving underneath him," Marjorie said, and it was true. Herb worked on the lake boats, during the season, as a cook. Then he worked for Morgan until after Christmas. The rest of the time he helped around the poolroom, making hamburgers, sweeping up, stopping fights before they got started. That was where he lived; he had a room above the poolroom on the main street.

In all the operations at the Turkey Barn it seemed to be Herb who had the efficiency and honor of the business continually on his mind; it was he who kept everything under control. Seeing him in the yard talking to Morgan, who was a thick, short man, red in the face, an unpredictable bully, you would be sure that it was Herb who was the boss and Morgan the hired help. But it was not so.

If I had not had Herb to show me, I don't think I could have learned turkey gutting at all. I was clumsy with my hands and had been shamed for it so often that the least show of impatience on the part of the person instructing me could have brought on a dithering paralysis. I could not stand to be watched by anybody but Herb. Particularly, I couldn't stand to be watched by Lily and Marjorie, two middle-aged sisters, who were very fast and thorough and competitive gutters. They sang at their work and talked abusively and intimately to the turkey carcasses.

"Don't you nick me, you old bugger!"

"Aren't you the old crap factory!"

I had never heard women talk like that.

Gladys was not a fast gutter, though she must have been thorough; Herb would have talked to her otherwise. She never sang and certainly she never swore. I thought her rather old, though she was not as old as Lily and Marjorie; she must have been over thirty. She seemed offended by everything that went on and had the air of keeping plenty of bitter judgments to herself. I never tried to talk to her, but she spoke to me one day in the cold little washroom off the gutting shed. She was putting pancake makeup on her face. The color of the makeup was so distinct from the color of her skin that it was as if she were slapping orange paint over a whitewashed, bumpy wall.

She asked me if my hair was naturally curly.

I said yes.

"You don't have to get a permanent?"

"No."

"You're lucky. I have to do mine up every night. The chemicals in my system won't allow me to get a permanent."

There are different ways women have of talking about their looks. Some women make it clear that what they do to keep themselves up is for the sake of sex, for men. Others, like Gladys, make the job out to be a kind of housekeeping, whose very difficulties they pride themselves on. Gladys was genteel. I could see her in the bank, in a navy-blue dress with the kind of detachable white collar you can wash at night. She would be grumpy and correct.

Another time, she spoke to me about her periods, which were profuse and painful. She wanted to know about mine. There was an uneasy, prudish, agitated expression on her face. I was saved by Irene, who was using the toilet and called out, "Do like me, and you'll be rid of all your problems for a while." Irene was only a few years older than I was, but she was recently—tardily—married, and heavily pregnant.

Gladys ignored her, running cold water on her hands. The hands of all of us were red and sore-looking from the work. "I can't use that soap. If I use it, I break out in a rash," Gladys said. "If I bring my own soap in here, I can't afford to have other people using it, because I pay a lot for it—it's a special anti-allergy soap."

I think the idea that Lily and Marjorie promoted—that Gladys was after Herb Abbott—sprang from their belief that single people ought to be teased and embarrassed whenever possible, and from their interest in Herb, which led to the feeling that somebody ought to be after him. They wondered about him. What they wondered was: How can a man want so little? No wife, no family, no house. The details of his daily life, the small preferences, were of interest. Where had he been brought up? (Here and there and all over.) How far had he gone in school? (Far enough.) Where was his girlfriend? (Never tell.) Did he drink coffee or tea if he got the choice? (Coffee.)

When they talked about Gladys's being after him they must have really wanted to talk about sex—what he wanted and what he got. They must have felt a voluptuous curiosity about him, as I did. He aroused this feeling by being circumspect and not making the jokes some men did, and at the same time by not being squeamish or gentlemanly. Some men, showing me the testicles from the turkey, would have acted as if the very existence of testicles were somehow a bad joke on me, something a girl could be taunted about; another sort of man would have been embarrassed and would have thought he had to protect me from embarrassment. A man who didn't seem to feel one way or the other was an oddity—as much to older women, probably, as to me. But what was so welcome to me may have been disturbing to them. They wanted to jolt him. They even wanted Gladys to jolt him, if she could.

There wasn't any idea then—at least in Logan, Ontario, in the late for-ties—about homosexuality's going beyond very narrow confines. Women, cer-tainly, believed in its rarity and in definite boundaries. There were homosexuals in town, and we knew who they were: an elegant, light-voiced, wavy-haired paperhanger who called himself an interior decorator; the minister's widow's fat, spoiled only son, who went so far as to enter baking contests and had crocheted a tablecloth; a hypochondriacal church organist and music teacher who kept the choir and his pupils in line with screaming tantrums. Once the label was fixed, there was a good deal of tolerance for these people, and their talents for decorating, for crocheting, and for music were appreciated—especially by women. "The poor fellow," they said. "He doesn't do any harm." They really seemed to believe—the women did—that it was the penchant for baking or music that was the determin-ing factor, and that it was this activity that made the man what he was—not any other detours he might take, or wish to take. A desire to play the violin would be taken as more a deviation from manliness than would a wish to shun women. Indeed, the idea was that any manly man would wish to shun women but most of them were caught off guard, and for good.

I don't want to go into the question of whether Herb was homosexual or not, because the definition is of no use to me. I think that probably he was, but maybe he was not. (Even considering what happened later, I think that.) He is not a puzzle so arbitrarily solved.

The other plucker, who worked with Irene, was Henry Streets, a neighbor of ours. There was nothing remarkable about him except that he was eighty-six years old and still, as he said of himself, a devil for work. He had whiskey in his thermos, and drank it from time to time through the day. It was Henry who had said to me, in our kitchen, "You ought to get yourself a job at the Turkey Barn. They need another gutter." Then my father said at once, "Not her, Henry. She's got ten thumbs," and Henry said he was just joking—it was dirty work. But I was already determined to try it—I had a great need to be successful in a job like this. I was almost in the condition of a grownup person who is ashamed of never having learned to read, so much did I feel my ineptness at manual work. Work, to everybody I knew, meant doing things I was no good at doing, and work was what people prided themselves on and measured each other by. (It goes without saying that the things I was good at, like schoolwork, were suspect or held in plain contempt.) So it was a surprise and then a triumph for me not to get fired, and to be able to turn out clean turkeys at a rate that was not disgraceful. I don't know if I really understood how much Herb Abbott was responsible for this, but he would sometimes say, "Good girl," or pat my waist and say, "You're getting to be a good gutter—you'll go a long ways in the world," and when I felt his quick, kind touch through the heavy sweater and bloody smock I wore, I felt my face glow and I wanted to lean back against him as he stood behind me. I wanted to rest my head against his wide, fleshy shoulder. When I went to sleep at night, lying on my side, I would rub my cheek against the pillow and think of that as Herb's shoulder.

I was interested in how he talked to Gladys, how he looked at her or noticed her. This interest was not jealousy. I think I wanted something to happen with them. I quivered in curious expectation, as Lily and Marjorie did. We all wanted to see the flicker of sexuality in him, hear it in his voice, not because we thought it would make him seem more like other men but because we knew that with him it would be entirely different. He was kinder and more patient than most women, and as stern and remote, in some ways, as any man. We wanted to see how he could be moved.

If Gladys wanted this, too, she didn't give any signs of it. It is impossible for me to tell with women like her whether they are as thick and deadly as they seem, not wanting anything much but opportunities for irritation and contempt, or if they are all choked up with gloomy fires and useless passions.

Marjorie and Lily talked about marriage. They did not have much good to say about it, in spite of their feeling that it was a state nobody should be allowed to stay out of. Marjorie said that shortly after her marriage she had gone into the woodshed with the intention of swallowing Paris green.

"I'd have done it," she said. "But the man came along in the grocery truck and I had to go out and buy the groceries. This was when we lived on the farm."

Her husband was cruel to her in those days, but later he suffered an accident—he rolled the tractor and was so badly hurt he would be an invalid all his life. They moved to town, and Marjorie was the boss now.

"He starts to sulk the other night and says he don't want his supper. Well, I just picked up his wrist and held it. He was scared I was going to twist his arm. He could see I'd do it. So I say, 'You *what?*' And he says, 'I'll eat it.' "

They talked about their father. He was a man of the old school. He had a noose in the woodshed (not the Paris green woodshed—this would be an earlier one, on another farm), and when they got on his nerves he used to line them up and threaten to hang them. Lily, who was the younger, would shake till she fell down. This same father had arranged to marry Marjorie off to a crony of his when she was just sixteen. That was the husband who had driven her to the Paris green. Their father did it because he wanted to be sure she wouldn't get into trouble.

"Hot blood," Lily said.

I was horrified, and asked, "Why didn't you run away?"

"His word was law," Marjorie said.

They said that was what was the matter with kids nowadays—it was the kids that ruled the roost. A father's word should be law. They brought up their own kids strictly, and none had turned out bad yet. When Marjorie's son wet the bed she threatened to cut off his dingy with the butcher knife. That cured him.

They said ninety percent of the young girls nowadays drank, and swore, and took it lying down. They did not have daughters, but if they did and caught them at anything like that they would beat them raw. Irene, they said, used to go to the hockey games with her ski pants slit and nothing under them, for convenience in the snowdrifts afterward. Terrible.

I wanted to point out some contradictions. Marjorie and Lily themselves drank and swore, and what was so wonderful about the strong will of a father who would insure you a lifetime of unhappiness? (What I did not see was that Marjorie and Lily were not unhappy altogether—could not be, because of their sense of consequence, their pride and style.) I could be enraged then at the lack of logic in most adults' talk—the way they held to their pronouncements no matter what evidence might be presented to them. How could these women's hands be so gifted, so delicate and clever—for I knew they would be as good at dozens of other jobs as they were at gutting; they would be good at quilting and darning and painting and papering and kneading dough and setting out seedlings—and their thinking so slapdash, clumsy, infuriating?

Lily said she never let her husband come near her if he had been drinking. Marjorie said since the time she nearly died with a hemorrhage she never let her husband come near her, period. Lily said quickly that it was only when he'd been drinking that he tried anything. I could see that it was a matter of pride not to let your husband come near you, but I couldn't quite believe that "come near" meant "have sex." The idea of Marjorie and Lily being sought out for such purposes seemed grotesque. They had bad teeth, their stomachs sagged, their faces were dull and spotty. I decided to take "come near" literally.

The two weeks before Christmas was a frantic time at the Turkey Barn. I began to go in for an hour before school as well as after school and on weekends. In the morning, when I walked to work, the street lights would still be on and the morning stars shining. There was the Turkey Barn, on the edge of a white field, with a row of big pine trees behind it, and always, no matter how cold and still it was, these trees were lifting their branches and sighing and straining. It seems unlikely that on my way to the Turkey Barn, for an hour of gutting turkeys, I should have experienced such a sense of promise and at the same time of perfect, impenetrable mystery in the universe, but I did. Herb had something to do with that, and so did the cold snap—the series of hard, clear mornings. The truth is, such feelings weren't hard to come by then. I would get them but not know how they were to be connected with anything in real life.

One morning at the Turkey Barn there was a new gutter. This was a boy eighteen or nineteen years old, a stranger named Brian. It seemed he was a relative, or perhaps just a friend, of Herb Abbott's. He was staying with Herb. He had worked on a lake boat last summer. He said he had got sick of it, though, and quit.

What he said was, "Yeah, fuckin' boats, I got sick of that."

Language at the Turkey Barn was coarse and free, but this was one word never heard there. And Brian's use of it seemed not careless but flaunting, mixing insult and provocation. Perhaps it was his general style that made it so. He had amazing good looks: taffy hair, bright-blue eyes, ruddy skin, well-shaped body— the sort of good looks nobody disagrees about for a moment. But a single, relentless notion had got such a hold on him that he could not keep from turning all his assets into parody. His mouth was wet-looking and slightly open most of the time, his eyes were half shut, his expression a hopeful leer, his movements indolent, exaggerated, inviting. Perhaps if he had been put on a stage with a microphone and a guitar and let grunt and howl and wriggle and excite, he would have seemed a true celebrant. Lacking a stage, he was unconvincing. After a while he seemed just like somebody with a bad case of hiccups—his insistent sexuality was that monotonous and meaningless.

If he had toned down a bit, Marjorie and Lily would probably have enjoyed him. They could have kept up a game of telling him to shut his filthy mouth and keep his hands to himself. As it was, they said they were sick of him, and meant it. Once, Marjorie took up her gutting knife. "Keep your distance," she said. "I mean from me and my sister and that kid."

She did not tell him to keep his distance from Gladys, because Gladys wasn't there at the time and Marjorie would probably not have felt like protecting her anyway. But it was Gladys Brian particularly liked to bother. She would throw down her knife and go into the washroom and stay there ten minutes and come out with a stony face. She didn't say she was sick anymore and go home, the way she used to. Marjorie said Morgan was mad at Gladys for sponging and she couldn't get away with it any longer.

Gladys said to me, "I can't stand that kind of thing. I can't stand people mentioning that kind of thing and that kind of—gestures. It makes me sick to my stomach."

I believed her. She was terribly white. But why, in that case, did she not complain to Morgan? Perhaps relations between them were too uneasy, perhaps she could not bring herself to repeat or describe such things. Why did none of us complain—if not to Morgan, at least to Herb? I never thought of it. Brian seemed just something to put up with, like the freezing cold in the gutting shed and the smell of blood and waste. When Marjorie and Lily did threaten to complain, it was about Brian's laziness.

He was not a good gutter. He said his hands were too big. So Herb took him off gutting, told him he was to sweep and clean up, make packages of giblets, and help load the truck. This meant that he did not have to be in any one place or doing any one job at a given time, so much of the time he did nothing. He would start sweeping up, leave that and mop the tables, leave that and have a cigarette, lounge against the table bothering us until Herb called him to help load. Herb was very busy now and spent a lot of time making deliveries, so it was possible he did not know the extent of Brian's idleness.

"I don't know why Herb don't fire you," Marjorie said. "I guess the answer is he don't want you hanging around sponging on him, with no place to go."

"I know where to go," said Brian.

"Keep your sloppy mouth shut," said Marjorie. "I pity Herb. Getting saddled."

On the last school day before Christmas we got out early in the afternoon. I went home and changed my clothes and came into work at about three o'clock. Nobody was working. Everybody was in the gutting shed, where Morgan Elliott was swinging a cleaver over the gutting table and yelling. I couldn't make out what the yelling was about, and thought someone must have made a terrible mistake in his work; perhaps it had been me. Then I saw Brian on the other side of the table, looking very sulky and mean, and standing well back. The sexual leer was not altogether gone from his face, but it was flattened out and mixed with a look of impotent bad temper and some fear. That's it, I thought; Brian is getting fired for being so sloppy and lazy. Even when I made out Morgan saying "pervert" and "filthy" and "maniac," I still thought that was what was happening. Marjorie and Lily, and even brassy Irene, were standing around with downcast, rather pious looks, such as children get when somebody is suffering a terrible bawling out at school. Only old Henry seemed able to keep a cautious grin on his face. Gladys was not to be seen. Herb was standing closer to Morgan than anybody else. He was not interfering but was keeping an eye on the cleaver. Morgy was blubbering, though he didn't seem to be in any immediate danger.

Morgan was yelling at Brian to get out. "And out of this town—I mean it—and don't you wait till tomorrow if you still want your arse in one piece! Out!" he shouted, and the cleaver swung dramatically towards the door. Brian started in that direction but, whether he meant to or not, he made a swaggering, taunting motion of the buttocks. This made Morgan break into a roar and run after him, swinging the cleaver in a stagy way. Brian ran, and Morgan ran after him, and Irene screamed and grabbed her stomach. Morgan was too heavy to run any distance and probably could not have thrown the cleaver very far, either. Herb watched from the doorway. Soon Morgan came back and flung the cleaver down on the table.

"All back to work! No more gawking around here! You don't get paid for gawking! What are you getting under way at?" he said, with a hard look at Irene.

"Nothing," Irene said meekly.

"If you're getting under way get out of here."

"I'm not."

"All right, then!"

We got to work. Herb took off his blood-smeared smock and put on his jacket and went off, probably to see that Brian got ready to go on the suppertime bus. He did not say a word. Morgan and his son went out to the yard, and Irene and Henry went back to the adjoining shed, where they did the plucking, working knee-deep in the feathers Brian was supposed to keep swept up.

"Where's Gladys?" I said softly.

"Recuperating," said Marjorie. She, too, spoke in a quieter voice than usual, and "recuperating" was not the sort of word she and Lily normally used. It was a word to be used about Gladys, with a mocking intent.

They didn't want to talk about what had happened, because they were afraid Morgan might come in and catch them at it and fire them. Good workers as they were, they were afraid of that. Besides, they hadn't seen anything. They must have been annoyed that they hadn't. All I ever found out was that Brian had either done something or shown something to Gladys as she came out of the washroom and she had started screaming and having hysterics.

Now she'll likely be laid up with another nervous breakdown, they said. And he'll be on his way out of town. And good riddance, they said, to both of them.

I have a picture of the Turkey Barn crew taken on Christmas Eve. It was taken with a flash camera that was someone's Christmas extravagance. I think it was Irene's. But Herb Abbott must have been the one who took the picture. He was the one who could be trusted to know or to learn immediately how to manage anything new, and flash cameras were fairly new at the time. The picture was taken about ten o'clock on Christmas Eve, after Herb and Morgy had come back from making the last delivery and we had washed off the gutting table and swept and mopped the cement floor. We had taken off our bloody smocks and heavy sweaters and gone into the little room called the lunchroom, where there was a table and a heater. We still wore our working clothes: overalls and shirts. The men wore caps and the women kerchiefs, tied in the wartime style. I am stout and cheerful and comradely in the picture, transformed into someone I don't ever remember being or pretending to be. I look years older than fourteen. Irene is the only one who has taken off her kerchief, freeing her long red hair. She peers out from it with a meek, sluttish, inviting look, which would match her reputation but is not like any look of hers I remember. Yes, it must have been her camera; she is posing for it, with that look, more deliberately than anyone else is. Marjorie and Lily are smiling, true to form, but their smiles are sour and reckless. With their hair hidden, and such figures as they have bundled up, they look like a couple of tough and jovial but testy workmen. Their kerchiefs look misplaced; caps would be better. Henry is in high spirits, glad to be part of the work force, grinning and looking twenty years younger than his age. Then Morgy, with his hangdog look, not trusting the occasion's bounty, and Morgan very flushed and bosslike and satisfied. He has just given each of us our bonus turkey. Each of these turkeys has a leg or a wing missing, or a malformation of some kind, so none of them are salable at the full price. But Morgan has been at pains to tell us that you often get the best meat off the gimpy ones, and he has shown us that he's taking one home himself.

We are all holding mugs or large, thick china cups, which contain not the usual tea but rye whiskey. Morgan and Henry have been drinking since supper-time. Marjorie and Lily say they only want a little, and only take it at all because it's Christmas Eve and they are dead on their feet. Irene says she's dead on her feet as well but that doesn't mean she only wants a little. Herb has poured quite generously not just for her but for Lily and Marjorie, too, and they do not object. He has measured mine and Morgy's out at the same time, very stingily, and poured in Coca-Cola. This is the first drink I have ever had, and as a result I will believe for years that rye-and-Coca-Cola is a standard sort of drink and will always ask for it, until I notice that few other people drink it and that it makes me sick. I didn't get sick that Christmas Eve, though; Herb had not given me enough. Except for an odd taste, and my own feeling of consequence, it was like drinking Coca-Cola.

I don't need Herb in the picture to remember what he looked like. That is, if he looked like himself, as he did all the time at the Turkey Barn and the few times I saw him on the street—as he did all the times in my life when I saw him except one.

The time he looked somewhat unlike himself was when Morgan was cursing out Brian and, later, when Brian had run off down the road. What was this different look? I've tried to remember, because I studied it hard at the time. It wasn't much different. His face looked softer and heavier then, and if you had to describe the expression on it you would have to say it was an expression of shame. But what would he be ashamed of? Ashamed of Brian, for the way he had behaved? Surely that would be late in the day; when had Brian ever behaved otherwise? Ashamed of Morgan, for carrying on so ferociously and theatrically? Or of himself, because he was famous for nipping fights and displays of this sort in the bud and hadn't been able to do it here? Would he be ashamed that he hadn't stood up for Brian? Would he have expected himself to do that, to stand up for Brian?

All this was what I wondered at the time. Later, when I knew more, at least about sex, I decided that Brian was Herb's lover, and that Gladys really was trying to get attention from Herb, and that that was why Brian had humiliated her—with or without Herb's connivance and consent. Isn't it true that people like Herb— dignified, secretive, honorable people—will often choose somebody like Brian, will waste their helpless love on some vicious, silly person who is not even evil, or a monster, but just some importunate nuisance? I decided that Herb, with all his gentleness and carefulness, was avenging himself on us all—not just on Gladys but on us all—with Brian, and that what he was feeling when I studied his face must have been a savage and gleeful scorn. But embarrassment as well—embarrassment for Brian and for himself and for Gladys, and to some degree for all of us. Shame for all of us—that is what I thought then.

Later still, I backed off from this explanation. I got to a stage of backing off from the things I couldn't really know. It's enough for me now just to think of Herb's face with that peculiar, stricken look; to think of Brian monkeying in the shade of Herb's dignity; to think of my own mystified concentration on Herb, my need to catch him out, if I could ever get the chance, and then move in and stay close to him. How attractive, how delectable, the prospect of intimacy is, with the very person who will never grant it. I can still feel the pull of a man like that, of his promising and refusing. I would still like to know things. Never mind facts. Never mind theories, either.

When I finished my drink I wanted to say something to Herb. I stood beside him and waited for a moment when he was not listening to or talking with anyone else and when the increasingly rowdy conversation of the others would cover what I had to say.

"I'm sorry your friend had to go away."

"That's all right."

Herb spoke kindly and with amusement, and so shut me off from any further right to look at or speak about his life. He knew what I was up to. He must have known it before, with lots of women. He knew how to deal with it.

Lily had a little more whiskey in her mug and told how she and her best girlfriend (dead now, of liver trouble) had dressed up as men one time and gone into the men's side of the beer parlor, the side where it said "Men Only," because they wanted to see what it was like. They sat in a corner drinking beer and keeping their eyes and ears open, and nobody looked twice or thought a thing about them, but soon a problem arose.

"Where were we going to go? If we went around to the other side and anybody seen us going into the ladies', they would scream bloody murder. And if we went into the men's somebody'd be sure to notice we didn't do it the right way. Meanwhile the beer was going through us like a bugger!"

"What you don't do when you're young!" Marjorie said.

Several people gave me and Morgy advice. They told us to enjoy ourselves while we could. They told us to stay out of trouble. They said they had all been young once. Herb said we were a good crew and had done a good job but he didn't want to get in bad with any of the women's husbands by keeping them there too late. Marjorie and Lily expressed indifference to their husbands, but Irene announced that she loved hers and that it was not true that he had been dragged back from Detroit to marry her, no matter what people said. Henry said it was a good life if you didn't weaken. Morgan said he wished us all the most sincere Merry Christmas.

When we came out of the Turkey Barn it was snowing. Lily said it was like a Christmas card, and so it was, with the snow whirling around the street lights in town and around the colored lights people had put up outside their doorways. Morgan was giving Henry and Irene a ride home in the truck, acknowledging age and pregnancy and Christmas. Morgy took a shortcut through the field, and Herb walked off by himself, head down and hands in his pockets, rolling slightly, as if he were on the deck of a lake boat. Marjorie and Lily linked arms with me as if we were old comrades.

"Let's sing," Lily said. "What'll we sing?"

" 'We Three Kings'?" said Marjorie. " 'We Three Turkey Gutters'?"

" 'I'm Dreaming of a White Christmas.' "

"Why dream? You got it!"

So we sang.

EUROPE
AND
RUSSIA

THE
GIFTS OF
WAR

Margaret
Drabble

Great Britain

Timeo Danaos et dona ferentes.*

Aeneid II I 49

When she woke in the morning, she could tell at once, as soon as she reached consciousness, that she had some reason to feel pleased with herself, some rare cause for satisfaction. She lay there quietly for a time, enjoying the unfamiliar sensation, not bothering to place it, grateful for its vague comfortable warmth. It protected her from the disagreeable noise of her husband's snores, from the thought of getting breakfast, from the coldness of the linoleum when she finally dragged herself out of bed. She had to wake Kevin: he always overslept these days, and he took so long to get dressed and get his breakfast, she was surprised he wasn't always late for school. She never thought of making him go to bed earlier; she hadn't the heart to stop him watching the telly, and anyway she enjoyed his company, she liked having him around in the evenings, laughing in his silly seven-year-old way at jokes he didn't understand—jokes she didn't always under-

*'I fear the Greeks, even when they bring gifts.

stand herself, and which she couldn't explain when he asked her to. "You don't know *anything*, Mum," he would groan, but she didn't mind his condemnations; she didn't expect to know anything, it amused her to see him behaving like a man already, affecting superiority, harmlessly, helplessly, in an ignorance that was as yet so much greater than her own—though she would have died rather than have allowed him to suspect her amusement, her permissiveness. She grumbled at him constantly, even while wanting to keep him there: she snapped at his endless questions, she snubbed him, she repressed him, she provoked him. And she did not suffer from doing this, because she knew that they could not hurt each other: he was a child, he wasn't a proper man yet, he couldn't inflict true pain, any more than she could truly repress him, and his teasing, obligatory conventional school-boy complaints about her cooking and her stupidity seemed to exorcise, in a way, those other crueller onslaughts. It was as though she said to herself: if my little boy doesn't mean it when he shouts at me, perhaps my husband doesn't either: perhaps there's no more serious offence in my bruises and my greying hair than there is in those harmless childish moans. In the child, she found a way of accepting the man: she found a way of accepting, without too much submission, her lot.

She loved the child: she loved him with so much passion that a little of it spilled over generously onto the man who had misused her: in forgiving the child his dirty blazer and shirts and his dinner-covered tie, she forgave the man for his Friday nights and the childish vomit on the stairs and the bedroom floor. It never occurred to her that a grown man might resent more than hatred such second-hand forgiveness. She never thought of the man's emotions: she thought of her own, and her feelings for the child redeemed her from bitterness, and shed some light on the dark industrial terraces and the waste lands of the city's rubble. Her single-minded commitment was a wonder of the neighbourhood: she's a sour piece, the neighbours said, she keeps herself to herself a bit too much, but you've got to hand it to her, she's been a wonderful mother to that boy, she's had a hard life, but she's been a wonderful mother to that boy. And she, tightening her woolly headscarf over her aching ears as she walked down the cold steep windy streets to join the queue at the post office or the butcher's, would stiffen proudly, her hard lips secretly smiling as she claimed and accepted and nodded to her role, her place, her social dignity.

This morning, as she woke Kevin, he reminded her instantly of her cause for satisfaction, bringing to the surface the pleasant knowledge that had underlain her wakening.

"Hi, Mum," he said, as he opened his eyes to her, "how old am I today?"

"Seven, of course," she said, staring dourly at him, pretending to conceal her instant knowledge of the question's meaning, assuming scorn and dismissal. "Come on, get up, child, you're going to be late as usual."

"And how old am I tomorrow, Mum?" he asked, watching her like a hawk, waiting for that delayed, inevitable break.

"Come on, come on," she said crossly, affecting impatience, stripping the blankets off him, watching him writhe in the cold air, small and bony in his striped pyjamas.

"Oh, go on, Mum," he said.

"What d'you mean, 'go on,' " she said, "don't be so cheeky, come on, get a move on, you'll get no breakfast if you don't get a move on."

"Just think, Mum," he said, "how old am I tomorrow?"

"I don't know what you're talking about," she said, ripping his pyjama jacket off him, wondering how long to give the game, secure in her sense of her own thing.

"Yes you do, yes you do," he yelled, his nerve beginning, very slightly, to falter. "You know what day it is tomorrow."

"Why, my goodness me," she said, judging that the moment had come, "I'd quite forgotten. Eight tomorrow. My goodness me."

And she watched him grin and wriggle, too big now for embraces, his affection clumsy and knobbly; she avoided the touch of him these days, pushing him irritably away when he leant on her chair-arm, twitching when he banged into her in the corridor or the kitchen, pulling her skirt or overall away from him when he tugged at it for attention, regretting sometimes the soft and round docile baby that he had once been, and yet proud at the same time of his gawky growing, happier, more familiar with the hostilities between them (a better cover for love) than she had been with the tender wide smiles of adoring infancy.

"What you got me for my birthday?" he asked, as he struggled out of his pyjama trousers: and she turned at the door and looked back at him, and said,

"What d'you mean, what've I got you? I've not got you anything. Only good boys get presents."

"I *am* good," he said: "I've been ever so good all week."

"Not that I noticed, you weren't," she said, knowing that too prompt an acquiescence would ruin the dangerous pleasure of doubtful anticipation.

"Go on, tell me," he said, and she could tell from his whining plea that he was almost sure that she had got what he wanted, almost sure but not quite sure, that he was, in fact, in the grip of an exactly manipulated degree of uncertainty, a torment of hope that would last him for a whole twenty-four hours, until the next birthday morning.

"I'm telling you," she said, her hand on the door, staring at him sternly,

"I'm telling you, I've not got you anything." And then, magically, delightfully, she allowed herself and him that lovely moment of grace: "I've not got you anything—*yet,*" she said: portentous, conspiratorial, yet very very faintly threatening.

"You're going to get it today," he shrieked, unable to restrain himself, unable to keep the rules: and as though annoyed by his exuberance she marched smartly out of the small back room, and down the narrow stairs to the kitchen, shouting at him in an excessive parade of rigour, "Come on, get moving, get your things on, you'll be late for school, you're always late—": and she stood over him while he ate his flakes, watching each spoonful disappear, heaving a great sigh of resigned fury when he spilled on the oilcloth, catching his guilty glance as he wiped it with his sleeve, not letting him off, unwilling, unable to relax into a suspect tenderness.

He went out the back way to school: she saw him through the yard and stood in the doorway watching him disappear, as she always watched him, down the narrow alley separating the two rows of back-to-back cottages, along the ancient industrial cobbles, relics of another age: as he reached the Stephensons' door she called out to him, "Eight tomorrow, then," and smiled, and waved, and he smiled back, excited, affectionate, over the ten yards' gap, grinning, his grey knee socks pulled smartly up, his short cropped hair already standing earnestly on end, resisting the violent flattening of the brush with which she thumped him each morning: he reminded her of a bird, she didn't know why, she couldn't have said why, a bird, vulnerable, clumsy, tenacious, touching. Then Bill Stephenson emerged from his back door and joined him, and they went down the alley together, excluding her, leaving her behind, kicking at pebbles and fag packets with their scuffed much-polished shoes.

She went back through the yard and into the house, and made a pot of tea, and took it up to the man in bed. She dumped it down on the corner of the dressing-table beside him, her lips tight, as though she dared not loosen them: her face had only one expression, and she used it to conceal the two major emotions of her life, resentment and love. They were so violently opposed, these passions, that she could not move from one to the other: she lacked flexibility; so she inhabited a grim inexpressive no-man's-land between them, feeling in some way that she thus achieved a kind of justice.

"I'm going up town today," she said, as the man on the bed rolled over and stared at her.

He wheezed and stared.

"I'm going to get our Kevin his birthday present," she said, her voice cold and neutral, offering justice and no more.

"What'll I do about me dinner?" he said.

"I'll be back," she said. "And if I'm not, you can get your own. It won't kill you."

He mumbled and coughed, and she left the room. When she got downstairs, she began, at last, to enter upon the day's true enjoyment: slowly she took possession of it, this day that she had waited for, and which could not now be taken from her. She'd left herself a cup of tea on the table, but before she sat down to drink it she got her zip plastic purse from behind the clock on the dresser, and opened it, and got the money out. There it was, all of it: thirty shillings, three ten-bob notes, folded tightly up in a brown envelope: twenty-nine and eleven, she needed, and a penny over. Thirty shillings, saved, unspoken for, to spend. She'd wondered, from time to time, if she ought to use it to buy him something useful, but she knew now that she wasn't going to: she was going to get him what he wanted—a grotesque, unjustifiable luxury, a pointless gift. It never occurred to her that the pleasure she took in doing things for Kevin was anything other than selfish: she felt vaguely guilty about it, she would have started furtively, like a miser, had anyone knocked on the door and interrupted her contemplation, she would bitterly have denied the intensity of her anticipation.

And when she put her overcoat on, and tied on her headsquare, and set off down the road, she tried to appear to the neighbours as though she wasn't going anywhere in particular: she nodded calmly, she stopped to gape at Mrs. Phillips' new baby (all frilled up, poor mite, in ribbons and pink crochet, a dreadful sight poor little innocent like something off an iced cake, people should know better than to do such things to their own children); she even called in at the shop for a quarter of tea as a cover for her excursion, so reluctant was she to let anyone know that she was going to town, thus unusually, on a Wednesday morning. And as she walked down the steep hillside, where the abandoned tram-lines still ran, to the next fare stage of the bus, she could not have said whether she was making the extra walk to save two pence, or whether she was, more deviously, concealing her destination until the last moment from both herself and the neighbourhood.

Because she hardly ever went into town these days. In the old days she had come this way quite often, going down the hill on the tram with her girl friends, with nothing better in mind than a bit of window-shopping and a bit of a laugh and a cup of tea: penniless then as now, but still hopeful, still endowed with a touching faith that if by some miracle she could buy a pair of nylons or a particular blue lace blouse or a new brand of lipstick, then deliverance would be granted to her in the form of money, marriage, romance, the visiting prince who would glimpse her in the crowd, glorified by that seductive blouse, and carry her off to a better world. She could remember so well how hopeful they had been: even Betty Jones, fat, monstrous, ludicrous Betty Jones had cherished such rosy illusions, had gazed with them in longing at garments many sizes too small and far too expensive, somehow convinced that if she could by chance or good fortune acquire one all her flesh would melt away and reveal the lovely girl within. Time had taught Betty Jones: she shuffled now in shoes cracked and splitting beneath her own weight. Time had taught them all. The visiting prince, whom need and desire had once truly transfigured in her eyes, now lay there at home in bed, stubbly, disgusting, ill, malingering, unkind: she remembered the girl who had seen such other things in him with a contemptuous yet pitying wonder. What fools they all had been, to laugh, to giggle and point and whisper, to spend their small wages to deck themselves for such a sacrifice. When she saw the young girls today, of the age she had been then, still pointing and giggling with the same knowing ignorance, she was filled with a bitterness so acute that her teeth set against it, and the set lines of her face stiffened to resist and endure and conceal it. Sometimes she was possessed by a rash desire to warn them, to lean forward and tap on their shoulders, to see their astonished vacant faces, topped with their mad over-perfumed mounds of sticky hair, turn upon her in alarm and disbelief. What do you think you're playing at, she would say to them, what do you think you're at? Where do you think it leads you, what do you think you're asking for? And they would blink at her, uncomprehending, like condemned cattle, the sacrificial virgins, not yet made restless by the smell of blood. I could tell you a thing or two, she wanted to say, I could tell you enough to wipe those silly grins off your faces: but she said nothing, and she could not have said that it was envy or a true charitable pity that most possessed and disturbed her when she saw such innocents.

What withheld her most from envy, pure and straight and voracious, was a sense of her own salvation. Because, amazingly, she had been saved, against all probability: her life which had seemed after that bridal day of white nylon net and roses to sink deeply and almost instantly into a mire of penury and beer and butchery, had been so redeemed for her by her child that she could afford to smile with a kind of superior wisdom, a higher order of knowledge, at those who had not known her trials and her comforts. They would never attain, the silly teenagers, her own level of consolation; they would never know what it was like to find in an object which had at first appeared to her as a yet more lasting sentence, a death blow to the panic notions of despair and flight—to find in such a thing love, and identity, and human warmth. When she thought of this—which she did, often, though not clearly, having little else to think of—she felt as though she alone, or she one of the elected few, had been permitted to glimpse something of the very nature of the harsh, mysterious processes of human survival; and she could induce in herself a state of recognition that was almost visionary. It was all she had: and being isolated by pride from more neighbourly and everyday and diminishing attempts at commiseration, she knew it. She fed off it: her maternal role, her joy, her sorrow. She gazed out of the bus window now, as the bus approached the town centre and the shops, and as she thought of the gift she was going to buy him, her eyes lit on the bombed sites, and the rubble and decay of decades, and the exposed walls where dirty fading wallpapers had flapped in the wind for years, and she saw where the willowherb grew, green and purple, fields of it amongst the brick, on such thin soil, on the dust of broken bricks and stones, growing so tall in tenacious aspiration out of such shallow infertile ground. It was significant: she knew, as she looked at it, that it was significant. She herself had grown out of this landscape, she had nourished herself and her child upon it. She knew what it meant.

Frances Janet Ashton Hall also knew what it meant, for she too had been born and bred there; although, being younger, she had not lived there for so long, and, having been born into a different class of society, she knew that she was not sentenced to it for life, and was indeed upon the verge of escape, for the next autumn she was to embark upon a degree in economics at a southern University. Nevertheless, she knew what it meant. She was a post-war child, but it was not for nothing that she had witnessed since infancy the red and smoking skies of the steel-works (making arms for the Arabs, for the South Africans, for all those wicked countries)—it was not for nothing that she had seen the deep scars in the city's centre, not all disguised quite comfortably as car parks. In fact, she could even claim the distinction of having lost a relative in the air raids: her great-aunt Susan, who had refused to allow herself to be evacuated to the Lake District, had perished from a stray bomb in the midst of a highly residential suburban area. Frances was not yet old enough to speculate upon the effect that this tale, oft-repeated, and with lurid details, had had upon the development of her sensibility; naturally she ascribed her ardent pacifism and her strong political convictions to her own innate radical virtue, and when she did look for ulterior motives for her faith she was far more likely to relate them to her recent passion for a newfound friend, one Michael Swaines, than to any childhood neurosis.

She admired Michael. She also liked him for reasons that had nothing to do with admiration, and being an intelligent and scrupulous girl she would spend fruitless, anxious and enjoyable hours trying to disentangle and isolate her various emotions, and to assess their respective values. Being very young, she set a high value on disinterest: standing now, for his sake, on a windy street corner in a conspicuous position outside the biggest department store in town, carrying a banner and wearing (no less) a sandwich-board, proclaiming the necessity for Peace in Vietnam, and calling for the banning of all armaments, nuclear or otherwise, she was carrying on a highly articulate dialogue with her own conscience, by means of which she was attempting to discover whether she was truly standing there for Michael's sake alone, or whether she would have stood there anyway, for the sake of the cause itself. What, she asked herself, if she had been solicited to make a fool of herself in this way merely by that disagreeable Nicholas, son of the Head of the Adult Education Centre? Would she have been prepared to oblige? No, she certainly would not, she would have laughed the idea of sandwich-boards to scorn, and would have found all sorts of convincing arguments against the kind of public display that she was now engaged in. But, on the other hand, this did not exactly invalidate her actions, for she *did* believe, with Michael, that demonstrations were necessary and useful: it was just that her natural reluctance to expose herself would have conquered her, had not Michael himself set about persuading her. So she was doing the right thing but for the wrong reason, like that man in *Murder in the Cathedral.* And perhaps it was for a *very* wrong reason, because she could not deny that she even found a sort of corrupt pleasure in doing things she didn't like doing—accosting strangers, shaking collection-boxes, being stared at—when she knew that it was being appreciated by other people: a kind of yearning for disgrace and martyrdom. Like stripping in public. Though not, surely, *quite* the same, because stripping didn't do any good, whereas telling people about the dangers of total war was a useful occupation. So doing the right thing for the wrong reason could at least be said to be better than doing the wrong thing for the wrong reason, couldn't it? Though her parents, of course, said it was the wrong thing anyway, and that one shouldn't molest innocent shoppers: Oh Lord, she thought with sudden gloom, perhaps my *only* reason for doing this is to annoy my parents: and bravely, to distract herself from the dreadful suspicion, she stepped forward and asked a scraggy thin woman in an old red velvet coat what she thought of the American policy in Vietnam.

"What's that?" said the woman, crossly, annoyed at being stopped in mid-stride, and when Frances repeated her question she gazed at her as though she were an idiot and walked on without replying. Frances, who was becoming used to such responses, was not as hurt as she had been at the beginning of the morning: she was even beginning to think it was quite funny. She wondered if she might knock off for a bit and go and look for Michael: he had gone into the store, to try to persuade the manager of the Toy Department not to sell toy machine-guns and toy bombs and toy battleships. She thought she would go and join him; and when a horrid man in a cloth cap spat on the pavement very near her left shoe and muttered something about bloody students bugger off ruining the city for decent folk, she made up her mind. So she ditched her sandwich-board and rolled her banner up, and set off through the swing doors into the cosy warmth: although it was Easter the weather was bitterly cold, spring seemed to reach them two months later than anywhere else in England. It was a pity, she thought, that there weren't any more Easter marches: she would have liked marching, it would have been more sociable; but Michael believed in isolated pockets of resistance. Really, what he meant was, he didn't like things that he wasn't organising himself. She didn't blame him for that, he was a marvellous organiser, it was amazing the amount of enthusiasm he'd got up in the Students' Union for what was after all rather a dud project: no, not dud, she hadn't meant that, what she meant was that it was no fun, and anyone with a lower sense of social responsibility than herself couldn't have been expected to find it very interesting. Very nice green stockings on the stocking counter, she wondered if she could afford a pair. This thing that Michael had about children and violence, it really was very odd: he had a brother who was writing a thesis on violence on the television and she supposed it must have affected him. She admired his faith. Although at the same time she couldn't help remembering a short story by Saki that she had read years ago, called "The Toys of Peace," which had been about the impossibility of making children play with anything but soldiers, or something to that effect.

When she reached the toy department, she located Michael immediately, because she could hear his voice raised in altercation. In fact, as she approached, she could see that quite a scene was going on, and if Michael hadn't looked quite so impressive when he was making a scene she would have lost nerve and fled: but as it was she approached, discreetly, and hovered on the outskirts of the centre of activity. Michael was arguing with a man in a black suit, some kind of manager figure she guessed (though what managers were or did she had no idea) and a woman in an overall: the man, she could see, was beginning to lose his patience, and was saying things like:

"Now look here, young man, we're not here to tell our customers what they ought to do, we're here to sell them what they want," and Michael was producing his usual arguments about responsibility and education and having to make a start somewhere and why not here and now; he'd already flashed around his leaflets on violence and delinquency, and was now offering his catalogue of harmless constructive wooden playthings.

"Look," he was saying, "look how much more attractive these wooden animals are, I'm sure you'd find they'd sell just as well, and they're far more durable"—whereat the woman in an overall sniffed and said since when had salesmen dressed themselves up as University students, if he wanted to sell them toys he ought to do it in the proper way; an interjection which Michael ignored, as he proceeded to pick up off the counter in front of him a peculiarly nasty piece of clockwork, a kind of car-cum-aeroplane thing with real bullets and knives in the wheels and hidden bomb-carriers and God knows what, she rather thought it was a model from some television puppet programme, it was called the Desperado Destruction Machine. "I mean to say, look at this horrible thing," Michael said to the manager, pressing a knob and nearly slicing off his own finger as an extra bit of machinery jumped out at him, "whatever do you think can happen to the minds of children who play with things like this?"

"That's a very nice model," said the manager, managing to sound personally grieved and hurt, "it's a very nice model, and you've no idea how popular it's
been for the price. It's not a cheap foreign thing, that, you know, it's a really
well-made toy. Look—" and he grabbed it back off Michael and pulled another
lever, to display the ejector-seat mechanism. The driver figure was promptly
ejected with such violence that he shot right across the room, and Michael, who
was quite well brought up really, dashed off to retrieve it: and by the time he got
back the situation had been increasingly complicated by the arrival of a real live
customer who had turned up to buy that very object. Though if it really was as
popular as the manager had said, perhaps that wasn't such a coincidence. Anyway,
this customer seemed very set on purchasing one, and the overalled woman
detached herself from Michael's scene and started to demonstrate one for her,
trying to pretend as she did so that there was no scene in progress and that nothing
had been going on at all: the manager too tried to hush Michael up by engaging
him in conversation and backing him away from the counter and the transaction,
but Michael wasn't so easy to silence: he continued to argue in a loud voice, and
stood his ground. Frances wished that he would abandon this clearly pointless
attempt, and all the more as he had by now noticed her presence, and she knew
that at any moment he would appeal for her support. And finally the worst
happened, as she had known it might; he turned to the woman who was trying to
buy the Desperado Destruction Machine, and started to appeal to her, asking her
if she wouldn't like to buy something less dangerous and destructive. The woman
seemed confused at first, and when he asked her for whom she was buying it, she
said that it was for her little boy's birthday, and she hadn't realised it was a
dangerous toy, it was just something he'd set his heart on, he'd break his heart if
he didn't get it, he'd seen it on the telly and he wanted one just like that:
whereupon the manager, who had quite lost his grip, intervened and started to
explain to her that there was nothing dangerous about the toy at all, on the
contrary it was a well-made pure British product, with no lead paint or sharp edges,
and that if Michael didn't shut up he'd call the police: whereupon Michael said that
there was no law to stop customers discussing products in shops with one another,
and he was himself a bona-fide customer, because look, he'd got a newly-pur-
chased pair of socks in his pocket in a Will Baines bag. The woman continued to
look confused, so Frances thought that she herself ought to intervene to support
Michael, who had momentarily run out of aggression: and she said to the woman,
in what she thought was a very friendly and reasonable tone, that nobody was
trying to stop her buying her little boy a birthday present, they just wanted to
point out that with all the violence in the world today anyway it was silly to add
to it by encouraging children to play at killing and exterminating and things like
that, and hadn't everyone seen enough bombing, particularly here (one of Mi-

chael's favourite points, this), and why didn't she buy her boy something constructive like Meccano or a farmyard set: and as she was saying all this she glanced from
time to time to the woman's face, and there was something in it, she later
acknowledged, that should have warned her. She stood there, the woman, her
woollen headscarf so tight round her head that it seemed to clamp her jaws
together into a violently imposed silence; her face unnaturally drawn, prematurely
aged; her thickly-veined hands clutching a zip plastic purse and that stupid piece
of clockwork machinery: and as she listened to Frances's voice droning quietly and
soothingly and placatingly away her face began to gather a glimmering of expression, from some depths of reaction too obscure to guess at: and as Frances finally
ran down to a polite and only very faintly hopeful enquiring standstill, she opened
her mouth and spoke. She said only one word, and it was a word that Frances had
never heard before, though she had seen it in print in a once-banned book; and
by some flash of insight, crossing the immeasurable gap of quality that separated
their two lives, she knew that the woman herself had never before allowed it to
pass her lips, that to her too it was a shocking syllable, portentous, unforgettable,
not a familiar word casually dropped into the dividing spaces. Then the woman,
having spoken, started to cry: incredibly, horribly, she started to cry. She dropped
the clockwork toy on to the floor, and it fell so heavily that she could almost have
been said to have thrown it down, and she stood there, staring at it, as the tears
rolled down her face. Then she looked at them, and walked off. Nobody followed
her: they stood there and let her go. They did not know how to follow her, nor
what appeasement to offer for her unknown wound. So they did nothing. But
Frances knew that in their innocence they had done something dreadful to her,
in the light of which those long-since ended air raids and even distant Vietnam
itself were an irrelevance, a triviality: but she did not know what it was, she could
not know. At their feet, the Destruction Machine buzzed and whirred its way to
a broken immobility, achieving a mild sensation in its death-throes by shooting a
large spring coil out of its complex guts; she and Michael, after lengthy apologies,
had to pay for it before they were allowed to leave the store.

THE NOTHINGNESS FOREST

Margareta Ekström

Sweden

First there was laughter and play. The lamp that dazzled. And she screwed up her eyes. Her toes struggled inside the warm hand. But she didn't remember that now.

The smell and the smoothness of the ointment. Someone who carefully touches her skin where it's most sensitive. The voice that blows well-known breath into her nostrils. The delicate cleanliness of the paper diaper. The rustling of plastic. Tight clothes that are forced over one's head and entangle one's legs. Someone puts her on a stool and her feet don't reach the floor.

She thinks she's flying, and is dizzy with glee. Then she hits the ground and her laughter turns to crying without one second's hesitation.

She stops crying and listens. No answer. She cries harder. But the only thing she hears is the echo of a closing door. And the silence becomes deeper.

The silence is so deep that it makes her silent too. Smothered and scared by the silence, she crawls and slides across the floor, bumps her forehead and comes to a stop on her hands and knees, as immobile as a railroad car at the terminal.

Then she hears something scratching and whining. Scratching and whining and enticing. Like laughing. Like feeling a woolly coat of fur.

She gurgles with delight and gets up. She stands unsteadily with the diaper hanging heavy in the back. The door handle moves up and down and the dog comes in.

They hug each other. The four shaggy legs hug the four that are crooked and clothed. The tongue licks warmly and pleasantly. She chokes and struggles. Long before the dog manages to put a stop to the bowing and scraping of his affection, she is interested in something else. Her back straight, she stands determined, with one hand deep in his fur.

Although the dog is several times her size, he feels the human power of that little fist. He succeeds in controlling the waggings and droolings of his bliss, and he, too, looks forward with determination. Now they see the gate.

Two pairs of eyes at an equal level above the ground see a gate. It cuts freedom and air and greenery into thin strips. The handle rests like a punctuation dash for reflection, horizontally in the air. But reflection is not their specialty. And without a thought, without a stumble, without delay, they reach the gate.

The dog, having practiced on many handles, manages the gate handle easily. Now there is the crunch of gravel under their paws and soles. They're on their way!

On that day a high-pressure system over central Sweden has decided to move southward. It does so slowly and reluctantly. It has lain comfortably over the swaybacked meadows of Upland, and it has clung to the rugged branches of the juniper pine covered hillsides. It has filtered through the newly unfolded birch foliage, and sniffed along fields of wood anemones, bitter vetch, and the just-formed little leaves that can become anything when summer comes.

The winds of departure come in gusts. They give and they take. There's an excitement in the air. Do they feel it, perhaps, the dog and the child, as they start out?

Behind them in the villa no one suspects anything. It is an uneventful weekday. No one suspects that everything is about to change, just as no one suspects a change in the beautiful spring weather. There are no foreboding signs. Except perhaps the calm, the very silence.

All at once walking is so very easy. The four paws tramp eagerly. The two feet stamp in their cotton socks. Her hand deeply imbedded in the fur: a fistful of security, shaggy and strong.

And so, without stopping, they wander down the street where all the windows seem to look the other way, and they disappear on the path into the forest. A schoolboy on his bicycle turns a corner one second too late. He had had trouble with his shoestrings. The lady who is beating her rugs got dust in her eyes and runs into the house to look in the mirror. As though enveloped in a cloak of invisibility, they enter the realm of the blueberry bushes.

She starts humming to herself. The dog walks on and listens. His ears bend forward, to the side: What is she saying? Shall I obey? But the sounds aren't really human sounds yet. I won't pay attention to them, he decides. Just then she suddenly says clearly and loudly: "Doggy!"

He jumps with surprise. With his front paws apart, he stands there and wags his tail.

As a result of his sudden reaction, she falls down on her bottom. But gets up right away, and walks on. Alone.

The dog barks.

"Doggy," she repeats stubbornly. And he joins her.

Now she is the leader. She is singing something incomprehensible while beating time with her arms. She laughs when the gusts of wind whisk around her legs, and at the wagtail that's there one minute, gone the next, and then back again. They play at peekaboo like Mommy and Daddy.

"Peekaboo," says the child. And the bird disappears.

The dog has started to run around in circles. Catches the scent of mice and rabbits on the wet reception tip of his muzzle. The chattering of squirrels makes him stand on his hind legs with his eyes riveted upon a pine. Then, down on all fours again, he circles around the child, who as though pulled by a string is advancing straight as an arrow into the forest.

A coast guard helicopter skims the tree tops. Had it not received orders to look for imagined enemies, it would have noticed the geometric figure described by the dog and the child: a circle with a moving radius.

Airplanes and helicopters are nothing new for the child and the dog. They walk happily in the dark forest. The temperature falls a few degrees. The food in their stomachs settles down. An uncertainty about direction and goal intrudes upon their spirit of adventure. But these signals aren't strong enough to stop them. They continue to quickly move away from the town.

Someone looking at the community from above, with the eyes of an interested giant bending down to see, hands on his knees and with his shoulders at the level of the lowest clouds, would observe a strange commotion, like a whirlwind of people and feelings, of exclaiming and lamenting. Also, cars are crowding around one of the villas. People get out and get back in. Exhaust fumes shine with a bluish hue in the midday sunshine. Someone is crying and cannot be comforted.

But in the dark of the forest there is a smell of resin, and the pine needles glitter. Feet leave no tracks. The scent of violets and pine combines with a pungent odor from the ever heavier contents of the child's plastic pants. She tries to scratch, and the dog sniffs with interest several times. Then she grabs hold of his fur, and they do another kilometer at a slow trot.

A squirrel drops gnawed-off pine cones on the pair. A flock of bullfinches shines like toadstools against golden maidenhair. The silence thickens under the low branches. The lichen retains the warmth of the day and so doesn't heed the signals of change in the weather. The child walks more slowly now and her socks have absorbed moisture from the path.

At that moment someone calls the child's name. It is a long and mournful call. An enormous voice that seems to swallow them both, that seems to take them into its round mouth and then slowly drop them again onto the path.

They listen in the same direction, the child and the dog. Try to take a few steps towards it. But last year's brown meadowsweet is thick there and a fallen tree blocks their way with its pointed roots. So they continue along the path, slowly and hesitatingly. Soon they forget the call, but its echo makes them uneasy.

There it is again: the child's name. A man's deep voice. Nobody they know. The voice is vehement and urgent. It sounds like an order and the dog looks questioningly at the child. He stands in the child's way, inclines his head and waits for an initiative from this very small human being.

But she looks at him and laughs and says her "Doggy!"

That awakens his sense of duty and he bumps into her so that she has to sit down on the path. When she tries to get up, he bumps her again. The dog is trying to shove her in the direction of the calls, but the child is only aware of his keeping her from the one thing that is important and fun: walking. For the first time in her life she has discovered the trick of walking, and so wants to keep going and going to see how long it can last.

Now the name is blaring through the forest, and the dog is very worried. He stands over the child and gently takes hold of the back of her jumper with his teeth, as though she were a puppy.

That makes the child angry.

"Bad!" she says. "Bad dog!"

That makes the dog meek and submissive. But when the child's name resounds again and again, further away this time, his excitement returns. Something is expected of him, he is sure of that, something is happening, there is a connection between the shouts and the little child who is lying on her back now looking at him with angry eyes, her forehead creased.

"Bad doggy! Go away!"

The dog steps away from the child and thoughtfully lies down on the mossy ground. With his muzzle resting on his front paws, he looks at the cotton-clothed mystery, who, although almost hairless and with crooked legs, has the commanding glint in her eyes which he has learned to obey, always.

He whines and whisks his tail around ingratiatingly. The shouts come from a greater distance now. When he attempts to bark, his conflicting emotions transform the bark into a squeak.

Once again he tries to persuade the child by standing close to her. She has gotten up and is standing unsteadily, looking hard at him. He comes closer and opens his jaws as much as he can: she is a foolish and disobedient puppy who has to be carried home to her basket.

At that, the child's fist lands full force right on his soft upper lip. Behind it is the hard jawbone, so the effect is considerable. The dog howls and retreats.

"Go away! Bad dog!" the child commands and takes a few steps towards him.

Ashamed and confused, dragging his tail, the dog disappears like a shadow. The loud human voices attract him with their promise of more certain commands and soothing pats on the back. Like a shadow he disappears. Then all is quiet.

The shouts are only a mumble now, and easily drowned by low-flying bumblebees. There is a rumbling in the child's stomach that commands all of her attention. She listens to it. Food. Water. She trots on.

At a bend in the road, she meets loneliness. All at once she realizes without any words: far away, no mommy, no daddy, no lady, no dog. Hungry and lonely.

She cries with a loud and reproachful voice. But the pine seedlings don't pay any attention to her accusations, and the gathering clouds that she can see, now that the forest has thinned, are only gray and uninterested.

Her howling rises and falls. She has to sit down in order to have enough strength to cry as she clenches her fists, and her feet inside the dirty, wet cotton socks. So that's what the world is like. Once upon a time there was a bright light that dazzled, and a warm hand around her feet. She doesn't remember it, but misses it anyway. Because it's not that way now.

Here, the pine needles stick and hunger aches and the low clouds are damp and uncomfortably cold. Here there is loneliness without bounds.

As though the child could see the hopelessness in her situation from the outside, she stops crying. For what good is it to cry at the threshold of horror and the utmost limit of misery?

Quietly she sits there and picks up earth and tender grass. Drops it again. She plucks with her fingers and her hands in the same way as the very old do with the roses on their last blanket, the folds in their sheets. As though she wanted to prepare, gather strength to meet the Horrible.

But the Horrible doesn't come. Only dusk gathering more and more. Only fog that licks her cheeks, and sleep that moves inside of her warm and soft. Mild gray Nothingness is all there is, and it is worse than fear.

The cold rises from the earth. Slowly her eyes turn inward. An erring ant examines the seam of her jumper.

The evening tide wipes away the last remains of day. Outlines are erased. Pines and stones, moss and child, all sink into the fog. She learns that the created can be lifeless, can be a thing, and that the joy of life needs both a striking surface and a match in order to glimmer. She sits there, heavy with hunger and loneliness and turns into a thing.

Therefore, she doesn't move when the man in the windbreaker bends over her with a happy cry and lifts her into his arms. Therefore, she turns away when Mommy's teary face, an eon later, bends down over her.

For many days she avoids meeting their eyes. They are so inexperienced, so young, they know nothing about life. They have not seen, and some of them will never see, the great nothingness she met in the forest.

Translated by Eva Claeson

CHRISTMAS

John
McGahern

Ireland

As well as a railway ticket they gave me a letter before I left the Home to work for Moran. They warned me to give the letter unopened to Moran, which was why I opened it on the train; it informed him that since I was a ward of state if I caused trouble or ran away he was to contact the guards at once. I tore it up, since it occurred to me that I might well cause trouble or run away, resolving to say I lost it if asked, but he did not ask for any letter.

Moran and his wife treated me well. The food was more solid than at the Home, a roast always on Sundays, and when the weather grew hard they took me to the town and bought me wellingtons and an overcoat and a cap with flaps that came down over the ears. After the day's work when Moran had gone to the pub, I was free to sit at the fire while Mrs Moran knitted, and listened to the wireless—what I enjoyed most were the plays—and Mrs Moran told me she was knitting a pullover for me for Christmas. Sometimes she asked me about life at the Home and when I'd tell her she'd sigh, 'You must be very glad to be with us instead,' and I would tell her, which was true, that I was. I usually went to bed before Moran came back from the pub, as they often quarrelled then, and I considered I had no place in that part of their lives.

Moran made his living by buying cheap branches or uncommercial timber the sawmills couldn't use and cutting them up to sell as firewood. I delivered the timber with an old jennet Moran had bought from the tinkers. The jennet squealed, a very human squeal, any time a fire of branches was lit, and ran, about the only time he did run, to stand in rigid contentment with his nostrils in the thick of the wood smoke. When Moran was in good humour it amused him greatly to light a fire to see the jennet's excitement at the prospect of smoke.

There was no reason this life shouldn't have gone on for long but for a stupid wish on my part, which set off an even more stupid wish in Mrs Grey, and what happened has struck me ever since as usual when people look to each other for their happiness or whatever it is called. Mrs Grey was Moran's best customer. She'd come from America and built the huge house on top of Mounteagle after her son had been killed in aerial combat over Italy.

The thaw overhead in the bare branches had stopped the evening we filled that load for Mrs Grey. There was no longer the dripping on the dead leaves, the wood clamped in the silence of white frost except for the racket some bird made in the undergrowth. Moran carefully built the last logs above the crates of the cart and I threw him the bag of hay that made the load look bigger than it was. 'Don't forget to call at Murphy's for her paraffin,' he said. 'No, I'll not forget.' 'She's bound to tip you well this Christmas. We could use money for the Christmas.' He'd use it to pour drink down his gullet. 'Must be time to be moving,' I said. 'It'll be night before you're there,' he answered.

The cart rocked over the roots between the trees, cold steel of the bridle ring in the hand close to the rough black lips, steam of the breath wasting on the air to either side. We went across the paddocks to the path round the lake, the wheels cutting two tracks on the white stiff grass, crush of the grass yielding to the iron. I had to open the wooden gate to the pass. The small shod hooves wavered between the two ridges of green inside the wheeltracks on the pass, the old body swaying to each drive of the shafts as the wheels fell from rut to rut.

The lake was frozen over, a mirror fouled by white blotches of the springs, and rose streaks from the sun were impaled on the firs of Oakport across the bay.

The chainsaw started up in the wood again. He'd saw while there was light. 'No joke to make a living, a drink or two for some relief, all this ballsing. May be better if we stayed in bed, conserve our energy, eat less,' but in spite of all he said he went on buying the branches cheap from McAnnish after the boats had taken the trunks down the river to the mill.

I tied the jennet to the chapel gate and crossed to Murphy's shop.

'I want Mrs Grey's paraffin.'

The shop was full of men. They sat on the counter or on wooden fruit boxes and upturned buckets along the walls. They used to trouble me at first. I supposed it little different from going into a shop in a strange country without its language, but they learned they couldn't take a rise out of me, that was their phrase. They used to lob tomatoes at the back of my head in the hope of some reaction, but they left me mostly alone when they saw none was forthcoming. If I felt anything for them it was a contempt tempered by fear: I was here, and they were there.

'You want her paraffin, do you? I know the paraffin I'd give her if I got your chance,' Joe Murphy said from the centre of the counter where he presided, and a loyal guffaw rose from around the walls.

'Her proper paraffin,' someone shouted, and it drew even more applause, and when it died a voice asked, 'Before you get off the counter, Joe, throw us an orange.'

Joe stretched to the shelf and threw the orange to the man who sat on a bag of Spanish onions. As he stretched forward to catch the fruit the red string bag collapsed and he came heavily down on the onions. 'You want to bruise those onions with your dirty awkward arse. Will you pay for them now, will you?' Joe shouted as he swung his thick legs down from the counter.

'Everybody's out for their onions these days.' The man tried to defend himself with a nervous laugh as he fixed the string bag upright and changed his seat to an orange box.

'You've had your onions: now pay for them.'

'Make him pay for his onions,' they shouted.

'You must give her her paraffin first.' Joe took the tin, and went to the barrel raised on flat blocks in the corner, and turned the copper tap.

'Now give her the proper paraffin. It's Christmas time,' Joe said again as he screwed the cap tight on the tin, the limp black hair falling across the bloated face.

'Her proper paraffin,' the approving cheer followed me out of the door.

'He never moved a muscle, the little fucker. Those homeboys are a bad piece of work,' I heard with much satisfaction as I stowed the tin of paraffin securely among the logs of the cart. Ice over the potholes of the road was catching the first stars. Lights of bicycles—it was a confession night—hesitantly approached out of the night. Though exposed in the full glare of their lamps I was unable to recognize the bicyclists as they pedalled past in dark shapes behind their lamps, and this made raw the fear I'd felt but had held down in the shop. I took a stick and beat the reluctant jennet into pulling the load uphill as fast as he was able.

After I'd stacked the logs in the fuel shed I went and knocked on the back door to see where they wanted me to put the paraffin. Mrs Grey opened the door.

'It's the last load until after Christmas,' I said as I put the tin down.

'I haven't forgotten.' She smiled and held out a pound note.

'I'd rather not take it.' It was there the first mistake was made, playing for higher stakes.

'You must have something. Besides the firewood you've brought us so many messages from the village that we don't know what we'd have done without you.'

'I don't want money.'

'Then what would you like me to give you for Christmas?'

'Whatever you'd prefer to give me.' I thought *prefer* was well put for a homeboy.

'I'll have to give it some thought, then,' she said as I led the jennet out of the yard, delirious with stupid happiness.

'You got the paraffin and logs there without trouble?' Moran beamed when I came in to the smell of hot food. He'd changed into good clothes and was finishing his meal at the head of the big table in tired contentment.

'There was no trouble,' I answered.

'You've fed and put in the jennet?'

'I gave him crushed oats.'

'I bet you Mrs Grey was pleased.'

'She seemed pleased.'

He'd practically his hand out. 'You got something good out of it, then?'

'No.'

'You mean to say she gave you nothing?'

'Not tonight but maybe she will before Christmas.'

'Maybe she will but she always gave a pound with the last load before,' he said suspiciously. His early contentment was gone.

He took his cap and coat to go for a drink or two for some relief.

'If there's an international crisis in the next few hours you know where I'll be found,' he said to Mrs Moran as he left.

Mrs Grey came Christmas Eve with a large box. She smelled of scent and gin and wore a fur coat. She refused a chair saying she'd to rush, and asked me to untie the red twine and paper.

A toy airplane stood inside the box. It was painted white and blue. The tyres smelled of new rubber.

'Why don't you wind it up?'

I looked up at the idiotically smiling face, the tear-brimmed eyes.

'Wind it up for Mrs Grey,' I heard Moran's voice.

I was able to do nothing. Moran took the toy from my hand and wound it up. A light flashed on and off on the tail and the propellors turned as it raced across the cement.

'It was too much for you to bring,' Moran said in his politic voice.

'I thought it was rather nice when he refused the money. My own poor boy loved nothing better than model airplanes for Christmas.' She was again on the verge of tears.

'We all still feel for that tragedy,' Moran said. 'Thank Mrs Grey for such a lovely present. It's far too good.'

I could no longer hold back rage: 'I think it's useless,' and began to cry.

I have only a vague memory afterwards of the voice of Moran accompanying her to the door with excuses and apologies.

'I should have known better than to trust a homeboy,' Moran said when he came back. 'Not only did you do me out of the pound but you go and insult the woman and her dead son. You're going to make quick time back to where you came from, my tulip.' Moran stirred the airplane with his boot as if he wished to kick it but dared not out of respect for the money it had cost.

'Well, you'll have a good flight in it this Christmas.'

The two-hour bell went for Midnight Mass, and as Moran hurried for the pub to get drinks before Mass, Mrs Moran started to strip the windows of curtains and to set a single candle to burn in each window. Later, as we made our way to the church, candles burned in the windows of all the houses and the church was ablaze with light. I was ashamed of the small old woman, afraid they'd identify me with her as we walked up between the crowded benches to where a steward directed us to a seat in the women's side-altar. In the smell of burning wax and flowers and damp stone, I got out the brown beads and the black prayerbook with the gold cross on the cover they'd given me in the Home and began to prepare for the hours of boredom Midnight Mass meant. It did not turn out that way.

A drunken policeman, Guard Mullins, had slipped past the stewards on guard at the door and into the women's sidechapel. As Mass began he started to tell the schoolteacher's wife how available her arse had been for handling while she'd worked in the bar before assuming the fur coat of respectability, 'And now, O Lordy me, a prize rose garden wouldn't get a luk in edgeways with its grandeur.' The stewards had a hurried consultation whether to eject him or not and decided it'd probably cause less scandal to leave him as he was. He quietened into a drunken stupor until the Monsignor climbed into the pulpit to begin his annual hour of the season of peace and glad tidings. As soon as he began, 'In the name of the Father and of the Son and of the Holy Ghost. This Christmas, my dearly beloved children in Christ, I wish . . .' Mullins woke to applaud with a hearty, 'Hear, hear. I couldn't approve more. You're a man after my own heart. Down with the hypocrites!' The Monsignor looked towards the policeman and then at the stewards, but as he was greeted by another, 'Hear, hear!' he closed his notes and in a voice of acid wished everybody a holy and happy Christmas and climbed angrily from the pulpit to conclude the shortest Midnight Mass the church had ever known. It was not, though, the end of the entertainment. As the communicants came from the rails Mullins singled out the tax collector, who walked down the aisle with closed, bowed head, and hands rigidly joined, to shout, 'There's the biggest hypocrite in the parish,' which delighted almost everybody.

As I went past the lighted candles in the window, I thought of Mullins as my friend and for the first time felt proud to be a ward of state. I avoided Moran and his wife, and from the attic I listened with glee to them criticizing Mullins. When the voices died I came quietly down to take a box of matches and the airplane and go to the jennet's stable. I gathered dry straw in a heap, and as I lit it and the smoke rose the jennet gave his human squeal until I untied him and he was able to put his nostrils in the thick of the smoke. By the light of the burning straw I put the blue and white toy against the wall and started to kick. With each kick I gave a new sweetness was injected into my blood. For such a pretty toy it took few kicks to reduce it to shapelessness, and then, in the last flames of the straw, I flattened it on the stable floor, the jennet already nosing me to put more straw on the dying fire.

As I quietened, I was glad that I'd torn up the unopened letter in the train that I was supposed to have given to Moran. I felt a new life had already started to grow out of the ashes, out of the stupidity of human wishes.

THAT WALL, THAT MIMOSA

Mercè Rodoreda

Catalonia/Spain

My girlfriends laughed a lot when Miquel left me. A mania seized him for seeing the world. He said he'd come back, and they still say he will, but while they say it they're thinking I'll never see him again. And that's what I think too. Because Miquel . . . right away he wanted to sleep with me, and I really wasn't in the mood. I just wanted to go out together. I didn't know how to say no, because he told me if I didn't he'd really go astray. Maybe he'll come back someday, and if he does I wouldn't take him as a gift. Not even if they gold-plated him.

What my girlfriends all want to know is why I'm so happy when I have a cold. Let them wonder. They're surprised how I sing when I'm coughing like a dog and my nose is running like a drainpipe. I never told them how much I like soldiers, and how I fall in love when I see one. It hurts me to see them with those heavy shoes and those jackets. They wear such heavy clothes. They even do their exercises in them, out in the heat. But some of them when they cock their helmets a little over one eye . . . When they go around in threes and walk by and say things to the girls they pass, because they're homesick. They're like uprooted plants. The ones from the villages are so homesick when they get here! They're homesick for their mothers, their way of life, their normal food. They're homesick for the girls who go to the fountain and they long for everything. And with those heavy clothes to top it all off.

The three of them passed me when I was out for a walk. I was wearing a pink frock with a little shawl tied at the neck in that same pink, because I'd had some fabric left over. And a tortoise-shell barrette with an imitation gold ring, that caught my hair in a wave. The three of them stopped in front of me and blocked my way. One who had a very round face asked me if I had a streetcar ticket and if I'd sell it to him. I told him I didn't have any streetcar tickets, and the other soldier said, "Not even an old one?" And they looked at each other and laughed, but the one who'd stayed off to one side didn't say a thing. He had a freckle on the top of his cheek, and another little one on his neck, near the ear. They were both the same color: dark earth.

The two who'd wanted a streetcar ticket asked me what my name was, and I told them straight out, since I had nothing to hide . . . I said "Crisantema," and they said I was an autumn flower, and how strange it was—that I, so young, could be an autumn flower. The soldier who hadn't spoken yet said "Come on, let's go," and the others said wait a minute, so Crisantema can tell us what she does on weekends. And finally, just when I was feeling comfortable, they walked away laughing and the one who hadn't said anything came up beside me. He'd left his buddies. He said he'd like very much to see me again, because I reminded him of a girl from his village named Jacinta . . . "What's a good day?" he asked me. And I said "Friday evening." That's when the masters were going to Tarragona to meet their grandson, and I was going to watch the house and wait for Senyora Carlota, who was coming from Valencia . . . I told him where I was working and said he should write it down, but he didn't bother since he had a good memory.

When Friday came he was already there, waiting for me in the street. And some strange indescribable thing came over me, I don't know where, maybe in my veins, maybe in my skin, I don't know, but it was something very strange, since I thought if he wanted to see me it was because he was homesick. I brought along two rolls with slices of roast meat inside them. After we'd been walking a while I asked if he was hungry. I unwrapped the rolls and gave him one. We sat down to eat on a garden wall, with branches from trees and a rosebush falling over it. I ate mine in bites, pulling on it, but he had a different way of doing it. He pinched off a bit of bread and a piece of meat with his hand, and put them in his mouth. Country people are sometimes very delicate. He ate slowly, and as I watched him eat I stopped being hungry. I couldn't finish my roll, so I gave it to him, and he ate that one too.

His name was Angel. I've always liked that name. We hardly said a word to each other that day, but we got to know each other well. And when we were coming back, a gang of boys thumbed their noses at us and yelled out: "They're going to get married, they're going to get married!" The littlest boy threw a dirt bomb at us and Angel chased him, because when he saw Angel coming after him he started to run. Angel grabbed his ear and pulled it, just a little bit, gently, to give him a scare. And said he was going to lock him in the brig, and afterwards put him in the soldiers' mess and make him peel potatoes for two straight years. That's all for the first day.

The second day we walked along that street again and stopped to talk on the wall, which had one side all caked. On the other side there was a row of little houses, with a gate that had windows with grills on both sides of it. And the little houses were always shut, because the people who lived in them spent most of their time around back, which is where the front door and the garden are supposed to be. One time, when we were standing at the foot of the wall, and the sky was that dusky blue that still doesn't blur things, they lit the streetlamps. I saw that the tree we'd seen up above was a mimosa. It was coming into bloom, and it was just lovely the whole time it had flowers. It was a good mimosa, the kind with a few ash-colored leaves and lots of little flowers. The branches were all like yellow clouds. Because some of them have dark leaves, and flowers as long as a worm, and more leaves than flowers. In the light from the streetlamp, it seemed like the mimosa's branches were coming from heaven.

We got used to eating before they lit the streetlamps. I always brought along two rolls with a little meat inside, and while he was eating his slowly in little pinches I'd be dying to kiss that freckle on his neck. One of those nights I caught a chill, because to look pretty I'd put on a pear-colored silk blouse. When I got home my eyes were running and my head felt like it was about to split. The next day I went to the drugstore. My mistress made me go, because she said that was no cold I had but the flu. The clerk at the counter had very pale eyes, almost grey. I've never seen a snake's eyes, but I'm sure that clerk's eyes were the kind snakes have. He said I had a spring cold. I told him how I'd spent two hours in a silk blouse under a mimosa. And he said "It's the pollen. Don't ever stand under a mimosa again."

One afternoon when I was on the wall with Angel, I saw a head on the street corner nearest us. It couldn't have been a vision, and it wasn't a chopped-off head either. It was a young man's head. That night, thinking about the head on the corner, staring at us till it realized I'd seen it, I felt like I knew it. I could almost have sworn it was one of those soldiers who were with Angel the first time I'd seen him, and who'd asked me for a streetcar ticket. I told Angel about it. He said it couldn't be, because they'd already finished their time and gone back to their villages.

That was the last time I saw him. I never saw him again. Lots of times I'd go back to the wall and wait for him, and finally I stopped going. But sometimes it would really hurt just to think maybe he was there . . . He never even kissed me. All he did was take my hand, and hold it for a long time under the mimosa. One day, after we'd eaten, he stared at me so long and so hard that I asked him what he was looking at. He shrugged his shoulders, as if to say "If I only knew!" I gave him a piece of my bread, and he went on looking at me for a while. My cold hung on like it was planning to stay forever. Just when it seemed better, it'd break out again. Itchy nose and sneezing, and coughing fits at night. And I was happy. Afterwards when I went to the drugstore, even if it was only to buy boric acid, the clerk would say "Watch out for that mimosa . . ." And when I get a cold now, it's like I just caught it on the wall, like I was still there.

By this time Miquel's turned my head of course, and I've promised myself to him, because a good girl has to get married. But sometimes when I was with Miquel, I'd close my hand because I felt like Angel's hand was inside it. And then open it, so he could take it out if he wanted . . . so not to force him. And when my girlfriends think I'm only living for Miquel, who's gone off to see the world, I think of Angel, who disappeared like a puff of smoke. But I don't really mind. When I think of him he's mine. There's one thing that's kind of sad though . . . they have a new clerk at the drugstore. And if I ask for a package of aspirin, the new clerk, who doesn't know me, says "Here, two and a half *pessetes*." And clack!, the cash register opens. And if I ask for some citronella he looks at me and says "Two *rals*." And clack!, the cash register opens. Then I leave, but before opening the door I stand quietly for a moment. I don't really know why. As if I'd forgotten something.

Translated by David H. Rosenthal

DATE
WITH A
BIRD

Tatyana
Tolstaya

Russia

"Boys! Dinner time!"

The boys, up to their elbows in sand, looked up and came back to the real world: their mother was on the wooden porch, waving; this way, come on, come on! From the door came the smells of warmth, light, an evening at home.

Really, it was already dark. The damp sand was cold on their knees. Sand castles, ditches, tunnels—everything had blurred into impenetrability, indistinguishability, formlessness. You couldn't tell where the path was, where the damp growths of nettles were, where the rain barrel was . . . But in the west, there was still dim light. And low over the garden, rustling the crowns of the dark wooded hills, rushed a convulsive, sorrowful sigh: that was the day, dying.

Petya quickly felt around for the heavy metal cars—cranes, trucks; Mother was tapping her foot impatiently, holding the doorknob, and little Lenechka had already made a scene, but they swooped him up, dragged him in, washed him, and wiped his struggling face with a sturdy terry towel.

Peace and quiet in the circle of light on the white tablecloth. On saucers, fans of cheese, of sausage, wheels of lemon as if a small yellow bicycle had been broken; ruby lights twinkled in the jam.

Petya was given a large bowl of rice porridge; a melting island of butter floated in the sticky Sargasso Sea. Go under, buttery Atlantis. No one is saved. White palaces with emerald scaly roofs, stepped temples with tall doorways covered with streaming curtains of peacock feathers, enormous golden statues, marble staircases going deep into the sea, sharp silver obelisks with inscriptions in an unknown tongue—everything, everything vanished under water. The transparent green ocean waves were licking the projections of the temples; tanned, crazed people scurried to and fro, children wept. . . . Looters hauled precious trunks made of aromatic wood and dropped them; a whirlwind of flying clothing spread. . . . Nothing will be of use, nothing will help, no one will be saved, everything will slip, list, into the warm, transparent waves. . . . The gold eight-story statue of the main god, with a third eye in his forehead, sways, and looks sadly to the east. . . .

"Stop playing with your food!"

Petya shuddered and stirred in the butter. Uncle Borya, Mother's brother—we don't like him—looks unhappy; he has a black beard and a cigarette in his white teeth; he smokes, having moved his chair closer to the door, open a crack into the corridor. He keeps bugging, nagging, mocking—what does he want?

"Hurry up, kids, straight to bed. Leonid is falling asleep."

And really, Lenechka's nose is in his porridge, and he's dragging his spoon slowly through the viscous mush. But Petya has no intention of going to bed. If Uncle Borya wants to smoke freely, let him go outside. And stop interrogating him.

Petya ate doomed Atlantis and scraped the ocean clean with his spoon, and then stuck his lips into his cup of tea—buttery slicks floated on the surface. Mother took away sleeping Lenechka, Uncle Borya got more comfortable and smoked openly. The smoke from him was disgusting, heavy. Tamila always smoked something aromatic. Uncle Borya read Petya's thoughts and started probing.

"You've been visiting your dubious friend again?"

Yes, again. Tamila wasn't dubious, she was an enchanted beauty with a magical name, she lived on a light blue glass mountain with impenetrable walls, so high up you could see the whole world, as far as the four posts with the signs: South, East, North, West. But she was stolen by a red dragon who flew all over the world with her and brought her here, to this colony of summer dachas. And now she lived in the farthest house, in an enormous room with a veranda filled with tubs of climbing Chinese roses and piled with old books, boxes, chests, and candlesticks; smoked thin cigarettes in a long cigarette holder with jangling copper rings, drank something from small shot glasses, rocked in her chair, and laughed as if she were crying. And in memory of the dragon, Tamila wore a black shiny robe with wide sleeves and a mean red dragon on the back. And her long tangled hair reached down to the armrests of the chair. When Petya grew up he would marry Tamila and lock Uncle Borya in a high tower. But later—maybe—he would have mercy, and let him out.

Uncle Borya read Petya's mind again, laughed, and sang—for no one in particular, but insulting anyway.

> *A-a-ana was a seamstress,*
> *And she did embroidery.*
> *Then she went on sta-age*
> *And became an actress!*
> *Tarum-pam-pam!*
> *Tarum-pam-pam!*

No, he wouldn't let him out of the tower.

Mother came back to the table.

"Were you feeding Grandfather?" Uncle Borya sucked his tooth as if nothing were wrong.

Petya's grandfather was sick in bed in the back room, breathing hard, looking out the low window, depressed.

"He's not hungry," Mother said.

"He's not long for this world," Uncle Borya said, and sucked his tooth. And then he whistled that sleazy tune again: *tarum-pam-pam!*

Petya said thank you, made sure the matchbox with his treasure was still in his pocket, and went to bed—to feel sorry for his grandfather and to think about his life. No one was allowed to speak badly of Tamila. No one understood anything.

. . . Petya was playing ball at the far dacha, which went down to the lake. Jasmine and lilacs had grown so luxuriantly that you couldn't find the gate. The ball flew over the bushes and disappeared in the garden. Petya climbed over the fence and through the bushes—and found a flower garden with a sundial in the center, a spacious veranda, and on it, Tamila. She was rocking in a black rocker, in the bright-black robe, legs crossed, pouring herself a drink from a black bottle; her eyelids were black and heavy and her mouth was red.

"Hi!" Tamila shouted and laughed as if she were crying. "I was waiting for you."

The ball lay at her feet, next to her flower-embroidered slippers. She was rocking back and forth, back and forth, and blue smoke rose from her jangling cigarette holder, and there was ash on her robe.

"I was waiting for you," Tamila repeated. "Can you break the spell on me? No? Oh dear . . . I thought . . . Well, come get your ball."

Petya wanted to stand there and look at her and hear what she would say next.

"What are you drinking?" he asked.

"*Panacea*," Tamila said, and drank some more. "Medicine for all evil and suffering, earthly and heavenly, for evening doubts, for nocturnal enemies. Do you like lemons?"

Petya thought and said: I do.

"Well, when you eat lemons, save the pits for me, all right? If you collect one hundred thousand pits and make them into a necklace, you can fly even higher than the trees, did you know that? If you want, we can fly together, I'll show you a place where there's buried treasure—but I forgot the word to open it up. Maybe we'll think of it together."

Petya didn't know whether to believe her or not, but he wanted to keep looking at her, to watch her speak, watch her rock in that crazy chair, watch the copper rings jangle. She wasn't teasing him, slyly watching his eyes to check: Well? This is interesting, isn't it? Do you like it? She simply rocked and jangled, black and long, and consulted with Petya, and he understood: she would be his friend ages unto ages.

He came closer to look at the amazing rings shining on her hand. A snake with a blue eye circled her finger three times; next to it squatted a squashed silver toad. Tamila took off the snake and let him look at it, but she wouldn't let him see the toad.

"Oh no, oh no; if you take that off, it's the end of me. I'll turn into black dust and the wind will scatter me. It protects me. I'm seven thousand years old, didn't you know?"

It's true, she's seven thousand years old, but she should go on living, she shouldn't take off the ring. She's seen so much. She saw Atlantis perish—as she flew over the doomed world wearing her lemon-pit necklace. They had wanted to burn her at the stake for witchcraft, they were dragging her when she struggled free and soared up to the clouds: why else have the necklace? But then a dragon kidnapped her, carried her away from her glass mountain, from the glass palace, and the necklace was still there, hanging from her mirror.

"Do you want to marry me?"

Petya blushed and replied: I do.

"That's settled. Just don't let me down! We'll ratify our union with a word of honor and some chocolates."

And she handed him a whole dish of candies. That's all she ate. And drank from that black bottle.

"Want to look at the books? They're piled over there."

Petya went over to the dusty mound and opened a book at random. It was a color picture: like a page from a book, but he couldn't read the letters, and on top in the corner there was a big colored letter, all entwined with flat ribbon, grasses, and bells, and above that a creature, half-bird, half-woman.

"What's that?" Petya asked.

"Who knows. They're not mine," Tamila said, rocking, jangling, and exhaling.

"Why is the bird like that?"

"Let me see. Ah, that bird. That's the Sirin, the bird of death. Watch out for it: it will choke you. Have you heard somebody wailing, cuckooing in the woods at night? That's this bird. It's a night bird. There's also the Finist. It used to fly to me often, but then we had a fight. And there's another bird, the Alkonost. It gets up in the morning at dawn, all pink and transparent, you can see through it, and it sparkles. It makes its nest in water lilies. It lays one egg, very rare. Do you know why people pick lilies? They're looking for the egg. Whoever finds it will feel a sense of longing all their life. But they still look for it, they still want it. Why, *I* have it. Would you like it?"

Tamila rocked once on the black bentwood rocker and went into the house. A beaded cushion fell from the seat. Petya touched it; it was cool. Tamila came back, and in her hand, jingling against the inside of her rings, was the magical egg, pink glass, tightly stuffed with golden sparkles.

"You're not afraid? Hold it! Well, come visit me." She laughed and fell into the rocker, moving the sweet, aromatic air.

Petya didn't know what it was to be depressed for life, and took the egg.

Definitely, he would marry her. He had planned to marry his mother, but now that he had promised Tamila . . . He would definitely take his mother with him, too; and if it came to that, he could take Lenechka, as well . . . but Uncle Borya—no way. He loved his mother very, very much, but you'd never hear such strange and marvelous stories as Tamila's from her. Eat and wash up—that was her whole conversation. And what they bought; onions or fish or something.

And she'd never even heard of the Alkonost bird. Better not tell her. And he'd put the egg in a matchbox and not show it to anybody.

Petya lay in bed and thought about how he would live with Tamila in the big room with the Chinese roses. He would sit on the veranda steps and whittle sticks for a sailboat he'd call *The Flying Dutchman*. Tamila would rock in her chair, drink the panacea, and talk. Then they would board *The Flying Dutchman*, the dragon flag on the mast, Tamila in her black robe on the deck, sunshine and salt spray, and they would set sail in search of Atlantis, lost in the shimmering briny deep.

He used to live a simple life: whittling, digging in the sand, reading adventure books; lying in bed, he would listen to the night trees anxiously moving outside his window, and think that miracles happened on distant islands, in parrot-filled jungles, or in tiny South America, narrowing downward, with its plastic Indians and rubber crocodiles. But the world, it turned out, was imbued with mystery, sadness, and magic, rustling in the branches, swaying in the dark waters. In the evenings, he and his mother walked along the lake: the sun set in the crenellated forest, the air smelled of blueberries and pine resin, and high above the ground red fir cones glimmered gold. The water in the lake looks cold, but when you put your hand in it, it's even hot. A large gray lady in a cream dress walks along the high shore: she walks slowly, using a stick, smiles gently, but her eyes are dark and her gaze empty. Many years ago her little daughter drowned in the lake, and she is waiting for her to come home: it's bedtime, but the daughter still hasn't come. The gray lady stops and asks, "What time is it?" When she hears the reply, she shakes her head. "Just think." And when you come back, she'll stop and ask again, "What time is it?"

Petya had felt sorry for the lady ever since he learned her secret. But Tamila says little girls don't drown, they simply *cannot* drown. Children have gills: when they get underwater they turn into fish, though not right away. The girl is swimming around, a silver fish, and she pokes her head out, wanting to call to her mother. But she has no voice . . .

And here, not far away, is a boarded-up dacha. No one comes to live there, the porch is rotted through, the shutters nailed, the paths overgrown. Evil had been done in that dacha, and now no one can live there. The owners tried to get tenants, even offered them money to live there; but no, no one will. Some people tried, but they didn't last three days: the lights went out by themselves, the water wouldn't come to a boil in the kettle, wet laundry wouldn't dry, knives dulled on their own, and the children couldn't shut their eyes at night, sitting up like white columns in their beds.

And on that side—see? You can't go there, it's a dark fir forest; twilight, smoothly swept paths, white fields with intoxicating flowers. And that's where the bird Sirin lives, amid the branches, the bird of death, as big as a wood grouse. Petya's grandfather is afraid of the bird Sirin, it might sit on his chest and suffocate him. It has six toes on each foot, leathery, cold, and muscular, and a face like a sleeping girl's. *Cu-goo! Cu-goo!* the Sirin bird cries in the evenings, fluttering in its fir grove. Don't let it near Grandfather, shut the windows and doors, light the lamp, let's read out loud. But Grandfather is afraid, he watches the window anxiously, breathes heavily, plucks at his blanket. *Cu-goo! Cu-goo!* What do you want from us, bird? Leave Grandfather alone! Grandfather, don't look at the window like that, what do you see there? Those are just fir branches waving in the dark, it's just the wind acting up, unable to fall asleep. Grandfather, we're all here. The lamp is on and the tablecloth is white and I've cut out a boat, and Lenechka has drawn a rooster. Grandfather?

"Go on, go on, children." Mother shoos them from Grandfather's room, frowning, with tears in her eyes. Black oxygen pillows lie on a chair in the corner—to chase away the Sirin bird. All night it flies over the house, scratching at windows; and toward morning it finds a crack, climbs up, heavy, on the windowsill, on the bed, walks on the blanket, looking for Grandfather. Mother grabs a scary black pillow, shouts, waves it about, chases the Sirin bird . . . gets rid of it.

Petya tells Tamila about the bird: maybe she knows a spell, a word to ward off the Sirin bird? But Tamila shakes her head sadly: no; she used to, but it's back on the glass mountain. She would give Grandfather her protective toad ring—but then she'd turn into black powder herself. . . . And she drinks from her black bottle.

She's so strange! He wanted to think about her, about what she said, to listen to her dreams; he wanted to sit on her veranda steps, steps of the house where everything was allowed: eat bread and jam with unwashed hands, slouch, bite your nails, walk with your shoes on—if you felt like it—right in the flower-beds; and no one shouted, lectured, called for order, cleanliness, and common sense. You could take a pair of scissors and cut out a picture you liked from any book—Tamila didn't care, she was capable of tearing out a picture and cutting it herself, except she always did it crooked. You could say whatever came into your head without fear of being laughed at: Tamila shook her head sadly, understanding; and if she did laugh, it was as if she were crying. If you ask, she'll play cards: Go Fish, anything; but she played badly, mixing up cards and losing.

Everything rational, boring, customary; all that remained on the other side of the fence overgrown with flowering bushes.

Ah, he didn't want to leave! At home he had to be quiet about Tamila (when I grow up and marry her, *then* you'll find out); and about the Sirin; and about the sparkling egg of the Alkonost bird, whose owner will be depressed for life. . . .

Petya remembered the egg, got it out of the matchbox, stuck it under his pillow, and sailed off on *The Flying Dutchman* over the black nocturnal seas.

In the morning Uncle Borya, with a puffy face, was smoking before breakfast on the porch. His black beard stuck out challengingly and his eyes were narrowed in disdain. Seeing his nephew, he began whistling yesterday's disgusting tune . . . and laughed. His teeth—rarely visible because of the beard—were like a wolf's. His black eyebrows crawled upward.

"Greetings to the young romantic." He nodded briskly. "Come on, Peter, saddle up your bike and go to the store. Your mother needs bread, and you can get me two packs of Kazbeks. They'll sell it to you, they will. I know Nina in the store, she'll give kids under sixteen anything at all."

Uncle Borya opened his mouth and laughed. Petya took the ruble and walked his sweaty bike out of the shed. On the ruble, written in tiny letters, were incomprehensible words, left over from Atlantis: *Bir sum. Bir som. Bir manat.* And beneath that, a warning: "Forging state treasury bills is punishable by law." Boring, adult words. The sober morning had swept away the magical evening birds, the girl-fish had gone down to the bottom of the lake, and the golden three-eyed statues of Atlantis slept under a layer of yellow sand. Uncle Borya had dissipated the fragile secrets with his loud, offensive laughter, had thrown out the fairy-tale rubbish—but not forever, Uncle Borya, just for a while. The sun would start leaning toward the west, the air would turn yellow, the oblique rays would spread, and the mysterious world would awaken, start moving, the mute silvery drowned girl would splash her tail, and the heavy, gray Sirin bird would bustle in the fir forest, and in some unpopulated spot, the morning bird Alkonost perhaps already would have hidden its fiery pink egg in a water lily, so that someone could long for things that did not come to pass. . . . *Bir sum, bir som, bir manat.*

Fat-nosed Nina gave him the cigarettes without a word, and asked him to say hello to Uncle Borya—a disgusting hello for a disgusting person—and Petya rode back, ringing his bell, bouncing on the knotty roots that resembled Grandfather's enormous hands. He carefully rode around a dead crow—a wheel had run over the bird, its eye was covered with a white film, the black dragged wings were covered with ashes, and the beak was frozen in a bitter avian smile.

At breakfast Mother looked concerned—Grandfather wouldn't eat again. Uncle Borya whistled, breaking the shell of his egg with a spoon, and watching the boys—looking for something to pick on. Lenechka spilled the milk and Uncle Borya was glad—an excuse to nag. But Lenechka was totally indifferent to his uncle's lectures: he was still little and his soul was sealed like a chicken egg; everything just rolled off. If, God forbid, he fell into the water, he wouldn't drown—he'd turn into a fish, a big-browed striped perch. Lenechka finished his milk and, without listening to the end of the lecture, ran out to the sand box: the sand had dried in the morning sun and his towers must have fallen apart. Petya remembered.

"Mama, did that girl drown a long time ago?"

"What girl?" his mother asked with a start.

"You know. The daughter of that old lady who always asks what time it is?"

"She never had any daughter. What nonsense. She has two grown sons. Who told you that?"

Petya said nothing. Mother looked at Uncle Borya, who laughed with glee.

"Drunken delirium of our shaggy friend! Eh? A girl, eh?"

"What friend?"

"Oh, nothing . . . Neither fish nor fowl."

Petya went out on the porch. Uncle Borya wanted to dirty everything. He wanted to grill the silver girl-fish and crunch her up with his wolf teeth. It won't work, Uncle Borya. The egg of the transparent morning bird Alkonost is glowing under my pillow.

Uncle Borya flung open the window and shouted into the dewy garden: "You should drink less!"

Petya stood by the gate and dug his nail into the ancient gray wood. The day was just beginning.

Grandfather wouldn't eat in the evening, either. Petya sat on the edge of the crumpled bed and patted his grandfather's wrinkled hand. His grandfather was looking out the window, his head turned. The wind had risen, the treetops were swaying, and Mama took down the laundry—it was flapping like *The Flying Dutchman*'s white sails. Glass jangled. The dark garden rose and fell like the ocean. The wind chased the Sirin bird from the branches; flapping its mildewed wings, it flew to the house and sniffed around, moving its triangular face with shut eyes: is there a crack? Mama sent Petya away and made her bed in Grandfather's room.

There was a storm that night. The trees rioted. Lenechka woke up and cried. Morning was gray, sorrowful, windy. The rain knocked Sirin to the ground, and Grandfather sat up in bed and was fed broth. Petya hovered in the doorway, glad to see his grandfather, and looked out the window—the flowers drooped under the rain, and it smelled of autumn. They lit the stove; wearing hooded jackets, they carried wood from the shed. There was nothing to do outside. Lenechka sat down to draw, Uncle Borya paced, hands behind his back, and whistled.

The day was boring: they waited for lunch and then waited for dinner. Grandfather ate a hard-boiled egg. It rained again at night.

That night Petya wandered around underground passages, staircases, in subway tunnels; he couldn't find the exit, kept changing trains: the trains traveled on ladders with the doors wide open and they passed through strange rooms filled with furniture; Petya had to get out, get outside, get up to where Lenechka and Grandfather were in danger: they forgot to shut the door, it was wide open, and the Sirin bird was walking up the creaking steps, its eyes shut; Petya's schoolbag was in the way, but he needed it. How to get out? Where was the exit? How do I get upstairs? "You need a bill." Of course, a bill to get out. There was the booth. Give me a bill. A treasury bill? Yes, yes, please! "Forging state treasury bills is punishable by law." There they were, the bills: long, black sheets of paper. Wait, they have holes in them. That's punishable by law. Give me some more. I don't want to! The schoolbag opens, and long black bills, holes all over, fall out. Hurry, pick them up, quick, I'm being persecuted, they'll catch me. They scatter all over the floor, Petya picks them up, stuffing them in any which way; the crowd separates, someone is being led through. . . . He can't get out of the way, so many bills, oh there it is, the horrible thing: they're leading it by the arms, huge, howling like a siren, its purple gaping face upraised; it's neither-fish-nor-fowl, it's the end!

Petya jumped up with a pounding heart; it wasn't light yet. Lenechka slept peacefully. He crept barefoot to Grandfather's room, pushed the door—silence. The night light was on. The black oxygen pillows were in the corner. Grandfather lay with open eyes, hands clutching the blanket. He went over, feeling cold; guessing, he touched Grandfather's hand and recoiled. Mama!

No, Mama will scream and be scared. Maybe it can still be fixed. Maybe Tamila can help?

Petya rushed to the exit—the door was wide open. He stuck his bare feet into rubber boots, put a hood over his head, and rattled down the steps. The rain had ended, but it still dripped from the trees. The sky was turning gray. He ran on legs that buckled and slipped in the mud. He pushed the veranda door. There was a strong waft of cold, stale smoke. Petya bumped into a small table: a jangle and rolling sound. He bent down, felt around, and froze: the ring with the toad, Tamila's protection, was on the floor. There was noise in the bedroom. Petya flung open the door. There were two silhouettes in the dim light in the bed: Tamila's tangled black hair on the pillow, her black robe on the chair; she turned and moaned. Uncle Borya sat up in bed, his beard up, his hair disheveled. Tossing the blanket over Tamila's leg and covering his own legs, he blustered and shouted, peering into the dark: "Eh? Who is it? What is it? Eh!"

Petya started crying and shouted, trembling in horrible understanding, "Grandfather's dead! Grandfather's dead! Grandfather's dead!"

Uncle Borya threw back the blanket and spat out horrible, snaking, inhuman words; Petya shuddered in sobs, and ran out blindly: boots in the flowerbeds; his soul was boiled like egg white hanging in clumps on the trees rushing toward him; sour sorrow filled his mouth and he reached the lake and fell down under the wet tree oozing rain; screeching, kicking his feet, he chased Uncle Borya's horrible words, Uncle Borya's horrible legs, from his mind.

He got used to it, quieted down, lay there. Drops fell on him from above. The dead lake, the dead forest: birds fell from the trees and lay feet up; the dead empty world was filled with gray thick oozing depression. Everything was a lie.

He felt something hard in his hand and unclenched his fist. The squashed silver guard toad popped its eyes at him.

The match box, radiating eternal longing, lay in his pocket.
The Sirin bird had suffocated Grandfather.
No one can escape his fate. It's all true, child. That's how it is.
He lay there a bit longer, wiped his face, and headed for the house.

Translated by Antonina W. Bouis

AFRICA AND
THE
MIDDLE EAST

TURKISH SOLDIER FROM EDIRNE

Nissim Aloni

Israel

On moonlit nights, when the dust in the street obscured the pallid light, stories were told in the lots of the neighborhood. At the end of the street in Mr. Pinto's cafe, the Devil sat sipping arak from a pouch made of bat skin. In the woods near the HaTikva Quarter lions who could down a horse with one blow were wandering around. In the attic of Salamon Cabillio's house a thousand-year-old owl lived, cursing all who dared approach him. Salamon saw him.

"My uncle Alberto got blinded because of it," Salamon said.

"And you?" Shmeel asked him.

"I'm blind!" rang out Salamon.

He had on a jockey's cap and smoked a stalk of straw. We used to smoke the cane from which the blind wove chairs.

There was a war in the world. Arcane secrets leapt about like wrestlers from the far corner of the lot up to and into the great darkness and we embarked, with the train, under the big bridge near Yaffo, to the battlefields in the desert, we galloped atop saddled white horses, we skipped over the face of the abyss, we sat in the whorehouses at the end of Allenby Street, by the sea, with the soldiers. Salamon told us that his blind uncle took him to Yaffo, on Saturdays. Near a monastery there are stands piled with red dates and the whores sit in the sun with their legs spread apart.

"Moise Lalo's daughter, the one that skipped home a long time ago, sits there," Salamon said, "fat, and between her legs there's a cross."

Sometimes, later on in the night, they whispered stories about Elohim, who was death, and whose picture was on all the electric lines, and who himself was colored blue, because of the war, at the end. The war was in Marseille-Matruch and in the street raging inspectors went around to see that there was darkness. But on moonlit nights death came down from the heights of the electric line and sat with us, in the lot, old and small, blue, bald.

He sat near me when I told the story of the Turkish soldier from Edirne.

One spring morning, having gotten his orders, the Turkish soldier from Edirne burst out of his trench, jumped over the wire lines and ran forward with his rifle extended to kill his enemies from Bulgaria. As he ran, a Bulgarian bomb hit him in the neck and severed his head. His head, detached from his body, flew in the air, but his mouth continued calling out the war cry of the Turks and his body continued running in murderous anger toward the Bulgarians.

It seemed to me that death laughed between his bones, as if I had made up the whole incident, yet I had heard the story from the mouth of the Turkish soldier from Edirne.

He used to shine shoes. During the day he sat on a stool near his shoeshine box, in the row of shoeshine stands on Allenby Street, very close to Rothschild Avenue, and I on my way back from school would slip away from my friends to hang around. He kept, for my sake, the pictures of Views of Our Country that could be found on every cigarette carton. His eyes were frantic, like the heads of the mice in Isidore Saporta's shoe repair shop. In the middle of his head there was a straight white streak and both sides of his black hair were smeared with brilliantine. He had a mustache whose ends covered up his mouth and on his neck there was a long white scar.

He always dressed in rumpled khakis. In his shirt pocket there was a small red pen and a jackknife, the shine of whose blade had long faded. He used to clean his fingernails with that knife. On his wrist he wore a strip of black leather and he always wore sneakers. Whenever a neighboring shoeshine man talked to him he answered in a whisper. I knew why he never raised his voice, ever. He never said his name. And he did not ask after mine.

Nights he used to sit in Mr. Pinto's cafe, at the end of the main street in the neighborhood, and with him the Devil and the sock salesman with the hooked teeth and Salamon's blind uncle and sometimes even Mr. Goldberg, the Pole who lived in the small room on the roof of Shmeel's house. But at night I did not recognize the shoeshine man.

If I passed there, in the evening hours before the windows darkened, I would avert my eyes so as not to look, even though I wanted very much to see the Devil sipping from his pouch. When the dates ripened on the trees the bats flew at them attacking with a twittering that resembled a cry. In the drink stand adorned with Avramino Kashi's colored pennants, near the picture of King George, there was a jar of date juice. I said to myself, nights the Devil latches onto the date trees grabbing the bats from their flight and makes wine skins out of them.

Once, at noon, I asked the Turkish soldier from Edirne:

"What does the Devil drink?"

"Beer."

In the afternoon, on my way back home, I used to stop by and take a rest. He on his stool and me on my school bag. We used to gaze at the street, our eyes glazed in a leaden stupor. Sometimes I would test him with things I had learned that morning in school. I told him about the turns the war was taking in the world. In the Western Desert there were sand storms. In Sebastapol battles raged tracked with blood. Is the war still raging in Edirne? Are the sand storms still howling? Are the Turks still overrunning their enemies from Bulgaria? He always nodded his head as if saying yes. In one of the drawers in his shoeshine box there was a tiny bottle of arak. When the Turk took in a sip his Adam's apple would jump and the white scar on his neck would turn red.

Afterward, he would wipe his mouth and look at me, cockeyed, like a mouse, with frantic eyes. Once he extended the bottle of arak over to me and my heart beat wildly. When he returned the bottle to the drawer his lips separated and the ends of his mouth extended out from under his mustache. He smiled.

I told him:

"Your throat is cut."

He looked at the empty street and the smile extended over his face.

"In the city of Edirne there isn't a man without a cut throat," he said, silently. His walk resembled that of a man slipping away. I saw him that way, from a distance, several times, his eyes glued to the sidewalk and his hands touching the walls of the houses. That's the way he goes (I said in my heart), in his sneakers, since his head was cut off and flew away, in the war between the Turks and the Bulgarians in the spring.

My friends called me Edirne.

Salamon Cabillio told stories about his uncle and his aunts and his brother Zakole mimicked him. Miko told detective stories. Shmeel told about his father's wars in the Western desert. I told stories about Edirne.

In Edirne there were mosques whose minarets bore unto heaven. There were men with squared beards and cut throats and curved swords. There was a sad king whose squared beard hid his cut throat. Around the city there were valleys filled with roses and rivers that came down from the mountains and watered the roses. Every night there was a high pitched piercing sound from the rivers, a sound of neighing, and it extended from the mouths of thousands of war horses who had drowned in the rivers. A war horse that drowns in the river, the Turkish soldier said, neighs once a night, and when there is neighing the famous singers of Edirne stop singing in the cafes.

The musicians of Edirne, said the soldier, are known throughout the world. If you check, he told me, you'll find that every famous musician comes from there.

"And Joseph Schmidt?" I asked.

"From Edirne."

Once when the Turkish king had been victorious over the Greek army he held a big feast in the city. They filled the big square in Edirne with the carcasses of Greek soldiers, stuck flags in them, and all the big singers came to sing songs to the king. That night the neighing of the drowning horses could not be heard, the voices of the singers were so tender. The king cried. When they finished singing he asked them:

"How is it that you are possessed of voices that burn the heart and fill it with honey?"

One musician came out and said:

"My king, my father was a furrier and when the Russians closed in on our city, the supply of salt ran out. What did my father do? He dipped morsels in water extracted from skins. From that, your highness, or at least my father told me it was so, my voice became sweet."

The king marvelled greatly:

"What, water extracted from skins mellows the voice?"

The Turkish musician from Edirne answered the king:

"Maybe the water from the skins or maybe the sorrows."

The Turkish soldier told me that the king succumbed to grief and told the musicians, "Merciful God, if there were no wars there would be no sweet voices." Afterwards they opened barrels of wine and drank at the king's expense.

"Was the Devil there?"

"A man," the Turkish soldier from Edirne answered, "will never drink at the expense of a king, even a sad king."

Sometimes, at night in my bed, I would see the shoeshine man, in his sneakers, on the battlefield, searching for his head, the king watching him in grief, the musicians singing with the drowning horses, and the Devil drinking from a pouch.

One evening, on my way back from the library, I passed by Mr. Pinto's cafe and saw the Turk sitting on the sidewalk with his head bowed down. I remember that the radio announcer said the humidity would be high; my shirt stuck to my skin. Blue lights already flashed on the electric lines and there were blankets on the windows. I wanted to slip by but he raised his head suddenly and his eyes barred my way. His hair hung loosely about his eyes but the streak flashed in the dimness, straight and white, as always. I said in my heart: another man. His shirt was open, his belt untied, and the seams of his pants were coming apart. When Salamon's blind uncle was drunk my mother used to close the shutters. He would piss into the middle of the street and cry out, "My eyes, my eyes."

"You'd think he was being slaughtered," my mother would say.

The Turk smiled, as one afflicted. I stood a few steps from him, alert and suspicious.

People passing scolded me.

"Get home, kid!"

The Turk, like a doll, continued smiling and fixed his shrouded eyes on me.

I knew, in the dimness, that there was no frenzy in his eyes.

I thought: another man. Maybe he would cry out, like Salamon's uncle. Maybe he would hit at something. I thought the Devil must have thrown him out of the cafe.

I said, from a distance, as if I did not know him:

"Why don't you go home?"

A rancid smell issued from him and entered the pages of the book. The librarian would sense it. The librarian handled each book that was returned as if in search, under the brown dust jacket, on the pages, between the lines, in the words, for signs of disgraceful acts. I pressed the book hard onto my back.

The Turk raised his head sluggishly and tried to wipe his mouth. Afterwards he tried to button the buttons on his pants but his hand dragged. As he lost hope, he smiled down toward his pants. His hand slipped down to the sidewalk. His head fell against his chest. He resembled a man sleeping.

"You live far?"

My voice was odd, shrill, abrasive and distant from me, as if I were a child who had thrown a rock and gone off to hide. I said to myself: They're waiting for me at home. My mother would be looking at the clock on the wall. My father would be looking at my mother from behind the paper. My mother would go to the lots in the neighborhood and call out my name.

"Where do you live?"

He raised his head, slowly, and looked at me for a long time, his smile crooked, his eyes blinking. As if he had uncovered my deceit in the dark. I said in my heart, the librarian is uncovering my deceit, the kids are uncovering my deceit, the Turk is uncovering my deceit.

"What?" he said, his voice inanimate, dull, disparate.

I stood up abruptly, like a belligerent soldier.

"A book, from the library."

He swung his head like the pendulum of our wall clock.

Afterward, as if reminiscing, he stretched his legs over the road and his hands began to search for the pockets of his pants.

"Where is your house?" I said, indignant.

Now he searched in the pockets of his shirt and did not find what he wanted. Finally he drew a picture from Views of Our Country out of his back pocket.

"My children," he said, extending the picture to me, "wife, far away."

In the picture there was a guard dressed in a kulpak hat, holding a rifle. The picture was not valuable, even though I would be able to get two "Paragons of Industriousness" or even three "Rachel Lamenting Her Sons" in exchange; I did not know whether or not to take it.

"Take it," the Turk said in his remote voice. "Wife. Children. There!"

Suddenly, with a ray of light, Mr. Pinto came out from behind the blinds. For a second the beam collared the Turk and me. Then, when only the sides of his immense body and curly hair were illuminated, I saw Mr. Pinto waving his huge hand, lit up behind me.

"Home! Get home!" Mr. Pinto called out to me. "What business you got over here?" Even though I saw his black eyebrows I only withdrew a step. The sidewalk isn't his, I told myself bravely.

The Turk seemed as if he did not see or hear the giant Mr. Pinto.

"Didn't you hear what I said?" Mr. Pinto yelled at me.

I did not move from my place. Mr. Pinto stepped toward me. I jumped like a grasshopper until I felt the wall of a house on my back. The book from the library got scratched. Mr. Pinto extended the open palm of one hand toward the Turk and with his other hand he spoke to me:

"Don't you have eyes, you bastard? He's sick!"

The Turk turned his head to Mr. Pinto. Now his lips were crooked, as if he were compelled to smile. A ray of light brightened his disheveled hair and his open shirt, his mustache twinkled. Another man, I cried out in my heart, a pirate with a mustache! But when he turned his head from me it swayed again, like the women in the neighborhood when they spoke of the war.

He lets his head sway as if he wants it to drop off, I said in my heart.

"Now I'll teach you a lesson!" Mr. Pinto growled, enveloping me with his flailing hands. An angry inspector making his rounds through the street warned Mr. Pinto.

Mr. Pinto, like a titanic clown, stopped, bowed down and disappeared behind the black shades of the cafe. The street was dark, only the blue lights from the height of the electric lines flashed over us, a pale island.

The inspector continued running, searching for illegal lights; I heard his voice in the distance shouting:

"Turn off the light!"

The Turk got to his feet, wavering. He searched for the wall and leaned on it with his hand. I stood once again in the middle of the sidewalk as if it were I who now barred his way. He stood by the wall a moment, his eyes lowered, like a child playing, whose turn it was to stand by the wall and count until all the others had hidden. I also counted, to a hundred, two hundred, more. He roused abruptly. He pushed his hair up with his hand and brushed it through. Then he hitched up his pants and girded them, like a soldier setting out on a long mission.

"Where's your house?"

He started walking. I went after him.

I thought that he would remove his head in his house.

I am in foreign territory, I said to myself, going after him.

The streets were dark. The openings of the houses were dark. The buses travelled with blue eyes. Angry people swore in the darkness. I tightened my grip on the book in my hand as I went along, a few steps behind him, along the lengths of the walls of the houses. When we arrived at the railroad crossing he stopped without warning, turned and looked at me. He waved his hand toward me, like Mr. Pinto, but I stood my ground, as in a game of freeze: when he cut across the tracks I cut across after him, in the trail of his sneakers. His tracks dissolved. Now he seemed like a man running and I ran on. On no account could I lose the book while running, I said in my heart, this alien land would consume it. Before I even realized it I saw that we were going by the Summer Eden Cinema. I had heard the voices of the heroes from the afternoon show but now they were of older people, strangers. My heart beat violently: even during the day I did not pass the border of the houses near the Summer Eden Cinema. Once we had had a war with a gang from Shabazi Street that had inadvertently wandered onto our street: they'd had us by the balls.

Was it possible we were running to Edirne? The Turk's house, surrounded by blue mountains and pink rivers. From the house a minaret rose high, topped by a crescent moon. He illuminated the house with the leather strap wrapped around his wrist. After, when the horses in the river neighed, he would remove his head. Maybe the Turkish king waits for him there, gloomy.

The Turk ran like a soldier, and I too, after him, ran like a soldier, over the face of the dark intersections, strange trees, other lots enveloped in darkness. We passed by the faces of soldiers dressed in mariner's caps, and strong, hostile children lining up against me with outstretched hands threw stones after me. Did they know me from my neighborhood? A woman yelled a word out after me that was consumed in the darkness. I thought: Thermos, thermos, land of the thermos, thermos children, thermos women, maybe they threw thermoses after me. My face was struck by wind from the sea.

There was dry sweat on my brow. I heard the sweet rumble of the sea. The water approached us like an unseen train. A keen smell, acrid, rose from the sea, the smell of drowning horses.

When I stood on the sand at the shoreline, not far from the first houses of Yaffo, I saw that the Turk was sitting on the sand and smoking a cigarette. The white waves of the sea were not dark, despite the war. Next to him was an orange crate that had been spewn forth by the sea. I sat on it, next to him. He looked past me.

"Get away, get away."

I sat on the orange crate like a righteous man, and he extended a cigarette to me, from a distance. I did not move from my place. My heart beat wildly, as on that day that he had offered me the tiny bottle of arak. A little more and I thought I would cry, and I said in my heart, I am the strongest man in the world. We sat like that, he on the sand and I on the crate, gazing in stupor at the brooding sea and the white waves.

I said to him:

"They said on the radio it would be wet."

The Turk threw his cigarette into the sea.

"Soon I will die."

Death, old and blue, twinkled over the face of the white waves.

"People die in Edirne?" I asked.

He laughed:

"One man, in Edirne, died eight times."

I thought that it would be my duty to tell of this in the neighborhood. Shmeel's father was liable to die in the Western Desert, but now Shmeel would know that his father could die seven more times.

I said to him proudly:

"My grandfather died only once. They buried him."

The white waves continued to lap the moist shore while the Turk told me about the dying; an instant before they died they leapt about in the air in the full splendor of their consummate might. That is the time when they are more graceful than they ever were and as mighty as the greatest heroes. They hang in the air, like frogs, with hands extended, and they have the power to do what is not in the power of a live man to do, if only they do not die and get buried. Because death sits among the mourners waiting to take them.

"Does death come from the electric line?"

"If the mourners rise from their places," the Turk said, "and man by man hold the one dying with two hands and if the dying man yokes himself to them strongly, he will return to life."

"All the dying?"

Without warning, as a wave disappearing in the darkness of night, yet still discernible, I noticed that he had risen from his place: the Turk disappeared in the darkness of the first houses of Yaffo. I knew because the picture of the guard in his kulpak hat remained in my hand.

I did not know even how to call out to him by name.

I walked the length of the dark promenade until I reached the bus station on the square. The sidewalk and the road were joined in black by the darkness and the moisture. The wetness was on my skin, my hair and in my nostrils. It descended on the face of the dark square like a black jelly-fish spreading its amorphous body up to the openings of the dark houses surrounding the square. Opposite the jelly-fish, from the lamps of the buses, came pale blue light. From the big cafe on the other side, women came out with soldiers, chattering and laughing like pieces of glass shattering, and with them a jazz tune broke through, and returned hastily, back to the hall, behind the dark shades, away from the anger of the wrathful inspectors.

One Saturday morning, when they cleaned the hall of the big cafe, we saw wooden huts and snow-covered awnings from Switzerland. Salamon said the huts were Swiss. He said it was a whorehouse. In Shauliko's cafe, on the main street of the neighborhood, there were only landscapes of woods and waterfalls with women stretched out on the green. A small whorehouse, Salamon said.

The sea rumbled incessantly. The darkness is indifferent, I said in my heart, as if the world belongs to it. I knew I was sad. I whistled an American tune. I heard a woman saying to a soldier, in English:

"Dance."

In the light of the blue lamps of a bus the head of a driver twinkled, like an evil spirit.

When I entered my neighborhood I saw my mother and father circling around trying to find me. In a panic I thought of how I could lie my way out, so as to gain their trust, but the book from the library cancelled all my plans.

My father asked me:

"Where were you?"

Since I did not answer he removed his belt.

"What did you do?" he said, and my mother repeated his question in a chirping, contemptuous voice.

Since I did not answer my father began to hit me in the street. My mother cried out for him to release me, but she also hit me, with her hand. In the darkness I saw the heads of the children, hostile.

I cried out, because of the blows, but there no longer remained any doubt: The shoeshine man from Allenby Street was the Turkish soldier from Edirne.

After that night I did not slip away from my friends to hang around the soldier for a few days. I also did not know what I would do with the picture of the Hebrew guard on his watch. I did not play with it and I did not deal it and I did not glue it into my album of Views of Our Country.

And already there was talk of the big vacation.

One day, after a quarrel, I returned to Allenby Street. I saw that the Turk's eyes were dull, dull as the blade of his jackknife. I sat on my school bag and told him that the city of London was being shelled with powerful bombs, but he continued shining a pair of shoes with no man in them, with great diligence. I told him about things I had heard in school but it seemed as if he were not listening. When I was quiet his expression did not change. A man came up and put his shoes up to be shined but the Turk smoked his cigarette, as if he were alone.

Again he did not give me pictures from Views of Our Country but only continued smoking. I stopped telling him about the turns the war was taking. Once I said, my mouth slack, that soon the big vacation would come, but he did not hear. We would both sit and gaze in the glazed stupor of mid-afternoon. I looked for excuses to get away.

One day, on my return from school, he was not in his place.

I asked some of the other shoeshine men, the ones usually next to him, but they shrugged their shoulders. When I came the next day, he was not there. After a few days another shoeshine man grabbed his place, a stranger.

Sometimes, evenings, I used to pass quickly by the front of Mr. Pinto's cafe, but if he was there he was behind the shades. I did not see either him, or the Devil. In the darkness I used to inspect the legs of passing men but I did not see his sneakers. A few times I passed near the walls of the houses neighboring the cafe, in the hope that maybe some sign had been left on them from his hand.

One day I thought that he might have changed his place.

I went the length of the street, waving my lunch bag for camouflage, from the Avenue up to Kikar HaMoshavot, but he was not there. The next day I went all along the street from the Avenue up to Magen David Square.

He went to Edirne, I said in my heart.

In the lot I said that every man in Edirne dies eight times but I did not want to reveal the secret of the dying; no one believed me.

"Eight times!" said Salamon Cabillio mockingly. And afterwards he cried out in the night:

"People die like flies!"

Everyone believed him.

One day, in the afternoon, on my way back from school, a lot of people were gathered in a crowd near Mr. Pinto's cafe at the end of the street. I was playing the whole way with two friends at Views of Our Country: whoever had the most pictures was the winner. Sometimes extremely valuable pictures were lost in this game. I was so absorbed in the game that I did not see the crowd until I stumbled upon some women standing on its periphery.

They held their heads with their hands and the voices of mourning could be heard. We rushed to press in under the stevedores and the crane operators and suddenly I saw the Turk, laid out on the sidewalk, in the heart of the crowd. The sun beat down on the heads of those standing around and on the full length of the Turk lying flat out on the wet sidewalk, his hair dishevelled, his mustache wet, his eyes shut and spittle dribbling from around his mouth.

My friends called out to me: "Edirne! Edirne!" But the Turk did not move. I raised my eyes to the big men around me, but they looked at the Turk with their arms crossed over their grey undershirts, as if they were watching a horse who would never get up again, even though the Turk's chest rose and fell.

He's dying, I thought, the Turk is dying, death is sitting on the face of the big men, the indifferent ones, like that moist darkness in the sea. Now I saw flies circling on the Turk's face as if they too knew that the Turk was ownerless property.

I approached and said quickly, in a whisper.

"Get up!"

I heard that the stevedores were yelling behind me but I did not know what they were saying. What kind of shout is that? And I waited that he jump from his place. I said to him in my heart, Jump, Turkish soldier, leap in the air, be a hero among heroes, get up, stand on your feet, and run, run, run the way you ran before your head was cut off, before you cried the war cry that spring, get up, you will live many more times, more, get up and yoke yourself to those standing, to the stevedores, the mourning women, the crane operators, get up, Turkish soldier, get up now so that the sign of death will not be upon you!

The stevedores, the crane operators, all the big men tried to shift me from my place near the Turk lying on the sidewalk as if he were dead, until he shook his head, straightened up, sat on the edge of the sidewalk and stood, wavering, with his eyes closed. He tried to wipe the spittle from around his mouth, he neared the wall and leaned on it. His clothes were dirty, torn, and his sneakers wet. The scar on his throat was crimson.

The women continued holding their heads in their hands and the voices of mourning could still be heard. The men shook their heads in disdain. Slowly they began to disperse. It seemed that he did not see me. After leaning on the wall for some time he took in a few deep breaths, raised the wet hair from his eyes and brushed it through with his hand. Then he straightened himself up, like a soldier, and went forth, tottering, on his mission, along the lengths of the walls.

Translated by Ammiel Alcalay

SOME ARE BORN TO SWEET DELIGHT

Nadine Gordimer

South Africa

> Some are Born to sweet delight,
> Some are Born to Endless Night.
> WILLIAM BLAKE, *'Auguries of Innocence'*

They took him in. Since their son had got himself signed up at sea for eighteen months on an oil rig, the boy's cubbyhole of a room was vacant; and the rent money was a help. There had rubbed off on the braid of the commissionaire father's uniform, through the contact of club members' coats and briefcases he relieved them of, loyal consciousness of the danger of bombs affixed under the cars of members of parliament and financiers. The father said 'I've no quarrel with that' when the owners of the house whose basement flat the family occupied stipulated 'No Irish'. But to discriminate against any other foreigners from the old Empire was against the principles of the house owners, who were also the mother's employers—cleaning three times a week and baby-sitting through the childhood of three boys she thought of as her own. So it was a way of pleasing Upstairs to let the room to this young man, a foreigner who likely had been turned away from other vacancies posted on a board at the supermarket. He was clean and tidy enough; and he didn't hang around the kitchen, hoping to be asked to eat with the family, the way one of their own kind would. He didn't eye Vera.

Vera was seventeen, and a filing clerk with prospects of advancement; her father had got her started in an important firm through the kindness of one of his gentlemen at the club. A word in the right place; and now it was up to her to become a secretary, maybe one day even a private secretary to someone like the members of the club, and travel to the Continent, America—anywhere.

—You have to dress decently for a firm like that. Let others show their backsides.—

—Dad!—The flat was small, the walls thin—suppose the lodger heard him. Her pupils dilated with a blush, half shyness, half annoyance. On Friday and Saturday nights she wore T-shirts with spangled graffiti across her breasts and went with girl-friends to the discothèque, although she'd had to let the pink side of her hair grow out. On Sundays they sat on wooden benches outside the pub with teasing local boys, drinking beer shandies. Once it was straight beer laced with something and they made her drunk, but her father had been engaged as doorman for a private party and her mother had taken the Upstairs children to the zoo, so nobody heard her vomiting in the bathroom.

So she thought.

He was in the kitchen when she went, wiping the slime from her panting mouth, to drink water. He always addressed her as 'miss'—Good afternoon, miss.—He was himself filling a glass.

She stopped where she was; sourness was in her mouth and nose, oozing towards the foreign stranger, she mustn't go a step nearer. Shame tingled over nausea and tears. Shame heaved in her stomach, her throat opened, and she just reached the sink in time to disgorge the final remains of a pizza minced by her teeth and digestive juices, floating in beer.—Go away. Go away!—her hand flung in rejection behind her. She opened both taps to blast her shame down the drain.—Get out!—

He was there beside her, in the disgusting stink of her, and he had wetted a dish-towel and was wiping her face, her dirty mouth, her tears. He was steadying her by the arm and sitting her down at the kitchen table. And she knew that his kind didn't even drink, he probably never had smelled alcohol before. If it had been one of her own crowd it would have been different.

She began to cry again. Very quietly, slowly, he put his hand on hers, taking charge of the wrist like a doctor preparing to follow the measure of a heart in a pulse-beat. Slowly—the pace was his—she quietened; she looked down, without moving her head, at the hand. Slowly, she drew her own hand from underneath, in parting.

As she left the kitchen a few meaningless echoes of what had happened to her went back and forth—are you all right yes I'm all right are you sure yes I'm all right.

She slept through her parents' return and next morning said she'd had flu.

He could no longer be an unnoticed presence in the house, outside her occupation with her work and the friends she made among the other junior employees, and her preoccupation, in her leisure, with the discothèque and cinema where the hand-holding and sex-tussles with local boys took place. He said, Good afternoon, as they saw each other approaching in the passage between the family's quarters and his room, or couldn't avoid coinciding at the gate of the tiny area garden where her mother's geraniums bloomed and the empty milk bottles were set out. He didn't say 'miss'; it was as if the omission were assuring, Don't worry, I won't tell anyone, *although I know all about what you do*, everything, I won't talk about you among my friends—did he even have any friends? Her mother told her he worked in the kitchens of a smart restaurant—her mother had to be sure a lodger had steady pay before he could be let into the house. Vera saw other foreigners like him about, gathered loosely as if they didn't know where to go; of course, they didn't come to the disco and they were not part of the crowd of familiars at the cinema. They were together but looked alone. It was something noticed the way she might notice, without expecting to fathom, the strange expression of a caged animal, far from wherever it belonged.

She owed him a signal in return for his trustworthiness. Next time they happened to meet in the house she said—I'm Vera.—

As if he didn't know, hadn't heard her mother and father call her. Again he did the right thing, merely nodded politely.

—I've never really caught your name.—

—Our names are hard for you, here. Just call me Rad.—His English was stiff, pronounced syllable by syllable in a soft voice.

—So it's short for something?—

—What is that?—

—A nickname. Bob for Robert.—

—Something like that.—

She ended this first meeting on a new footing the only way she knew how:—Well, see you later, then—the vague dismissal used casually among her friends when no such commitment existed. But on a Sunday when she was leaving the house to wander down to see who was gathered at the pub she went up the basement steps and saw that he was in the area garden. He was reading newspapers—three or four of them stacked on the mud-plastered grass at his side. She picked up his name and used it for the first time, easily as a key turning in a greased lock.—Hullo, Rad.—

He rose from the chair he had brought out from his room.—I hope your mother won't mind? I wanted to ask, but she's not at home.—

—Oh no, not Ma, we've had that old chair for ages, a bit of fresh air won't crack it up more than it is already.—

She stood on the short path, he stood beside the old rattan chair; then sat down again so that she could walk off without giving offence—she left to her friends, he left to his reading.

She said—I won't tell.—

And so it was out, what was between them alone, in the family house. And they laughed, smiled, both of them. She walked over to where he sat.—Got the day off? You work in some restaurant, don't you, what's it like?—

—I'm on the evening shift today.—He stayed himself a moment, head on one side, with aloof boredom.—It's something. Just a job. What you can get.—

—I know. But I suppose working in a restaurant at least the food's thrown in, as well.—

He looked out over the railings a moment, away from her.—I don't eat that food.—

She began to be overcome by a strong reluctance to go through the gate, round the corner, down the road to The Mitre and the whistles and appreciative pinches which would greet her in her new flowered Bermudas, his black eyes following her all the way, although he'd be reading his papers with her forgotten. To gain time she looked at the papers. The one in his hand was English. On the others, lying there, she was confronted with a flowing script of tails and gliding flourishes, the secret of somebody else's language. She could not go to the pub; she could not let him know that was where she was going. The deceptions that did for parents were not for him. But the fact was there was no deception: she *wasn't* going to the pub, she suddenly wasn't going.

She sat down on the motoring section of the English newspaper he'd discarded and crossed her legs in an X from the bare round knees.—Good news from home?—

He gestured with his foot towards the papers in his secret language; his naked foot was an intimate object, another secret.

—From my home, no good news.—

She understood this must be some business about politics, over there—she was in awe and ignorance of politics, nothing to do with her.—So that's why you went away.—

He didn't need to answer.

—You know, I can't imagine going away.—

—You don't want to leave your friends.—

She caught the allusion, pulled a childish face, dismissing them.—Mum and Dad . . . everything.—

He nodded, as if in sympathy for her imagined loss, but made no admission of what must be his own.

—Though I'm mad keen to travel. I mean, that's my idea, taking this job. Seeing other places—just visiting, you know. If I make myself capable and that, I might get the chance. There's one secretary in our offices who goes everywhere with her boss, she brings us all back souvenirs, she's very generous.—

—You want to see the world. But now your friends are waiting for you—

She shook off the insistence with a laugh.—And you want to go home!—

—No.—He looked at her with the distant expression of an adult before the innocence of a child.—Not yet.—

The authority of his mood over hers, that had been established in the kitchen that time, was there. She was hesitant and humble rather than flirtatious when she changed the subject.—Shall we have—will you have some tea if I make it? Is it all right?—He'd never eaten in the house; perhaps the family's food and drink were taboo for him in his religion, like the stuff he could have eaten free in the restaurant.

He smiled.—Yes it's all right.—And he got up and padded along behind her on his slim feet to the kitchen. As with a wipe over the clean surfaces of her mother's sink and table, the other time in the kitchen was cleared by ordinary business about brewing tea, putting out cups. She set him to cut the gingerbread:— Go on, try it, it's my mother's homemade.—She watched with an anxious smile, curiosity, while his beautiful teeth broke into its crumbling softness. He nodded, granting grave approval with a full mouth. She mimicked him, nodding and smiling; and, like a doe approaching a leaf, she took from his hand the fragrant slice with the semicircle marked by his teeth, and took a bite out of it.

Vera didn't go to the pub any more. At first they came to look for her—her chums, her mates—and nobody believed her excuses when she wouldn't come along with them. She hung about the house on Sundays, helping her mother.—Have you had a tiff or something?—

As she always told her bosom friends, she was lucky with her kind of mother, not strict and suspicious like some.—No, Ma. They're okay, but it's always the same thing, same things to say, every weekend.—

—Well . . . shows you're growing up, moving on—it's natural. You'll find new friends, more interesting, more your type.—

Vera listened to hear if he was in his room or had had to go to work—his shifts at the restaurant, she had learnt from timing his presence and absences, were irregular. He was very quiet, didn't play a radio or cassettes but she always could feel if he was there, in his room. That summer was a real summer for once; if he was off shift he would bring the old rattan chair into the garden and read, or stretch out his legs and lie back with his face lifted to the humid sun. He must be thinking of where he came from; very hot, she imagined it, desert and thickly-white cubes of houses with palm trees. She went out with a rug—nothing unusual about wanting to sunbathe in your own area garden—and chatted to him as if just because he happened to be there. She watched his eyes travelling from right to left along the scrolling print of his newspapers, and when he paused, yawned, rested his head and closed his lids against the light, could ask him about home—his home. He described streets and cities and cafés and bazaars—it wasn't at all like her idea of desert and oases.—But there are palm trees?—

—Yes, nightclubs, rich people's palaces to show tourists, but there are also factories and prison camps and poor people living on a handful of beans a day.— She picked at the grass: I see.—Were you—were your family—do you like beans?—

He was not to be drawn; he was never to be drawn.

—If you know how to make them, they are good.—

—If we get some, will you tell us how they're cooked?—

—I'll make them for you.—

So one Sunday Vera told her mother Rad, the lodger, wanted to prepare a meal for the family. Her parents were rather touched; nice, here was a delicate mark of gratitude, such a glum character, he'd never shown any sign before. Her father was prepared to put up with something that probably wouldn't agree with him.—Different people, different ways. Maybe it's a custom with them, when they're taken in, like bringing a bunch of flowers.—The meal went off well. The dish was delicious and not too spicy; after all, gingerbread was spiced, too. When her father opened a bottle of beer and put it down at Rad's place, Vera quickly lifted it away.—He doesn't drink, Dad.—

Graciousness called forth graciousness; Vera's mother issued a reciprocal invitation.—You must come and have our Sunday dinner one day—my chicken with apple pie to follow.—

But the invitation was in the same code as 'See you later'. It was not mentioned again. One Sunday Vera shook the grass from her rug.—I'm going for a walk.—And the lodger slowly got up from his chair, put his newspaper aside, and they went through the gate. The neighbours must have seen her with him. The pair went where she led, although they were side by side, loosely, the way she'd seen young men of his kind together. They went on walking a long way, down streets and then into a park. She loved to watch people flying kites; now he was the one who watched her as she watched. It seemed to be his way of getting to know her; to know anything. It wasn't the way of other boys—her kind—but then he was a foreigner here, there must be so much he needed to find out. Another weekend she had the idea to take a picnic. That meant an outing for the whole day. She packed apples and bread and cheese—remembering no ham—under the eyes of her mother. There was a silence between them. In it was her mother's recognition of the accusation she, Vera, knew she ought to bring against herself: Vera was 'chasing' a man; this man. All her mother said was—Are you joining other friends?—She didn't lie.—No. He's never been up the river. I thought we'd take a boat trip.—

In time she began to miss the cinema. Without guile she asked him if he had seen this film or that; she presumed that when he was heard going out for the evening the cinema would be where he went, with friends of his—his kind—she never saw. What did they do if they didn't go to a movie? It wouldn't be bars, and she knew instinctively he wouldn't be found in a disco, she couldn't see him shaking and stomping under twitching coloured lights.

He hadn't seen any film she mentioned.—Won't you come?—It happened like the first walk. He looked at her again as he had then.—D'you think so?—

—Why ever not. Everybody goes to movies.—

But she knew why not. She sat beside him in the theatre with solemnity. It was unlike any other time, in that familiar place of pleasure. He did not hold her hand; only that time, that time in the kitchen. They went together to the cinema regularly. The silence between her and her parents grew; her mother was like a cheerful bird whose cage had been covered. Whatever her mother and father thought, whatever they feared—nothing had happened, nothing happened until one public holiday when Vera and the lodger were both off work and they went on one of their long walks into the country (that was all they could do, he didn't play sport, there wasn't any activity with other young people he knew how to enjoy). On that day celebrated for a royal birthday or religious anniversary that couldn't mean anything to him, in deep grass under profound trees he made love to Vera for the first time. He had never so much as kissed her, before, not on any evening walking home from the cinema, not when they were alone in the house and the opportunity was obvious as the discretion of the kitchen clock sounding through the empty passage, and the blind eye of the television set in the sitting-room. All that he had never done with her was begun and accomplished with unstoppable passion, summoned up as if at a mere command to himself; between this and the placing of his hand on hers in the kitchen, months before, there was nothing. Now she had the lips from which, like a doe, she had taken a morsel touched with his saliva, she had the naked body promised by the first glimpse of the naked feet. She had lost her virginity, like all her sister schoolgirls, at fourteen or fifteen, she had been fucked, half-struggling, by some awkward local in a car or a back room, once or twice. But now she was overcome, amazed, engulfed by a sensuality she had no idea was inside her, a bounty of talent unexpected and unknown as a burst of song would have been welling from one who knew she had no voice. She wept with love for this man who might never, never have come to her, never have found her from so far away. She wept because she was so afraid it might so nearly never have happened. He wiped her tears, he dressed her with the comforting resignation to her emotion a mother shows with an over-excited child.

She didn't hope to conceal from her mother what they were doing; she knew her mother knew. Her mother felt her gliding silently from her room down the passage to the lodger's room, the room that still smelt of her brother, late at night, and returning very early in the morning. In the dark Vera knew every floorboard that creaked, how to avoid the swish of her pyjamas touching past a wall; at dawn saw the squinting beam of the rising sun sloped through a window that she had never known was so placed it could let in any phase of the sun's passage across the sky. Everything was changed.

What could her mother have said? Maybe he had different words in his language; the only ones she and her mother had wouldn't do, weren't meant for a situation not provided for in their lives. *Do you know what you're doing? Do you know what he is? We don't have any objection to them, but all the same. What about your life? What about the good firm your father's got you into? What'll it look like, there?*

The innocent release of sensuality in the girl gave her an authority that prevailed in the house. She brought him to the table for meals, now; he ate what he could. Her parents knew this presence, in the code of their kind, only as the signal by which an 'engaged' daughter would bring home her intended. But outwardly between Vera and her father and mother the form was kept up that his position was still that of a lodger, a lodger who had somehow become part of the household in that capacity. There was no need for him to pretend or assume any role; he never showed any kind of presumption towards their daughter, spoke to her with the same reserve that he, a stranger, showed to them. When he and the girl rose from the table to go out together it was always as if he accompanied her, without interest, at her volition.

Because her father was a man, even if an old one and her father, he recognized the power of sensuality in a female and was defeated, intimidated by its obstinacy. *He* couldn't take the whole business up with her; her mother must do that. He quarrelled with his wife over it. So she confronted their daughter. *Where will it end?* Both she and the girl understood: he'll go back where he comes from, and where'll you be? He'll drop you when he's had enough of what he wanted from you.

Where would it end? Rad occasionally acknowledged her among his friends, now—it turned out he did have some friends, yes, young men like him, from his home. He and she encountered them on the street and instead of excusing himself and leaving her waiting obediently like one of those pet dogs tied up outside the supermarket, as he usually had done when he went over to speak to his friends, he took her with him and, as if remembering her presence after a minute or two of talk, interrupted himself: She's Vera. Their greetings, the way they looked at her, made her feel that he had told them about her, after all, and she was happy. They made remarks in their own language she was sure referred to her. If she had moved on, from the pub, the disco, the parents, she was accepted, belonged somewhere else.

And then she found she was pregnant. She had no girlfriend to turn to who could be trusted not to say those things: he'll go back where he comes from he'll drop you when he's had enough of what he wanted from you. After the second month she bought a kit from the pharmacy and tested her urine. Then she went to a doctor because that do-it-yourself thing might be mistaken.

—I thought you said you would be all right.—

That was all he said, after thinking for a moment, when she told him.

—Don't worry, I'll find something. I'll do something about it. I'm sorry, Rad. Just forget it.—She was afraid he would stop loving her—her term for love-making.

When she went to him tentatively that night he caressed her more beauti-fully and earnestly than ever while possessing her.

She remembered reading in some women's magazine that it was dangerous to do anything to get rid of 'it' (she gave her pregnancy no other identity) after three months. Through roundabout enquiries she found a doctor who did abor-tions, and booked an appointment, taking an advance on her holiday bonus to meet the fee asked.

—By the way, it'll be all over next Saturday. I've found someone.— Timidly, that week, she brought up the subject she had avoided between them.

He looked at her as if thinking very carefully before he spoke, thinking apart from her, in his own language, as she was often sure he was doing. Perhaps he had forgotten—it was really her business, her fault, she knew. Then he pronounced what neither had:—The baby?—

—Well . . .—She waited, granting this.

He did not take her in his arms, he did not touch her.—You will have the baby. We will marry.—

It flew from her awkward, unbelieving, aghast with joy:—You want to marry me!—

—Yes, you're going to be my wife.—

—Because of this?—a baby?—

He was gazing at her intensely, wandering over the sight of her.—Because I've chosen you.—

Of course, being a foreigner, he didn't come out with things the way an English speaker would express them.

And I love *you*, she said, I love you, I love you—babbling through vows and tears. He put a hand on one of hers, as he had done in the kitchen of her mother's house; once, and never since.

She saw a couple in a mini-series standing hand-in-hand, telling them; 'We're getting married'—hugs and laughter.

But she told her parents alone, without him there. It was safer that way, she thought, for him. And she phrased it in proof of his good intentions as a triumphant answer to her mother's warnings, spoken and unspoken.—Rad's going to marry me.—

—He wants to marry you?—Her mother corrected. The burst of a high-pitched cry. The father twitched an angry look at his wife.

Now it was time for the scene to conform to the TV family announcement.—We're going to get married.—

Her father's head flew up and sank slowly, he turned away.

—You want to be married to him?—Her mother's palm spread on her breast to cover the blow.

The girl was brimming feeling, reaching for them.

Her father was shaking his head like a sick dog.

—And I'm pregnant and he's glad.—

Her mother turned to her father but there was no help coming from him. She spoke impatiently, flatly.—So that's it.—

—No, that's not it. It's not it at all.—She would not say to them 'I love him', she would not let them spoil that by trying to make her feel ashamed.—It's what I want.—

—It's what she wants.—Her mother was addressing her father.

He had to speak. He gestured towards his daughter's body, where there was no sign yet to show life growing there.—Nothing to be done then.—

When the girl had left the room he glared at his wife.—Bloody bastard.—

—Hush. Hush.—There was a baby to be born, poor innocent.

And it was, indeed, the new life the father had gestured at in Vera's belly that changed everything. The foreigner, the lodger—had to think of him now as the future son-in-law, Vera's intended—told Vera and her parents he was sending her to his home for his parents to meet her.—To your country?—

He answered with the gravity with which, they realized, marriage was regarded where he came from.—The bride must meet the parents. They must know her as I know hers.—

If anyone had doubted the seriousness of his intentions—well, they could be ashamed of those doubts, now; he was sending her home, openly and proudly, his foreigner, to be accepted by his parents.—But have you told them about the baby, Rad?—She didn't express this embarrassment in front of her mother and father.—What do you think? That is why you are going.—He slowed, then spoke again.—It's a child of our family.—

So she was going to travel at last! In addition to every other joy! In a state of continual excitement between desire for Rad—now openly sharing her room with her—and the pride of telling her work-mates why she was taking her annual leave just then, she went out of her way to encounter former friends whom she had avoided. To say she was travelling to meet her fiancé's family; she was getting married in a few months, she was having a baby—yes—proof of this now in the rounding under the flowered jumpsuit she wore to show it off. For her mother, too, a son-in-law who was not one of their kind became a distinction rather than a shame.—Our Vera's a girl who's always known her own mind. It's a changing world, she's not one just to go on repeating the same life as we've had.—The only thing that hadn't changed in the world was joy over a little one coming. Vera was thrilled, they were all thrilled at the idea of a baby, a first grandchild. Oh that one was going to be spoilt all right! The prospective grandmother was knitting, although Vera laughed and said babies weren't dressed in that sort of thing any more, hers was going to wear those little unisex frog suits in bright colours. There was a deposit down on a pram fit for an infant prince or princess.

It was understood that if the intended could afford to send his girl all the way home just to meet his parents before the wedding, he had advanced himself in the restaurant business, despite the disadvantages young men like him had in an unwelcoming country. Upstairs was pleased with the news; Upstairs came down one evening and brought a bottle of champagne as a gift to toast Vera, whom they'd known since she was a child, and her boy—much pleasant laughter when the prospective husband filled everyone's glass and then served himself with orange juice. Even the commissionaire felt confident enough to tell one of his gentlemen at the club that his daughter was getting married, but first about to go abroad to meet the young man's parents. His gentlemen's children were always travelling; in his ears every day were overheard snatches of destinations—'by bicycle in China, can you believe it' . . . 'two months in Peru, rather nice . . .' . . . 'snorkeling on the Barrier Reef, last I heard'. *Visiting her future parents-in-law where there is desert and palm trees; not bad!*

The parents wanted to have a little party, before she left, a combined engagement party and farewell. Vera had in mind a few of her old friends brought together with those friends of his she'd been introduced to and with whom she knew he still spent some time—she didn't expect to go along with him, it wasn't their custom for women, and she couldn't understand their language, anyway. But he didn't seem to think a party would work. She had her holiday bonus (to remember what she had drawn it for, originally, was something that, feeling the baby tapping its presence softly inside her, she couldn't believe of herself) and she kept asking him what she could buy as presents for his family—his parents, his sisters and brothers, she had learnt all their names. He said he would buy things, he knew what to get. As the day for her departure approached, he still had not done so.—But I want to pack! I want to know how much room to leave, Rad!—He brought some men's clothing she couldn't judge and some dresses and scarves she didn't like but didn't dare say so—she supposed the clothes his sisters liked were quite different from what she enjoyed wearing—a good thing she hadn't done the choosing.

She didn't want her mother to come to the airport; they'd both be too emotional. Leaving Rad was strangely different; it was not leaving Rad but going, carrying his baby, to the mystery that was Rad, that was in Rad's silences, his blind love-making, the way he watched her, thinking in his own language so that she could not follow anything in his eyes. It would all be revealed when she arrived where he came from.

He had to work, the day she left, until it was time to take her to the airport. Two of his friends, whom she could scarcely recognize from the others in the group she had met occasionally, came with him to fetch her in the taxi one of them drove. She held Rad's hand, making a tight double fist on his thigh, while the men talked in their language. At the airport the others left him to go in alone with her. He gave her another, last-minute gift for home.—Oh Rad—where'm I going to put it? The ticket says one hand-baggage!—But she squeezed his arm in happy recognition of his thoughts for his family.—It can go in—easy, easy.—He unzipped her carryall as they stood in the queue at the check-in counter. She knelt with her knees spread to accommodate her belly, and helped him.—What is it, anyway—I hope not something that's going to break?—He was making a bed for the package.—Just toys for my sister's kid. Plastic.——I could have put them in the suitcase—oh Rad . . . what room'll I have for duty-free!—In her excitement, she was addressing the queue for the American airline's flight which would take her on the first leg of her journey. These fellow passengers were another kind of foreigner, Americans, but she felt she knew them all; they were going to be travelling in her happiness, she was taking them with her.

She held him with all her strength and he kept her pressed against his body; she could not see his face. He stood and watched her as she went through passport control and she stopped again and again to wave but she saw Rad could not wave, could not wave. Only watch her until he could not see her any longer. And she saw him in her mind, still looking at her, as she had done at the beginning when she had imagined herself as still under his eyes if she had gone to to the pub on a Sunday morning.

Over the sea, the airliner blew up in midair. Everyone on board died. The black box was recovered from the bed of the sea and revealed that there had been an explosion in the tourist-class cabin followed by a fire; and there the messages ended; silence, the disintegration of the plane. No one knows if all were killed outright or if some survived to drown. An inquiry into the disaster continued for a year. The background of every passenger was traced, and the circumstances that led to the journey of each. There were some arrests; people detained for questioning and then released. They were innocent—but they were foreigners, of course. Then there was another disaster of the same nature, and a statement from a group with an apocalyptic name representing a faction of the world's wronged, claiming the destruction of both planes in some complication of vengeance for holy wars, land annexation, invasions, imprisonments, cross-border raids, territorial disputes, bombings, sinkings, kidnappings no one outside the initiated could understand. A member of the group, a young man known as Rad among many other aliases, had placed in the hand-baggage of the daughter of the family with whom he lodged, and who was pregnant by him, an explosive device. Plastic. A bomb of a plastic type undetectable by the usual procedures of airport security.

Vera was chosen.

Vera had taken them all, taken the baby inside her; down, along with her happiness.

THE CONJURER MADE OFF WITH THE DISH

Naguib Mahfouz

Egypt

"The time has come for you to be useful," said my mother to me. And she slipped her hand into her pocket, saying, "Take this piaster and go off and buy some beans. Don't play on the way and keep away from the carts."

I took the dish, put on my clogs, and went out, humming a tune. Finding a crowd in front of the bean seller, I waited until I discovered a way through to the marble counter.

"A piaster's worth of beans, mister," I called out in my shrill voice.

He asked me impatiently, "Beans alone? With oil? With cooking butter?"

I did not answer, and he said roughly, "Make way for someone else."

I withdrew, overcome by embarrassment, and returned home defeated.

"Returning with the dish empty?" my mother shouted at me. "What did you do—spill the beans or lose the piaster, you naughty boy?"

"Beans alone? With oil? With cooking butter?—you didn't tell me," I protested.

"Stupid boy! What do you eat every morning?"

"I don't know."

"You good-for-nothing, ask him for beans with oil."

I went off to the man and said, "A piaster's worth of beans with oil, mister."

With a frown of impatience he asked, "Linseed oil? Vegetable oil? Olive oil?"

I was taken aback and again made no answer.

"Make way for someone else," he shouted at me.

I returned in a rage to my mother, who called out in astonishment, "You've come back empty-handed—no beans and no oil."

"Linseed oil? Vegetable oil? Olive oil? Why didn't you tell me?" I said angrily.

"Beans with oil means beans with linseed oil."

"How should I know?"

"You're a good-for-nothing, and he's a tiresome man—tell him beans with linseed oil."

I went off quickly and called out to the man while still some yards from his shop, "Beans with linseed oil, mister."

"Put the piaster on the counter," he said, plunging the ladle into the pot.

I put my hand into my pocket but did not find the piaster. I searched for it anxiously. I turned my pocket inside out but found no trace of it. The man withdrew the ladle empty, saying with disgust, "You've lost the piaster—you're not a boy to be depended on."

"I haven't lost it," I said, looking under my feet and round about me. "It was in my pocket all the time."

"Make way for someone else and stop bothering me."

I returned to my mother with an empty dish.

"Good grief, are you an idiot, boy?"

"The piaster . . ."

"What of it?"

"It's not in my pocket."

"Did you buy sweets with it?"

"I swear I didn't."

"How did you lose it?"

"I don't know."

"Do you swear by the Koran you didn't buy anything with it?"

"I swear."

"Is there a hole in your pocket?"

"No, there isn't."

"Maybe you give it to the man the first time or the second."

"Maybe."

"Are you sure of nothing?"

"I'm hungry."

She clapped her hands together in a gesture of resignation.

"Never mind," she said. "I'll give you another piaster but I'll take it out of your money-box, and if you come back with an empty dish, I'll break your head."

I went off at a run, dreaming of a delicious breakfast. At the turning leading to the alleyway where the bean seller was, I saw a crowd of children and heard merry, festive sounds. My feet dragged as my heart was pulled toward them. At least let me have a fleeting glance. I slipped in among them and found the conjurer looking straight at me. A stupefying joy overwhelmed me; I was completely taken out of myself. With the whole of my being I became involved in the tricks of the rabbits and the eggs, and the snakes and the ropes. When the man came up to collect money, I drew back mumbling, "I haven't got any money."

He rushed at me savagely, and I escaped only with difficulty. I ran off, my back almost broken by his blow, and yet I was utterly happy as I made my way to the seller of beans.

"Beans with linseed oil for a piaster, mister," I said.

He went on looking at me without moving, so I repeated my request.

"Give me the dish," he demanded angrily.

The dish! Where was the dish? Had I dropped it while running? Had the conjurer made off with it?

"Boy, you're out of your mind!"

I retraced my steps, searching along the way for the lost dish. The place where the conjurer had been, I found empty, but the voices of children led me to him in a nearby lane. I moved around the circle. When the conjurer spotted me, he shouted out threateningly, "Pay up or you'd better scram."

"The dish!" I called out despairingly.

"What dish, you little devil?"

"Give me back the dish."

"Scram or I'll make you into food for snakes."

He had stolen the dish, yet fearfully I moved away out of sight and wept in grief. Whenever a passerby asked me why I was crying, I would reply, "The conjurer made off with the dish."

Through my misery I became aware of a voice saying, "Come along and watch!"

I looked behind me and saw a peep show had been set up. I saw dozens of children hurrying toward it and taking it in turns to stand in front of the peepholes, while the man began his tantalizing commentary to the pictures.

"There you've got the gallant knight and the most beautiful of all ladies, Zainat al-Banat."

My tears dried up, and I gazed in fascination at the box, completely forgetting the conjurer and the dish. Unable to overcome the temptation, I paid over the piaster and stood in front of the peephole next to a girl who was standing in front of the other one, and enchanting picture stories flowed across our vision. When I came back to my own world I realized I had lost both the piaster and the dish, and there was no sign of the conjurer. However, I gave no thought to the loss, so taken up was I with the pictures of chivalry, love, and deeds of daring. I forgot my hunger. I forgot even the fear of what threatened me at home. I took a few paces back so as to lean against the ancient wall of what had once been a treasury and the chief cadi's seat of office, and gave myself up wholly to my reveries. For a long while I dreamed of chivalry, of Zainat al-Banat and the ghoul. In my dream I spoke aloud, giving meaning to my words with gestures. Thrusting home the imaginary lance, I said, "Take that, O ghoul, right in the heart!"

"And he raised Zainat al-Banat up behind him on the horse," came back a gentle voice.

I looked to my right and saw the young girl who had been beside me at the performance. She was wearing a dirty dress and colored clogs and was playing with her long plait of hair. In her other hand were the red-and-white sweets called "lady's fleas," which she was leisurely sucking. We exchanged glances, and I lost my heart to her.

"Let's sit down and rest," I said to her.

She appeared to go along with my suggestion, so I took her by the arm and we went through the gateway of the ancient wall and sat down on a step of its stairway that went nowhere, a stairway that rose up until it ended in a platform behind which there could be seen the blue sky and minarets. We sat in silence, side by side. I pressed her hand, and we sat on in silence, not knowing what to say. I experienced feelings that were new, strange, and obscure. Putting my face close to hers, I breathed in the natural smell of her hair mingled with an odor of dust, and the fragrance of breath mixed with the aroma of sweets. I kissed her lips. I swallowed my saliva, which had taken on a sweetness from the dissolved "lady's fleas." I put my arm around her, without her uttering a word, kissing her cheek and lips. Her lips grew still as they received the kiss, then went back to sucking at the sweets. At last she decided to get up. I seized her arm anxiously. "Sit down," I said.

"I'm going," she replied simply.

"Where to?" I asked dejectedly.

"To the midwife Umm Ali," and she pointed to a house on the ground floor of which was a small ironing shop.

"Why?"

"To tell her to come quickly."

"Why?"

"My mother's crying in pain at home. She told me to go to the midwife Umm Ali and tell her to come along quickly."

"And you'll come back after that?"

She nodded her head in assent and went off. Her mentioning her mother reminded me of my own, and my heart missed a beat. Getting up from the ancient stairway, I made my way back home. I wept out loud, a tried method by which I would defend myself. I expected she would come to me, but she did not. I wandered from the kitchen to the bedroom but found no trace of her. Where had my mother gone? When would she return? I was fed up with being in the empty house. A good idea occurred to me. I took a dish from the kitchen and a piaster from my savings and went off immediately to the seller of beans. I found him asleep on a bench outside the shop, his face covered by his arm. The pots of beans had vanished and the long-necked bottles of oil had been put back on the shelf and the marble counter had been washed down.

"Mister," I whispered, approaching.

Hearing nothing but his snoring, I touched his shoulder. He raised his arm in alarm and looked at me through reddened eyes.

"Mister."

"What do you want?" he asked roughly, becoming aware of my presence and recognizing me.

"A piaster's worth of beans with linseed oil."

"Eh?"

"I've got the piaster and I've got the dish."

"You're crazy, boy," he shouted at me. "Get out or I'll bash your brains in."

When I did not move, he pushed me so violently I went sprawling onto my back. I got up painfully, struggling to hold back the crying that was twisting my lips. My hands were clenched, one on the dish and the other on the piaster. I threw him an angry look. I thought about returning home with my hopes dashed, but dreams of heroism and valor altered my plan of action. Resolutely I made a quick decision and with all my strength threw the dish at him. It flew through the air and struck him on the head, while I took to my heels, heedless of everything. I was convinced I had killed him, just as the knight had killed the ghoul. I did not stop running till I was near the ancient wall. Panting, I looked behind me but saw no signs of any pursuit. I stopped to get my breath, then asked myself what I should do now that the second dish was lost? Something warned me not to return home directly, and soon I had given myself over to a wave of indifference that bore me off where it willed. It meant a beating, neither more nor less, on my return, so let me put it off for a time. Here was the piaster in my hand, and I could have some sort of enjoyment with it before being punished. I decided to pretend I had forgotten I had done anything wrong—but where was the conjurer, where was the peep show? I looked everywhere for them to no avail.

Worn out by this fruitless searching, I went off to the ancient stairway to keep my appointment. I sat down to wait, imagining to myself the meeting. I yearned for another kiss redolent with the fragrance of sweets. I admitted to myself that the little girl had given me lovelier sensations than I had ever experienced. As I waited and dreamed, a whispering sound came from behind me. I climbed the stairs cautiously, and at the final landing I lay down flat on my face in order to see what was beyond, without anyone being able to notice me. I saw some ruins surrounded by a high wall, the last of what remained of the treasury and the chief cadi's seat of office. Directly under the stairs sat a man and a woman, and it was from them that the whispering came. The man looked like a tramp; the woman like one of those Gypsies that tend sheep. A suspicious inner voice told me that their meeting was similar to the one I had had. Their lips and the looks they exchanged spoke of this, but they showed astonishing expertise in the unimaginable things they did. My gaze became rooted upon them with curiosity, surprise, pleasure, and a certain amount of disquiet. At last they sat down side by side, neither of them taking any notice of the other. After quite a while the man said, "The money!"

"You're never satisfied," she said irritably.

Spitting on the ground, he said, "You're crazy."

"You're a thief."

He slapped her hard with the back of his hand, and she gathered up a handful of earth and threw it in his face. Then, his face soiled with dirt, he sprang at her, fastening his fingers on her windpipe, and a bitter fight ensued. In vain she gathered all her strength to escape from his grip. Her voice failed her, her eyes bulged out of their sockets, while her feet struck out at the air. In dumb terror, I stared at the scene till I saw a thread of blood trickling down from her nose. A scream escaped from my mouth. Before the man raised his head, I had crawled backward. Descending the stairs at a jump, I raced off like mad to wherever my legs might carry me. I did not stop running till I was breathless. Gasping for breath, I was quite unaware of my surroundings, but when I came to myself I found I was under a raised vault at the middle of a crossroads. I had never set foot there before and had no idea of where I was in relation to our quarter. On both sides sat sightless beggars, and crossing from all directions were people who paid attention to no one. In terror I realized I had lost my way and that countless difficulties lay in wait for me before I found my way home. Should I resort to asking one of the passersby to direct me? What, though, would happen if chance should lead me to a man like the seller of beans or the tramp of the waste plot? Would a miracle come about whereby I would see my mother approaching so that I could eagerly hurry toward her? Should I try to make my own way, wandering about till I came across some familiar landmark that would indicate the direction I should take?

I told myself that I should be resolute and make a quick decision. The day was passing, and soon mysterious darkness would descend.

Translated by Denys Johnson-Davies

WHO WILL STOP THE DARK?

Charles Mungoshi

Zimbabwe

The boy began to believe what the other boys at school said about his mother. In secret he began to watch her—her face, words and actions. He would also watch his father's bare arched back as he toiled at his basket-weaving from day to day. His mother could go wherever she wanted to go. His father could not. Every morning he would drag his useless lower limbs out of the hut and sit under the *muonde* tree. He would not leave the tree till late in the evening when he would drag himself again back into the hut for his evening meal and bed. And always the boy felt a stab of pain when he looked at the front of his father's wet urine-stiffened trousers.

The boy knew that his mother had something to do with this condition of his father. The tight lines round her mouth and her long silences that would sometimes erupt into unexpected bursts of red violence said so. The story was that his father had fallen off the roof he had been thatching and broken his back. But the boy didn't believe it. It worried him. He couldn't imagine it. One day his father had just been like any other boy's father in their village, and the next day he wasn't. It made him wonder about his mother. He felt that it wasn't safe in their house. So he began to spend most of his time with the old man, his grandfather.

"I want you in the house," his mother said, when she could afford words, but the boy knew she was saying it all the time by the way she tightened her mouth and lowered her looking-away-from-people eyes.

The boy remembered that his grandfather had lived under the same roof with them for a long time. He couldn't remember how he had then come to live alone in his own hut half-a-mile from their place.

"He is so childish," he heard his mother say one day.

"He is old," his father said, without raising his head from his work.

"And how old do you think my mother is?" The lines round his mother's mouth drew tighter and tauter.

"Women do not grow as weak as men in their old age," his father persisted.

"Because it's the men who have to bear the children—so they grow weak from the strain!" His mother's eyes flashed once—so that the boy held his breath—and then she looked away, her mouth wrinkled tightly into an obscene little hole that reminded the boy of a cow's behind just after dropping its dung. He thought now his father would keep quiet. He was surprised to hear him say, "A man's back is the man. Once his back is broken—" another flash of his mother's eye silenced him and the boy couldn't stand it. He stood up to go out.

"And where are you going?" his mother shouted after him.

"To see grandfather."

"What do you want there with him?"

The boy turned back and stayed round the yard until his mother disappeared into the house. Then he quietly slid off for his grandfather's place through the bush. His father pretended not to see him go.

The old man had a way of looking at the boy: like someone looking into a mirror to see how badly his face had been burned.

"A, Zakeo," the old man said when the boy entered the yard. He was sitting against the wall of his hut, smoking his pipe quietly, looking into the distance. He hadn't even looked in Zakeo's direction.

"Did you see me this time?" Zakeo asked, laughing. He never stopped being surprised by the way his grandfather seemed to know everyone by their footfalls and would greet them by their names without even looking at them.

"I don't have to look to know it's you," the old man said.

"But today I have changed my feet to those of a bird," the boy teased him.

"No," the old man shook his head. "You are still the cat in my ears."

The boy laughed over that and although the old man smoked on without changing his expression, the boy knew that he was laughing too.

"Father said to ask you how you have spent the day," the boy said, knowing that the old man would know that it was a lie. The boy knew he would be forgiven this lie because the old man knew that the boy always wished his father would send him with such a message to his own father.

"You don't have to always protect him like that," the old man growled, almost to himself.

"*Sekuru?*" the boy didn't always understand most of the grown-up things the old man said.

"I said get on with the work. Nothing ever came out of a muscular mouth and snail-slime hands."

The boy disappeared into the hut while the old man sat on, smoking.

Zakeo loved doing the household chores for his grandfather: sweeping out the room and lighting the fire, collecting firewood from the bush and fetching water from the well and cooking. The old man would just look on, not saying anything much, just smoking his pipe. When he worked the boy didn't talk. Don't use your mouth and hands at the same time, the old man had told him once and whenever he forgot the old man reminded him by not answering his questions. It was a different silence they practiced in the old man's house, the boy felt. Here, it was always as if his grandfather was about to tell him a secret. And when he left his parents' place he felt he must get back to the old man at the earliest opportunity to hear the secret.

"Have you ever gone hunting for rabbits, boy?" his grandfather asked him one day.

"No, *Sekuru.* Have you?"

The old man didn't answer. He looked away at the darkening landscape, puffing at his pipe.

"Did you like it?" the boy asked.

"Like it? We lived for nothing else, boy. We were born hunters, stayed hunters all our life and most of us died hunters."

"What happened to those who weren't hunters?"

"They became tillers of the land, and some, weavers of bamboo baskets."

"You mean Father?"

"I am talking of friends I used to know."

"But didn't you ever teach Father to hunt, *Sekuru?*" The boy's voice was strained, anxious, pained. The old man looked at him briefly and then quickly away.

"I taught him everything a man ought to know," he said distantly.

"Basket-weaving too?"

"That was his mother," the old man said and then silently went on, *his mother, your grandmother, my wife, taught your father basket-weaving. She also had been taught by a neighbor who later gave me the lumbago.*

"You like basket-weaving?" he asked the boy.

"I hate it!" The old man suddenly turned, surprised at the boy's vehemence. He took the pipe out of his mouth for a minute, looking instantly at the boy, then he looked away, returning the pipe to his mouth.

"Do you think we could go hunting together, *Sekuru?*" the boy asked.

The old man laughed.

"Sekuru?" the boy was puzzled.

The old man looked at him.

"Please?"

The old man stroked the boy's head. "Talk of fishing," he said. "Or mouse-trapping. Ever trapped for mice?"

"No."

"Of course, you wouldn't have." He looked away. "You go to school these days."

"I don't like school!" Again, the old man was taken by surprise at the boy's violence. He looked at his grandson. The first son of his first son and only child. The boy's thirteen-year-old fists were clenched tightly and little tears danced in his eyes. *Could he believe in a little snotty-arse boy's voice? He looks earnest enough. But who doesn't, at the I-shall-never-die age of thirteen?* The old man looked away as if from the sight of the boy's death.

"I tell you I *hate* school!" the boy hissed.

"I hear you," the old man said quietly but didn't look at him. He was aware of the boy looking at him, begging him to believe him, clenching tighter his puny fists, his big ignorant eyes daring him to try him out on whatever milk-scented dream of heroics the boys might be losing sleep over at this difficult time of his life. The old man felt desolate.

"You don't believe me, do you, *Sekuru?*"

"Of course. I do!"

The boy suddenly uncoiled, ashamed and began to wring his hands, looking down at the ground.

That was unnecessarily harsh, the old man felt. So he stroked the boy's head again. *Thank you, ancestors, for our physical language that will serve our sons and daughters till we are dust.* He wished he could say something in words, something that the boy would clearly remember without it creating echoes in his head. He didn't want to give the boy an echo which he would later on mistake for the genuine thing.

"Is mouse-trapping very hard, *Sekuru?*" the boy asked, after some time.

"Nothing is ever easy, boy. But then, nothing is ever really hard for one who wants to learn."

"I would like to try it. Will you teach me?"

Physically, the old man didn't show anything, but he recoiled inwardly, the warmth in the center of him turned cold. *Boys' pranks, like the honey-bird luring you to a snake's nest. If only it were not this world, if only it were some other place where what we did today weren't our future, to be always there, held against us, to always see ourselves in . . .*

"And school?" he asked, as if he needed the boy to remind him again.

It was the boy's turn to look away, silent, unforgiving, betrayed.

As if stepping on newly-laid eggs, the old man learned a new language: not to touch the boy's head any more.

"There is your mother," he said, looking away, the better to make his grandson realize the seriousness of what he was talking about. From the corner of his eye he watched his grandson struggling with it, and saw her dismissed—not quite in the old way—but in a way that filled him with regrets for opportunities lost and a hopeless future.

"And if she doesn't mind?" the boy asked mischievously.

"You mean you will run away from school?" The old man restrained from stroking the boy's head.

"Maneto ran away from school and home two weeks ago. They don't know where he is right now."

Echoes, the old man repeated to himself. "But your mother is your mother," he said. *After all is said and done, basket-weaving never killed anyone. What kills is the rain and the hailstorms and the cold and the hunger when you are like this, when the echoes come.*

"I want to learn mouse-trapping, *Sekuru,*" the boy said. "At school they don't teach us that. It's always figures and numbers and I don't know what they mean and they all laugh at me."

The grandfather carefully pinched, with right forefinger and thumb, the ridge of flesh just above the bridge of his nose, closed his eyes and sighed. The boy looked at him eagerly, excited, and when he saw his grandfather settle back comfortably against the wall, he clapped his hands, rising up. The old man looked at him and was touched by the boy's excitement and not for the first time, he wondered at the mystery that is called life.

"Good night, *Sekuru,*" the boy said.

"Sleep well, Zakeo. Tell her that I delayed you if she asks where you have been." But the boy had already gone. The old man shook his head and prepared himself for another night of battle with those things that his own parents never told him exist.

· · ·

They left the old man's hut well before sunrise the following day.

The boy had just come in and dumped his books in a corner of the room and they had left without any questions from the old man.

The grandfather trailed slowly behind the boy who ran ahead of him, talking and gesticulating excitedly. The old man just listened to him and laughed with him.

It was already uncomfortably warm at this hour before sunrise. It was October. The white cowtracks spread out straight and flat before them, through and under the new thick flaming *musasa* leaves, so still in the morning air. Through patches in the dense foliage the sky was rusty-metal blue, October-opaque: the end of the long dry season, towards the *gukurahundi*, the very first heavy rains that would cleanse the air and clean the cowdung threshing floors of chaff, change and harden the crimson and bright-yellow leaves into hard green flat blades and bring back the stork, the millipede and the centipede, the fresh water crickets and the frogs, and the tiny yellow bird—*jesa*—that builds its nest on the river-reeds with the mouth of the nest facing down.

The air was harsh and still, and the old man thought, with renewed pleasure, of how he had almost forgotten the piercing whistle of that October-thirst bird, the *nonono*, and the shrill jarring ring of the *cicada*.

The cowtracks fell toward the river. They left the bush and came out into the open where the earth, bare and black from the *chirimo* fires, was crisscrossed with thousands of cattle-tracks which focused on the water-holes. The old man smelt wet river clay.

"It's hot," the boy said.

"It's October, *Gumiguru*, the tenth and hottest month of the year." The old man couldn't resist telling the boy a bit of what he must be going through.

The boy took off his school shirt and wound it round his waist.

"With a dog worth the name of dog—when dogs were still dogs—a rabbit goes nowhere in this kind of terrain," the old man said, seeing how naturally the boy responded to—blended in with—the surroundings.

"Is that why people burn the grass?"

"Aa, so you know that, too?"

"Maneto told me."

"Well, it's partly why we burn the grass but mainly we burn it so that new grass grows for our animals."

Finally, the river, burnt down now by the long rainless months to a thin trickle of blood, running in the shallow, sandy bottom of a vlei. But there were still some fairly deep water-holes and ponds where fish could be found.

"These ponds are great for *muramba*," the old man said. "You need fairly clean flowing water for *magwaya*—the flat short-spear-blade fish."

They dug for worms in the wet clay on the river banks. The old man taught the boy how to break the soft earth with a digging stick for the worms.

"Worms are much easier to find," the old man said. "They stay longer on the hook. But a maggot takes a fish faster." Here the old man broke off, suddenly assailed with a very vivid smell of three-day-old cowdung, its soft cool feel and the entangled wriggling yellow mass of maggots packed in it.

"Locusts and hoppers are good too, but in bigger rivers, like Munyati where the fish are so big they would take another fish for a meal. Here the fish are smaller and cleverer. They don't like hoppers."

The old man looked into the coffee tin into which they were putting the worms and said, "Should be enough for me one day. There is always some other place we can get some more when these are finished. No need to use more than we should."

"But if they should get finished, *Sekuru?* Look, the tin isn't full yet." Zakeo looked intently at his grandfather. He wanted to fit in all the fishing that he would ever do before his mother discovered that he was playing truant from school. The old man looked at him. He understood. But he knew the greed of thirteen-year-olds and the retribution of the land and the soil when well-known laws were not obeyed.

"There will always be something when we get where these worms run out."

They walked downstream along the bank, their feet kicking up clouds of black and white ash.

The sun came up harsh and red-eyed upstream. They followed a tall straight shadow and a short stooped one along the stream until they came to a dark pool where the water, though opaque, wasn't really dirty.

"Here we are. I will get us some reeds for fishing rods while you prepare the lines. The hooks are already on the lines."

The old man produced from a plastic bag a mess of tangled lines and metal blue-painted hooks.

"Here you are. Straighten these out."

He then proceeded to cut some tall reeds on the river bank with a pocket knife the boy had seen him poking tobacco out of his pipe with.

"Excellent rods, look." He bent one of the reeds till the boy thought it was going to break, and when he let go, the rod shot back like a whip!

"See?" the old man said.

The boy smiled and the old man couldn't resist slapping him on the back.

The boy then watched the old man fasten the lines to the rods.

"In my day," the old man said, "there were woman knots and men knots. A woman knot is the kind that comes apart when you tug the line. A knot worth the name of whoever makes it shouldn't fall apart. Let the rod break, the line snap, but a knot, a real man's knot, should stay there."

They fished from a rock by a pool.

"Why do you spit on the bait before you throw the line into the pool, *Sekuru?*"

The old man grinned. "For luck, boy, there is nothing you do that fate has no hand in. Having a good hook, a good line, a good rod, good bait or a good pool is no guarantee that you will have good fishing. So little is knowledge, boy. The rest is just mere luck."

Zakeo caught a very small fish by the belly.

"What's this?" he aksed.

"A very good example of what I call luck! They aren't usually caught by the belly. You need several all-way facing hooks in very clear water even without bait—for you to catch them like that!"

The boy laughed brightly and the old man suddenly heard the splash of a kingfisher as it flew away, fish in beak, and this mixed with the smell of damp-rotting leaves and moisty river clay, made the old man think: nothing is changed since our time. Then, a little later: except me. Self-consciously, with a sly look at the boy to make sure he wasn't seeing him, the old man straightened his shoulders.

The boy's grandfather hooked a frog and dashed it against a rock.

"What's that?" the boy asked.

"Know why I killed that—that—criminal?" he asked the boy.

"No, *Sekuru.*"

"Bad luck. Throw it back into the pool and it's going to report to the fish."

"But what is it?"

"Uncle Frog."

"A frog!" The boy was surprised.

"Shhh," the old man said. "Not a frog. Uncle Frog. You hear?"

"But why Uncle Frog, *Sekuru?*"

"Just the way it is, boy. Like the rain. It comes on its own."

Once again, the boy didn't understand the old man's grown-up talk. The old man saw it and said, "That kind of criminal is only good for dashing against the rock. You don't eat frogs, do you?"

The boy saw that the old man was joking with him. "No," he said.

"So why should we catch him on our hook when we don't eat him or need him?"

"I don't know, *Sekuru.*" The boy was clearly puzzled.

"He is the spy of the fish," the old man said in such a way that the boy sincerely believed him.

"But won't the fish notice his absence and wonder where he has gone to?"

"They won't miss him much. When they begin to do we will be gone. And when we come back here, they will have forgotten. Fish are just like people. They forget too easily."

It was grown-up talk again but the boy thought he would better not ask the man what he meant because he knew he wouldn't be answered.

They fished downriver till they came to where the Chambara met the Suka River.

"From here they go into Munyati," the old man said to himself, talking about his old hunting grounds; and to the boy, talking about the rivers.

"Where the big fish are," the boy said.

"You know that too?" the old man said, surprised.

"Maneto and his father spent days and days fishing the Munyati and they caught fish as big as men," the boy said seriously.

"Did Maneto tell you that?"

"Yes. And he said his father told him that *you, Sekuru*, were the only hunter who ever got to where the Munyati gets into the big water, the sea. Is that true?"

The old man pulled out his pipe and packed it. They were sitting on a rock. He took a long time packing and lighting the pipe.

"Is it true?" the boy asked.

"I was lost once," the old man said. "The Munyati goes into just another small water—but bigger than itself—and more powerful."

The boy would have liked to ask the man some more questions on this one but he felt that the old man wouldn't talk about it.

"You aren't angry, *Sekuru?*" the boy asked, looking up earnestly at his grandfather.

The old man looked at him, surprised again. *How do these milk-nosed ones know what we feel about all this?*

"Let's get back home," he said.

Something was bothering the old man, the boy realized, but what it was he couldn't say. All he wanted him to tell him was the stories he had heard from Maneto—whether they were true or not.

They had caught a few fish, enough for their supper, the boy knew, but the old man seemed angry. And that, the boy couldn't understand.

When they got back home the boy lit the fire, and with directions from the old man helped him to gut and salt the fish. After a very silent supper of sadza and salted fish the boy said he was going.

"Be sure to come back tomorrow," the old man said.

And the boy knew that whatever wrong he had done the old man, he would be told the following day.

Very early the following morning the boy's mother paid her father-in-law a visit. She stood in front of the closed door for a long time before she knocked. She had to collect herself.

"Who is there?" the old man answered from within the hut. He had heard the footsteps approaching but he did not leave his blankets to open up for her.

"I would like to talk to you," she said, swallowing hard to contain her anger.

"Ah, it's Zakeo's mother?"

"Yes."

"And what bad winds blow you this way this early, *muroora?*"

"I want to talk to you about my son."

"Your son?"

She caught her breath quickly. There was a short silence. The old man wouldn't open the door.

"I want to talk about Zakeo," she called.

"What about him?"

"Please leave him alone."

"You are telling me that?"

"He must go to school."

"And so?"

She was quiet for a minute, then she said, "Please."

"What have I done to him?"

"He won't eat, he won't listen to me, and he doesn't want to go to school."

"And he won't listen to his father?" the old man asked.

"He listens to *you.*"

"And you have come here this early to beat me up?"

She swallowed hard. "He is the only one I have. Don't let him destroy his future."

"He does what he wants."

"At his age? What does he know?"

"Quite a lot."

She was very angry, he could feel it through the closed door.

She said, "He will only listen to you. Please, help us."

Through the door the old man could feel her tears coming. He said, "He won't even listen to his father?"

"His father?" he heard her snort.

"Children belong to the man, *you* know that," the old man warned her.

And he heard her angry feet as she went away.

Zakeo came an hour after his mother had left the old man's place. His grandfather didn't say anything to him. He watched the boy throw his school bag in the usual corner of the hut, then after the usual greetings, he went out to bring in the firewood.

"Leave the fire alone," the old man said. "I am not cold."

"*Sekuru?*" The boy looked up, hurt.

"Today we go mouse-trapping in the fields."

"Are we going right now?"

"Yes."

"I'll make the fire if you like. We can go later."

"No. Now." The old man was quiet for some time, looking away from the boy.

"Are you all right, *Sekuru?*"

"Yes."

"We will go later when it's warm if you like."

The old man didn't answer him.

And as they came into the open fields with the last season's corn crop stubble, the boy felt that the old man wasn't quite well.

"We can do it some other day, *Sekuru.*"

His grandfather didn't answer.

They looked for the smooth mouse-tracks in the corn stubble and the dry grass. Zakeo carried the flat stones that the old man pointed out to him to the places where he wanted to set up the traps. He watched his grandfather setting the traps with the stone and two sticks. The sticks were about seven inches long each. One of them was the male and the other the female stick. The female was in the shape of a Y and the male straight.

The old man would place the female stick upright in the ground with the forked end facing up. The male would be placed in the fork parallel to the ground to hold up one end of the stone across the mousepath. The near end of the male would have a string attached to it and at the other end of the string would be the "trigger"—a match-stick-sized bit of straw that would hold the bait-stick against the male stick. The stone would be kept one end up by the delicate tension in the string and if a mouse took the bait the trigger would fly and the whole thing fall across the path onto the unfortunate victim.

The boy learned all this without words from the old man, simply by carefully watching him set about ten traps all over the field that morning. Once he tried to ask a question and he was given a curt, "Mouths are for women." Then he too set up six traps and around noon the old man said, "Now we will wait."

They went to the edge of the field where they sat under the shade of a *mutsamwi* tree. The old man carefully, tiredly, rested his back against the trunk of the tree, stretched himself out, sighed, and closing his eyes, took out his pipe and tobacco pouch and began to load. The boy sat beside him, looking on. He sensed a tension he had never felt in his grandfather. Suddenly it wasn't fun any more. He looked away at the distant hills in the west. Somewhere behind those hills the Munyati went on to the sea, or the other bigger river which the old man hadn't told him about.

"Tell me a story, *Sekuru*," Zakeo said, unable to sit in his grandfather's silence.

"Stories are for the night," the old man said without opening his mouth or taking out the pipe. "The day is for watching and listening and learning."

Zakeo stood up and went a little way into the bush at the edge of the field. Tears stung his eyes but he would not let himself cry. He came back a little later and lay down beside the old man. He had hardly closed his eyes in sleep, just at that moment when the voices of sleep were beginning to talk, when he felt the old man shaking him up.

"The day is not for sleeping," the old man said quietly but firmly. He still wasn't looking at Zakeo. The boy rubbed the sleep out of his eyes and blinked.

"Is that what they teach you at school?"

"*Sekuru?*"

The old man groaned in a way that told Zakeo what he thought of school. The boy felt ashamed that he had hurt his grandfather. "I am sorry."

The grandfather didn't answer or look at him. Some time later he said, "Why don't you go and play with the other boys of your own age?"

"Where?"

"At school. Anywhere. Teach them what you have learned."

The boy looked away for some time. He felt deserted, the old man didn't want him around any more. Things began to blur in his eyes. He bit his lip and kept his head stiffly turned away from his grandfather.

"You can teach them all I have taught you. Huh?"

"I don't think they would listen to me," the boy answered, still looking away, trying to control his voice.

"Why?"

"They never listen to me."

"Why?"

"They—they—just don't." He bit his lower lip harder but a big tear plopped down on his hand. He quickly wiped away the tear and then for a terrible second they wouldn't stop coming. He was ashamed in front of his grandfather. The old man, who had never seen any harm in boys crying, let him be.

When the boy had stopped crying he said, "Forget them."

"Who?"

"Your friends."

"They are not my friends. They are always laughing at me."

"What about?"

"Oh, all sorts of silly things."

"That doesn't tell me what sort of things."

"O, O, *lots of things!*" The boy's face was contorted in an effort to contain himself. Then he couldn't stop himself, "They are always at me saying your father is your mother's horse. Your mother rides hyenas at night. Your mother is a witch. Your mother killed so-and-so's child. Your mother digs up graves at night and you all eat human flesh which she hunts for you." He stopped. "O, lots of things I don't know!" The boy's whole body was tensed with violent hatred. The old man looked at him, amused.

"Do they really say that, now?"

"Yes, and I know I could beat them all in a fight but the headmaster said we shouldn't fight and father doesn't want me to fight either. But I know I can lick them all in a fight."

The old man looked at the boy intensely for some time, his pipe in his hand, then he looked away to the side and spat out brown spittle. He returned the pipe to his mouth and said, "Forget them. They don't know a thing." He then sighed and closed his eyes once more and settled a little deeper against the tree.

The boy looked at him for a long time and said, "I don't want to go to school, *Sekuru.*"

"Because of your friends?"

"They are not *my friends!*" He glared blackly at his grandfather, eyes flashing brilliantly and then, ashamed, confused, rose and walked a short distance away.

The old man looked at him from the corner of his eyes and saw him standing, looking away, body tensed, stiff and stubborn. He called out to him quietly, with gentleness, "Come back, Zakeo. Come and sit here by me."

Later on the boy woke up from a deep sleep and asked the old man whether it was time yet for the traps. He had come out of sleep with a sudden startled movement as if he were a little strange animal that had been scared by hunting dogs.

"That must have been a very bad dream," the old man said.

Zakeo rubbed the sleep out of his eyes and blinked. He stared at the old man, then the sun which was very low in the west, painting everything with that ripe mango hue that always made him feel sad. Tall dark shadows were creeping eastward. He had that strange feeling that he had overslept into the next day. In his dream his mother had been shouting at him that he was late for school. A rather chilly wind was blowing across the desolate fields.

"Sit down here beside me and relax," the old man said. "We will give the mice one more hour to return home from visiting their friends. Or to fool themselves that it's already night and begin hunting."

Zakeo sat beside his grandfather and then he felt very relaxed.

"You see?" the old man said. "Sleep does you good when you are tired or worried. But otherwise don't trust sleeping during the day. When you get to my age you will learn to sleep without sleeping."

"How is that?"

"Never mind. It just happens."

Suddenly, sitting in silence with the old man didn't bother him any more.

"You can watch the shadows or the setting sun or the movement of the leaves in the wind—or the sudden agitation in the grass that tells you some little animal is moving in there. The day is for watching and listening and learning."

He had got lost somewhere in his thoughts when the old man said, "Time for the traps."

That evening the old man taught him how to gut the mice, burn off the fur in a low-burning flame, boil them till they were cooked and then arrange them in a flat open pan close to the fire to dry them so that they retained as little moisture as possible which made them firm but solidly pleasant on eating.

After supper the old man told him a story in which the hero seemed to be always falling into one misfortune after another, but always getting out through his own resourcefulness only to fall into a much bigger misfortune—on and on without the possibility of a happily ever after. It seemed as if the old man could go on and on inventing more and more terrible situations for his hero and improvising solutions as he went on till the boy thought he would never hear the end of the story.

"The story had no ending," the old man told him when he asked. He was feeling sleepy and he was afraid his mother would put a definite stop to his visits to the old man's place, even if it meant sending him out to some distant relative.

"Carry her these mice," the old man said when Zakeo said good night and stood up to go. "I don't think she will beat you tonight. She loves mice," he said with a little laugh.

But when he got home his mother threw the mice to the dog.

"What did I tell you?" she demanded of him, holding the oxhide strop.

Zakeo didn't answer. He was looking at his mother without blinking, ready to take the strop like Ndatofa, the hero in the old man's story. In the corner of his eye he saw his father working at his baskets, his eyes watering from the guttering smoking lamp he used to give him light. The crow's feet round his eyes made him appear as if he were wincing from some invisible pain.

"Don't you answer when I am talking to you?" his mother said.

The boy kept quiet, sitting erect, looking at his mother. Then she made a sound which he couldn't understand, a sound which she always uttered from some unliving part of her when she was mad. She was blind with rage but the boy held in his screams right down there where he knew screams and sobs came from. He gritted his teeth and felt the scalding lashes cutting deep into his back, right down to where they met the screams, where they couldn't go any farther. And each time the strop cut into him and he didn't scream his mother seemed to get madder and madder. His father tried to intervene but he quickly returned to his basket-weaving when the strop cracked into *his* back twice in quick merciless succession. It was then that Zakeo almost let out a deafening howl. He closed his eyes so tightly that veins stood out in his face. He felt on fire.

"I could kill you—you—you!" He heard his mother scream and he waited, tensed, for the strop and then suddenly as if someone had told him, he knew it wasn't coming. He opened his eyes and saw that his mother had dropped the strop and was crying herself. She rushed at him and began to hug him.

"My Zakeo! My own son. What are you doing this to me for? Tell me. What wrong have I done to you, ha? O, I know! I know very well who is doing this to you. He never wanted your father to marry me!"

He let her hug him without moving but he didn't let her hugging and crying get as far as the strop lashes. *That* was his own place. He just stopped her hugs and tears before they got *there*. And when he had had enough, he removed her arms from round him and stood up. His mother looked at him, surprised, empty hands that should have contained his body becoming emptier with the expression on her face.

"Where are you going, Zakeo?" It was as if *he* had slapped her.

"Do you care?"

"Zakeo! I am *your* mother! Do you know that? No one here cares for you more than I do! Not *him!*" pointing at his father. "And *not* even him!"—indicating in the direction of his grandfather's hut.

"You don't know anything," Zakeo said, without understanding what he meant by that but using it because he had heard it used of his classmates by the old man.

"You don't know anything," he repeated it, becoming more and more convinced of its magical effect on his mother who gaped at him as if she was about to sneeze.

As he walked out he caught sight of his father who was working furiously at his baskets, his head almost touching his knees and his back bent double.

The old man was awake when Zakeo walked in.

"Put another log on the fire," the old man said.

Zakeo quietly did so. His back ached but the heat had gone. He felt a little relaxedly cool.

"You didn't cry today."

The boy didn't answer.

"But you will cry one day."

The boy stopped raking the coals and looked at the old man, confused.

"You will cry one day and you will think your mother was right."

"But—" the boy stopped, lost. The night had turned suddenly chilly, freaky weather for October. He had been too involved with something else to notice it when he walked the half-mile between their place and the old man's. Now he felt it at his back and he shivered.

"Get into the blankets, you will catch a cold," the old man said.

Zakeo took off his shirt and left the shorts on. He got into the blankets beside the old man, on the side away from the fire.

"One day you will want to cry but you won't be able to," the old man said.

"Sekuru?"

"I said get into the blankets."

The boy lay down on his left side, facing the wall, away from the old man and drew up his knees with his hands between them. He knew he wouldn't be able to sleep on his back that night.

"Thirteen," the old man said, shaking his head.

"Sekuru?"

"Sleep now. I must have been dreaming."

Zakeo pulled the smoke-and-tobacco-smelling ancient blankets over his head.

"Who doesn't want to cry a good cry once in a while but there are just not enough tears to go round all of us?"

"Sekuru?"

"You still awake?"

"Yes."

"You want to go school?"

"No."

"Go to sleep then."

"I can't."

"Why?"

"I just can't."

"Try. It's good for you. Think of fishing."

"Yes, *Sekuru.*"

"Or mouse-trapping."

"And hunting?"

"Yes. Think all you like of hunting."

"You will take me hunting some day, won't you, *Sekuru?*"

"Yes," the old man said and then after some time, "When the moon becomes your mother's necklace."

"You spoke, *Sekuru?*"

"I said yes."

"Thank you, *Sekuru.* Thank you very much."

"Thank you, *Sekuru,* thank you very much," the old man mimicked the boy, shook his head sadly—knowing that the following day the boy would be going to school. Soon, he too was fast asleep, dreaming of that mountain which he had never been able to climb since he was a boy.

IN
THE SHADOW
OF WAR

Ben
Okri

Nigeria

That afternoon three soldiers came to the village. They scattered the goats and chickens. They went to the palm-frond bar and ordered a calabash of palm-wine. They drank amidst the flies.

Omovo watched them from the window as he waited for his father to go out. They both listened to the radio. His father had bought the old Grundig cheaply from a family that had to escape the city when the war broke out. He had covered the radio with a white cloth and made it look like a household fetish. They listened to the news of bombings and air raids in the interior of the country. His father combed his hair, parted it carefully, and slapped some aftershave on his unshaven face. Then he struggled into the shabby coat that he had long outgrown.

Omovo stared out of the window, irritated with his father. At that hour, for the past seven days, a strange woman with a black veil over her head had been going past the house. She went up the village paths, crossed the Express road, and disappeared into the forest. Omovo waited for her to appear.

The main news was over. The radio announcer said an eclipse of the moon was expected that night. Omovo's father wiped the sweat off his face with his palm and said, with some bitterness:

'As if an eclipse will stop this war.'

'What is an eclipse?' Omovo asked.

'That's when the world goes dark and strange things happen.'

'Like what?'

His father lit a cigarette.

'The dead start to walk about and sing. So don't stay out late, eh.'

Omovo nodded.

'Heclipses hate children. They eat them.'

Omovo didn't believe him. His father smiled, gave Omovo his ten kobo allowance, and said:

'Turn off the radio. It's bad for a child to listen to news of war.'

Omovo turned it off. His father poured a libation at the doorway and then prayed to his ancestors. When he had finished he picked up his briefcase and strutted out briskly. Omovo watched him as he threaded his way up the path to the bus-stop at the main road. When a danfo bus came, and his father went with it, Omovo turned the radio back on. He sat on the window-sill and waited for the woman. The last time he saw her she had glided past with agitated flutters of her yellow smock. The children stopped what they were doing and stared at her. They had said that she had no shadow. They had said that her feet never touched the ground. As she went past, the children began to throw things at her. She didn't flinch, didn't quicken her pace, and didn't look back.

The heat was stupefying. Noises dimmed and lost their edges. The villagers stumbled about their various tasks as if they were sleep-walking. The three soldiers drank palm-wine and played draughts beneath the sun's oppressive glare. Omovo noticed that whenever children went past the bar the soldiers called them, talked to them, and gave them some money. Omovo ran down the stairs and slowly walked past the bar. The soldiers stared at him. On his way back one of them called him.

'What's your name' he asked.

Omovo hesitated, smiled mischievously, and said:

'Heclipse.'

The soldier laughed, spraying Omovo's face with spit. He had a face crowded with veins. His companions seemed uninterested. They swiped flies and concentrated on their game. Their guns were on the table. Omovo noticed that they had numbers on them. The man said:

'Did your father give you that name because you have big lips?'

His companions looked at Omovo and laughed. Omovo nodded.

'You are a good boy,' the man said. He paused. Then he asked, in a different voice:

'Have you seen that woman who covers her face with a black cloth?'

'No.'

The man gave Omovo ten kobo and said:

'She is a spy. She helps our enemies. If you see her come and tell us at once, you hear?'

Omovo refused the money and went back upstairs. He re-positioned himself on the window-sill. The soldiers occasionally looked at him. The heat got to him and soon he fell asleep in a sitting position. The cocks, crowing dispiritedly, woke him up. He could feel the afternoon softening into evening. The soldiers dozed in the bar. The hourly news came on. Omovo listened without comprehension to the day's casualties. The announcer succumbed to the stupor, yawned, apologized, and gave further details of the fighting.

Omovo looked up and saw that the woman had already gone past. The men had left the bar. He saw them weaving between the eaves of the thatch houses, stumbling through the heat-mists. The woman was further up the path. Omovo ran downstairs and followed the men. One of them had taken off his uniform top. The soldier behind had buttocks so big they had begun to split his pants. Omovo followed them across the Express road. When they got into the forest the men stopped following the woman, and took a different route. They seemed to know what they were doing. Omovo hurried to keep the woman in view.

He followed her through the dense vegetation. She wore faded wrappers and a grey shawl, with the black veil covering her face. She had a red basket on her head. He completely forgot to determine if she had a shadow, or whether her feet touched the ground.

He passed unfinished estates, with their flaking ostentatious signboards and their collapsing fences. He passed an empty cement factory: blocks lay crumbled in heaps and the workers' sheds were deserted. He passed a baobab tree, under which was the intact skeleton of a large animal. A snake dropped from a branch and slithered through the undergrowth. In the distance, over the cliff edge, he heard loud music and people singing war slogans above the noise.

He followed the woman till they came to a rough camp on the plain below. Shadowy figures moved about in the half-light of the cave. The woman went to them. The figures surrounded her and touched her and led her into the cave. He heard their weary voices thanking her. When the woman reappeared she was without the basket. Children with kwashiorkor stomachs and women wearing rags led her half-way up the hill. Then, reluctantly, touching her as if they might not see her again, they went back.

He followed her till they came to a muddied river. She moved as if an invisible force were trying to blow her away. Omovo saw capsized canoes and trailing waterlogged clothes on the dark water. He saw floating items of sacrifice:

loaves of bread in polythene wrappings, gourds of food, Coca-Cola cans. When he looked at the canoes again they had changed into the shapes of swollen dead animals. He saw outdated currencies on the riverbank. He noticed the terrible smell in the air. Then he heard the sound of heavy breathing from behind him, then someone coughing and spitting. He recognized the voice of one of the soldiers urging the others to move faster. Omovo crouched in the shadow of a tree. The soldiers strode past. Not long afterwards he heard a scream. The men had caught up with the woman. They crowded round her.

'Where are the others?' shouted one of them.

The woman was silent.

'You dis witch! You want to die, eh? Where are they?'

She stayed silent. Her head was bowed. One of the soldiers coughed and spat towards the river.

'Talk! Talk!' he said, slapping her.

The fat soldier tore off her veil and threw it to the ground. She bent down to pick it up and stopped in the attitude of kneeling, her head still bowed. Her head was bald, and disfigured with a deep corrugation. There was a livid gash along the side of her face. The bare-chested soldier pushed her. She fell on her face and lay still. The lights changed over the forest and for the first time Omovo saw that the dead animals on the river were in fact the corpses of grown men. Their bodies were tangled with river-weed and their eyes were bloated. Before he could react, he heard another scream. The woman was getting up, with the veil in her hand. She turned to the fat soldier, drew herself to her fullest height, and spat in his face. Waving the veil in the air, she began to howl dementedly. The two other soldiers backed away. The fat soldier wiped his face and lifted the gun to the level of her stomach. A moment before Omovo heard the shot a violent beating of wings just above him scared him from his hiding place. He ran through the forest screaming. The soldiers tramped after him. He ran through a mist which seemed to have risen from the rocks. As he ran he saw an owl staring at him from a canopy of leaves. He tripped over the roots of a tree and blacked out when his head hit the ground.

When he woke up it was very dark. He waved his fingers in front of his face and saw nothing. Mistaking the darkness for blindness he screamed, thrashed around, and ran into a door. When he recovered from his shock he heard voices outside and the radio crackling on about the war. He found his way to the balcony, full of wonder that his sight had returned. But when he got there he was surprised to find his father sitting on the sunken cane chair, drinking palm-wine with the three soldiers. Omovo rushed to his father and pointed frantically at the three men.

'You must thank them,' his father said. 'They brought you back from the forest.'

Omovo, overcome with delirium, began to tell his father what he had seen. But his father, smiling apologetically at the soldiers, picked up his son and carried him off to bed.

WHEN THE TRAIN COMES

Zoe Wicomb

South Africa

I am not the kind of girl whom boys look at. I have known this for a long time, but I still lower my head in public and peep through my lashes. Their eyes leap over me, a mere obstacle in a line of vision. I should be pleased; boys can use their eyes shamelessly to undress a girl. That is what Sarie says. Sarie's hand automatically flutters to her throat to button up her orlon cardigan when boys talk to her. I have tried that, have fumbled with buttons and suffered their perplexed looks or reddened at the question, 'Are you cold?'

I know that it is the fact of guiding the buttons through their resistant holes that guides the eyes to Sarie's breasts.

Today I think that I would welcome any eyes that care to confirm my new ready-made polyester dress. Choosing has not brought an end to doubt. The white, grey and black stripes run vertically, and from the generous hem I have cut a strip to replace the treacherous horizontal belt. I am not wearing a cardigan, even though it is unusually cool for January, a mere eighty degrees. I have looked once or twice at the clump of boys standing with a huge radio out of which the music winds mercurial through the rise and fall of distant voices. There is no music in our house. Father says it is distracting. We stand uneasily on the platform. The train is late or perhaps we are early. Pa stands with his back to the boys who have greeted him deferentially. His broad shoulders block my view but I can hear their voices flashing like the village lights on Republic Day. The boys do not look at me and I know why. I am fat. My breasts are fat and, in spite of my uplift bra, flat as a vetkoek.

There is a lump in my throat which I cannot account for. I do of course cry from time to time about being fat, but this lump will not be dislodged by tears. I am pleased that Pa does not say much. I watch him take a string out of his pocket and wind it nervously around his index finger. Round and round from the base until the finger is encased in a perfect bandage. The last is a loop that fits the tip of his finger tightly; the ends are tied in an almost invisible knot. He hopes to hold my attention with this game. Will this be followed by cat's cradle with my hands foolishly stretched out, waiting to receive? I smart at his attempts to shield me from the boys; they are quite unnecessary.

Pa knows nothing of young people. On the morning of my fourteenth birthday he quoted from Genesis III . . . in pain you shall bring forth children. I had been menstruating for some time and so knew what he wanted to say. He said, 'You must fetch a bucket of water in the evenings and wash the rags at night . . . have them ready for the next month . . . always be prepared . . . it does not always come on time. Your mother was never regular . . . the ways of the Lord . . .' and he shuffled off with the bicycle tyre he was pretending to repair.

'But they sell things now in chemists' shops, towels you can throw away,' I called after him.

'Yes,' he looked dubiously at the distant blue hills, 'perhaps you could have some for emergencies. Always be prepared,' and lowering his eyes once again blurted, 'And don't play with boys now that you're a young lady, it's dangerous.'

I have never played with boys. There were none to play with when we lived on the farm. I do not know why. The memory, of a little boy boring a big toe into the sand, surfaces. He is staring enviously at the little house I have carved into the sandbank. There are shelves on which my pots gleam and my one-legged Peggy sleeps on her bank of clay. In my house I am free to do anything, even invite the boy to play. I am proud of the sardine can in which two clay loaves bake in the sun. For my new china teapot I have built a stone shrine where its posy of pink roses remains forever fresh. I am still smiling at the boy as he deftly pulls a curious hose from the leg of his khaki shorts and, with one eye shut, aims an arc of yellow pee into the teapot. I do not remember the teapot ever having a lid.

There is a lump in my throat I cannot account for. I sometimes cry about being fat, of course, especially after dinner when the zip of my skirt sinks its teeth into my flesh. Then it is reasonable to cry. But I have after all stood on this platform countless times on the last day of the school holidays. Sarie and I, with

Pa and Mr Botha waving and shouting into the clouds of steam, Work Hard or Be Good. Here, under the black and white arms of the station sign, where succulents spent and shrivelled in autumn grow once again plump in winter before they burst into shocking spring flower. So that Pa would say, 'The quarters slip by so quickly, soon the sun will be on Cancer and you'll be home again.' Or, 'When the summer train brings you back with your First Class Junior Certificate, the aloe will just be in flower.' And so the four school quarters clicked by under the Kliprand station sign where the jewelled eyes of the iceplant wink in the sun all year round.

The very first lump in my throat he melted with a fervent whisper, 'You must, Friedatjie, you must. There is no high school for us here and you don't want to be a servant. How would you like to peg out the madam's washing and hear the train you once refused to go on rumble by?' Then he slipped a bag of raisins into my hand. A terrifying image of a madam's menstrual rags that I have to wash swirls liquid red through my mind. I am grateful to be going hundreds of miles away from home; there is so much to be grateful for. One day I will drive a white car.

Pa takes a stick of biltong out of his pocket and the brine in my eyes retreats. I have no control over the glands under my tongue as they anticipate the salt. His pocketknife lifts off the seasoned and puckered surface and leaves a slab of marbled meat, dry and mirror smooth so that I long to rest my lips on it. Instead my teeth sink into the biltong and I am consoled. I eat everything he offers.

We have always started our day with mealie porridge. That is what miners eat twice a day, and they lift chunks of gypsum clean out of the earth. Father's eyes flash a red light over the breakfast table: 'Don't leave anything on your plate. You must grow up to be big and strong. We are not paupers with nothing to eat. Your mother was thin and sickly, didn't eat enough. You don't want cheekbones that jut out like a Hottentot's. Fill them out until they're shiny and plump as pumpkins.' The habit of obedience is fed daily with second helpings of mealie porridge. He does not know that I have long since come to despise my size. I would like to be a pumpkin stored on the flat roof and draw in whole beams of autumn's sunlight so that, bleached and hardened, I could call upon the secret of my glowing orange flesh.

A wolf whistle from one of the boys. I turn to look and I know it will upset Pa. Two girls in identical flared skirts arrive with their own radio blaring Boeremusiek. They nod at us and stand close by, perhaps seeking protection from the boys. I hope that Pa will not speak to me loudly in English. I will avoid calling him Father for they will surely snigger under cover of the whining concertina. They must know that for us this is no ordinary day. But we all remain silent and I am inexplicably ashamed. What do people say about us? Until recently I believed that I was envied; that is, not counting my appearance.

The boys beckon and the girls turn up their radio. One of them calls loudly, 'Turn off that Boere-shit and come and listen to decent American music.' I wince. The girls do as they are told, their act of resistance deflated. Pa casts an anxious glance at the white policeman pacing the actual platform, the paved white section. I take out a paper handkerchief and wipe the dust from my polished shoes, a futile act since this unpaved strip for which I have no word other than the inaccurate platform, is all dust. But it gives me the chance to peer at the group of young people through my lowered lashes.

The boys vie for their attention. They have taken the radio and pass it round so that the red skirts flare and swoop, the torsos in T-shirts arch and taper into long arms reaching to recover their radio. Their ankles swivel on the slender stems of high heels. Their feet are covered in dust. One of the arms adjusts a chiffon headscarf that threatens to slip off, and a pimply boy crows at his advantage. He whips the scarf from her head and the tinkling laughter switches into a whine.

'Give it back . . . You have no right . . . It's mine and I want it back . . . Please, oh please.'

Her arm is raised protectively over her head, the hand flattened on her hair.

'No point in holding your head now,' he teases. 'I've got it, going to try it on myself.'

Her voice spun thin on threads of tears, abject as she begs. So that her friend consoles, 'It doesn't matter, you've got plenty of those. Show them you don't care.' A reproachful look but the friend continues, 'Really, it doesn't matter, your hair looks nice enough. I've told you before. Let him do what he wants with it, stuff it up his arse.'

But the girl screams, 'Leave me alone,' and beats away the hand reaching out to console. Another taller boy takes the scarf and twirls it in the air. 'You want your doekie? What do you want it for hey, come on tell us, what do you want it for? What do you want to cover up?'

His tone silences the others and his face tightens as he swings the scarf slowly, deliberately. She claws at his arm with rage while her face is buried in the other crooked arm. A little gust of wind settles the matter, whips it out of his hand and leaves it spreadeagled against the eucalyptus tree where its red pattern licks the bark like flames.

I cannot hear their words. But far from being penitent, the tall boy silences the bareheaded girl with angry shaking of the head and wagging of the finger. He runs his hand through an exuberant bush of fuzzy hair and my hand involuntarily flies to my own. I check my preparations: the wet hair wrapped over large rollers to separate the strands, dried then swirled around my head, secured overnight with a nylon stocking, dressed with vaseline to keep the strands smooth and straight and then pulled back tightly to stem any remaining tendency to curl. Father likes it pulled back. He says it is a mark of honesty to have the forehead and ears exposed. He must be thinking of Mother, whose hair was straight and trouble-free. I would not allow some unkempt youth to comment on my hair.

The tall boy with wild hair turns to look at us. I think that they are talking about me. I feel my body swelling out of the dress rent into vertical strips that fall to my feet. The wind will surely lift off my hair like a wig and flatten it, a sheet of glossy dead bird, on the eucalyptus tree.

The bareheaded girl seems to have recovered; she holds her head reasonably high.

I break the silence. 'Why should that boy look at us so insolently?' Pa looks surprised and hurt. 'Don't be silly. You couldn't possibly tell from this distance.' But his mouth puckers and he starts an irritating tuneless whistle.

On the white platform the policeman is still pacing. He is there because of the Blacks who congregate at the station twice a week to see the Springbok train on its way to Cape Town. I wonder whether he knows our news. Perhaps their servants, bending over washtubs, ease their shoulders to give the gossip from Wesblok to madams limp with heat and boredom. But I dismiss the idea and turn to the boys who certainly know that I am going to St Mary's today. All week the grown-ups have leaned over the fence and sighed, Ja, ja, in admiration, and winked at Pa: a clever chap, old Shenton, keeps up with the Boers all right. And to me, 'You show them, Frieda, what we can do.' I nodded shyly. Now I look at my hands, at the irrepressible cuticles, the stubby splayed fingernails that will never taper. This is all I have to show, betraying generations of servants.

I am tired and I move back a few steps to sit on the suitcases. But Father leaps to their defence. 'Not on the cases, Frieda. They'll never take your weight.' I hate the shiny suitcases. As if we had not gone to enough expense, he insisted on new imitation leather bags and claimed that people judge by appearances. I miss my old scuffed bag and slowly, as if the notion has to travel through folds of fat, I realise that I miss Sarie and the lump in my throat hardens.

Sarie and I have travelled all these journeys together. Grief gave way to excitement as soon as we boarded the train. Huddled together on the cracked green seat, we argued about who would sleep on the top bunk. And in winter when the nights grew cold we folded into a single S on the lower bunk. As we tossed through the night in our magic coupé, our fathers faded and we were free. Now Sarie stands in the starched white uniform of a student nurse, the Junior Certificate framed in her father's room. She will not come to wave me goodbye.

Sarie and I swore our friendship on the very first day at school. We twiddled our stiff plaits in boredom; the *First Sunnyside Reader* had been read to us at home. And Jos. Within a week Jos had mastered the reader and joined us. The three of us hand in hand, a formidable string of laughing girls tugging this way and that, sneering at the Sunnyside adventures of Rover, Jane and John. I had no idea that I was fat. Jos looped my braids over her beautiful hands and said that I was pretty, that my braids were a string of sausages.

Jos was bold and clever. Like a whirlwind she spirited away the tedium of exhausted games and invented new rules. We waited for her to take command. Then she slipped her hand under a doekie of dyed flourbags and scratched her head. Her ear peeped out, a faded yellow-brown yearning for the sun. Under a star-crammed sky Jos had boldly stood for hours, peering through a crack in the shutter to watch their fifth baby being born. Only once had she looked away in agony and then the Three Kings in the eastern sky swiftly swopped places in the manner of musical chairs. She told us all, and with an oath invented by Jos we swore that we would never have babies. Jos knew everything that grown-ups thought should be kept from us. Father said, 'A cheeky child, too big for her boots, she'll land in a madam's kitchen all right.' But there was no need to separate us. Jos left school when she turned nine and her family moved to the village where her father had found a job at the garage. He had injured his back at the mine. Jos said they were going to have a car; that she would win one of those competitions, easy they were, you only had to make up a slogan.

Then there was our move. Pa wrote letters for the whole community, bit his nails when he thought I was not looking and wandered the veld for hours. When the official letter came the cooped-up words tumbled out helter-skelter in his longest monologue.

'In rows in the village, that's where we'll have to go, all boxed in with no room to stretch the legs. All my life I've lived in the open with only God to keep an eye on me, what do I want with the eyes of neighbours nudging and jostling in cramped streets? How will the wind get into those back yards to sweep away the smell of too many people? Where will I grow things? A watermelon, a pumpkin need room to spread, and a turkey wants a swept yard, the markings of a grass broom on which to boast the pattern of his wingmarks. What shall we do, Frieda? What will become of us?' And then, calmly, 'Well, there's nothing to be done. We'll go to Wesblok, we'll put up our curtains and play with the electric lights and find a corner for the cat, but it won't be our home. I'm not clever old Shenton for nothing, not a wasted drop of Scots blood in me. Within five years we'll have enough to buy a little place. Just a little raw brick house and somewhere to tether a goat and keep a few chickens. Who needs a water lavatory in the veld?'

The voice brightened into fantasy. 'If it were near a river we could have a pond for ducks or geese. In the Swarteberg my pa always had geese. Couldn't get to sleep for months here in Namaqualand without the squawking of geese. And ostriches. There's nothing like ostrich biltong studded with coriander seeds.' Then he slowed down. 'Ag man, we won't be allowed land by the river but nevermind hey. We'll show them, Frieda, we will. You'll go to high school next year and board with Aunt Nettie. We've saved enough for that. Brains are for making money and when you come home with your Senior Certificate, you won't come back to a pack of Hottentots crouching in straight lines on the edge of the village. Oh no, my girl, you won't.' And he whipped out a stick of beef biltong and with the knife shaved off wafer-thin slices that curled with pleasure in our palms.

We packed our things humming. I did not really understand what he was fussing about. The Coloured location did not seem so terrible. Electric lights meant no more oil lamps to clean and there was water from a tap at the end of each street. And there would be boys. But the children ran after me calling, 'Fatty fatty vetkoek.' Young children too. Sarie took me firmly by the arm and said that it wasn't true, that they were jealous of my long hair. I believed her and swung my stiff pigtails haughtily. Until I grew breasts and found that the children were right.

Now Sarie will be by the side of the sick and infirm, leaning over high hospital beds, soothing and reassuring. Sarie in a dazzling white uniform, her little waist clinched by the broad blue belt.

If Sarie were here I could be sure of climbing the two steel steps on to the train.

The tall boy is now pacing the platform in unmistakable imitation of the policeman. His face is the stern mask of someone who does not take his duties lightly. His friends are squatting on their haunches, talking earnestly. One of them illustrates a point with the aid of a stick with which he writes or draws in the sand. The girls have retreated and lean against the eucalyptus tree, bright as stars against the grey of the trunk. Twelve feet apart the two radios stand face to face, quarrelling quietly. Only the female voices rise now and again in bitter laughter above the machines.

Father says that he must find the station master to enquire why the train has not come. 'Come with me,' he commands. I find the courage to pretend that it is a question but I flush with the effort.

'No, I'm tired, I'll wait here.' And he goes. It is true that I am tired. I do not on the whole have much energy and I am always out of breath. I have often consoled myself with an early death, certainly before I become an old maid. Alone with my suitcases I face the futility of that notion. I am free to abandon it since I am an old maid now, today, days after my fifteenth birthday. I do not in any case think that my spirit, weightless and energetic like smoke from green wood, will soar to heaven.

I think of Pa's defeated shoulders as he turned to go and I wonder whether I ought to run after him. But the thought of running exhausts me. I recoil again at the energy with which he had burst into the garden only weeks ago, holding aloft *Die Burger* with both hands, shouting, 'Frieda, Frieda, we'll do it. It's all ours, the whole world's ours.'

It was a short report on how a Coloured deacon had won his case against the Anglican Church so that the prestigious St Mary's School was now open to non-whites. The article ended sourly, calling it an empty and subversive gesture, and warning the deacon's daughters that it would be no bed of roses.

'You'll have the best, the very best education.' His voice is hoarse with excitement.

'It will cost hundreds of rand per year.'

'Nonsense, you finish this year at Malmesbury and then there'll be only the two years of Matric left to pay for. Really, it's a blessing that you have only two years left.'

'Where will you find the money?' I say soberly.

'The nest egg of course, stupid child. You can't go to a white school if you're so stupid. Shenton has enough money to give his only daughter the best education in the world.'

I hesitate before asking, 'But what about the farm?' He has not come to like the Wesblok. The present he wraps in a protective gauze of dreams; his eyes have grown misty with focusing far ahead on the unrealised farm.

A muscle twitches in his face before he beams, 'A man could live any-where, burrow a hole like a rabbit in order to make use of an opportunity like this.' He seizes the opportunity for a lecture. 'Ignorance, laziness and tobacco have been the downfall of our people. It is our duty to God to better ourselves, to use our brains, our talents, not to place our lamps under bushels. No, we'll do it. We must be prepared to make sacrifices to meet such a generous offer.'

His eyes race along the perimeter of the garden wall then he rushes indoors, muttering about idling like flies in the sun, and sets about writing to St Mary's in Cape Town.

I read novels and kept in the shade all summer. The crunch of biscuits between my teeth was the rumble of distant thunder. Pimples raged on my chin, which led me to Madame Rose's Preparation by mail order. That at least has fulfilled its promise.

I was surprised when Sarie wept with joy or envy, so that the tears spurted from my own eyes on to the pages of *Ritchie's First Steps in Latin*. (Father said that they pray in Latin and that I ought to know what I am praying for.) At night a hole crept into my stomach, gnawing like a hungry mouse, and I fed it with Latin declensions and Eetsumor biscuits. Sarie said that I might meet white boys and for the moment, fortified by conjugations of *Amo*, I saw the eyes of Anglican boys, remote princes leaning from their carriages, penetrate the pumpkin-yellow of my flesh.

Today I see a solid stone wall where I stand in watery autumn light waiting for a bell to ring. The Cape southeaster tosses high the blond pigtails and silvery laughter of girls walking by. They do not see me. Will I spend the dinner breaks hiding in lavatories?

I wish I could make this day more joyful for Pa but I do not know how. It is no good running after him now. It is too late.

The tall boy has imperceptibly extended his marching ground. Does he want to get closer to the policeman or is he taking advantage of Father's absence? I watch his feet, up, down, and the crunch of his soles on the sand explodes in my ears. Closer, and a thrilling thought shoots through the length of my body. He may be looking at me longingly, probing; but I cannot bring my eyes to travel up, along his unpressed trousers. The black boots of the policeman catch my eye. He will not be imitated. His heavy legs are tree trunks rooted in the asphalt. His hand rests on the bulge of his holster. I can no longer resist the crunch of the boy's soles as they return. I look up. He clicks his heels and halts. His eyes are narrowed with unmistakable contempt. He greets me in precise mocking English. A soundless shriek for Pa escapes my lips and I note the policeman resuming his march before I reply. The boy's voice is angry and I wonder what aspect of my dress offends him.

'You are waiting for the Cape Town train?' he asks unnecessarily. I nod.

'You start at the white school tomorrow?' A hole yawns in my stomach and I long for a biscuit. I will not reply.

'There are people who bury dynamite between the rails and watch whole carriages of white people shoot into the air. Like opening the door of a birdcage. Phsssh!' His long thin arms describe the spray of birdflight. 'Perhaps that is why your train has not come.'

I know he is lying. I would like to hurl myself at him, stab at his eyes with my blunt nails, kick at his ankles until they snap. But I clasp my hands together piously and hold, hold the tears that threaten.

'Your prayer is answered, look, here's Fa-atherrr,' and on the held note he clicks his heels and turns smartly to march off towards his friends.

Father is smiling. 'She's on her way, should be here any second now.' I take his arm and my hand slips into his jacket pocket where I trace with my finger the withered potato he wears for relief of rheumatism.

'No more biltong, girlie,' he laughs. The hole in my stomach grows dangerously.

The white platform is now bustling with people. Porters pile suitcases on to their trolleys while men fish in their pockets for sixpence tips. A Black girl staggers on to the white platform with a suitcase in each hand. Her madam ambles amiably alongside her to keep up with the faltering gait. She chatters without visible encouragement and, stooping, takes one of the bags from the girl who clearly cannot manage. The girl is big-boned with strong shapely arms and calves. What can the suitcase contain to make her stagger so? Her starched apron sags below the waist and the crisp servant's cap is askew. When they stop at the far end of the platform she slips a hand under the edge of the white cap to scratch. Briefly she tugs at the tip of her yellow-brown earlobe. My chest tightens. I turn to look the other way.

Our ears prick at a rumbling in the distance which sends as scout a thin squeal along the rails. A glass dome of terror settles over my head so that the chatter about me recedes and I gulp for air. But I do not faint. The train lumbers to a halt and sighs deeply. My body, all but consumed by its hole of hunger, swings around lightly, even as Father moves forward with a suitcase to mount the step. And as I walk away towards the paling I meet the triumphant eyes of the tall boy standing by the whitewashed gate. Above the noise of a car screeching to a halt, the words roll off my tongue disdainfully:

> *Why you look and kyk gelyk,*
> *Am I miskien of gold gemake?*

ASIA
AND THE
SOUTH PACIFIC

AMERICAN DREAMS

Peter Carey

Australia

No one can, to this day, remember what it was we did to offend him. Dyer the butcher remembers a day when he gave him the wrong meat annd another day when he served someone else first by mistake. Often when Dyer gets drunk he recalls this day and curses himself for his foolishness. But no one seriously believes that it was Dyer who offended him.

But one of us did something. We slighted him terribly in some way, this small meek man with the rimless glasses and neat suit who used to smile so nicely at us all. We thought, I suppose, he was a bit of a fool and sometimes he was so quiet and grey that we ignored him, forgetting he was there at all.

When I was a boy I often stole apples from the trees at his house up in Mason's Lane. He often saw me. No, that's not correct. Let me say I often sensed that he saw me. I sensed him peering out from behind the lace curtains of his house. And I was not the only one. Many of us came to take his apples, alone and in groups, and it is possible that he chose to exact payment for all these apples in his own peculiar way.

Yet I am sure it wasn't the apples.

What has happened is that we all, all eight hundred of us, have come to remember small transgressions against Mr. Gleason who once lived amongst us.

My father, who has never borne malice against a single living creature, still believes that Gleason meant to do us well, that he loved the town more than any of us. My father says we have treated the town badly in our minds. We have used it, this little valley, as nothing more than a stopping place. Somewhere on the way to somewhere else. Even those of us who have been here many years have never taken the town seriously. Oh yes, the place is pretty. The hills are green and the woods thick. The stream is full of fish. But it is not where we would rather be.

For years we have watched the films at the Roxy and dreamed, if not of America, then at least of our capital city. For our own town, my father says, we have nothing but contempt. We have treated it badly, like a whore. We have cut down the giant shady trees in the main street to make doors for the school house and seats for the football pavilion. We have left big holes all over the countryside from which we have taken brown coal and given back nothing.

The commercial travellers who buy fish and chips at George the Greek's care for us more than we do, because we all have dreams of the big city, of wealth, of modern houses, of big motor cars: American Dreams, my father has called them.

Although my father ran a petrol station he was also an inventor. He sat in his office all day drawing strange pieces of equipment on the back of delivery dockets. Every spare piece of paper in the house was covered with these little drawings and my mother would always be very careful about throwing away any piece of paper no matter how small. She would look on both sides of any piece of paper very carefully and always preserved any that had so much as a pencil mark.

I think it was because of this that my father felt that he understood Gleason. He never said as much, but he inferred that he understood Gleason because he, too, was concerned with similar problems. My father was working on plans for a giant gravel crusher, but occasionally he would become distracted and become interested in something else.

There was, for instance, the time when Dyer the butcher bought a new bicycle with gears, and for a while my father talked of nothing else but the gears. Often I would see him across the road squatting down beside Dyer's bicycle as if he were talking to it.

We all rode bicycles because we didn't have the money for anything better. My father did have an old Chev truck, but he rarely used it and it occurs to me now that it might have had some mechanical problem that was impossible to solve, or perhaps it was just that he was saving it, not wishing to wear it out all at once. Normally, he went everywhere on his bicycle and, when I was younger, he carried me on the cross bar, both of us dismounting to trudge up the hills that led into and out of the main street. It was a common sight in our town to see people pushing bicycles. They were as much a burden as a means of transport.

Gleason also had his bicycle and every lunchtime he pushed and pedalled it home from the shire offices to his little weatherboard house out at Mason's Lane. It was a three-mile ride and people said that he went home for lunch because he was fussy and wouldn't eat either his wife's sandwiches or the hot meal available at Mrs. Lessing's café.

But while Gleason pedalled and pushed his bicycle to and from the shire offices everything in our town proceeded as normal. It was only when he retired that things began to go wrong.

Because it was then that Mr. Gleason started supervising the building of the wall around the two-acre plot up on Bald Hill. He paid too much for this land. He bought it from Johnny Weeks, who now, I am sure, believes the whole episode was his fault, firstly for cheating Gleason, secondly for selling him the land at all. But Gleason hired some Chinese and set to work to build his wall. It was then that we knew that we'd offended him. My father rode all the way out to Bald Hill and tried to talk Mr. Gleason out of his wall. He said there was no need for us to build walls. That no one wished to spy on Mr. Gleason or whatever he wished to do on Bald Hill. He said no one was in the least bit interested in Mr. Gleason. Mr. Gleason, neat in a new sportscoat, polished his glasses and smiled vaguely at his feet. Bicycling back, my father thought that he had gone too far. Of course we had an interest in Mr. Gleason. He pedalled back and asked him to attend a dance that was to be held on the next Friday, but Mr. Gleason said he didn't dance.

"Oh well," my father said, "any time, just drop over."

Mr. Gleason went back to supervising his family of Chinese labourers on his wall.

Bald Hill towered high above the town and from my father's small filling station you could sit and watch the wall going up. It was an interesting sight. I watched it for two years, while I waited for customers who rarely came. After school and on Saturdays I had all the time in the world to watch the agonizing progress of Mr. Gleason's wall. It was as painful as a clock. Sometimes I could see the Chinese labourers running at a jog-trot carrying bricks on long wooden planks. The hill was bare, and on this bareness Mr. Gleason was, for some reason, building a wall.

In the beginning people thought it peculiar that someone would build such a big wall on Bald Hill. The only thing to recommend Bald Hill was the view of the town, and Mr. Gleason was building a wall that denied that view. The top soil was thin and bare clay showed through in places. Nothing would ever grow there. Everyone assumed that Gleason had simply gone mad and after the initial interest they accepted his madness as they accepted his wall and as they accepted Bald Hill itself.

Occasionally someone would pull in for petrol at my father's filling station and ask about the wall and my father would shrug and I would see, once more, the strangeness of it.

"A house?" the stranger would ask. "Up on that hill?"

"No," my father would say, "chap named Gleason is building a wall."

And the strangers would want to know why, and my father would shrug and look up at Bald Hill once more. "Damned if I know," he'd say.

Gleason still lived in his old house at Mason's Lane. It was a plain weatherboard house with a rose garden at the front, a vegetable garden down the side, and an orchard at the back.

At night we kids would sometimes ride out to Bald Hill on our bicycles. It was an agonizing, muscle-twitching ride, the worst part of which was a steep, unmade road up which we finally pushed our bikes, our lungs rasping in the night air. When we arrived we found nothing but walls. Once we broke down some of the brickwork and another time we threw stones at the tents where the Chinese labourers slept. Thus we expressed our frustration at this inexplicable thing.

The wall must have been finished on the day before my twelfth birthday. I remember going on a picnic birthday party up to Eleven Mile Creek and we lit a fire and cooked chops at a bend in the river from where it was possible to see the walls on Bald Hill. I remember standing with a hot chop in my hand and someone saying, "Look, they're leaving!"

We stood on the creek bed and watched the Chinese labourers walking their bicycles slowly down the hill. Someone said they were going to build a chimney up at the mine at A.1 and certainly there is a large brick chimney there now, so I suppose they built it.

When the word spread that the walls were finished most of the town went up to look. They walked around the four walls which were as interesting as any other brick walls. They stood in front of the big wooden gates and tried to peer through, but all they could see was a small blind wall that had obviously been constructed for this special purpose. The walls themselves were ten feet high and topped with broken glass and barbed wire. When it became obvious that we were not going to discover the contents of the enclosure, we all gave up and went home.

Mr. Gleason had long since stopped coming into town. His wife came instead, wheeling a pram down from Mason's Lane to Main Street and filling it with groceries and meat (they never bought vegetables, they grew their own) and wheeling it back to Mason's Lane. Sometimes you would see her standing with the pram halfway up the Gell Street hill. Just standing there, catching her breath. No one asked her about the wall. They knew she wasn't responsible for the wall and they felt sorry for her, having to bear the burden of the pram and her husband's madness. Even when she began to visit Dixon's hardware and buy plaster of paris and tins of paint and waterproofing compound, no one asked her what these things were for. She had a way of averting her eyes that indicated her terror of questions. Old Dixon carried the plaster of paris and the tins of paint out to her pram for her and watched her push them away. "Poor woman," he said, "poor bloody woman."

From the filling station where I sat dreaming in the sun, or from the enclosed office where I gazed mournfully at the rain, I would see, occasionally, Gleason entering or leaving his walled compound, a tiny figure way up on Bald Hill. And I'd think "Gleason," but not much more.

Occasionally strangers drove up there to see what was going on, often egged on by locals who told them it was a Chinese temple or some other silly thing. Once a group of Italians had a picnic outside the walls and took photographs of each other standing in front of the closed door. God knows what they thought it was.

But for five years between my twelfth and seventeenth birthdays there was nothing to interest me in Gleason's walls. Those years seem lost to me now and I can remember very little of them. I developed a crush on Susy Markin and followed her back from the swimming pool on my bicycle. I sat behind her in the pictures and wandered past her house. Then her parents moved to another town and I sat in the sun and waited for them to come back.

We became very keen on modernization. When coloured paints became available the whole town went berserk and brightly coloured houses blossomed overnight. But the paints were not of good quality and quickly faded and peeled, so that the town looked like a garden of dead flowers. Thinking of those years, the only real thing I recall is the soft hiss of bicycle tyres on the main street. When I think of it now it seems very peaceful, but I remember then that the sound induced in me a feeling of melancholy, a feeling somehow mixed with the early afternoons when the sun went down behind Bald Hill and the town felt as sad as an empty dance hall on a Sunday afternoon.

And then, during my seventeenth year, Mr. Gleason died. We found out when we saw Mrs. Gleason's pram parked out in front of Phonsey Joy's Funeral Parlour. It looked very sad, that pram, standing by itself in the windswept street. We came and looked at the pram and felt sad for Mrs. Gleason. She hadn't had much of a life.

Phonsey Joy carried old Mr. Gleason out to the cemetery by the Parwan Railway Station and Mrs. Gleason rode behind in a taxi. People watched the old hearse go by and thought, "Gleason," but not much else.

And then, less than a month after Gleason had been buried out at the lonely cemetery by the Parwan Railway Station, the Chinese labourers came back.

We saw them push their bicycles up the hill. I stood with my father and Phonsey Joy and wondered what was going on.

And then I saw Mrs. Gleason trudging up the hill. I nearly didn't recognize her, because she didn't have her pram. She carried a black umbrella and walked slowly up Bald Hill and it wasn't until she stopped for breath and leant forward that I recognized her.

"It's Mrs. Gleason," I said, "with the Chinese."

But it wasn't until the next morning that it became obvious what was happening. People lined the main street in the way they do for a big funeral but, instead of gazing towards the Grant Street corner, they all looked up at Bald Hill.

All that day and all the next people gathered to watch the destruction of the walls. They saw the Chinese labourers darting to and fro, but it wasn't until they knocked down a large section of the wall facing the town that we realized there really was something inside. It was impossible to see what it was, but there was something there. People stood and wondered and pointed out Mrs. Gleason to each other as she went to and fro supervising the work.

And finally, in ones and twos, on bicycles and on foot, the whole town moved up to Bald Hill. Mr. Dyer closed up his butcher shop and my father got out the old Chev truck and we finally arrived up at Bald Hill with twenty people on board. They crowded into the back tray and hung on to the running boards and my father grimly steered his way through the crowds of bicycles and parked just where the dirt track gets really steep. We trudged up this last steep track, never for a moment suspecting what we would find at the top.

It was very quiet up there. The Chinese labourers worked diligently, removing the third and fourth walls and cleaning the bricks which they stacked neatly in big piles. Mrs. Gleason said nothing either. She stood in the only remaining corner of the walls and looked defiantly at the townspeople who stood open-mouthed where another corner had been.

And between us and Mrs. Gleason was the most incredibly beautiful thing I had ever seen in my life. For one moment I didn't recognize it. I stood open-mouthed, and breathed the surprising beauty of it. And then I realized it was our town. The buildings were two feet high and they were a little rough but very correct. I saw Mr. Dyer nudge my father and whisper that Gleason had got the faded "U" in the BUTCHER sign of his shop.

I think at that moment everyone was overcome with a feeling of simple joy. I can't remember ever having felt so uplifted and happy. It was perhaps a childish emotion but I looked up at my father and saw a smile of such warmth spread across his face that I knew he felt just as I did. Later he told me that he thought Gleason had built the model of our town just for this moment, to let us see the beauty of our own town, to make us proud of ourselves and to stop the

American Dreams we were so prone to. For the rest, my father said, was not Gleason's plan and he could not have foreseen the things that happened afterwards.

I have come to think that this view of my father's is a little sentimental and also, perhaps, insulting to Gleason. I personally believe that he knew everything that would happen. One day the proof of my theory may be discovered. Certainly there are in existence some personal papers, and I firmly believe that these papers will show that Gleason knew exactly what would happen.

We had been so overcome by the model of the town that we hadn't noticed what was the most remarkable thing of all. Not only had Gleason built the houses and the shops of our town, he had also peopled it. As we tip-toed into the town we suddenly found ourselves. "Look," I said to Mr. Dyer, "there you are."

And there he was, standing in front of his shop in his apron. As I bent down to examine the tiny figure I was staggered by the look on its face. The modelling was crude, the paintwork was sloppy, and the face a little too white, but the expression was absolutely perfect: those pursed, quizzical lips and the eyebrows lifted high. It was Mr. Dyer and no one else on earth.

And there beside Mr. Dyer was my father, squatting on the footpath and gazing lovingly at Mr. Dyer's bicycle's gears, his face marked with grease and hope.

And there was I, back at the filling station, leaning against a petrol pump in an American pose and talking to Brian Sparrow who was amusing me with his clownish antics.

Phonsey Joy standing beside his hearse. Mr. Dixon sitting inside his hardware store. Everyone I knew was there in that tiny town. If they were not in the streets or in their backyards they were inside their houses, and it didn't take very long to discover that you could lift off the roofs and peer inside.

We tip-toed around the streets peeping into each other's windows, lifting off each other's roofs, admiring each other's gardens, and, while we did it, Mrs. Gleason slipped silently away down the hill towards Mason's Lane. She spoke to nobody and nobody spoke to her.

I confess that I was the one who took the roof from Cavanagh's house. So I was the one who found Mrs. Cavanagh in bed with young Craigie Evans.

I stood there for a long time, hardly knowing what I was seeing. I stared at the pair of them for a long, long time. And when I finally knew what I was seeing I felt such an incredible mixture of jealousy and guilt and wonder that I didn't know what to do with the roof.

Eventually it was Phonsey Joy who took the roof from my hands and placed it carefully back on the house, much, I imagine, as he would have placed the lid on a coffin. By then other people had seen what I had seen and the word passed around very quickly.

And then we all stood around in little groups and regarded the model town with what could only have been fear. If Gleason knew about Mrs. Cavanagh and Craigie Evans (and no one else had), what other things might he know? Those who hadn't seen themselves yet in the town began to look a little nervous and were unsure of whether to look for themselves or not. We gazed silently at the roofs and felt mistrustful and guilty.

We all walked down the hill then, very quietly, the way people walk away from a funeral, listening only to the crunch of the gravel under our feet while the women had trouble with their high-heeled shoes.

The next day a special meeting of the shire council passed a motion calling on Mrs. Gleason to destroy the model town on the grounds that it contravened building regulations.

It is unfortunate that this order wasn't carried out before the city newspapers found out. Before another day had gone by the government had stepped in.

The model town and its model occupants were to be preserved. The minister for tourism came in a large black car and made a speech to us in the football pavilion. We sat on the high, tiered seats eating potato chips while he stood against the fence and talked to us. We couldn't hear him very well, but we heard enough. He called the model town a work of art and we stared at him grimly. He said it would be an invaluable tourist attraction. He said tourists would come from everywhere to see the model town. We would be famous. Our businesses would flourish. There would be work for guides and interpreters and caretakers and taxi drivers and people selling soft drinks and ice creams.

The Americans would come, he said. They would visit our town in buses and in cars and on the train. They would take photographs and bring wallets bulging with dollars. American dollars.

We looked at the minister mistrustfully, wondering if he knew about Mrs. Cavanagh, and he must have seen the look because he said that certain controversial items would be removed, had already been removed. We shifted in our seats, like you do when a particularly tense part of a film has come to its climax, and then we relaxed and listened to what the minister had to say. And we all began, once more, to dream our American Dreams.

We saw our big smooth cars cruising through cities with bright lights. We entered expensive night clubs and danced till dawn. We made love to women like Kim Novak and men like Rock Hudson. We drank cocktails. We gazed lazily into refrigerators filled with food and prepared ourselves lavish midnight snacks which we ate while we watched huge television sets on which we would be able to see American movies free of charge and forever.

The minister, like someone from our American Dreams, reentered his large black car and cruised slowly from our humble sportsground, and the newspaper men arrived and swarmed over the pavilion with their cameras and notebooks. They took photographs of us and photographs of the models up on Bald Hill. And the next day we were all over the newspapers. The photographs of the model people side by side with photographs of the real people. And our names and ages and what we did were all printed there in black and white.

They interviewed Mrs. Gleason but she said nothing of interest. She said the model town had been her husband's hobby.

We all felt good now. It was very pleasant to have your photograph in the paper. And, once more, we changed our opinion of Gleason. The shire council held another meeting and named the dirt track up Bald Hill "Gleason Avenue." Then we all went home and waited for the Americans we had been promised.

It didn't take long for them to come, although at the time it seemed an eternity, and we spent six long months doing nothing more with our lives than waiting for the Americans.

Well, they did come. And let me tell you how it has all worked out for us.

The Americans arrive every day in buses and cars and sometimes the younger ones come on the train. There is now a small airstrip out near the Parwan cemetery and they also arrive there, in small aeroplanes. Phonsey Joy drives them to the cemetery where they look at Gleason's grave and then up to Bald Hill and then down to the town. He is doing very well from it all. It is good to see someone doing well from it. Phonsey is becoming a big man in town and is on the shire council.

On Bald Hill there are half a dozen telescopes through which the Americans can spy on the town and reassure themselves that it is the same down there as it is on Bald Hill. Herb Gravney sells them ice creams and soft drinks and extra film for their cameras. He is another one who is doing well. He bought the whole model from Mrs. Gleason and charges five American dollars admission. Herb is on the council now too. He's doing very well for himself. He sells them the film so they can take photographs of the houses and the model people and so they can come down to the town with their special maps and hunt out the real people.

To tell the truth most of us are pretty sick of the game. They come looking for my father and ask him to stare at the gears of Dyer's bicycle. I watch my father cross the street slowly, his head hung low. He doesn't greet the Americans any more. He doesn't ask them questions about colour television or Washington, D.C. He kneels on the footpath in front of Dyer's bike. They stand around him. Often they remember the model incorrectly and try to get my father to pose in the wrong way. Originally he argued with them, but now he argues no more. He does what they ask. They push him this way and that and worry about the expression on his face which is no longer what it was.

Then I know they will come to find me. I am next on the map. I am very popular for some reason. They come in search of me and my petrol pump as they have done for four years now. I do not await them eagerly because I know, before they reach me, that they will be disappointed.

"But this is not the boy."

"Yes," says Phonsey, "this is him alright." And he gets me to show them my certificate.

They examine the certificate suspiciously, feeling the paper as if it might be a clever forgery. "No," they declare. (Americans are so confident.) "No," they shake their heads, "this is not the real boy. The real boy is younger."

"He's older now. He used to be younger." Phonsey looks weary when he tells them. He can afford to look weary.

The Americans peer at my face closely. "It's a different boy."

But finally they get their cameras out. I stand sullenly and try to look amused as I did once. Gleason saw me looking amused but I can no longer remember how it felt. I was looking at Brian Sparrow. But Brian is also tired. He finds it difficult to do his clownish antics and to the Americans his little act isn't funny. They prefer the model. I watch him sadly, sorry that he must perform for such an unsympathetic audience.

The Americans pay one dollar for the right to take our photographs. Having paid the money they are worried about being cheated. They spend their time being disappointed and I spend my time feeling guilty that I have somehow let them down by growing older and sadder.

IN BROAD DAYLIGHT

Ha Jin

China

While I was eating corn cake and jellyfish at lunch, our gate was thrown open and Bare Hips hopped in. His large wooden pistol was stuck partly inside the waist of his blue shorts. "White Cat," he called me by my nickname, "hurry, let's go. They caught Old Whore at her home. They're going to take her through the streets this afternoon."

"Really?" I put down my bowl, which was almost empty, and rushed to the inner room for my undershirt and sandals. "I'll be back in a second."

"Bare Hips, did you say they'll parade Mu Ying today?" I heard Grandma ask in her husky voice.

"Yes, all the kids on our street have left for her house. I came to tell White Cat." He paused. "Hey, White Cat, hurry up!"

"Coming," I cried out, still looking for my sandals.

"Good, good!" Grandma said to Bare Hips, while flapping at flies with her large palm-leaf fan. "They should burn the bitch on Heaven Lamp like they did in the old days."

"Come, let's go," Bare Hips said to me the moment I was back. He turned to the door; I picked up my wooden scimitar and followed him.

"Put on your shoes, dear." Grandma stretched out her fan to stop me.

"No time for that, Grandma. I've got to be quick, or I'll miss something and won't be able to tell you the whole story when I get back."

We dashed into the street while Grandma was shouting behind us. "Come back. Take the rubber shoes with you."

We charged toward Mu Ying's home on Eternal Way, waving our weapons above our heads. Grandma was crippled and never came out of our small yard. That was why I had to tell her about what was going on outside. But she knew Mu Ying well, just as all the old women in our town knew Mu well and hated her. Whenever they heard that she had a man in her home again, these women would say, "This time they ought to burn Old Whore on Heaven Lamp."

What they referred to was the old way of punishing an adulteress. Though they had lived in New China for almost two decades, some ancient notions still stuck in their heads. Grandma told me about many of the executions in the old days that she had seen with her own eyes. Officials used to have the criminals of adultery executed in two different ways. They beheaded the man. He was tied to a stake on the platform at the marketplace. At the first blare of horns, a masked headsman ascended the platform holding a broad ax before his chest; at the second blare of horns, the headsman approached the criminal and raised the ax over his head; at the third blare of horns, the head was lopped off and fell to the ground. If the man's family members were waiting beneath the platform, his head would be picked up to be buried together with his body; if no family member was nearby, dogs would carry the head away and chase each other around until they ate up the flesh and returned for the body.

Unlike the man, the woman involved was executed on Heaven Lamp. She was hung naked upside down above a wood fire whose flames could barely touch her scalp. And two men flogged her away with whips made of bulls' penises. Meanwhile she screamed for help and the whole town could hear her. Since the fire merely scorched her head, it took at least half a day for her to stop shrieking and a day and a night to die completely. People used to believe that the way of punishment was justified by Heaven, so the fire was called Heaven Lamp. But that was an old custom; nobody believed they would burn Mu Ying in that way.

Mu's home, a small granite house with cement tiles built a year before, was next to East Wind Inn on the northern side of Eternal Way. When we entered that street, Bare Hips and I couldn't help looking around tremulously, because that area was the territory of the children living there. Two of the fiercest boys, who would kill without having second thoughts, ruled that part of our town. Whenever a boy from another street wandered into Eternal Way, they'd capture him and beat him up. Of course we did the same thing; if we caught one of them in our territory, we'd at least confiscate whatever he had with him: grasshopper cages, slingshots, bottle caps, marbles, cartridge cases, and so on. We would also make him call every one of us "Father" or "Grandfather." But today hundreds of children and grown-ups were pouring into Eternal Way; two dozen urchins on that street surely couldn't hold their ground. Besides, they had already adopted a truce, since they were more eager to see the Red Guards drag Mu Ying out of her den.

When we arrived, Mu was being brought out through a large crowd at the front gate. Inside her yard there were three rows of colorful washing hung on iron wires, and there was also a grape trellis. Seven or eight children were in there, plucking off grapes and eating them. Two Red Guards held Mu Ying by the arms, and the other Red Guards, about twenty of them, followed behind. They were all from Dalian City and wore home-made army uniforms. God knew how they came to know that there was a bad woman in our town. Though people hated Mu and called her names, no one would rough her up. Those Red Guards were strangers, so they wouldn't mind doing it.

Surprisingly, Mu looked rather calm; she neither protested nor said a word. The two Red Guards let go of her arms, and she followed them quietly into West Street. We all moved with them. Some children ran several paces ahead to look back at her.

Mu wore a sky-blue dress, which made her different from the other women who always wore jackets and pants suitable for honest work. In fact, even we small boys could tell that she was really handsome, perhaps the best looking woman of her age in our town. Though in her fifties, she didn't have a single gray hair; she was a little plump, but because of her long legs and arms she appeared rather queenly. While most of the women had sallow faces, hers looked white and healthy like fresh milk.

Skipping in front of the crowd, Bare Hips turned around and cried out at her, "Shameless Old Whore!"

She glanced at him, her round eyes flashing; the purple wart beside her left nostril grew darker. Grandma had assured me that Mu's wart was not a beauty-wart but a tear-wart. This meant that her life would be soaked in tears.

We knew where we were going, to White Mansion, which was our class-room building, the only two-storied house in the town. As we came to the end of West Street, a short man ran out from a street corner, panting for breath and holding a sickle. He was Meng Su, Mu Ying's husband, who sold bean jelly in summer and sugar-coated haws in winter at the marketplace. He paused in front of the large crowd, as though having forgotten why he had rushed over. He turned his head around to look back; there was nobody behind him. After a short moment he moved close, rather carefully.

"Please let her go," he begged the Red Guards. "Comrade Red Guards, it's all my fault. Please let her go." He put the sickle under his arm and held his hands together before his chest.

"Get out of the way!" commanded a tall young man, who must have been the leader.

"Please don't take her away. It's my fault. I haven't disciplined her well. Please give her a chance to be a new person. I promise, she won't do it again."

The crowd stopped to circle about. "What's your class status?" a square-faced young woman asked in a sharp voice.

"Poor peasant," Meng replied, his small eyes tearful and his cupped ears twitching a little. "Please let her go, sister. Have mercy on us! I'm kneeling down to you if you let her go." Before he was able to fall on his knees, two young men held him back. Tears were rolling down his dark fleshy cheeks, and his gray head began waving about. The sickle was taken away from him.

"Shut up," the tall leader yelled and slapped him across the face. "She's a snake. We traveled a hundred and fifty *li* to come here to wipe out poisonous snakes and worms. If you don't stop interfering, we'll parade you with her together. Do you want to join her?"

Silence. Meng covered his face with his large hands as though feeling dizzy.

A man in the crowd said aloud, "If you can share the bed with her, why can't you share the street?"

Many of the grown-ups laughed. "Take him, take him too!" someone told the Red Guards. Meng looked scared, sobbing quietly.

His wife stared at him without saying a word. Her teeth were clenched; a faint smile passed the corners of her mouth. Meng seemed to wince under her stare. The two Red Guards let his arms go, and he stepped aside, watching his wife and the crowd move toward the school.

Of Meng Su people in our town had different opinions. Some said he was a born cuckold who didn't mind his wife's sleeping with any man as long as she could bring money home. Some believed he was a good-tempered man who had stayed with his wife mainly for their children's sake; they forgot that the three children had grown up long before and were working in big cities far away. Some thought he didn't leave his wife because he had no choice—no woman would marry such a dwarf. Grandma, for some reason, seemed to respect Meng. She told me that Mu Ying had once been raped by a group of Russian soldiers under Northern Bridge and was left on the river bank afterwards. That night her husband sneaked there and carried her back. He looked after her for a whole winter till she recovered. "Old Whore doesn't deserve that good-hearted man," Grandma would say. "She's heartless and knows only how to sell her thighs."

We entered the school's playground where about two hundred people had already gathered. "Hey, White Cat and Bare Hips," Big Shrimp called us, waving his claws. Many boys from our street were there too. We went to join them.

The Red Guards took Mu to the front entrance of the building. Two tables had been placed between the stone lions that crouched on each side of the entrance. On one of the tables stood a tall paper hat with the big black characters on its side: "Down with Old Bitch!"

A young man in glasses raised his bony hand and started to address us, "Folks, we've gathered here today to denounce Mu Ying, who is a demon in this town."

"Down with Bourgeois Demons!" a slim woman Red Guard shouted. We raised our fists and repeated the slogan.

"Down with Old Bitch Mu Ying," a middle-aged man cried out with both hands in the air. He was an active revolutionary in our commune. Again we shouted, in louder voices.

The nearsighted man went on, "First, Mu Ying must confess her crime. We must see her attitude toward her own crime. Then we'll make the punishment fit both her crime and her attitude. All right, folks?"

"Right," some voices replied from the crowd.

"Mu Ying," he turned to the criminal, "you must confess everything. It's up to you now."

She was forced to stand on a bench. Staying below the steps, we had to raise our heads to see her face.

The questioning began. "Why do you seduce men and paralyze their revolutionary will with your bourgeois poison?" the tall leader asked in a solemn voice.

"I've never invited any man to my home, have I?" she said rather calmly. Her husband was standing at the front of the crowd, listening to her without showing any emotion, as though having lost his mind.

"Then why did they go to your house and not to others' houses?"

"They wanted to sleep with me," she replied.

"Shameless!" Several women hissed in the crowd.

"A true whore!"

"Scratch her!"

"Rip apart her filthy mouth!"

"Sisters," she spoke aloud. "All right, it was wrong to sleep with them. But you all know what it feels like when you want a man, don't you? Don't you once in a while have that feeling in your bones?" Contemptuously, she looked at the few withered middle-aged women standing in the front row, then closed her eyes. "Oh, you want that real man to have you in his arms and let him touch every part of your body. For that man alone you want to blossom into a woman, a real woman—"

"Take this, you Fox Spirit!" A stout young fellow struck her on the side with a fist like a sledgehammer. The heavy blow silenced her at once. She held her sides with both hands, gasping for breath.

"You're wrong, Mu Ying," Bare Hips's mother spoke from the front of the crowd, her forefinger pointing upward at Mu. "You have your own man, who doesn't lack an arm or a leg. It's wrong to have others' men and more wrong to pocket their money."

"I have my own man?" Mu glanced at her husband and smirked. She straightened up and said, "My man is nothing. He is no good, I mean in bed. He always comes before I feel anything."

All the adults burst out laughing. "What's that? What's so funny?" Big Shrimp asked Bare Hips.

"You didn't get it?" Bare Hips said impatiently. "You don't know anything about what happens between a man and a woman. It means that whenever she doesn't want him to come close to her he comes. Bad timing."

"It doesn't sound like that," I said.

Before we could argue, a large bottle of ink smashed on Mu's head and knocked her off the bench. Prone on the cement terrace, she broke into swearing and blubbering. "Oh, damn your ancestors! Whoever hit me will be childless!" Her left hand was rubbing her head. "Oh Lord of Heaven, they treat their grandma like this!"

"Serves you right!"

"A cheap weasel."

"Even a knife on her throat can't stop her."

"A pig is born to eat slop!"

When they put her back up on the bench, she became another person— her shoulders covered with black stains, and a red line trickling down her left temple. The scorching sun was blazing down on her as though all the black parts on her body were about to burn up. Still moaning, she turned her eyes to the spot where her husband had been standing a few minutes before. But he was no longer there.

"Down with Old Whore!" a farmer shouted in the crowd. We all followed him in one voice. She began trembling slightly.

The tall leader said to us, "In order to get rid of her counterrevolutionary airs, first, we're going to cut her hair." With a wave of his hand, he summoned the Red Guards behind him. Four men moved forward and held her down. The square-faced woman raised a large pair of scissors and thrust them into the mass of the dark hair.

"Don't, don't, please. Help, help! I'll do whatever you want me to—"

"Cut!" someone yelled.

"Shave her head bald!"

The woman Red Guard applied the scissors skillfully. After four or five strokes, Mu's head looked like the tail of a molting hen. She started blubbering again, her nose running and her teeth chattering.

A breeze came and swept away the fluffy curls from the terrace and scattered them on the sandy ground. It was so hot that some people took out fans, waving them continuously. The crowd stank of sweat.

Wooooo, wooooo, woo, woo. That was the train coming from Sand County at 3:30. It was a freight train, whose young drivers would toot the steam horn whenever they saw a young woman in a field beneath the track.

The questioning continued. "How many men have you slept with these years?" the nearsighted man asked.

"Three."

"She's lying," a woman in the crowd cried out.

"I told the truth, sister." She wiped off the tears from her cheeks with the back of her hand.

"Who are they?" the young man asked again. "Tell us more about them."

"An officer from the Little Dragon Mountain, and—"

"How many times did he come to your house?"

"I can't remember. Probably twenty."

"What's his name?"

"I don't know. He told me he was a big officer."

"Did you take money from him?"

"Yes."

"How much for each time?"

"Twenty *yuan.*"

"How much altogether?"

"Probably five hundred."

"Comrades and Revolutionary Masses," the young man turned to us, "how shall we handle this parasite that sucked blood out of a revolutionary officer?"

"Quarter her with four horses!" an old woman yelled.

"Burn her on Heaven Lamp!"

"Poop on her face!" a small fat girl shouted, her hand raised like a tiny pistol with the thumb cocked up and the forefinger aimed at Mu. Some grown-ups snickered.

Then a pair of old cloth-shoes, a symbol for a promiscuous woman, were passed to the front. The slim young woman took the shoes and tied them together with the laces. She climbed on a table and was about to hang the shoes around Mu's neck. Mu elbowed the woman aside and knocked the shoes to the ground. The stout young fellow picked up the shoes, and jumped twice to slap her on the cheeks with the soles. "You're so stubborn. Do you want to change yourself or not?" he asked.

"Yes, I do," she replied meekly and dared not stir a bit. Meanwhile the shoes were being hung around her neck.

"Now she looks like a real whore," a woman commented.

"Sing us a tune, Sis," a farmer demanded.

"Comrades," the man in glasses resumed, "let us continue the denunciation." He turned to Mu and asked, "Who are the other men?"

"A farmer from Apple Village."

"How many times with him?"

"Once."

"Liar!"

"She's lying!"

"Give her one on the mouth!"

The young man raised his hands to calm the crowd down and questioned her again, "How much did you take from him?"

"Eighty *yuan*."

"One night?"

"Yes."

"Tell us more about it. How can you make us believe you?"

"That old fellow came to town to sell piglets. He sold a whole litter for eighty, and I got the money."

"Why did you charge him more than the officer?"

"No, I didn't. He did it four times in one night."

Some people were smiling and whispering to each other. A woman said that old man must have been a widower or never married.

"What's his name?" the young man went on.

"No idea."

"Was he rich or poor?"

"Poor."

"Comrades," the young man addressed us, "here we have a poor peasant who worked with his sow for a whole year and got only a litter of piglets. That money is the salt and oil money for his family, but this snake swallowed the money with one gulp. What shall we do with her?"

"Kill her!"

"Break her skull!"

"Beat the piss out of her!"

A few farmers began to move forward to the steps, waving their fists or rubbing their hands.

"Hold," a woman Red Guard with a huge Chairman Mao badge on her chest spoke in a commanding voice. "The Great Leader has instructed us: 'For our struggle we need words but not force.' Comrades, we can easily wipe her out with words. Force doesn't solve ideological problems." What she said restrained those enraged farmers, who remained in the crowd.

Wooo, woo, wooo, woooooooooooo, an engine screamed in the south. It was strange, because the drivers of the four o'clock train were a bunch of old men who seldom blew the horn.

"Who is the third man?" the nearsighted man continued to question Mu.

"A Red Guard."

The crowd broke into laughter. Some women asked the Red Guards to give her another bottle of ink. "Mu Ying, you're responsible for your own words," the young man said in a serious voice.

"I told you the truth."

"What's his name?"

"I don't know. He led the propaganda team that passed here last month."

"How many times did you sleep with him?"

"Once."

"How much did you make out of him?"

"None. That stingy dog wouldn't pay a cent. He said he was the worker who should be paid."

"So you were outsmarted by him?"

Some men in the crowd guffawed. Mu wiped her nose with her thumb, and at once she wore a thick mustache. "I taught him a lesson, though," she said.

"How?"

"I tweaked his ears, gave him a bleeding nose, and kicked him out. I told him never come back."

People began talking to each other. Some said that she was a strong woman who knew what was hers. Some said the Red Guard was no good; if you got something you had to pay for it. A few women declared that the rascal deserved such a treatment.

"Dear Revolutionary Masses," the tall leader started to speak. "We all have heard the crime Mu Ying committed. She lured one of our officers and one of our poor peasants into the evil water, and she beat a Red Guard black and blue. Shall we let her go home without punishment or shall we teach her an unforgettable lesson so that she won't do it again?"

"Teach her a lesson!" some voices cried out in unison.

"Then we're going to parade her through the streets."

Two Red Guards pulled Mu off the bench, and another picked up the tall hat. "Brothers and sisters," she begged, "please let me off just for once. Don't, don't! I promise I'll correct my fault. I'll be a new person. Help! Oh, help!"

It was no use resisting; within seconds the huge hat was firmly planted on her head. They also hung a big placard between the cloth-shoes lying against her chest. The words on the placard read:

I Am a Broken Shoe
My Crime Deserves Death

They put a gong in her hands and ordered her to strike it when she announced the words written on the inner side of the gong.

My pals and I followed the crowd, feeling rather tired. Boys from East Street were wilder; they threw stones at Mu's back. One stone struck the back of her head and blood dropped on her neck. But they were stopped immediately by the Red Guards, because a stone missed Mu and hit a man on the shoulder. Old people, who couldn't follow us, were standing on chairs and windowsills with pipes and towels in their hands. We were going to parade her through every street. It would take several hours to finish the whole thing, as the procession would stop for a short while at every street corner.

Bong, Mu struck the gong and declared, "I am an evil monster."

"Louder!"

Dong, bong—"I have stolen men. I stink for a thousand years."

When we were coming out of the marketplace, Cross Eyes emerged from a narrow lane. He grasped my wrist and Bare Hips's arm and said, "Someone is dead at the train station. Come, let's go there and have a look." The word "dead" at once roused us. We, half a dozen boys, set out running to the train station.

The dead man was Meng Su. A crowd had gathered at the railroad a hundred meters east of the station house. A few men were examining the rail that was stained with blood and studded with bits of flesh. One man paced along the darker part of the rail and announced that the train had dragged Meng at least twenty meters.

Beneath the track, Meng's headless body lay in a ditch. One of his feet was missing, and the whitish shinbone stuck out several inches long. There were so many openings on his body that he looked like a large piece of fresh meat on the counter in the butcher's. Beyond him, ten paces away, a big straw hat remained on the ground. We were told that his head was under the hat.

Bare Hips and I went down the slope to have a glimpse at the head. Other boys dared not take a peep. We two looked at each other, asking with our eyes who should raise the straw hat. I held out my wooden scimitar and lifted the rim of the hat a little with the sword. A swarm of bluebottles charged out, droning like provoked wasps. We bent over to peek at the head. Two long teeth pierced through the upper lip. An eyeball was missing. The gray hair was no longer perceivable, as it was covered with mud and dirt. The open mouth filled with purplish mucus. A tiny lizard skipped, sliding away into the grass.

"Oh!" Bare Hips began vomiting. Sorghum gruel mixed with bits of string beans splashed on a yellowish boulder. "Leave it alone, White Cat."

We lingered at the station, listening to different versions of the accident. Some people said that Meng had gotten drunk and dropped asleep on the track. Some said he hadn't slept at all but laughed hysterically walking in the middle of the track toward the coming train. Some said he had not drunk a drop, as he had spoken with tears in his eyes to a few persons he had run into on his way to the station. In any case, he was dead, torn to pieces.

That evening when I was coming home, I heard Mu Ying groaning in the smoky twilight. "Take me home. Oh, help me. Who can help me? Where are you? Why don't you come and carry me home?"

She was lying at the bus stop, alone.

MR. TANG'S GIRLS

Shirley Geok-lin Lim

Malaysia

Kim Mee caught her sister smoking in the garden. It was a dry hot day with sunshine bouncing off the Straits. The mix of blue waves and light cast an unpleasant glare in the garden, whose sandy soil seemed to burn and melt under her feet. Everyone stayed indoors on such Saturday afternoons; Ah Kong and Mother sleeping in the darkened sunroom and the girls reading magazines or doing homework throughout the house. Kim Mee had painted her toenails a new dark red color; she was going to a picnic in Tanjong Bederah on Sunday and wanted to see the effect of the fresh color on her feet bare on sand. The garden behind the house sloped down to the sea in a jungle of sea-almond trees and pandanus; a rusted barbed-wire fence and a broken gate were the only signs which marked when the garden stopped being a garden and became sea-wilderness. A large ciku tree grew by the fence, its branches half within the garden and half flung over the stretch of pebbles, driftwood, ground-down shells, and rotting organisms which lead shallowly down to the muddy tidal water. It was under the branches hidden by the trunk that Kim Li was smoking. She was taken by surprise, eyes half-shut, smoke gently trailing from her nostrils, and gazing almost tenderly at the horizon gleaming like a high-tension wire in the great distance.

"Ah ha! Since when did you start smoking?" Kim Mee said softly, coming suddenly around the tree trunk.

Unperturbed, without a start, Kim Li took another puff, elegantly holding the cigarette to the side of her mouth. Her fingers curled exaggeratedly as she slowly moved the cigarette away. She said with a drawl, "Why should I tell you?"

"Ah Kong will slap you."

She snapped her head around and frowned furiously. "You sneak! Are you going to tell him?"

"No, of course not!" Kim Mee cried, half-afraid. There were only two years' difference in age between them, but Kim Li was a strange one. She suffered from unpredictable moods which had recently grown more savage. "You're so mean. Why do you think I'll tell?" Kim Mee was angry now at having been frightened. In the last year, she had felt herself at an advantage over her eldest sister, whose scenes, rages, tears, and silences were less and less credited. The youngest girl, Kim Yee, at twelve years old, already seemed more mature than Kim Li. And she, at fifteen, was clearly superior. She didn't want to leave Kim Li smoking under the cool shade with eyes sophisticatedly glazed and looking advanced and remote. Moving closer, she asked, "Where did you get the cigarette?"

"Mind your own business," Kim Li replied calmly.

"Is it Ah Kong's cigarette? Yes, I can see it's a Lucky Strike."

Kim Li dropped the stub and kicked sand over it. Smoke still drifted from the burning end, all but buried under the mound. "What do you know of life?" she asked loftily and walked up the white glaring path past the bathhouse and up the wooden side stairs.

Kim Mee felt herself abandoned as she watched her sister's back vanish through the door. "Ugly witch!" She glanced at her feet, where the blood red toenails twinkled darkly.

Saturdays were, as long as she could remember, quiet days, heavy and slow with the gray masculine presence of their father, who spent most of the day, with Mother beside him, resting, gathering strength in his green leather chaise in the sunroom. Only his bushy eyebrows, growing in a straight line like a scar across his forehead, seemed awake. The hair there was turning white, bristling in wisps that grew even more luxuriant as the hair on his head receded and left the tight high skin mottled with discolored specks. Now and again he would speak in sonorous tones, but, chiefly, he dozed or gazed silently out of the windows which surrounded the room to the low flowering trees which Ah Chee, the family servant, tended, and, through the crisp green leaves, to his private thoughts.

They were his second family. Every Friday he drove down from Kuala Lumpur, where his first wife and children lived, in time for dinner. On Saturdays, the girls stayed home. No school activity, no friend, no party, no shopping trip took them out of the house. Their suppressed giggles, lazy talk, muted movements, and uncertain sighs constituted his sense of home, and every Saturday, the four girls played their part: they became daughters whose voices were to be heard like a cheerful music in the background, but never loudly or intrusively.

Every Saturday they made high tea at five. The girls peeled hard-boiled eggs, the shells carefully cracked and coming clean off the firm whites, and mashed them with butter into a spread. They cut fresh loaves of bread into thick yellow slices and poured mugs of tea into which they stirred puddles of condensed milk and rounded teaspoons of sugar. Ah Kong would eat only fresh bread, thickly buttered and grained with sprinkles of sugar, but he enjoyed watching his daughters eat like European mems. He brought supplies from Kuala Lumpur: tomatoes, tins of deviled ham and Kraft cheese, and packages of Birds' blancmange. Saturday tea was when he considered himself a successful father and fed on the vision of his four daughters eating toast and tomato slices while his quiet wife poured tea by his side.

"I say, Kim Bee," Kim Yee said, swallowing a cracker, "are you going to give me your blouse?"

The two younger girls were almost identical in build and height. Kim Yee, in the last year shooting like a vine, in fact being slightly stockier and more long-waisted than Kim Bee. Teatime with Ah Kong was the occasion to ask for dresses, presents, money, and other favors, and Kim Yee, being the youngest, was the least abashed in her approach.

"Yah! You're always taking my clothes. Why don't you ask for the blouse I'm wearing?"

"May I? It's pretty, and I can wear it to Sunday School."

Breathing indignation, Kim Bee shot a look of terrible fury and imploration to her mother. "She's impossible . . ." But she swallowed the rest of her speech, for she also had a request to make to Ah Kong, who was finally paying attention to the squabble.

"Don't you girls have enough to wear? Why must you take clothes from each other?"

Like a child who knows her part, Mother shifted in her chair and said good-naturedly, "Girls grow so fast, Peng. Their clothes are too small for them in six months. My goodness, Kim Yee's dresses are so short she doesn't look decent in them."

"Me too, Ah Kong!" Kim Mee added. "I haven't had a new dress since Chinese New Year."

"Chinese New Year was only three months ago," Ah Kong replied, shooting up his eyebrows, whether in surprise or annoyance no one knew.

"But I've grown an inch since then!"

"And I've grown three inches in one year," Kim Bee said.

"Ah Kong, your daughters are becoming women," Kim Li said in an aggressive voice. She was sitting to one side of her father, away from the table, not eating or drinking, kicking her long legs rhythmically throughout the meal. She wore her blue school shorts, which fitted tightly above the thighs and stretched across the bottom, flattening the weight which ballooned curiously around her tall skinny frame. Her legs, like her chest, were skinny, almost fleshless. They were long and shapeless; the knees bumped out like rock outcroppings, and the ankles rose to meet the backs of her knees with hardly a suggestion of a calf. In the tight shorts she didn't appear feminine or provocative, merely unbalanced, as if the fat around the hips and bottom were a growth, a goiter draped on the lean trunk.

Everyone suddenly stopped talking. Mother opened her mouth and brought out a gasp; the sisters stopped chewing and looked away into different directions. Kim Mee was furious because Ah Kong's face was reddening. There would be no money for new clothes if he lost his temper.

"And you, you are not dressed like a woman," he replied without looking at her. "How dare you come to the table like a half-naked slut!" He had always been careful to avoid such language in his house, but her aggressive interruption aroused him.

"At least I don't beg you for clothes. And what I wear is what you give me. It's not . . ."

"Shut up!" he roared. "You . . ."

"Go to your room," Mother said to Kim Li before he could finish. Her voice was placid as if such quarrels were an everyday occurrence. If Ah Kong's bunched-up brows and protruding veins all balled up like a fist above his bony beak put her off, she didn't show it. "Peng," she continued, sweet-natured as ever, "maybe tomorrow we can go over the cost of some new clothes. The girls can shop for some cheap materials, and Ah Chee and I will sew a few simple skirts and blouses. We won't have to pay a tailor. They'll be very simple clothes, of course, because it's been so long since I've stitched anything . . ." So she chatted on, rolling a cozy domestic mat before him, and soon, they were spreading more butter and drinking fresh cups of tea.

Kim Li did not leave the table till Ah Kong's attention was unraveled; then she stretched herself out of the chair, hummed, and sauntered to her room, casual as a cat and grinning from ear to ear. Her humming wasn't grating, but it was loud enough to reach the dining room. What could Ah Kong do about it? He had again slipped into silence, drowsing along with the buzz of feminine discussion, acknowledging that, Sunday, he would once again open his purse and drive off in the warm evening to their grateful good-byes.

But there was Saturday night and the evening meal late at nine and the soft hours till eleven when his girls would sit in the living room with long washed hair reading *Her World* and *Seventeen*, selecting patterns for their new frocks. And by midnight, everyone would be asleep.

There was Ah Chee snoring in her back room among empty cracker tins and washed Ovaltine jars. He had acquired her when his second wife had finally given in to his determined courting and, contrary to her Methodist upbringing, married him in a small Chinese ceremony. The three of them had moved in immediately after the ceremony to this large wooden house on Old Beach Road, and, gradually, as the rooms filled up with beds and daughters, so also Ah Chee's room had filled up with the remains of meals. She never threw out a tin, bottle, or jar. The banged-up tins and tall bottles she sold to the junk man; those biscuit tins stamped with gaudy roses or toffee tins painted with ladies in crinoline gowns or Royal Guardsmen in fat fur hats she hoarded and produced each New Year to fill with love letters, bean cakes, and *kueh bulu*. Ah Kong approved of her as much as, perhaps even more than, he approved of his wife. Her parsimonious craggy face, those strong bulging forearms, the loose folds of her black trousers flapping as she padded barefoot and cracked sole from kitchen to garden, from one tidied room to another waiting to be swept, these were elements he looked forward to each Friday as much as he looked forward to his wife's vague smile and soft shape in bed. Ah Chee had lived in the house for seventeen years, yet her influence was perceivable only in a few rooms.

Ah Kong seldom looked into Ah Chee's room, which, he knew, was a junk heap gathered around a narrow board bed with a chicken wire strung across the bare window. But, at midnight, when he rose to check the fastenings at the back door and the bolts on the front, he looked into every room where his daughters slept. Here was Bee's, connected to her parents' through a bathroom. A Bible lay on her bed. She slept, passionately hugging a bolster to her face, half-suffocated, the pajama top riding high and showing a midriff concave and yellow in the dimness. Across the central corridor Kim Yee stretched corpselike and rigid, as if she had willed herself to sleep or were still awake under the sleeping mask, the stuffed bear and rabbit exhibited at the foot of her bed like nursery props, unnecessary now that the play was over. He sniffed in Kim Mee's room; it smelt of talcum and hairspray. The memory of other rooms came to mind, rooms which disgusted him as he wrestled to victory with their occupants. But no pink satin pillows or red paper flowers were here; a centerfold of the British singers the Beatles was taped to one wall and blue checked curtains swayed in the night breeze. Kim Mee slept curled against her bolster. In a frilly babydoll, her haunches curved and enveloped the pillow like a woman with her lover. He hated the sight but didn't cover her in case she should wake. There was a time when he would walk through the house looking into every room, and each silent form would fill him with pleasure, that they should belong to him, depend on his homecoming, and fall asleep in his presence, innocent and pure. Now the harsh scent of hairspray stagnated in the air; its metallic fragrance was clammy and chilled, a cheap and thin cover over the daughter whose delicate limbs were crowned with an idol's head aureoled and agonized by bristling rollers. Again the recollection of disgust tinged his thoughts, and he hesitated before Kim Li's room. He didn't know what to expect anymore of his daughters, one spending her allowance on lipstick, nail polish, Blue Grass cologne, and this other somehow not seeming quite right.

Kim Li was not yet asleep. With knees raised up, she sat in bed reading in the minute diagonal light of the bed lamp. He stopped at the door but could not retreat quickly enough. She turned a baleful look. "What do you want?"

"It's twelve o'clock. Go to sleep," he said curtly, feeling that that was not exactly what he should say; however, he seldom had to think about what to say in this house, and his self-consciousness was extreme. Suddenly he noticed her. She had cut her hair short, when he couldn't tell. He remembered once noticing that her hair was long and that she had put it up in a ponytail, which made her unpretty face as small as his palm. Tonight, her hair was cropped short carelessly in the front and sides so that what might have been curls shot away from her head like bits of string. She's ugly! he thought and turned away, not staying to see if she would obey him.

He stayed awake most of the night. This had been true every Saturday night for many years. Sleeping through the mornings, drowsing in the lounge chair through the afternoons, and sitting somnolent through tea and dinner hours, his life, all expended in the noise, heat, and rackety shuttle of the mines during the week, would gradually flow back to being. The weakness that overcame him as soon as he arrived at the front door each Friday night would ebb away; slowly, the movements of women through the rooms returned to him a masculine vitality. Their gaiety aroused him to strength, and his mind began turning again, although at first numb and weary.

He was supine and passive all through Saturday, but by nightfall he was filled with nervous energy. After his shower he would enter his bedroom with head and shoulders erect. His round soft wife in her faded nightgown was exactly what he wanted then; he was firm next to her slack hips, lean against her plump rolling breasts; he could sink into her submissive form like a bull sinking into a mudbank, groaning with pleasure. Later, after she was asleep, his mind kept churning. Plans for the week ahead were meticulously laid: the lawyer to visit on Monday; the old *klong* to be shut and the machinery moved to the new site; Jason, his eldest son, to be talked to about his absences from the office; the monthly remittance to be sent to Wanda, his second daughter, in Melbourne; old Chong to be retired. His mind worked thus, energetically and unhesitatingly, while he listened to his daughters settle for the night, the bathrooms eventually quiet, Ah Chee dragging across the corridor to bolt the doors, and soft clicks as one light and then another was switched off. Then, after the clock struck its twelve slow chimes, he walked through the house, looking into each room while his mind and body ran in electrical fusion, each female form in bed renewing his pleasure with his life, leaving each room with a fresh vibrance to his body. So he would lie awake till the early hours of Sunday, calm yet vibrating strongly, breathing deeply, for he believed in the medicinal value of fresh night air, while his mind struggled with problems and resolved them for the next week.

Tonight, however, his sleeplessness was not pleasurable. Old, he thought, old and wasted his daughters had made him. He couldn't lie relaxed and immobile; the bodies of women surrounded him in an irritating swarm. He heard Kim Li slapping a book shut, footsteps moving toward the dining room; a refrigerator door opening and its motor running. "Stupid girl!" he muttered, thinking of the cold flooding out of the machine, ice melting in trays, the tropical heat corrupting the rectangles of butter still hard and satiny in their paper wrappers. But he didn't get up to reprimand her.

All day Ah Kong would not speak to Kim Li; this wouldn't have appeared out of the ordinary except that she sat in the sunroom with him most of the morning.

Kim Bee and Kim Yee escaped to church at nine. In white and pink, wearing their grown-up heels and hair parted in braids, they looked like brides-maids, ceremoniously stiff with a sparkle of excitement softening their faces. The Methodist Church was ten minutes' walk away. Mother no longer went to church, but her younger daughters went every Sunday, since it was still their mother's faith, and were greeted by women their mother's age, who sent regards but never visited themselves. The pastor was especially nice to them, having participated in the drama eighteen years ago.

She's a stray lamb. Those were barbaric times after the Japanese Occupation; otherwise, she would probably not have consented to live in sinful relationship as a second wife. And, although I suppose it doesn't matter who the sin is committed with, Mr. Tang is a well-known, respectable man. Her situation is more understandable when you know how careful and correct Mr. Tang is with everything concerning himself and his family. It's a pity he is so Chinese, although, of course, divorces weren't as acceptable until a few years ago, and, even now, one shouldn't encourage it. Yet, if only he would divorce his first wife, she could return to the Church and the children . . . They're lovely girls, all of them, although the oldest hasn't been to service in a while, and the second seems excitable. The two young ones are so good, volunteer-ing for the Sunday School Drive, singing in the choir (they have such sweet tones!)

and so cheerful. A little anxious about the Scriptures. They want to know especially what has been written about the Day of Judgment, which isn't surprising seeing . . . Now, if Mr. Tang weren't a pagan, he couldn't maintain this terrible life, keeping two households in separate towns, but, of course, he's old-fashioned and believes in the propriety of polygamy. Pagans have their own faith, I have no doubt, and Christ will consider this when the Day comes, but for the mother . . .

For Kim Bee and Kim Yee, Sunday service was one of the more enjoyable events in a dull weekend. Fresh as frangipani wreaths, they walked companionably to church, for once in full charge of themselves. They radiated health and cheerfulness from the hours of imposed rest, from their gladness at meeting the friends their parents never met but still approved of, and from the simple encouraging emotions of welcome, love, and forgiveness which welled up in hymns, and which were the open subjects of the pastor's sermon.

"Love, love, love," sang the choir. "Our Father, Our Father," they murmured and flooded their hearts with gratitude, with desire. Radiant, they returned from church at noon, in time for lunch and, later, to say good-bye to Ah Kong, who drove back to Kuala Lumpur every Sunday at two.

All morning Kim Li sat cross-legged on the floor next to Ah Kong's chair. Now and again she attempted to clip a toenail, but her toes seemed to have been too awkwardly placed, or, perhaps, she had grown too ungainly; she could not grip the foot securely. It wasn't unusual for the girls to sit on the floor by Ah Kong's feet. As children they had read the Sunday comics sprawled on the sunroom floor. Or Mother would bake scones, and they would eat them hot from the oven around their father. It was a scene he particularly savored, a floury, milling hour when he was most quiescent, feeling himself almost a baby held in the arms of his womanly family. This morning, however, Kim Li's struggles to clip her toenails forced his attention. Her silent contortions exaggerated by the shorts she was wearing bemused him. Was she already a woman as she had claimed last evening? Ah Kong felt a curious pity for her mixed with anger. Yes, he would have to marry her off. She moved her skinny legs and shot a look at him slyly as if to catch him staring. If she weren't his daughter, he thought, he could almost believe she was trying to arouse him. But he couldn't send her out of the room without admitting that she disturbed him. Once he had watched a bitch in heat lick itself and had kicked it in disgust. He watched her now and was nauseated at the prospect of his future: all his good little girls turning to bitches and licking themselves.

Leaving promptly at two, Mr. Tang told his wife that he might not be coming next Friday; he had unexpected business and would call. He didn't tell her he was planning to find a husband for Kim Li. Complaisant as his wife was, he suspected she might not like the idea of an arranged marriage; nor would the girls. By midweek, he had found a man for Kim Li, the assistant to his general manager, a capable, China-born, Chinese-educated worker who had left his wife and family in Fukien eleven years ago and now couldn't get them out; he'd been without a woman since and had recently advised his Clan Association that he was looking for a second wife. Chan Kow had worked well for Mr. Tang for eight years. What greater compliment to his employees than to marry one of them, albeit one in a supervisory position, to his daughter? Chan Kow was overwhelmed by the proposal; he wasn't worthy of the match; besides, he was thirty-three and Mr. Tang's young daughter might not want him. But he would be honored, deeply honored.

Ah Kong called Mother with the match sealed. Would she inform Kim Li and have her agreeable for a wedding in July, the next month, which was the date the fortune-teller had selected as propitious for the couple? When he arrived on Friday night, he was surprised and relieved to find the family unchanged by his precipitous decision. "You did the right thing," his wife said late at night after the girls had gone to their own rooms. "My goodness, I was afraid Kim Li would yell and scream. You don't know the tantrums she can throw. Well, she took it so calmly. Wanted to know his name, his age, what he looks like. The girls were quite upset. Kim Mee is so sensitive. She was crying because she was afraid you will arrange a marriage for her also, and I couldn't say a thing to her. But you should have seen Kim Li. She was so excited about it. Started boasting that soon she was going to be a married woman and so on."

Ah Kong grunted.

"I told her a married woman has all kinds of responsibilities. She's lucky she'll have a husband who'll take care of her, but she will have to learn to get along with him. Well, she didn't like that. She wants to let her hair grow long now, and she needs some new dresses and nightclothes, of course. And we have to shop for towels and sheets for when she goes to her own house . . ."

"Spend whatever you like," Ah Kong said, and his wife fell silent. He had never said that before. She began calculating all she could buy for the other girls and for the house as well as long as he was in a generous mood.

"When am I going to meet the lucky man, ha, ha!" Kim Li asked the next morning, appearing suddenly in the sunroom. Startled, he opened his eyes with a groan. He thought he might have been asleep and had wakened on a snore. "When am I going to meet this Chan Kow?" she repeated loudly. His wife came hurrying in from their bedroom next door. He said nothing and closed his eyes again. "Ah Kong, I want to meet my husband-to-be. Maybe I can go to Kuala Lumpur with you and have a date with him, ha, ha!" Behind his shut eyes, he sensed her looming figure; her voice had grown strident.

Without opening his eyes, he said, "In an arranged marriage, the woman doesn't see the man till the day of the wedding. You can have a photograph of Chan Kow if you like."

"No, I want to go out with him first."

"Kim Li, you're having a traditional wedding. The man cannot go out with the woman until after they're married," the mother said in a mild tone. "You mustn't spoil the match by acting in a Western manner."

The other three girls huddled by the door listening to the argument. Kim Mee felt a great sympathy for her sister. It wasn't fair of Ah Kong to rush off and pick a husband for Kim Li. What about love? It was true that Kim Li was stupid and had been rude to Ah Kong, but this wasn't China. She wouldn't accept such an arranged marriage even if it meant that she had to leave home and support herself. She looked at her sister curiously. Imagine, she would be married next month! In bed with a stranger, an old man who only speaks Chinese! Kim Mee couldn't think of a worse fate.

Kim Li left the sunroom scowling; her mother couldn't persuade her that she didn't have a right to a few dates with Chan Kow. She didn't appear for tea, and, all through Sunday, she was languid; she walked slowly through the rooms as if she were swimming underwater, lazily moving one leg and then the other, falling into every chair on her way, and staring blankly at the walls. Ah Kong ignored her; she was as good as out of the house.

When he came back next Friday, Kim Li had gone through a total change. "I'm a woman now," she had said to her sisters and began using Kim Mee's makeup every day. She penciled her eyebrows crudely, rubbed two large red patches on her cheeks, and drew in wide lips with the brightest crimson lipstick in Kim Mee's collection. After every meal, she went to her room and added more color. Blue shadow circled her eyes, and her clumsy application of the mascara stick left blotches below her lids like black tearstains. She teased her short hair into a bush of knots and sprayed cologne till it dripped down her neck. Kim Mee didn't complain. Her sister who roamed up and down the house peering into every mirror and rubbing the uneven patches on her face had all her sympathy. To be married off just like that! No wonder Kim Li was acting crazy.

Ah Kong stood at the door afraid. No, he could not possibly allow Chan Kow to meet his daughter before the wedding, this painted woman who was smiling at him provocatively from her bedroom door. He could not understand from where Kim Li had picked up her behavior; in her blue shorts with her wide hips tilted, she presented a picture he was familiar with and had never associated with his home. No, his wife was always submissive, a good woman who could never suggest an immodest action. Was there something innate about a woman's evil that no amount of proper education or home life could suppress? It was good she was marrying soon, for her stance, her glances, her whole appearance indicated a lewd desire. He turned his eyes away from her and stayed in his room all night.

Lying in bed on Saturday morning, he asked the mother to take the girls to town. "I've work to do, and they are too noisy," he said. He was very tired. That he had to lie to his wife with whom he'd always had his way! He felt this other half of life falling apart. The shelter he had built for eighteen years was splintered by the very girls he supported, by their wagging hips and breasts.

"I don't wanna go," Kim Li was yelling. "I'm setting my hair."

"You must come along," Mother was patient. "We're shopping for your trousseau. You have to pick your clothes. Then we're going to the tailor shop and you have to be measured."

"All right, all right. I'm going to be a married woman, ha ha! Do you wanna know about my wedding night, Kim Mee? You have to be nice to me. I'll have all kinds of secrets then."

Only after the front door shut behind their chatter did Mr. Tang go to the sunroom, where Ah Chee had pulled down and closed the louvers. Next to his chair she had placed a plate of freshly ripened cikus. Because it grew so close to salty water, the tree usually bore small bitter fruit, but this season, it was loaded with large brown fruit which needed only a few days in the rice bin to soften to a sweet pulp. Stubbornly refusing to throw any out, Ah Chee was serving ciku to everyone every day. Mr. Tang slowly lowered himself onto his green leather chaise. Using the fruit knife carefully, he peeled a fruit. It was many years since he had last tasted one. Juice splattered onto his pajamas. He spat out the long shiny black seeds on the plate. His hands were sticky with pulp, but he kept them carelessly on the arms of his chair and let his head drop back. Gradually the cool dark room merged into his vision; Ah Chee's banging in the kitchen faded, and the silence flowed around his shallow breathing, flowed and overcame it until he felt himself almost asleep.

A body pressed against him softly. It was his wife's rolling on him in their sleep. He sighed and shifted his weight to accommodate her. The body was thin and sharp; it pressed against him in a clumsy embrace. He opened his eyes and saw Kim Li's black and blue eyes tightly shut, her white and red face screwed up in a smile. His heart was hammering urgently; he could feel his jaws tighten as if at the taste of something sour. "Bitch!" he shouted and slapped her hard. Kim Li's eyes blazed open. He saw her turn, pick something up, and turn to him again with her arms open as if in a gesture of love or hope. Then he felt the knife between his ribs. Just before he fell into the black water, he saw the gleaming fish eyes of the fish woman rise from the *klong* to greet him.

MARTYRDOM

Yukio Mishima

Japan

A diminutive Demon King ruled over the dormitory. The school in question was a place where large numbers of sons of the aristocracy were put through their paces. Equipped by the age of thirteen or fourteen with a coldness of heart and an arrogance of spirit worthy of many a grown-up, they were placed in this dormitory in their first year at middle school in order to experience communal life; this was one of the traditions of the spartan education, devised several decades earlier by the principal of the school, General Ogi. The members of any one year had all been to the same primary school, so that their training in mischief had taken thorough effect in the six years before entering the dormitory, and facilitated an astonishing degree of collaboration among them. A "graveyard" would be arranged in a corner of the classroom with a row of markers bearing the teachers' names; a trap would be set so that when an elderly, bald teacher came into the room a blackboard duster fell precisely onto his bald patch, coating it with white; on a winter morning, a lump of snow would be flung to stick on the ceiling, bright in the morning sun, so that it dripped steadily onto the teacher's platform; the matches in the teachers' room would be mysteriously transformed into things that spouted sparks like fireworks when struck; a dozen drawing pins would be introduced into the chair where the teacher sat, with their points just showing above the surface—these and a host of other schemes that seemed the work of unseen elves were all in fact carried out by two or three masterminds and a band of well-trained terrorists.

"Come on—let's see it! What's wrong with showing me anyway?"

The older boy who had turned up in the lunch break lounged astride the broken dormitory chair. He could sense the itching curiosity in himself that crawled vaguely, like soft incipient beard, right up to his ears, but in trying to conceal it from the other, his junior by a year, he was only making his face turn all the pinker. At the same time, it was necessary to sit in as slovenly a way as possible in order to show his independence of the rules.

"I'll show you, don't worry. But you'll have to wait another five minutes. What's up, K?—it's not like you to be so impatient."

The Demon King spoke boldly, gazing steadily at the older boy with mild, beautiful eyes. He was well developed for a mere fourteen, and looked in fact at least sixteen or seventeen. He owed his physique to something called the "Danish method" of child rearing—which involved among other things dangling the baby by one leg and kneading its soft, plump body like so much dough—and to the fact that he'd been brought up in a Western house with huge plate-glass windows standing on high ground in the Takanawa district of Tokyo, where breezes borne on bright wings from the distant sea would occasionally visit the lawn. Naked, he had the figure of a young man. During physical checkups, when the other boys were pale with dire embarrassment, he was a Daphnis surveying his nanny goats with cool, scornful eyes.

The dormitory was the farthest from the main school buildings, and the Demon King's room on the second floor looked out over the shimmering May woods covering the gentle slope of the school grounds. The long grass and undergrowth seemed almost tipsy as it swayed in the wind. It was morning, and the chirping of the birds in the woods was particularly noisy. Now and again, a pair of them would take off from the sea of young foliage and fly up like fish leaping from its surface, only to produce a sudden, furious twittering, turn a somersault, and sink down again between the waves of greenery.

When K, his senior, came to see him in his room bearing sandwiches and the like, it had been instantly apparent to the Demon King—young Hatakeyama—that the motive was a desire to see the book that everyone found so fascinating. To tease a senior pupil over something of this sort gave him a sweet sense of complicity, as though he too were being teased.

"Five minutes is up."

"No it isn't—it's only three minutes yet."

"It's five minutes!"

Quite suddenly, Hatakeyama gave him an almost girlish smile, the vulnerable smile of someone who had never yet had anyone be rude to him.

"Oh well, I suppose it can't be helped," he said. "I'll let you see it."

With his left hand thrust in his trouser pocket, as was his usual habit (in imitation of a cousin, a college student, whom he'd much admired for the way he let his shiny metal watchstrap show between the pocket and his sweater), he went lazily to open the bookcase. There, among the textbooks that he'd never once laid hands on after returning to the dorm, and the books his parents had bought for him—a grubby *Collected Boys' Tales*, the *Jungle Book*, and *Peter Pan* in paperback editions—there ought to have stood a volume with *"Plutarch's Lives"* inscribed in immature lettering on its spine. This book, whose red cover he had wrapped in uninviting brown paper and labeled with a title that he had memorized from a work of about the same thickness seen in the library, was constantly being passed from hand to hand, during classes and in recess alike. People would have been startled to find, on the page that should have portrayed a statue of Alexander the Great, an odd, complex sectional diagram in color.

"It's no use suddenly pretending you can't find it!" Gazing at the Demon King's rear view as he ferreted through the contents of the bookshelves, K was less concerned with the desire to see the book as such than with making sure, first, that he wasn't cheated by this formidable younger schoolmate, and then that he didn't put himself at a disadvantage by clumsy bullying.

"Somebody's stolen it!" shouted Hatakeyama, standing up. He'd been looking down as he searched, and his face was flushed, his eyes gleaming. Rushing to his desk, he frantically opened and closed each drawer in turn, talking to himself all the while:

"I made a point of getting everyone who came to borrow that book to sign for it. I mean, I couldn't have people taking my stuff out without my permission, could I? That book was the class's special secret. It meant a lot to everybody. I was particularly careful with it—I'd never have let anyone I didn't like read it. . . ."

"It's a bit late to get so angry about it, surely," said K with an assumed maturity, then, noticing the brutal glint in Hatakeyama's eye, suddenly shut up. More than anything, the look reminded him of a child about to kill a snake.

"I'm *sure* it's Watari," said his crony Komiyama, writing the name "Watari" twice in small letters on the blackboard and pointing to the bright-lit doorway through which the boy in question, by himself as usual, had just gone out into the school yard. Beyond the doorway a cloud was visible, smooth and glossy, floating in the sky beyond the spacious playground. Its shadow passed ponderously across the ground.

"Watari? Come off it! What does a kid like him understand about a book like that?"

"A lot—you wait and see! Haven't you ever heard of the quiet lecher? It's types with saintly expressions like him who're most interested in that kind of thing. Try barging in on him in his room tonight before supper, when all the rest have gone for exercise and there's nobody in the dorm. You'll see!"

Alone of their group, Watari had come to them from another primary school, and was thus a comparative outsider. There was something about him that kept others at a distance. Although he was particular about his clothes—he changed his shirt every day—he would go for weeks without cutting his nails, which were always an unhealthy black. His skin was a yellowish, lusterless white like a gardenia. His lips, in contrast, were so red that you wanted to rub them with your finger to see if he was wearing lipstick. Seen close to, it was an astonishingly beautiful face, though from a distance quite unprepossessing. He reminded you of an art object in which excessive care over detail has spoiled the effect of the whole; the details were correspondingly seductive in a perverse way.

He had begun to be bullied almost as soon as he appeared at the school. He gave the impression of looking disapprovingly on the tendency, common to all boys, to worship toughness as a way of making up for their awareness of the vulnerability peculiar to their age. If anything, Watari sought to preserve the vulnerability. The young man who seeks to be himself is respected by his fellows; the boy who tries to do the same is persecuted by other boys, it being a boy's business to become something else just as soon as he can.

Watari had the habit, whenever he was subjected to particularly vile treatment by his companions, of casting his eyes up at the clear blue sky. The habit was itself another source of mockery.

"Whenever he's picked on, he stares up at the sky as if he was Christ," said M, the most persistent of his tormentors. "And you know, when he does it, his nose tips back so you can see right up his nostrils. He keeps his nose so well blown, it's a pretty pink color round the edges inside. . . ."

Watari was, of course, banned from seeing *"Plutarch's Lives."*

The sun had set on all but the trees in the woods. The dark mass of foliage, minutely catching the lingering rays of the setting sun, trembled like the flame of a guttering candle. As he stealthily opened the door and went in, the first thing Hatakeyama saw was the wavering trees through the window directly ahead. The sight of Watari registered next; he was seated at his desk, gazing down with his head in his delicate white hands, intent on something. The open pages of the book and the hands stood out in white relief.

He turned around at the sound of footsteps. The next instant, his hands covered the book with an obstinate strength.

Moving swiftly and easily across the short space that separated them, Hatakeyama had seized him by the scruff of the neck almost before he realized it himself. Watari's large, expressionless eyes, wide open like a rabbit's, were suddenly close to his own face. He felt his knees pressing into the boy's belly, eliciting a strange sound from it as he sat on the chair; then he knocked aside the hands that tried to cling to him, and dealt a smart slap to his cheek. The flesh looked soft, as though it might stay permanently dented. For one moment, indeed, Watari's face seemed to tilt in the direction in which it had been struck, assuming an oddly placid, helpless expression. But then the cheek rapidly flooded with red and a thin, stealthy trickle of blood ran from the finely shaped nostrils. Seeing it, Hatakeyama felt a kind of pleasant nausea. Taking hold of the collar of Watari's blue shirt, he dragged him toward the bed, moving with unnecessarily large strides as though dancing. Watari let himself be dragged, limp as a puppet; curiously, he didn't seem to grasp the situation he was in, but gazed steadily at the evening sky over the woods with their lingering light. Or perhaps those big, helpless eyes simply let in the evening light quite passively, taking in the sky without seeing anything. The blood from his nose, though, cheerfully seemed to flaunt its glossy brightness as it dribbled down his mouth and over his chin.

"You thief!"

Dumping Watari on the bed, Hatakeyama climbed onto it himself and started trampling and kicking him. The bed creaked, sounding like ribs breaking. Watari had his eyes shut in terror. At times, he bared his over-regular teeth and gave a thin wail like a small sick bird. Hatakeyama thumped him in the side for a while, then, seeing that he had turned toward the wall and gone still, like a corpse, jumped down from the bed in one great leap. As a finishing touch, he remembered to thrust one guilty hand elegantly into the pocket of his narrow slacks and tilt himself slightly to one side. Then, whisking up *"Plutarch's Lives"* from the desk with his right hand, he tucked it stylishly under his arm and ran up the stairs to his second-floor room.

He had read the dubious book in question quite a few times. Each time, the first frenzied excitement seemed to fade a little. Recently in fact he had begun to get more pleasure, if anything, out of observing the powerful spell the book exerted over his friends as they read it for the first time. But now, reading it again himself after getting it back and roughing up Watari in the process, the original, wild excitement emerged as a still fiercer pleasure. He couldn't get through a single page at a time. Each appearance of one of those words of almost mystic power brought a myriad associations crowding, plunged him into an ever deeper intoxication. His breath grew shallower, his hand trembled, the bell for supper that happened just then to resound through the dormitory almost made him panic: how could he appear before the others in this state? He had entirely forgotten Watari.

That night, a dream woke Hatakeyama from a troubled sleep. The dream had led him to the lairs of various illnesses that he had suffered from in childhood. In actual fact, few children could have been healthier than he: the only illnesses he'd succumbed to were of the order of whooping cough, measles, and intestinal catarrh. Nevertheless, the diseases in his dream were all acquainted with him, and greeted him accordingly. Whenever one of them approached him, there was a disagreeable smell; if he tried to shove it away, "disease" transferred itself stickily to his hand like oil paint. One disease was even tickling his throat with its finger. . . .

When he awoke, he found himself staring, wide-eyed like a rabbit, in just the way that Watari had done earlier that day. And there, floating above the covers, was Watari's startled face, a mirror of his own. As their eyes met, the face rose slowly into the air.

Hatakeyama let out a high-pitched yell. At least, he thought he did: in fact his voice rose only as far as his throat.

Something was pressing down steadily, with cold hands, on his throat; yet the pressure was slight enough to be half pleasant. Deciding that it was a continuation of his dream after all, he extracted a hand unhurriedly from the bedclothes and stroked himself experimentally around the neck. It appeared that something like a cloth sash, about two inches wide, had been wrapped snugly around it.

He had the courage and good sense to fling it off without further ado. He sat up in bed, looking much older than he was, more like a young man of twenty. A chain of ivory clouds, lit up by the moon, was passing across the window outside, so that he was silhouetted against it like the statue of some god of old.

The thing that crouched like a dog at the foot of the bed had a white, human face turned resolutely toward him. It seemed to be breathing heavily, for the face as a whole appeared to swell and shrink; the eyes alone were still, overflowing with a shining light as they gazed, full of hostility (or was it longing?), at Hatakeyama's shadowed features.

"Watari. You came to get even, didn't you?"

Watari said nothing, the lips that were like a rose in the dark night quivering painfully. Finally, he said as though in a dream:

"I'm sorry."

"You wanted to kill me, I suppose."

"I'm sorry." He made no attempt to run away, simply repeating the same phrase.

Without warning, Hatakeyama flew at him and, propelled by the bed-springs, carried him face down onto the floor. There, kneeling astride him, he subjected him to a full twenty minutes' violence. "I'm going to make sure you feel ashamed in front of everyone in the bath!" he promised, then splashed his bare buttocks with blue-black ink; prodded them with the points of a pair of compasses to see their reaction; reared up, hauling the boy up by the ears as he did so. . . . He was brilliantly methodical, as though everything had been thought out in advance. There was no chance, even, for Watari to look up at the sky this time. He lay still, his cheek pressed against a join in the linoleum.

Two boys were allotted to each room in the dormitory, but Hatakeyama's roommate was home on sick leave. So long as he was careful not to be overheard downstairs, Hatakeyama could do as he wished.

Eventually, both of them began to tire. Before they realized it they were dozing, sprawled on the floor; Watari had even forgotten to cover his pale behind.

Their nap lasted no more than a moment. Hatakeyama awoke first. Pillowing his chin on clasped hands, he gazed at the moonlit window. All that was visible from the floor where he lay was the sky. The moon was below the frame of the window, but two or three clouds could be seen in the sky's fullness of limpid light. The scene had the impersonal clarity, precision, and fineness of detail of a scene reflected in the polished surface of a piece of machinery. The clouds seemed stationed as immovably as some majestic man-made edifice.

An odd desire awoke in Hatakeyama, taking him by surprise. It wasn't so much a break with the mood of tranquillity as a natural transition from it, and in a strange way it was linked with the terrifying sensation of the cord around his neck that he'd experienced a while before. This, he thought, is the fellow who tried to kill me. And suddenly a peculiar sense of both superiority and inferiority, a nagging humiliation at not in fact having been killed, made it impossible for him to stay still.

"You asleep?" he said.

"No," said Watari. As he replied, his eyes turned to look straight at Hatakeyama. He began to stretch out his thin right arm, then drew it in again and pressed it to his side, saying,

"It hurts here."

"Really? Does it *really* hurt?"

Hatakeyama rolled over twice. It brought him a little too close, so that he was lying half on top of Watari. Just as this happened, the latter gave a faint little chuckle, a sound—like the cry of a shellfish—he had never heard before. The

Demon King sought out the sound, then pressed his whole face against Watari's lips and the soft down around them.

There was something going on between Hatakeyama and Watari: their classmates passed on the rumor in hushed voices. The scandal possessed a mysterious power; thanks to it, Hatakeyama became increasingly influential, and even Watari was taken into their circle. The process was similar to that whereby a woman so far generally ignored suddenly acquires value in everyone's eyes if the dandy of the group takes a fancy to her. And it was totally unclear how Hatakeyama himself responded to this general reaction.

Before long, it was felt that his authority as Demon King required some kind of strict legal system. They would draft the necessary laws during their English and spelling lessons. The criminal code, for example, must be an arbitrary one, based on the principle of intimidation. A strong urge to self-regulation had awoken in the boys. One morning in the dormitory, the gang insisted that their leader pick out someone for them to punish. They were sitting in their chairs in a variety of bizarre postures; some were not so much seated in them as clinging to them. One first-grader had turned his chair upside down and was sitting holding on to two projecting legs.

"Hatakeyama—you've got to name somebody. You name him, and the rest of us'll deal with him. Isn't there anyone who's been getting above himself lately?"

"No, no one." He spoke in a surly voice, his mature-looking back turned to them.

"You sure? Then we'll choose the person ourselves."

"Wait a minute! What I said wasn't true. Listen: I'll name someone. But I won't say why."

They waited breathlessly; there wasn't one of them who didn't want to hear his own name mentioned.

"Where's Watari?"

"Watari?—he went off somewhere just now."

"OK, it's him. He's been getting uppish. If we don't put a stop to it, he'll get completely out of hand."

This was pure imitation of fifth-grader talk. Even so, having got it out, Hatakeyama looked cheerfully relieved, like someone remembering something till then forgotten. It provoked a happy clamor among the others:

"Let's fix the time—the lunch break!"

"And the place—by Chiarai Pond."

"I'll take my jackknife."

"And I'll bring a rope. If he struggles we can tie him up."

* * *

On a pond already green with slime the surrounding trees spread an even reflection of lush young foliage, so that anyone who walked beside it was steeped in its green light. They were all privately enjoying the important sound of their own feet tramping through the bamboo grass, and the party with Hatakeyama and Watari at its center exchanged no words. Watari showed no sign of fear as he walked, a fact that had a disturbing effect on his classmates, as though they were watching a very sick man, supposedly on his last legs, suddenly striding along. From time to time, he glanced up at the sky visible through the new leaves of the treetops. But the others were all too sunk in their own thoughts for anyone to remark on his behavior. Hatakeyama walked with long strides, head bent, left hand in pocket. He avoided looking at Watari.

Halting, Hatakeyama raised both arms in their rolled-up sleeves above his head:

"Stop! Quiet!"

An elderly gardener was pushing a wheelbarrow along the path above them toward the flower beds.

"Well, well—up to some mischief, I suppose," he said, seeing them.

"Dirty old scrounger!" someone replied. It was rumored that the old man lived off free dormitory leftovers.

"He's gone." M gave a signal with his eyes.

"Right. Here, Watari—"

For the first time, Hatakeyama looked straight into his eyes. Both Watari and his companions had unusually grave expressions.

"You've been getting too big for your boots."

No more was said: the sentence was passed; but nothing was done to carry it out. The judge stood with bare arms folded, slowly stroking them with his fingertips. . . . At that moment, Watari seemed to see his chance. Quite suddenly, he lunged toward Hatakeyama as though about to cling to him. Behind the latter lay the pond. As he braced his legs, stones and soil rolled down into it with a faint splashing. That was the only sound; to those around them, the two seemed locked in an embrace, silently consoling each other. But in steadying himself to avoid falling backward, Hatakeyama had exposed his arms to an attack already planned. Watari's teeth—regular and sharp as a girl's, or perhaps a cat's—sank into his young flesh. Blood oozed out along the line between teeth and skin, yet biter and bitten remained still. Hatakeyama didn't even groan.

A slight movement separated them. Wiping his lips, more crimson than ever with the blood, Watari stood still, his eyes fixed on Hatakeyama's wound. A second or two before the members of the group had grasped what had happened, Watari had started running. But his pursuers were six tough boys. He lost his footing on the clay by the pond. He resisted, so that his blue shirt tore to give a glimpse of one shoulder, almost pathologically white. The boy with the rope tied his hands behind his back. His trousers, soiled by the red clay, were an oddly bright, shiny color.

Hatakeyama had made no move to chase him. His left hand was thrust casually into his pocket, with no care for his wound. The blood dripped down steadily, making a red rim around the glass of his wristwatch, then seeping from his fingertips into the bottom of his pocket. He felt no pain, aware only of something that hardly seemed like blood, something warm and familiar and intensely personal, caressing the surface of his skin as it went. But he had made up his mind on one thing: in his friend's faces when they brought Watari back, he would see nothing but an embodiment of his own decision, inviting him to proceed.

After that, he didn't look at Watari but gazed steadily at the long rope to which he was tied, with the slack wound round and round him and its end held in the hand of one of his classmates.

"Let's go somewhere quiet," he said. "The little wood behind the pigeon lofts."

Prodded, Watari began walking. As they filed along the red clay path, he staggered again and fell to his knees. With a coarse "heave-ho," they yanked him to his feet. His shoulder stood out so white in the light reflected from the foliage that it was as though the bone was sticking out of the rent in his blue shirt.

All the time as Watari walked, the incorrigible M hung about him, tickling him under the arms, pinching his backside, roaring with laughter because the boy, he said, had looked up at the sky. What if he had known that only two things in the whole world were visible to Watari's eyes: the blue sky—the eye of God, forever striking down into men's eyes through the green leaves of the treetops—and the precious blood spilled on his own account down here on earth, the lifeblood staining Hatakeyama's arm? His gaze went continually from one to the other of these two things. Hatakeyama was looking straight ahead, walking with a confident step more adult than any adult's. On his left arm, just in front of Watari, the blood was slowly drying, showing up a bright purple whenever it passed through the sun's rays.

The grove behind the pigeon lofts was a sunny patch of widely spaced trees, little frequented, where the pigeons often came to pass the time. An undistinguished collection of smallish deciduous trees, it had, at its very center, one great pine with gently outstretched branches on which the birds were fond of lining up to coo at one another. The rays of the afternoon sun picked out the trunk of the pine in a bright, pure light so that the resin flowing from it looked like veins of agate.

Hatakeyama came to a halt and said to the boy holding the rope:

"All right—this'll do. Take the rope off Watari. But don't let him get away. Throw the thing up like a lasso and put it over that big branch on the pine tree."

The rich jest of this sent the others into ecstasies. Watari was being held down by two of them. The remaining four danced like little demons on the grass as they helped hitch up the rope. One end of it was tied in a loop. Then one of the boys mounted a handy tree stump, poked his head through the noose, and stuck out his tongue.

"That's no good—it'll have to be higher."

The boy who'd stuck his tongue out was the shortest of them all. Watari would need at least another two or three inches.

They were all scared, scared by the occasional, shadowy suggestion that their prank might possibly be in earnest. As they led Watari, pale and trembling slightly, to the waiting noose, one waggish youth delivered a funeral address. All the while, Watari continued to gaze up at the sky with his idiotically wide-open eyes.

Abruptly, Hatakeyama raised a hand by way of a signal. His eyes were shut tight.

The rope went up.

Startled by the sudden beating of many pigeons' wings and by the glow on Watari's beautiful face, astonishingly high above them, they fled the grove, each in a different direction, unable to bear the thought of staying at the scene of such dire murder.

They ran at a lively pace, each boyish breast still swelling with the pride of having killed someone.

A full thirty minutes later, they reentered the wood as though by agreement and, huddling together, gazed up fearfully at the branch of the great pine.

The rope was dangling free, the hanged corpse nowhere to be seen.

Translated by John Bester

ONE SUNDAY

Rohinton
Mistry

India

Najamai was getting ready to lock up her flat in Firozsha Baag and take the train to spend the day with her sister's family in Bandra.

She bustled her bulk around, turning the keys in the padlocks of her seventeen cupboards, then tugged at each to ensure the levers had tumbled properly. Soon, she was breathless with excitement and exertion.

Her breathlessness reminded her of the operation she had had three years ago to remove fat tissue from the abdomen and breasts. The specialist had told her, "You will not notice any great difference in the mirror. But you will appreciate the results when you are over sixty. It will keep you from sagging."

Here she was at fifty-five, and would soon know the truth of his words if merciful God kept her alive for five more years. Najamai did not question the ways of merciful God, even though her Soli was taken away the very year after first Dolly and then Vera went abroad for higher studies.

Today would be the first Sunday that the flat would be empty for the whole day. "In a way it is good," she reflected, "that Tehmina next door and the Boyces downstairs use my fridge as much as they do. Anyone who has evil intentions about my empty flat will think twice when he sees the coming-going of neighbours."

Temporarily reconciled towards the neighbours whom she otherwise regarded as nuisances, Najamai set off. She nodded at the boys playing in the
compound. Outside, it did not feel as hot, for there was a gentle breeze. She felt
at peace with the world. It was a twenty-minute walk, and there would be plenty
of time to catch the ten-fifteen express. She would arrive at her sister's well before
lunch-time.

At eleven-thirty Tehmina cautiously opened her door and peered out. She made
certain that the hallway was free of the risk of any confrontation with a Boyce on
the way to Najamai's fridge. "It is shameful the way those people misuse the poor
lady's goodness," thought Tehmina. "All Najamai said when she bought the fridge
was to please feel free to use it. It was only out of courtesy. Now those Boyces
behave as if they have a share in the ownership of the fridge."

She shuffled out in slippers and duster-coat, clutching one empty glass and
the keys to Najamai's flat. She reeked of cloves, lodged in her mouth for two
reasons: it kept away her attacks of nausea and alleviated her chronic toothaches.

Cursing the poor visibility in the hallway, Tehmina, circumspect, moved
on. Even on the sunniest of days, the hallway persisted in a state of half-light.
She fumbled with the locks, wishing her cataracts would hurry and ripen for
removal.

Inside at last, she swung open the fridge door to luxuriate in the delicious
rush of cold air. A curious-looking package wrapped in plastic caught her eye; she
squeezed it, sniffed at it, decided against undoing it. The freezer section was almost
bare; the Boyces' weekly packets of beef had not yet arrived.

Tehmina placed two ice-cubes in the empty glass she had brought along—
the midday drink of chilled lemonade was as dear to her as the evening Scotch and
soda—and proceeded to lock up the place. But she was startled in her battle with
Najamai's locks and bolts by footsteps behind her.

"Francis!"

Francis did odd jobs. Not just for Tehmina and Najamai in C Block, but for
anyone in Firozsha Baag who required his services. This was his sole means of
livelihood ever since he had been laid off or dismissed, it was never certain which,
from the furniture store across the road where he used to be a delivery boy. The
awning of that store still provided the only roof he had ever known. Strangely, the
store owner did not mind, and it was a convenient location—all that Tehmina or
Najamai or any of the other neighbours had to do was lean out of their verandas
and wave or clap hands and he would come.

Grinning away as usual, Francis approached Tehmina.

"Stop staring, you idiot," started Tehmina, "and check if this door is
properly locked."

"Yes, *bai*. But when will Najamai return? She said she would give me some work today."

"Never. Could not be for today. She won't be back till very late. You must have made a mistake." With a loud suck she moved the cloves to the other cheek and continued, "So many times I've told you to open your ears and listen properly when people tell you things. But no. You never listen."

Francis grinned again and shrugged his shoulders. In order to humour Tehmina he replied, "Sorry, *bai*, it is my mistake." He stood only about five feet two but possessed strength which was out of all proportion to his light build. Once, in Tehmina's kitchen during a cleaning spree he had picked up the stone slab used for grinding spices. It weighed at least fifty pounds, and it was the way in which he lifted it, between thumb and fingertips, that amazed Tehmina. Later, she had reported the incident to Najamai. The two women had marvelled at his strength, giggling at Tehmina's speculation that he must be built like a bull.

As humbly as possible Francis now asked, "Do you have any work for me today?"

"No. And I do not like it, you skulking here in the hallway. When there is work we will call you. Now go away."

Francis left. Tehmina could be offensive, but he needed the few paise the neighbours graciously let him earn and the leftovers Najamai allowed him whenever there were any. So he returned to the shade of the furniture store awning.

While Tehmina was chilling her lemonade with Najamai's ice, downstairs, Silloo Boyce cleaned and portioned the beef into seven equal packets. She disliked being obligated to Najamai for the fridge, though it was a great convenience. "Besides," she argued with herself, "we do enough to pay her back, every night she borrows the newspaper. And every morning I receive her milk and bread so she does not have to wake up early. Madam will not even come down, my sons must carry it upstairs." Thus she mused and reasoned each Sunday, as she readied the meat in plastic bags which her son Kersi later stacked in Najamai's freezer.

Right now, Kersi was busy repairing his cricket bat. The cord around the handle had come unwound and had gathered in a black cluster at its base, leaving more than half the length of the handle naked. It looked like a clump of pubic hair, Kersi thought, as he untangled the cord and began gluing it back around the handle.

The bat was a size four, much too small for him, and he did not play a lot of cricket any more. But for some reason he continued to care for it. The willow still possessed spring enough to send a ball to the boundary line, in glaring contrast to his brother Percy's bat. The latter was in sad shape. The blade was dry and cracked in places; the handle, its rubber grip and cord having come off long ago, had split; and the joint where the blade met the handle was undone. But Percy did not care. He never had really cared for cricket, except during that one year when the Australian team was visiting, when he had spent whole days glued to the radio, listening to the commentary. Now it was aeroplanes all the time, model kits over which he spent hours, and Biggles books in which he buried himself.

But Kersi had wanted to play serious cricket ever since primary school. In the fifth standard he was finally chosen for the class team. On the eve of the match, however, the captain contracted mumps, and the vice-captain took over, promptly relegating Kersi to the extras and moving up his own crony. That was the end of serious cricket for Kersi. For a short while, his father used to take him and his Firozsha Baag friends to play at the Marine Drive *maidaan* on Sunday mornings. And nowadays, they played a little in the compound. But it was not the same. Besides, they were interrupted all the time by people like that mean old Rustomji in A Block. Of all the neighbours who yelled and scolded, Rustomji-the-curmudgeon did the loudest and the most. He always threatened to confiscate their bat and ball if they didn't stop immediately.

Kersi now used his bat mainly for killing rats. Rat poison and a variety of traps were also employed with unflagging vigilance. But most of the rat population, with some rodent sixth sense, circumnavigated the traps. Kersi's bat remained indispensable.

His mother was quite proud of his skill, and once she had bragged about it to Najamai upstairs: "So young, and yet so brave, the way he runs after the ugly things. And he never misses." This was a mistake, because Kersi was promptly summoned the next time Najamai spied a rat in her flat. It had fled into the daughters' room and Kersi rushed in after it. Vera had just finished her bath and was not dressed. She screamed, first when she saw the rat, and again, when Kersi entered after it. He found it hard to keep his eyes on the rat—it escaped easily. Soon after, Vera had gone abroad for higher studies, following her sister Dolly's example.

The first time that Kersi successfully used his bat against a rat, it had been quite messy. Perhaps it was the thrill of the chase, or his rage against the invader, or just an ignorance about the fragility of that creature of fur and bone. The bat had come down with such vehemence that the rat was badly squashed. A dark red stain had oozed across the floor, almost making him sick. He discovered how sticky that red smear was only when he tried to wipe it off with an old newspaper.

The beef was now ready for the freezer. With seven packets of meat, and Najamai's latchkeys in his pocket, Kersi plodded upstairs.

When Najamai's daughters had gone abroad, they took with them the youthful sensuality that once filled the flat, and which could drive Kersi giddy with excitement on a day like this, with no one home, and all before him the prospect of exploring Vera and Dolly's bedroom, examining their undies that invariably lay scattered around, running his hands through lacy frilly things, rubbing himself with these and, on one occasion, barely rescuing them from a sticky end. Now, exploration would yield nothing but Najamai's huge underclothes. Kersi could not think of them as bras and panties—their vastness forfeited the right to these dainty names.

Feeling sadness, loss, betrayal, he descended the stairs lifelessly. Each wooden step, with the passage of years and the weight of tenants, was worn to concavity, and he felt just as worn. Not so long ago, he was able to counter spells of low spirits and gloominess by turning to his Enid Blyton books. A few minutes was all it took before he was sharing the adventures of the Famous Five or the Secret Seven, an idyllic existence in a small English village, where he would play with dogs, ride horses in the meadows, climb hills, hike through the countryside, or, if the season was right, build a snowman and have a snowball fight.

But lately, this had refused to work, and he got rid of the books. Percy had made fun of him for clinging to such silly and childish fantasy, inviting him to share, instead, the experience of aerial warfare with Biggles and his men in the RAF.

Everything in Firozsha Baag was so dull since Pesi *paadmaroo* had been sent away to boarding school. And all because of that sissy Jehangir, the Bulsara Bookworm.

Francis was back in the hallway, and was disappointed when Kersi did not notice him. Kersi usually stopped to chat; he got on well with all the servants in the building, especially Francis. Kersi's father had taught him to play cricket but Francis had instructed him in kite-flying. With a kite and string bought with fifty paise earned for carrying Najamai's quota of rice and sugar from the rationing depot, and with the air of a mentor, he had taught Kersi everything he knew about kites.

But the time they spent together was anathema to Kersi's parents. They looked distastefully on the growing friendship, and all the neighbours agreed it was not proper for a Parsi boy to consort in this way with a man who was really no better than a homeless beggar, who would starve were it not for their thoughtfulness in providing him with odd jobs. No good would come of it, they said.

Much to their chagrin, however, when the kite-flying season of high winds had passed, Kersi and Francis started spinning tops and shooting marbles. These, too, were activities considered inappropriate for a Parsi boy.

At six-thirty, Tehmina went to Najamai's flat for ice. This was the hour of the most precious of all ice-cubes—she'd just poured herself two fingers of Scotch.

A red glow from the Ambica Saris neon display outside Firozsha Baag floated eerily over the compound wall. Though the street lamps had now come on, they hardly illuminated the hallway, and tonight's full moon was no help either. Tehmina cursed the locks eluding her efforts. But as she continued the unequal struggle by twilight, her armpits soaked with sweat, she admitted that life before the fridge had been even tougher.

In those days she had to venture beyond the compound of Firozsha Baag and buy ice from the Irani Restaurant in Tar Gully. It was not the money she minded but the tedium of it all. Besides, the residents of Tar Gully amused themselves by spitting from their tenement windows on all comers who were better-heeled than they. In impoverished Tar Gully she was certainly considered better-heeled, and many well-aimed globs had found their mark. On such evenings Tehmina, in tears, would return to her flat and rush to take a bath, cursing those satanic animals and fiends of Tar Gully. Meanwhile, the ice she had purchased would sit melting to a sliver.

As the door finally unlocked, Tehmina spied a figure at the far end of the darkened hallway. Heart racing a little, she wondered who it might be, and called out as authoritatively as she could, *"Kaun hai?* What do you want?"

The answer came: *"Bai,* it's only Francis."

The familiar voice gave her courage. She prepared to scold him. "Did I not tell you this morning not to loiter here? Did I not say we would call if there was work? Did I not tell you that Najamai would be very late? Tell me then, you rascal, what are you doing here?"

Francis was hungry. He had not eaten for two whole days, and had been hoping to earn something for dinner tonight. Unable to tolerate Tehmina much longer, he replied sullenly, "I came to see if Najamai had arrived," and turned to go.

But Tehmina suddenly changed her mind. "Wait here while I get my ice," she said, realizing that she could use his help to lock the door.

Inside, she decided it was best not to push Francis too far. One never knew when this type of person would turn vicious. If he wanted to, he could knock her down right now, ransack Najamai's flat and disappear completely. She shuddered at these thoughts, then composed herself.

From downstairs came the strains of "The Blue Danube." Tehmina swayed absently. Strauss! The music reminded her of a time when the world was a simpler, better place to live in, when trips to Tar Gully did not involve the risk of spit globs. She reached into the freezer, and "The Blue Danube" concluded. Grudgingly, Tehmina allowed that there was one thing about the Boyces: they had good taste in music. Those senseless and monotonous Hindi film-songs never blared from their flat as they did sometimes from the other blocks of Firozsha Baag.

In control of herself now, she briskly stepped out. "Come on, Francis," she said peremptorily, "help me lock this door. I will tell Najamai that you will be back tomorrow for her work." She held out the ring of keys and Francis, not yet appeased by her half-hearted attempt at pacification, slowly and resentfully reached for them.

Tehmina was thankful at asking him to wait. "If it takes him so long, I could never do it in this darkness," she thought, as he handed back the keys.

Silloo downstairs heard the door slam when Tehmina returned to her own flat. It was time to start dinner. She rose and went to the kitchen.

Najamai stepped off the train and gathered together her belongings: umbrella, purse, shopping-bag of leftovers, and cardigan. Sunday night had descended in full upon the station, and the platforms and waiting-rooms were deserted. She debated whether to take the taxi waiting in the night or to walk. The station clock showed nine-thirty. Even if it took her forty minutes to walk instead of the usual twenty, it would still be early enough to stop at the Boyces' before they went to bed. Besides, the walk would be healthy and help digest her sister's *pupeta-noo-gose* and *dhandar-paatyo*. With any luck, tonight would be a night unencumbered by the pressure of gas upon her gut.

The moon was full, the night was cool, and Najamai enjoyed her little walk. She neared Firozsha Baag and glanced quickly at the menacing mouth of Tar Gully. In there, streetlights were few, and sections of it had no lights at all. Najamai wondered if she would be able to spot any of the pimps and prostitutes who were said to visit here after dark even though Tar Gully was not a red-light district. But it looked deserted.

She was glad when the walk was over. Breathing a little rapidly, she rang the Boyce doorbell.

"Hullo, hullo—just wanted to pick up today's paper. Only if you've finished with it."

"Oh yes," said Silloo, "I made everyone read it early."

"This is very sweet of you," said Najamai, raising her arm so Silloo could tuck the paper under it. Then, as Silloo reached for the flashlight, she protested: "No no, the stairs won't be dark, there's a full moon."

Lighting Najamai's way up the stairs at night was one of the many things Silloo did for her neighbour. She knew that if Najamai ever stumbled in the dark and fell down the stairs, her broken bones would be a problem for the Boyces. It was simpler to shine the flashlight and see her safely to the landing.

"Good-night," said Najamai and started up. Silloo waited. Like a spotlight in some grotesque cabaret, the torch picked up the arduous swaying of Najamai's buttocks. She reached the top of the stairs, breathless, thanked Silloo and disappeared.

Silloo restored the flashlight to its niche by the door. The sounds of Najamai's preparation for bed and sleep now started to drip downstairs, as relentlessly as a leaky tap. A cupboard slammed . . . the easy chair in the bedroom, next to the window by day, was dragged to the bedside . . . footsteps led to the extremities of the flat . . . after a suitable interval, the flush . . . then the sound of water again, not torrential this time but steady, gentle, from a faucet . . . footsteps again . . .

The flow of familiar sounds was torn out of sequence by Najamai's frantic cries.

"Help! Help! Oh quickly! Thief!"

Kersi and his mother were the first to reach the door. They were outside in time to see Francis disappear in the direction of Tar Gully. Najamai, puffing, stood at the top of the stairs. "He was hiding behind the kitchen door," she gasped. "The front door—Tehmina as usual—"

Silloo was overcome by furious indignation. "I don't know why, with her bad eyes, that woman must fumble and mess with your keys. What did he steal?"

"I must check my cupboards," Najamai panted. "That rascal of a loafer will have run far already."

Tehmina now shuffled out, still clad in the duster-coat, anxiously sucking cloves and looking very guilty. She had heard everything from behind her door but asked anyway, "What happened? Who was screaming?"

The senseless fluster irritated Kersi. He went indoors. Confused by what had happened, he sat on his bed and cracked the fingers of both hands. Each finger twice, expertly, once at the knuckle, then at the joint closest to the nail. He could also crack his toes—each toe just once, though—but he did not feel like it right now. Don't crack your fingers, they used to tell him, your hands will become fat and ugly. For a while then he had cracked his knuckles more fervently than ever, hoping they would swell into fists the size of a face. Such fists would be useful to scare someone off in a fight. But the hands had remained quite normal.

Kersi picked up his bat. The cord had set firmly around the handle and the glue was dry; the rubber grip could go back on. There was a trick to fitting it right; if not done correctly, the grip would not cover the entire handle, but hang over the tip, like uncircumcised foreskin. He rolled down the cylindrical rubber tube onto itself, down to a rubber ring. Then he slipped the ring over the handle and unrolled it. A condom was probably put on the same way, he thought; someone had showed him those things at school, only this looked like one with the tip lopped off. Just as in that joke about a book called *The Unwanted Child* by F. L. Burst.

He posed before the mirror and flourished the bat. Satisfied with his repair work, he sat down again. He felt angry and betrayed at the thought of Francis vanishing into Tar Gully. His anger, coupled with the emptiness of this Sunday which, like a promise unfulfilled, had primed him many hours ago, now made him succumb to the flush of heroics starting to sweep through him. He glanced at himself in the mirror again and went outside with the bat.

A small crowd of C Block neighbours and their servants had gathered around Najamai, Silloo, and Tehmina. "I'm going to find him," Kersi announced grimly to this group.

"What rubbish are you talking?" his mother exclaimed. "In Tar Gully, alone at night?"

"Oh what a brave boy!" cried Najamai. "But maybe we should call the police."

Tehmina, by this time, was muttering *non sequiturs* about ice-cubes and Scotch and soda. Kersi repeated: "I'm going to find him."

This time Silloo said, "Your brother must go with you. Alone you'll be no match for that rascal. Percy! Bring the other bat and go with Kersi."

Obediently, Percy joined his brother and they set off in the direction of Tar Gully. Their mother shouted instructions after them: "Be careful for God's sake! Stay together and don't go too far if you cannot find him."

In Tar Gully the two drew a few curious glances as they strode along with cricket bats. But the hour was late and there were not many people around. Those who were, waited only for the final *Matka* draw to decide their financial destinies. Some of these men now hooted at Kersi and Percy. "Parsi *bawaji!* Cricket at night? Parsi *bawaji!* What will you hit, boundary or sixer?"

"Just ignore the bloody *ghatis,*" said Percy softly. It was good advice; the two walked on as if it were a well-rehearsed plan, Percy dragging his bat behind him. Kersi carried his over the right shoulder to keep the puddles created by the overflowing gutters of Tar Gully from wetting it.

"It's funny," he thought, "just this morning I did not see any gutter spilling over when I went to the *bunya* for salt." Now they were all in full spate. The gutters of Tar Gully were notorious for their erratic habits and their stench, although the latter was never noticed by the denizens.

The *bunya*'s shop was closed for regular business but a small window was still open. The *bunya*, in his nocturnal role of bookie, was accepting last-minute *Matka* bets. Midnight was the deadline, when the winning numbers would be drawn from the earthen vessel that gave the game its name.

There was still no sign of Francis. Kersi and Percy approached the first of the tenements, with the familiar cow tethered out in front—it was the only one in this neighbourhood. Each morning, accompanied by the owner's comely daughter and a basket of cut green grass, it made the round of these streets. People would reverently feed the cow, buying grass at twenty-five paise a mouthful. When the basket was empty the cow would be led back to Tar Gully.

Kersi remembered one early morning when the daughter was milking the cow and a young man was standing behind her seated figure. He was bending over the girl, squeezing her breasts with both hands, while she did her best to work the cow's swollen udder. Neither of them had noticed Kersi as he'd hurried past. Now, as Kersi recalled the scene, he thought of Najamai's daughters, the rat in the bedroom, Vera's near-nude body, his dispossessed fantasy, and once again felt cheated, betrayed.

It was Percy who first spotted Francis and pointed him out to Kersi. It was also Percy who yelled *"Chor! Chor!* Stop him!" and galvanized the waiting *Matka* patrons into action.

Francis never had a chance. Three men in the distance heard the uproar and tripped him as he ran past. Without delay they started to punch him. One tried out a clumsy version of a dropkick but it did not work so well, and he diligently resumed with his fists. Then the others arrived and joined in the pounding.

The ritualistic cry of *"Chor! Chor!"* had rendered Francis into fair game in Tar Gully. But Kersi was horrified. This was not the way he had wanted it to end when he'd emerged with his bat. He watched in terror as Francis was slapped and kicked, had his arms twisted and his hair pulled, and was abused and spat upon. He looked away when their eyes met.

Then Percy shouted: "Stop! No more beating! We must take the thief back to the *bai* from whom he stole. She will decide!"

The notion of delivering the criminal to the scene of his crime and to his victim, like something out of a Hindi movie, appealed to this crowd. Kersi managed to shake off his numbness. Following Percy's example, he grabbed Francis by the arm and collar, signifying that this was their captive, no longer to be bashed around.

In this manner they led Francis back to Firozsha Baag—past the tethered cow, past the *bunya*'s shop, past the overflowing gutters of Tar Gully. Every once in a while someone would punch Francis in the small of his back or on his head. But Percy would remind the crowd of the *bai* who had been robbed, whereupon the procession would resume in an orderly way.

A crowd was waiting outside C Block. More neighbours had gathered, including the solitary Muslim tenant in Firozsha Baag, from the ground floor of B Block, and his Muslim servant. Both had a long-standing grudge against Francis over some incident with a prostitute, and were pleased at his predicament.

Francis was brought before Najamai. He was in tears and his knees kept buckling. "Why, Francis?" asked Najamai. "Why?"

Suddenly, a neighbour stepped out of the crowd and slapped him hard across the face: "You *budmaash!* You have no shame? Eating her food, earning money from her, then stealing from her, you rascal?"

At the slap, the gathering started to move in for a fresh round of thrashing. But Najamai screamed and the crowd froze. Francis threw himself at her feet, weeping. *"Bai,"* he begged, "you hit me, you kick me, do whatever you want to me. But please don't let them, please!"

While he knelt before her, the Muslim servant saw his chance and moved swiftly. He swung his leg and kicked Francis powerfully in the ribs before the others could pull him away. Francis yelped like a dog and keeled over.

Najamai was formally expressing her gratitude to Silloo. "How brave your two sons are. If they had not gone after that rogue I would never have seen my eighty rupees again. Say thanks to Percy and Kersi, God bless them, such fine boys." Both of them pointedly ignored Tehmina who, by this time, had been established as the minor villain in the piece, for putting temptation in Francis's path.

Meanwhile, the crowd had dispersed. Tehmina was chatting with the Muslim neighbour. Having few friends in this building, he was endeavouring to ingratiate himself with her while she was still vulnerable, and before she recovered from C Block's excommunication. By the light of the full moon he sympathized with her version of the episode.

"Najamai knows my eyes are useless till these cataracts are removed. Yet she wants me to keep her keys, look after her flat." The cloves ventured to her lips, agitated, but she expertly sucked them back to the safety of her cheeks. "How was I to know what Francis would do? If only I could have seen his eyes. It is always so dark in that hallway." And the Muslim neighbour shook his head slowly, making clucking sounds with his tongue to show he understood perfectly.

Back in her flat, Najamai chuckled as she pictured the two boys returning with Francis. "How silly they looked. Going after poor Francis with their big bats! As if he would ever have hurt them. Wonder what the police will do to him now." She went into the kitchen, sniffing. A smell of ammonia was in the air and a pool of yellowish liquid stood where Francis had been hiding behind the kitchen door. She bent down, puzzled, and sniffed again, then realized he must have lost control of his bladder when she screamed.

She mopped and cleaned up, planning to tell Silloo tomorrow of her discovery. She would also have to ask her to find someone to bring the rations next week. Maybe it was time to overcome her aversion to full-time servants and hire one who would live here, and cook and clean, and look after the flat. Someone who would also provide company for her, sometimes it felt so lonely being alone in the flat.

Najamai finished in the kitchen. She went to the bedroom, lowered her weight into the easy chair and picked up the Boyces' Sunday paper.

Kersi was in the bathroom. He felt like throwing up, but returned to the bedroom after retching without success. He sat on the bed and picked up his bat. He ripped off the rubber grip and slowly, meditatively, started to tear the freshly glued cord from around the handle, bit by bit, circle by circle.

Soon, the cord lay on the floor in a black tangled heap, and the handle looked bald, exposed, defenceless. Never before had Kersi seen his cricket bat in this flayed and naked state. He stood up, grasped the handle with both hands, rested the blade at an angle to the floor, then smashed his foot down upon it. There was a loud crack as the handle snapped.

B A B A R U,
T H E   F A M I L Y

B.
Wongar

Australia

Our Mother has left us. She has not died or run away but has changed into a crocodile. Maybe it is better that way—not that we will see much of her but it helps to know that she is not far off; should anything like that happen to any of us we will be around in the bush together again.

I hope Padre does not find out what has happened to Mother. He says that whenever any of us leaves we go to Heaven; the white man's boss called Jesus boils a huge billy in a campfire and the people, black and white, sit around and sip tea—you can put as many lumps of sugar in your cup as you like.

What should I say to the other children? There are two more of us— Anabrn and Purelko—and they are still asleep in the sandpit behind the fire, curled together like a couple of puppies. Mother called the pit *murlg*, the shelter, though it is nothing but a sheet of corrugated iron stuck sideways into the ground; it makes no cover from the rain but is a shield from the cold winds at night.

The sun has shot spear-high in the sky—the children will be up soon; they will nag me about Mother and ask for food. I had better see to the fire. A big log lies partly sunk in the ashes with a cluster of red coals buried beneath it—a few pokes with a stick and a chunk or two of wood will make it flare up again. I'm glad that Mother thought of it when she left; I was half awake and saw her waddling over the dusty ground. Her tail was swinging around the fire, slashing the ashes now and then; a log was clamped in her jaws, then dragged and pushed over the dying coals on top of the mound of ashes.

One of the children mumbles something; it is Purelko, my brother. He struggles to move his hand through the air to . . . tell me, perhaps, that he knows about Mother too. The boy, the youngest, is often awake at night and stares at the fire. When the flames go out he calls; sometimes he jerks his limbs to make me and Mother get up and do something about it. When we find food I have to feed him, the same as Mother did—hold a piece of yam in front of his mouth and wait for his lips to stretch open. With *njuga*, the mangrove crabs, you have to break off the tough pieces and chew them for him first. Padre says the boy will never get better; once a child is crippled like that he will be no different when he grows up.

Mother will be back, for sure, not now during the day, but at night. She will sneak in to check on the fire and see that we are all properly buried in the sand to keep warm. There is a big hole dug under the chain-wire fence, just over there at the far corner of the compound where the ground makes a small rise. Lucky the ground around is sandy and it is not hard to break out. She won't be far off; perhaps she's hiding in the mangroves farther down toward the bay.

Look, Padre is already up and has gone to open the gate. He only does it once a day for us to go out and look for bush tucker, but never so early. The gate squeaks—it sounds like a possum trapped in a hollow log. Once it leaves the compound, the track forks: one path goes up the river, passes a patch of thick forest, and leads to the scrub country stretching inland; the other branch follows the shore, passes the old jetty, and swings around the water. The outline of the bay looks like a badly thrown boomerang that fell short of coming back—as if it had hit the sea and made Warngi Cliff there across the entrance to the inlet.

Padre wears a white shirt and a dark wide-brimmed hat that has swallowed half his head. I saw him dressed like that long ago when Nati, Mother's father, left. Padre must have thought that the old man was on his way to Heaven and he gave him a good farewell, but Mother says our people go a different way.

"Should I come to sweep your hut?"

Mother did so every day. She made his fire and boiled the billy for tea. Once she even climbed up on the roof of the hut to prop up a sapling with a cross on top of it and fasten the lot with a piece of wire.

"Don't worry about it."

"We can bring you some wood from the bush."

"You will have plenty on your hands looking after those two. You're about grown up now."

Padre pats me on the cheek and walks slowly to our shelter. A track of freshly disturbed sand stretches from the fire right to that hole under the fence, but the claw marks can't be clearly seen. Good that Mother dragged her long tail to sweep the dusty ground behind her.

"How is the little albino; growing up?"

Anabrn steps out from the pit and allows the man to pat her on the head. She has fair hair; where she has slept a seashell has left a deep mark on the pale skin of her neck. Why does he call her albino? Mother thinks it means "white," but . . . all three of us show a bit of it. Padre says that some children will turn completely black only when they grow up; perhaps that means when they become *bala*, initiated. It should be about time for me to go through that now. There is a place Mother told me about, a billabong, I think, far off in the bush where the bay plunges its foamy snoot into the land. The men from Dulbu tribe sit on the ground in the shade of paperbark trees and sound out their *bilma*, clapping sticks, and didjeridu loud enough to please every spirit in the country. The sound tells you that the time has come to go there and be made into a woman. I hope there is somebody there to tell me how to go about the ceremony when the day comes. Our Nati will be there with his *bilma* for sure. By now he must be *marngit*, medicine man; he will know about us coming to life.

"Here is some tea and sugar. You still have that billy, I hope." On the ground near the fire Padre leaves two half-full jars and then stares into the ashes for a while. Look, there are paw marks on the ground from Mother's webbed feet; they are the same as those of ducks and other water birds but much bigger.

Purelko is up and crawls around the fire. The boy tries to tell us something but can't make the words; he just mumbles a sound or two. Maybe he is asking for tucker—his face is stained with charcoal and a layer of sand is stuck to the wet skin around his mouth. Even though he is crippled, the boy should know that you don't feed on sand whatever the color of your skin—black or white.

"Raunga, see that the boy is fed."

Padre walks back to his hut without saying more. He might come out later in the day to look around and tell us what to do. I should go up the rise there and cover that hole beneath the fence; it might be better if Padre knows nothing about it. Even if he does guess what has happened to Mother, let's hide the way she has gone. The man might be angry because she has not departed the same way as the white people do and he could set a trap to catch her when she comes back to see us tonight. Our Nati told us that the whites like to hunt every living soul in the bush. I have never seen Padre kill an animal but once long ago I peeped into his hut, and there was a stack of crocodile hides inside—I doubt whether the beast can live after you have skinned it.

If Nati were here he could tell us a lot about crocodiles. The animal is *marain*, sacred, to him and to all of us. The old man hardly said anything to Padre, and when he was here he kept away from the hut—his fire was behind that dead tree right over there on the top of the rise. Look, it is still there; the wind has blown off the ashes, but two partly burned pieces of wood remain on the ground. Mother thought he had gone back to his place along the long arm of the land stretching from here into the sea and had walked over to Warngi Cliff where the *marngit* should be. You can see the hill far across the bay, showing up above the forest like a cap of dark cloud. He will be down there now sitting on the rocks, clapping his sticks and chanting to call the spirits from Bralgu far across the sea to come back and look after us and the animals—the whole country. When they come, the spirits will bring *dal*, magic power, to heal Purelko and everyone else who needs help. I wish Nati would hurry them up; without Mother I may not be able to feed the poor boy.

I should climb up on that dead tree and look out. I did it a season ago and went up to the top branches. The arm of land stretches far out into the sea and then curls around the bay and ends at Warngi Cliff—it looks like the tail of a huge crocodile swinging about to poke at a monstrous porpoise asleep on the sea.

Let's push some sand in and fill up the hole. If Mother comes back at night she will dig it out again. Crocodiles have strong claws; they can burrow into the ground like anteaters and often make hollows to lie and wallow in. Look, Nati has left his *bilma* behind; I have never heard him chanting without them, but even if he does, the spirits might not be pleased to hear the voice. The sticks—just plain pieces of wood—must mean a lot. Look, they are smooth and worn from being handled for so long. The pair have been around . . . the man before Nati, and the healers before him, must have chanted with those sticks.

Padre has come out of the hut again; I'll rush back to our fire and not let him come this way. The man has brought a bundle of rags and hands it to me: "Each one of you must make a 'lap-lap.' Girls should have a cover."

Mother wore a cover made of a burlap bag and it had a few holes where patches of dark skin showed through; she called it *maidja* and . . . a fire caught her cover once and burned a whole chunk out of it. She did not wear the bag around here but had to put it on whenever she went inside the hut.

Maybe a barge is coming today and Padre is in a hurry to clear out the hut and make room for new goodies. No boat has been here for many seasons; when it sailed in last . . . I doubt whether Anabrn or Purelko were born then. Yes, that is why Padre is dressed. I wonder how the man found out these fellows are on the way here. Perhaps Jesus came in his dreams last night and told him that goodies are on the way.

"You can have some blankets; there are a few inside."

When the boat came before, there was a tall pole behind the hut with a long piece of wire stretched to it—a magic string. Mother reckoned it went all the way up to the sky to let the white man talk to his boss. They called it "radio." Padre never had to chant and clap with sticks—he talked into the wire instead whenever he wanted a barge to be sent here.

"Where's our Mummy?" Anabrn looks down to the ground and her voice quivers.

"Raunga will tell you that."

"Has she gone to the river or the sea?" The child is shy—dashes behind me and covers her face with both hands.

Padre walks off and, passing through the gate, turns back: "If I'm not back by evening, go inside the hut."

Maybe he knows about Mother and thinks she will come tonight to snatch us all. Our Nati thinks the whites are tough on crocodiles, and Padre may not be so different from that lot. Pity, he was around here before I was born, and even before our mother was born. Only Nati remembers him coming to Dulbu country. The other old fellows would have known about it too, but all of them are long gone. They say the white man landed from the sea, washed up on a small sandy patch among the boulders on the other side of Warngi Cliff. He was stiff like a log, with no word of our lingo to tell us where he came from.

The water has slipped back from the shore, leaving behind a long stretch of mud and sand—the bay looks like a water tank with the tap left open. It will be noon or even later before the sea comes back and the first waves show up; by then I will have gathered a whole bag of *njuga*, enough for a much bigger *babaru* than the three of us.

Perhaps I should go up to the top end of the bay while the shore remains dry, and then come back to look for tucker later. The old man doesn't like to wait and the quicker I go the better it will be. If . . . let's leave Purelko under that whistling tree; without him to carry I can run.

"Rest here, boy, the sand is soft and shaded . . . Anabrn will look after you for a while."

"Can I gather some crabs?"

"Do, but . . . don't let him crawl close to the water."

Anabrn did not ask where I was going—perhaps she knew that I had *bilma* with me. The sticks are in the bottom of the dilly bag that hangs around my neck. Nati will be pleased to have them. In the bush there, far beyond the bay, the other old men will gather too; a whole flock of them will sit near the billabong to chant and . . . how can they sing without *bilma?* I've watched Nati chanting in camp many times. He claps the sticks one against the other a few times and then throws his voice high into the air so that it floats above the forest and across the bay to the land beyond. The *bilma* clap now and then to warn the spirits to be on the lookout for his call. A chant like that is magic, and when it is well sung it cannot only heal humans but also bring back to life the dead trees and boulders scattered throughout Dulbu country.

Someone has just passed by here. Stretching along the shore toward the top of the bay there is a line of footprints in the wet sand: Padre—no one else around here wears shoes. Maybe he has gone for a walk. It will be quite a while before the tide comes in, and without the waves the barge will never be able to sail in. The boat has to come in right there, where those two rows of posts are stuck in the mud holding up a long platform made of saplings. There is hardly any water there now, but once the waves come back the sea will almost reach the top of the stilts. Padre calls it "jetty" and it has been there ever since I can remember. It must have been quite a job to drag all those trunks from the bush and sink them in the bay. All our fellows stuck to the job and struggled for a whole Dry to build that thing.

Mother didn't think that the jetty did any good, even though the barges called in a finger-count of time. They were loaded all right—our fellows had to drag bags and boxes of goodies ashore and then farther on up to the camp. Whenever the boat called, Padre's hut became like a hollow log packed up with honey. You only had to walk inside, look at the cross and whisper a few white man's words, then come out with a piece or two of barley sugar. I often got a handful of biscuits and learned to chant a little song, though I've never found out what the words meant. The women with small children each received a tin, not easy to open and the milk inside was too thick and hard to pour out—but it tasted nice. Mother often got a billycan full of flour; the powder had something . . . you could not tell if they were maggots or tiny weevils, but once the stuff was baked it tasted all right. Once she made *nadu,* damper, from . . . never knew whether it was dried milk or washing powder. Whatever the food came in, it always had shiny lettering on it to tell you how it should taste, but in the whole camp only Padre knew how to read.

Look, there is Padre, far away across the big bite of the bay; only his white shirt shows up, bobbing along the shore. He has gone a long way, almost to the patch of mangrove forest where the top part of the "tail" stretches out to bridge Warngi Cliff and the rest of the land. It's a tricky part of the country to go through—not so bad now, but once the tide is up the sea surges beyond the shore and moves inland through the mangroves to flood a whole chunk of the country. The water would almost cut off the whole of the cliff then if it were not for a long ridge of dunes that lies behind the mangrove forest shielding it from the open sea.

Yes, the *bilma* are in my bag all right. The sticks are our *ranga,* sacred, and when they are clapped, only old men and spirits can understand what they say.

I hope Nati will not be angry with me—we all know that woman is not supposed to come to this part of the country except to be initiated. He may not be at the billabong; the spirits often go over the dunes to fish or look for oysters. If Nati is not there I will leave the sticks and . . . when I get back to the camp he might appear in my dream to tell me when I should go to the billabong again.

Should I tell Nati that the boat is about to come again? No, the old man might not like the news. The last time the barge was here it brought in a pile of timber, stacks of corrugated iron sheets, doors, windows, and rolls of wire mesh. Padre wanted to build a church—nothing like that hut but much bigger. The building was to sit on that rise in the compound, and the whisper went around that once it was up Padre would climb to the top to look right over the forest to the billabong to see what our spirits were up to. He put the wire fence around all right to make that compound but went no further. The church is still down in the bush near the jetty. You can't see much of it now; the piles of corrugated iron have been swallowed up by vines and scrub, and as for the stacks of timber—the ants have eaten the lot. The windows are still there, hiding behind a thick cover of leaves, and it is only now and then when *walu*, the sun, peeps in that the glass blinks back to say the stuff is still there.

There is not much sea here, only one arm of water that has moved in from the main body of the bay to separate the shore on this side from Warngi Cliff over there; it looks like the tongue of a panting animal. The cliff looms above, tall— almost halfway to the clouds. The rocks facing the bay go straight up like a wall. The whole hill has the shape of a whale, and it was indeed once a *warngi*, sea monster. Our Nati says that at the Dreaming, the time when the spirits were about to make Dulbu country, a huge sea beast rushed toward the land to snatch them. One of our ancestors, Crocodile Man, rushed out from the billabong over there in the bush and dived into the bay. He moved about under the water for a while, and when he showed up again his jaws were wide open and he snapped at the monster, taking out a whole chunk before *warngi* could even see him properly.

The cliff side facing that small stretch of land. . . . Look—Padre is struggling up the craggy slopes and . . . he will not have far to go before he reaches the top of the wall. Quick, I'd better leave the shore and walk through the bush; I don't want him to see me. The billabong should not be far off now, tucked somewhere in the bush between here and the edge of the mangrove marsh.

I wonder what Padre is doing here. Maybe he wants to have a good look from the cliff to see how far out to sea the barge is. The boat might be passing Dulbu country and taking goodies to some other place; he will have to shout out or wave to make the white fellows call in. Before, there was a tall pole on the rise at our camp, and every time the barge was due to call, a flag flapped on the top. It helped, but the pole has long gone and . . . Padre might take off his shirt now and wave with it from the cliff to bring his fellows this way. Yes, that is what he is doing, I can see him between the branches; his shirt must be unbuttoned—it flaps about in the wind. I wonder how long he is going to be there. The tide hasn't turned yet, but it shouldn't be long before the waves come rolling across the shore to the mangrove marsh. It will be hard to get back from the cliff then.

I'll wander through the bush and look for the billabong; it can't be far off and . . . I hope it shows up soon—I'm getting thirsty. Padre might feel that way too. There won't be much to drink among the rocks there. His fellow whites might have forgotten about him and may never come. Mother says he spoke angry words to his boss. It happened not long after the barge was here last time and something went wrong with our people. A few children died first and then a whole mob of us, young and old, got sick.

"It's a plague—could wipe us all out!" Padre used to yell into the magic wire—you could hear his voice right across the camp. "Send us bloody doctors and medicine—come quickly, for Heaven's sake." His voice was heard for days. It seemed as though he would choke himself with the loud calls, but instead he grew angry and. . . . The radio was thrown out of a window and broke into pieces as it hit the ground.

"Bloody doctors" never came. Our Nati was right when he told us that the boat would not call again because there was nothing for them to take back from our country. A few bundles of crocodile skins were sent off but that was only a small crumb against all the loads of goodies that had been brought in—so little to please Padre's boss.

I have to kneel to get some water, maybe lie on the billabong bank and lean forward for a good drink. It is quite a big pool, well tucked into the bush. Huge paperbark trees have grown sky-tall, not so much to make shade but to hide the place from outside view. The ground over there near a huge boulder looks well cleared and bare—even the rock surface seems to be smooth, perhaps touched by humans and spirits alike.

Let's step about slowly; the men could be resting and elders do not like to be disturbed. They might be behind bushes, hiding in the shade, or . . . yes, they should be resting on the bottom of the billabong as all of our spirits do. I wonder if Nati will be there or . . . no, he is likely to be farther down at the top of Warngi Cliff. Look, there is a track going that way; the path swings around the mangrove marsh heading to the sandy ridge behind, and then a long neck of land heads toward the cliff. The old man must often come down here from the hill, chant and dance with the spirits, and then head back to Warngi—from there you can keep an eye on the whole Dulbu country.

I'd better be off. I'll just leave the *bilma* stick on top of the boulder and come in some other time when they want me. Look, something has just moved in the pool. On the surface two flower buds float; no, they are a pair of green eyes and . . . yes, the snout is over there—crocodiles often surface from underneath the lily pads to get a breath of air, and they don't show much of themselves if they want to rest in peace.

The sea is back, with the waves racing one another and rolling toward the shore. It will not be long now before the water slides over the small embankment and pours in to flood the mangrove forest behind. Padre should be down from the cliff by now if he is ever to come back. Maybe he has gone to the other side of the hill. Mother told us there are pieces of an airplane washed up on the shore there and stuck among the rocks. The metal does not rot quickly and could not be eaten by ants. The wrecked pieces have been there since "War," Mother thinks. However long ago that was, it is much further back than she remembers. When the airplane plunged into the sea it had aboard a whole bunch of white men. Maybe some of them made it to the shore farther up the coast but no one ever heard of them; we wouldn't have known about Padre either if Nati had not found him.

The sun is already hanging down from the sky; it will not be long now before it plunges into the sea. I'd better hurry back—Anabrn and Purelko will be angry with me for leaving them so long. They could already be calling for me, but children have weak voices and . . . they grow feebler when you are worn out with hunger. It would need to be like the roar of a didjeridu, not just a voice to match the howl of the sea, to reach this part of the bay.

Look, a white cloth lies washed up, the waves are still splashing against it: Padre's shirt—no, only half of it. His hat has come in too, sitting there on the water as though looking for the best spot to come ashore. Perhaps . . . Padre must have gone to see Nati and our other fellows. Good that they took him with them; he has been in our country ever since that day when Nati found him on the shore. The man must be too angry to go to his boss. Better this way; we may not see much of him, but now and then he will show up in our dreams.

I'll pick up the shirt and hat and take them down to the jetty and leave them on a log there. If the barge comes this way again the whites can have their clothes back.

BIOGRAPHICAL NOTES

NISSIM ALONI is an Israeli short-story writer, playwright, and Hebrew translator of French plays. His own plays have been performed regularly in Israel since the 1950s. "Turkish Soldier from Edirne" is taken from *The Owl*, a collection of his stories dealing with childhood in a Sephardic neighborhood of Tel Aviv.

PETER CAREY was born in Australia in 1943. He is the author of four novels, including *Oscar and Lucinda* and *The Tax Collector*, as well as two collections of short stories, *The Fat Man in History* and *War Crimes*.

MICHELLE CLIFF is the author of novels, poetry, and short stories. "Columba" is taken from her collection of stories, *Bodies of Water*, published in 1990. Cliff was born in Jamaica and currently lives in Santa Cruz, California.

MARGARET DRABBLE of Great Britain is better known as a novelist than a short-story writer. Her books include *A Summer Bird-Cage*, *The Garrick Year*, *The Millstone*, and *Realms of Gold*. She is also the author of a scholarly biography of the British novelist Arnold Bennett.

JORGE EDWARDS was born in Santiago, Chile, and worked as a lawyer, a farmer, and a journalist before entering the diplomatic service. He has published several volumes of short stories, one of which received the Santiago Literary Prize in 1961.

MARGARETA EKSTRÖM is a Swedish novelist, short-story writer, poet, diarist, critic, and columnist. The winner of several literary awards in Sweden, she has published nine volumes of short fiction. English translations of her stories have appeared in *London Magazine*, *Vogue*, and *Ontario Review*. She lives in Stockholm.

NADINE GORDIMER has long been recognized as one of the finest short-story writers and novelists of the century. Many of her stories, which are frequently published in *The New Yorker*, are set in South Africa and deal with generational and political conflict, family life, and apartheid. Gordimer, who was born and still lives in South Africa, won the Nobel Prize for Literature in 1991. "Some Are Born to Sweet Delight" is taken from her collection *Jump and Other Stories*.

HA JIN teaches creative writing at Emory University. He was born in the Liaoning province in China, where many of his short stories are set, and came to the United States in 1985. His fiction has appeared in *The Kenyon Review* and *The Atlantic*. "In Broad Daylight" was the winner of the Kenyon Review New Fiction prize in 1993. His book of poetry, *Between Silences*, was published by the University of Chicago Press in 1990.

CHARLES JOHNSON has worked as a director of the Creative Writing Program at the University of Washington, a reviewer for the *Los Angeles Times*, and a consulting editor for *The Seattle Review*. His PBS drama, *Booker*, won the Writers Guild Award. Johnson also won the National Book Award in 1990 for his novel *Middle Passage*, an account of the nineteenth-century slave trade through the eyes of a newly freed slave who unwittingly finds himself aboard a ship bound for Africa to abduct more slaves. "Exchange Value" is taken from his collection of stories, *The Sorcerer's Apprentice*.

THOMAS KING is the son of a Cherokee father and a mother of Greek and German descent, received his Ph.D. in literature from the University of Utah, and taught Native Studies for many years at the University of Lethbridge, Alberta. In 1989 he became the chairman of the Department of American Indian Studies at the University of Minnesota in Minneapolis. He lives in Toronto.

SHIRLEY GEOK-LIN LIM is a Chinese-Malaysian writer with a particular interest in the condition of women in Southeast Asia. She was the winner of the Commonwealth Poetry Prize in 1980 for her first book, *Crossing the Peninsula*, and established her international reputation with her collection of stories, *Another Country*, from which the dramatic "Mr. Tang's Girls" is taken. Lim currently lives and teaches in California. She is also the co-editor of the book, *The Forbidden Stitch: An Asian-American Women's Anthology*, which won an American Book Award in 1990.

MARIO VARGAS LLOSA, one of Latin America's most famous novelists, was born in Peru in 1936, was educated in Madrid, and has lived for many years in Europe. His novels include *The War of the End of the World*, *The Real Life of Alejandro Mayta*, *The Storyteller*, and *In Praise of the Stepmother*. "On Sunday" is a story in Vargas Llosa's book *The Cubs*, a book about the activities and friendships of an urban gang of Peruvian teenage boys. In 1990 Vargas Llosa returned to Peru to run for political office as a candidate with a coalition government.

NAGUIB MAHFOUZ, the author of more than thirty novels and fourteen volumes of short stories written in his native Arabic, reached a wide English-speaking audience in 1988, the year he was awarded the Nobel Prize for Literature. Since then, many of his stories and several of his novels, including the renowned *Cairo Trilogy*, have become available in English translations in the United States and Europe. Mahfouz was born in 1911 and has been writing since the age of seventeen.

GABRIEL GARCÍA MÁRQUEZ, winner of the Nobel Prize for Literature in 1982, is best known in the United States for his modern classic, *One Hundred Years of Solitude*, but he is also the author of several other novels and five books of short stories. Though Marquez has written (and continues to write) in the realist tradition, as in the story "Artificial Roses," he is highly regarded as one of the masters of the style known as Magic Realism, a blend of the fantastic and the everyday.

JOHN McGAHERN is the author of four novels, including *High Ground*, and has been the recipient of the Æ Memorial Award, one of Ireland's most prestigious literary honors. Whether about young people, middle-aged couples, or the elderly, McGahern's stories are usually set in rural Ireland, a place that for his characters is both charming and entrapping.

YUKIO MISHIMA remains the dominant name in twentieth-century Japanese literature. The autobiographical *Confessions of a Mask*, novels like *The Sailor Who Fell from Grace with the Sea*, and the great trilogy of novels, *The Sea of Fertility*, were among the most respected works of Asian literature in the 1950s and 1960s. An interest in macabre situations and extreme states of mind carried over from Mishima's writing to his personal life as well. His death was surely the most dramatic in the annals of literary history: in 1970 he and another member of a right-wing organization he had founded committed ritual *seppuku* after seizing control of a military installation outside Tokyo. Protesting Japan's neglect of its traditional values, Mishima stabbed himself with his sword and was in turn beheaded by his comrades.

ROHINTON MISTRY (whose name means "craftsman" in his native language) was born in Bombay in 1952 and at the age of twenty-three emigrated to Canada, where he worked in a bank for ten years and studied English and philosophy at the University of Toronto. He began publishing short stories in his early thirties; his first collection, *Swimming Lessons and Other Stories from Firozsha Baag*, was published in the United States in 1989, establishing him as one of the important new voices in modern fiction. The eleven stories in that collection, like his excellent first novel *Such a Long Journey* (1991), detail in both comic and tragic fashion the life of the Parsi community in his tumultuous homeland.

BHARATI MUKHERJEE is a native of Bombay who has lived in Canada and now resides in the United States, where she teaches creative writing and has been the recipient of grants from the Guggenheim Foundation and the National Endowment for the Arts. "Saints" is taken from Mukherjee's collection entitled *Darkness*. Her later book of short stories, *The Middleman and Other Stories*, won the National Book Critics Circle Award for Fiction in 1988. *The Holder of the World*, her 1993 novel, is concerned (like much of her other fiction) with identity and the clash of radically different cultures.

CHARLES MUNGOSHI was born in Zimbabwe in 1947 when that country was still known as Rhodesia. Some of his work was banned in his native land, although he enjoyed a striking success in his early twenties: his first novel was published in Shona, an African language, in 1970, and his short stories and poetry have been read throughout Africa and Europe. He was the winner of the Rhodesian PEN Award in 1976 and 1981. Since Zimbabwe attained its independence in 1981, he has become one of the most popular authors in that country and his work has been widely translated.

ALICE MUNRO, who lives in Clinton, Ontario, and often writes about life in the smaller towns of Canada, is a regular fiction contributor to many American periodicals, including *The New Yorker*, *Grand Street*, and *The Paris Review*. Although she has published novels, she is best known as one of the modern masters of the short story, with a particular focus on the lives of girls and women. "The Turkey Season" is taken from her 1983 collection, *The Moons of Jupiter and Other Stories*.

V. S. NAIPAUL is the grandson of Indians who emigrated to the Western hemisphere and settled finally in Trinidad. As a product of two cultures, in effect, he has written extensively (both fiction and nonfiction) about modern India and the Caribbean. Novels like *The Mystic Masseur*, *Miguel Street*, *The Mimic Men*, *In a Free State*, *Guerillas*, and *A House for Mr. Biswas* are modern classics, telling stories (like "The Raffle") that are both serious and droll and deal with the struggle to live and succeed in the economically troubled Caribbean.

BEN OKRI was born in Nigeria and grew up there and in England. In 1991 he won the Booker Prize for *The Famished Road*, the story of an African child in touch with the spirit world. He is also the author of the novel *Songs of Enchantment*. "In the Shadow of War" is from his collection, *Stars of the New Curfew*. Many of Okri's books deal with the modern landscape of Africa as a place of dreamlike fantasy and violent reality.

MERCÈ RODOREDA was born in 1909 in Catalonia and died in 1982. She began her life as a writer by publishing novels in the 1930s in the Catalan language. After Franco's rise to power at the end of the Spanish Civil War, her country's identity, culture, and language were suppressed by the government in Madrid; she became a woman without a homeland or a native language. For many years she lived in Paris and finally, in 1959, resumed publishing. "That Wall, That Mimosa" is taken from her collection *My Christina and Other Stories*. After the fall of Franco, Rodoreda was able to return to her native Barcelona. Her novel *Camellia Street* has also been published in the United States.

TATYANA TOLSTAYA, a resident of Moscow, was born in Leningrad in 1951 and began publishing short stories in her twenties in the major Soviet journals. She has lived briefly in the United States, having been a writer-in-residence at the University of Virginia in 1988. Tolstaya comes from a remarkable literary background: she is the granddaughter of the writer Alexis Tolstoy and the great-grandniece of Leo Tolstoy. "Date with a Bird" is taken from her collection, *On the Golden Porch*, published in the United States in 1990.

ZOE WICOMB is a native of Cape Province in South Africa. In 1970 she moved to England, where she works as an English teacher in Nottingham. "When the Train Comes" is from her 1987 collection of short stories, *You Can't Get Lost in Cape Town*, a book praised by Toni Morrison as one of the best works of modern fiction to come out of South Africa. The ten linked stories in that volume deal with a young black woman coming to terms with the racist world of a South African township and her attempts both to escape and acknowledge her past.

B. WONGAR is the pseudonym of a writer born in Yugoslavia who is married to an Aboriginal and has lived in Australia for many years. He has written many books in support of Aboriginal causes, calling international attention to important issues of culture and environment. *"Babaru, the Family"* is from his collection of stories, *Babaru*.

ACKNOWLEDGMENTS

Grateful acknowledgment is made to the authors, publishers, and literary agents for permission to reprint the stories in this collection.

NISSIM ALONI: "Turkish Soldier from Edirne" by Nissim Aloni, translated from the Hebrew by Ammiel Alcalay, translation copyright © 1983 by Ammiel Alcalay. First published in *The Denver Quarterly*, Vol. 18, No. 1. Reprinted by permission.

PETER CAREY: "American Dreams" from *The Fat Man in History* by Peter Carey, copyright © 1974, 1979 by Peter Carey. Published by Faber and Faber, University of Queensland Press, and Vintage Books. Reprinted by permission of the author and Rogers, Coleridge, and White Ltd.

MICHELLE CLIFF: "Columba" from *Bodies of Water* by Michelle Cliff, copyright © 1990 by Michelle Cliff. Reprinted by permission of Dutton Signet, a division of Penguin Books USA Inc.

MARGARET DRABBLE: "The Gifts of War" by Margaret Drabble, copyright © 1970 by Margaret Drabble. Used by permission of Peters, Fraser and Dunlop Group Ltd.

JORGE EDWARDS: "Weight-Reducing Diet" by Jorge Edwards, copyright © 1973 by Jorge Edwards, from *The Eye of the Heart: Short Stories from Latin America*, edited by Barbara Howes. Reprinted by permission of Avon Books, a division of the Hearst Corporation.

MARGARETA EKSTRÖM: "The Nothingness Forest" from *Death's Midwives* by Margareta Ekström, translated by Eva Claeson, translation copyright © 1985 by Eva Claeson. Reprinted by permission of Ontario Review Press, Inc.

NADINE GORDIMER: "Some Are Born to Sweet Delight" from *Jump and Other Stories* by Nadine Gordimer, copyright © 1991 by Felix Licensing, B.V. Reprinted by permission of Farrar, Straus & Giroux and Penguin Books Canada Limited.

HA JIN: "In Broad Daylight" by Ha Jin, copyright © 1993 by Ha Jin. First published in *The Kenyon Review*. Reprinted by permission of the author.

CHARLES JOHNSON: "Exchange Value" from *The Sorcerer's Apprentice* by Charles Johnson, copyright © 1986 by Charles Johnson. Reprinted by permission of Atheneum Publishers, an imprint of Macmillan Publishing Company. "Exchange Value" copyright © 1981 by Charles Johnson.

THOMAS KING: "Borders" from *One Good Story, That One* by Thomas King, published by HarperCollins Canada, copyright © 1993 by Thomas King. Reprinted by permission of The Bukowski Agency, Toronto.

SHIRLEY GEOK-LIN LIM: "Mr. Tang's Girls" from *Modern Secrets* by Shirley Geok-lin Lim, copyright © 1989 by Shirley Geok-lin Lim. Reprinted by permission of the author.

MARIO VARGAS LLOSA: "On Sunday" from *The Cubs and Other Stories* by Mario Vargas Llosa. Translated by Gregory Kolovakas and Ronald Christ. English translation copyright © 1979 by Harper and Row, Publishers, Inc. Reprinted by permission of Farrar, Straus and Giroux, Inc.

NAGUIB MAHFOUZ: "The Conjurer Made Off with the Dish" from *The Time and the Place and Other Stories* by Naguib Mahfouz, translated by Denys Johnson-Davies, translation copyright © 1978 by Denys Johnson-Davies. Used by permission of Doubleday, a division of Bantam Doubleday Dell Publishing Group, Inc.

GABRIEL GARCÍA MÁRQUEZ: "Artificial Roses" from *No One Writes to the Colonel* by Gabriel García Márquez, translated by Gregory Rabassa and S. J. Bernstein. English translation copyright © 1968 by Harper & Row, Publishers, Inc. Reprinted by permission of HarperCollins.

JOHN MCGAHERN: "Christmas" from *Collected Stories* by John McGahern, copyright © 1993 by John McGahern. Reprinted by permission of Alfred A. Knopf, Inc.

YUKIO MISHIMA: "Martyrdom" from *Acts of Worship: Seven Stories* by Yukio Mishima, translated by John Bester. Anthology copyright © 1989 by Kodansha International Ltd. Reprinted by permission of the publisher, Kodansha International Ltd. All rights reserved.

ROHINTON MISTRY: "One Sunday" from *Swimming Lessons and Other Stories from Firozsha Baag* by Rohinton Mistry, copyright © 1987 by Rohinton Mistry. Reprinted by permission of Houghton Mifflin Co. All rights reserved.

BHARATI MUKHERJEE: "Saints" from *Darkness* by Bharati Mukherjee, copyright © 1985 by Bharati Mukherjee. Reprinted by permission of Penguin Books Canada Ltd. and Russell and Volkening.

CHARLES MUNGOSHI: "Who Will Stop the Dark?" from *The Setting Sun and the Rolling World* by Charles Mungoshi, copyright © 1989 by Charles Mungoshi. Reprinted by permission of Beacon Press.

ALICE MUNRO: "The Turkey Season" from *The Moons of Jupiter and Other Stories* by Alice Munro, copyright © 1982 by Alice Munro. Reprinted by permission of Alfred A. Knopf, Inc. and Virginia Barber Literary Agency, Inc.

V. S. NAIPAUL: "The Raffle" from *A Flag on the Island* by V. S. Naipaul, copyright © 1967 by V. S. Naipaul. Used by permission of Viking Penguin, a division of Penguin Books USA Inc.

BEN OKRI: "In the Shadow of War" from *Stars of the Night Curfew* by Ben Okri, copyright © 1988 by Ben Okri. Used by permission of Viking Penguin, a division of Penguin Books USA Inc.

MERCÈ RODOREDA: "That Wall, That Mimosa" from *My Christina and Other Stories* by Mercè Rodoreda, translated by David H. Rosenthal, copyright © 1967 by Mercè Rodoreda, translation copyright © 1984 by David H. Rosenthal. Reprinted by permission of Graywolf Press, Saint Paul, Minnesota.

TATYANA TOLSTAYA: "Date with a Bird" from *On the Golden Porch* by Tatyana Tolstaya, translated by Antonina W. Bouis, copyright © 1989 by Tatyana Tolstaya. Reprinted by permission of Alfred A. Knopf, Inc.

ZOE WICOMB: "When the Train Comes" from *You Can't Get Lost in Cape Town* by Zoe Wicomb, copyright © 1987 by Zoe Wicomb. Reprinted by permission of Pantheon, a division of Random House, Inc.

B. WONGAR: "*Babaru*, the Family," from *Babaru* by B. Wongar, copyright © 1982 by B. Wongar. Reprinted by permission of the author.